Praise for *Ch*

'A terrifically good book, so clevely constructed and managed. It's a work of real tenderness . . . powerful and convincing.'
Jim Crace

'Wilkins is brilliant at character . . . the writing is full of verve. Wilkins has an eye for telling detail, a great ear for dialogue and a dark sense of humour. It is easy to understand the acclaim he has already won in his native New Zealand.' *Guardian*

Praise for *Nineteen Widows Under Ash*

'Wilkins reminds me of some of the great American writers—Faulkner, Lowry, Richard Ford—where the simple story you are apparently reading deepens and broadens and throws out layers and shadows, and you are conscious of an underwater life and a sky overhead, but all the time you are immersed in what seems a limpid, even transparent medium.' *Evening Post*

Praise for *Little Masters*

'*Little Masters* is an engrossing, fiercely readable book. It deals with classic themes of parents and children, love and exile, and the sadness of separation and dislocation. Damien Wilkins writes brilliantly about streetwise, smart children and adults searching for love and stability far away from home.'
Colm Tóibín

Praise for *The Miserables*

'Wilkins has constructed a powerful portrait of family life . . . He handles the temporal shifts of the narrative with delicacy, precision, remarkable grace and apparent lack of effort . . . the prose is controlled, elegant, almost deadpan . . . A moving and subtle piece of work.' *Times Literary Supplement*

Also by Damien Wilkins

The Veteran Perils (short stories)

The Miserables

The Idles (poems)

Little Masters

Nineteen Widows Under Ash

When Famous People Come to Town (essay)

Chemistry

Great Sporting Moments (as editor)

the fainter damien wilkins

victoria university press

VICTORIA UNIVERSITY PRESS
Victoria University of Wellington
PO Box 600 Wellington
vuw.ac.nz/vup

Copyright © Damien Wilkins 2006

First published 2006

ISBN-13: 978-0-86473-530-0
ISBN-10: 0-86473-530-8

This book is copyright. Apart from
any fair dealing for the purpose of private study,
research, criticism or review, as permitted under the
Copyright Act, no part may be reproduced by any
process without the permission of
the publishers

National Library of New Zealand Cataloguing-in-Publication Data

Wilkins, Damien, 1963-
The fainter / Damien Wilkins.
ISBN 0-86473-530-8
I. Title.
NZ823.2—dc 22

Published with the asssitance of a grant from

Printed by Astra Print, Wellington

for Maree

part one

What happened to Luke

Though he'd invited them in, telling them it was their house after all, his sister's boys stayed at the bedroom door. It made him think anthropologically, of pygmies observing at some threshold.

They were hardly mesmerised. They were watching Luke iron his shirt. 'It's a strange sight, isn't it?' he said. It had already been established that their father had never done such a thing. 'Quite right,' Luke had told them. 'Awful job.'

Finally, the younger one, Timmy, took a step into the room and saw inside the wardrobe where all the white shirts were hanging, crumpled from the suitcase still open on the bed. 'What team are you on?'

For a moment Luke didn't get it. Simon, who was thirteen and who'd refused to come closer—there might even have been some revulsion on his part—dismissed his little brother with a kind of cough. 'He thinks it's like a sports uniform.'

'It is, sort of,' said Luke.

'Who do you play for?'

'New Zealand.' Luke pressed down with the iron. 'We play in white.' He'd spoken jokily into the steam.

Simon made the sound again, aimed this time at his uncle. He was not a pygmy; Simon was almost Luke's height, with large hands that might already have reached inside animals for their young. 'Maybe he's a waiter. Anyway, dinner's ready is what we had to say.' He disappeared. Unfortunately, the small one remained. He came over and put a finger on the ironing board.

'Careful,' Luke said, feeling the temptation, 'you might lose it.'

'Why are you doing it?' asked the boy. Solemn creature.

Luke paused, staring at the shirt. Could this simple query now derail him? In looking into the pinched material of the cuff, he had a moment when he lost the room. Briefly, he forgot everything. Would he fall? The ironing board wasn't something to grip. It was a comic object always. He came back at once, however, and turned to his nephew. Dinner was ready and he would have to go downstairs and front. There was still so much to iron, though now he felt the senselessness of it. 'Good question,' he said. Along the length of the ironing board he made a hesitant smoothing motion with his hand, as if patting the back of a curiously tall dog. Good boy. He held the iron up towards his nephew. 'See how hot it is,' he said moronically.

Without hesitation the boy spat. 'Fried,' said Timmy. 'Now you.'

'Me?' His mouth was dry, his nostrils too, from the flights. He'd sprayed himself regularly with the demister, his self-consciousness, like everything in that setting, evaporating.

'Try it. The sound it makes, that's evaporation.' A mind-reader too. The boy spelled the word out, getting it wrong in the middle perhaps.

The English language was, as had been said to Luke more than once over the past few months, a living, breathing nightmare. 'Pity the poor foreigners,' his boss had whispered at an informal with the Norwegians, who actually handled it better than most. How had he, Luke, gained hold of it to the extent of winning a regional spelling bee at eleven? The question took its place in the queue of questions. His nephew was talking about the spelling lists he was given at school. It sounded like torture. 'Very good,' said Luke.

They stood looking at the surface of the iron which was browned in places. He liked a clean iron. He was proud of his shirts, without being silly about it. There were about thirty of them. Maybe that was silly. He believed his neck was one of his more sensitive areas. The shirts hadn't been bought in a Pierre Cardin job lot from the Kirks annual sale, as was the case with most of his colleagues. When he was travelling, he always carried a small bottle of distilled water for the ironing, which he knew was excessive. An hour before, when his sister Catherine had handed him the iron, Luke must have frowned. 'That's historic,' she said. He apologised at once and said it didn't matter at all, but she'd noted his unreasonableness and he'd seen again her sensitivity. The resolution on both sides was to bury these truths. He plunged the iron down again so a burst of steam covered his face, and he gave his 'horror' laugh from inside the heat.

His nephew, however—and good on him—was bored with the trick. 'Why are we waiting?' he said.

'No reason.' Then Luke leaned forward and tried to spit. There was the briefest sizzle. It sent the boy away rather puzzled. What was his uncle made of, or not made of?

He'd come down to his sister's South Canterbury farm, via Los Angeles, Auckland, Wellington, from New York, from the United Nations, if such a thing were possible—Luke himself had almost lost faith in the story, though it was only some thirty, forty, fifty hours old.

He'd turned in his keys, his swipe cards, his IDs. What was left? A lump of receipts—he was still in the habit of retaining all evidence, not for tax purposes but to prove to himself this was his life a wad of laundry stubs. Through August and September, he was changing at least twice a day, keeping fresh shirts in a locker at the Mission—an initiative which caught on more or less at once. He'd even persuaded Kerry, the Head of the Mission, to contract a laundry service direct from the office, to save them lugging dirty clothes home on the subway.

In rationalising the contents of his wallet, he'd come across his membership card to the gym on East 61st, where he'd been only a few times, the last one to play doubles on the rooftop tennis court with people from the office before heading to a place called Smorgas on 2nd Avenue—which had been recommended by one of the Norwegians—for shrimp sandwiches and cocktails. In throwing stuff away, he'd seen the receipt for this too. Here they also served New Zealand rack of lamb, an item that affected them all rather powerfully and oddly, he thought, though no one ordered it nor mentioned it to the waiter. The temptation had been strong. Despite their previous high spirits on the tennis court—no one had been good enough to sustain anything approaching a competitive streak—the atmosphere grew a little bleak. Homesickness was not, in his limited experience, a simple emotion. It lived quite comfortably alongside other feelings with which at first glance it might appear incompatible. Everyone at the table at Smorgas, with its apparently legitimate Scandinavian connection, had at some recent time announced his or her delight at leaving New Zealand. To lift things, he ordered Bjorn Borgs all round: crushed gooseberries and strawberries with bourbon and cranberry juice, and followed these with Stranded in Stockholms: lemon and orange juice, mint, with Cointreau and Magellan gin. Inevitably one of them—it was Alexandra, or Sandy as she was known—had been stranded in Stockholm. She tried to tell the story but by now the cocktails had done their work. Here was a form of drinking even more vastly self-reflexive than wine. To have a cocktail, Luke considered, was to enter its lore. By some force one was compelled to read the ingredients aloud from the menu, then try to remember whatever it was that had belonged in one's own favourites. He was a bit bored by this talk but also pleasantly drugged—both removed and attached. James, his age, a Classics background, who'd taken him to the gym the first time and who'd suggested the tennis, was debating with himself whether Aquavit was dominated by caraway or cumin. Yes, Luke thought to himself with affection, these are my people tonight. Someone began asking the waiter about the lingonberry, apparently native to Sweden though sourced on this occasion from Wisconsin. Not as bitter as the cranberry.

Weeks later, in his sister's spare room, Luke found at the bottom of his suitcase some dimes and quarters, which appeared suddenly curious to him. They belonged to another period. Rooftop tennis, Wisconsin lingonberries—hard to place all that now in its correct sequence. His American period. The coins looked positively Roman.

As a kid he'd collected coins, preferring them to stamps. Sometimes he'd thought along these lines: a stamp had been licked once, sent once; who knew how many hands a coin had passed through? A Day in the Life of a Penny and all that. Mostly, however, he liked the money aspect of coins. Against all advice in numismatist literature, Luke periodically emptied his albums on his bed so that the coins were in a heap, and then he ran his hands through them, whispering, 'I'm rich, I'm rich.' Embarrassing, but had things changed much since then? He loved his salary, spending it, naturally, but also dwelling on it. They were paying him for this? His posting allowance, though hardly a remarkable sum, was another thrill; it returned him again to childhood pocket money. If they'd given it out in coins, he may well have rolled around in it. He just wasn't serious—which might have been his problem all through. It was something teachers said, and his parents. It didn't seem to hold him back though.

Could this be true as well, that he'd also recently been at The Hague? But there he was in the photo—he drew in the lens, with his slightly large head and its tight dark curls—at the International Court of Justice, sitting just behind the three in wigs, part of his country's legal team trying to bring nuclear France once more to account. (Charles Fuge, a few rungs up the ladder, was beside him in the back row—another scene-stealer, since Fuge was looking away from the camera, his beaky profile, the upward curve of his chin, indicating a greater interest placed somewhere just beyond the group portrait. The effect of this relatively junior pair was to suggest off-stage dramas perhaps, giving the not inaccurate idea that all the important stuff had happened away from this table with its ceremonial aspect. Fuge was masterfully clandestine and spoke French well enough to whisper it. The judges, by contrast, seemed decorative, almost electively dumb. As if to underline this, Justice Carling, most prominent in the foreground, had his hand over his mouth.) In 1973, when they'd won, Luke was five. France pulled the plug on the tests, giving the Court nothing to rule on. Now, twenty-two years later, when the French announced their plan to conduct a further eight underground tests, he was in the right spot. Maybe it had been his talent up to this point, to be positioned correctly. Had he not, as a teenager, chanced upon the Oxford Union Debate on TV at the very moment the Prime Minister, David Lange, taking the affirmative on 'Nuclear Weapons are Morally Indefensible', was listening to some preppy fool with his interjection: 'And whether you are snuggling up to the bomb, or living in the peaceful shadow of the bomb, New Zealand benefits, sir. And that's the question with which we charge you. And that's the question with which we would like an answer, sir.' Lange, adjusting his glasses, grinning, had made his famous reply: 'And I'm going to give it to you if you hold your breath just for a moment. I can smell the uranium on it as you lean forward!'

Like all the best impromptu remarks, there was some evidence of preparation. Maybe the line had been written for him. Yet his delivery was genius. The audience loved it, loved Lange. A nation did. At the end, a standing ovation. It was a theory Luke had listened to more than once, that this had been the last unambivalent moment in the public life of his country. It was all downhill from here.

If Luke had missed the moment, would he have followed this course? Moral conscience attached to wit: it was an inspiration, even to one who lacked seriousness. He had none of Lange's amused religiosity, his slightly ironic though completely sincere sense of social engagement, nor even his physical bulk—a significant component, since the eloquence of the large is always more impressive than the small man's mouth, which might easily seem defensive or compensatory—yet Luke suspected he could think fast and on occasion speak winningly. It was also a lesson that the preppy fool opposite the Prime Minister had not been humiliated but slain in such a way as to feel gratitude to his slayer. It could be thought he had almost given Lange his line. Both bathed in the laughter and the applause.

Luke knew he too liked an audience. He took Law to make it to Foreign Affairs, MFAT, which he joined after a couple of years of postgraduate work. No getting around it, New Zealand was a piddly stage. He saw himself out there, amid the world, in reach of the uranium. He wanted to smell the world's breath as the world leaned forward towards him.

His first posting: junior legal adviser to the Permanent Mission. Environmental Law was his thing, or should have been his thing. Luke left New Zealand on a high. Anyone plotting his rise would have agreed it had been rapid but—to most who knew him—not unearned, and his work farewell party was the full affair, with dancing and vomiting. As tribute to his popularity, and because he was in with the bookings person, they let him use one of the boardrooms with Maori carvings and famous paintings on the walls worth a million, more. A colleague pointed to the brown landscapes: 'Will it be hard leaving all this, Luke?' It will, Luke said, and went to get the painting off the wall. He was restrained happily by an older woman from Treasury with whom he'd worked closely on several projects and who'd once sold him her tickets to a film at ten percent discount. All over he'd made her known as Ms Ten Per. She squeezed his shoulders, looked into his eyes, finally couldn't speak. Neither of them was in any way overcome. They'd simply reached the natural end of their acquaintance, and Luke, like many before him, bright recent recruits, was leaving. Probably she'd gripped them all like this, testing resolve or ambition, and perhaps a few had even broken down, wept on her shoulder. She was the diplomatic corps' mother. I may never see my mother again, he thought. He was leaving. It was this odd moment more than any other which brought home the fact to him. His own mother was no longer alive, yet he thought of her; she would have been proud. His father had remarried and shifted to Australia.

In connection with a not-so-elaborate gag—there was a nuclear theme—someone was serving French toast. 'If the Froggies fuck up with the nukes,' it was announced, 'we'll all be toast.'

The shout was: 'Luke will save us!'

He received advice from old heads, little of it cogent. He should take it easy for the first year away. He should throw himself into it. He shouldn't miss out on any new experience. He should be cautious, the diplomatic life was a long one. Reinvention was possible with each new posting. He should always be himself. He should serve the greater thing.

By 2 a.m. some senior people were still grimly hanging on. Most of the marrieds were gone. It was typical: down to gay men and single straight women confiding in one another. The proliferation in the room of facial tics, lips that drooped oddly, eyes that couldn't stop winking, also suggested that 'Doctor' Nick had been busy. Nick was Doctor of the Diplomatic Bag, with friends in the dance party scene around the world. He played keyboards in lounge bands wherever he was posted. He'd played in Soweto and in Rio. A generous guy, who sometimes got round in, and was forgiven for, a fez. On returning from Harare, his wardrobe for several months was East African, and he accepted, perhaps even created, the honorific 'Chief Nick'.

He now gave Luke the names of several clubs in Manhattan and several people in these clubs. 'For some reason,' he said, 'they know me as Raisin.'

Luke hardly had to think. 'Because you wanted to be a sultan, they reduced you. You're just a Raisin.'

Nick was half-pleased, eyeing Luke for the first time as a contender maybe. 'You know, I think that's right!'

There was someone from Editorial doing the dishes in the kitchenette; she'd been there seven hours. 'Let me help,' Luke said to her.

She looked at him, puzzled. 'I'm in here,' she said. Then she ran to him and hugged him.

The air was amorous. Two women, quite high up, both

married, were dancing together and kissing. 'In the morning,' one said to Luke, 'we start our lives over. I tell my children the news.' The other kissed Luke, and said, 'And I tell my husband.'

'What will you say?' said Luke.

'That we love each other.'

The other woman said, 'Kids are really adaptable.'

The three of them agreed with this. The women looked at each other. Then one of them said she felt sick and had to lie down.

Luke himself stayed away from the party drugs, but only for health reasons. He wouldn't have minded getting wasted and washing dishes all night or feeling loving. Yet it was out for him. A couple of years before, he'd been driving a golf ball into a practice net at a friend's house and the ball had missed the net, come back at him off a concrete wall and struck him in the left temple. So he'd not always been in the right spot. He'd had a few fainting spells in the weeks following that, and finally he was put on medication. He wasn't allowed to drive a car. They thought it might possibly be some sort of night epilepsy. Would he have fits? They thought perhaps not. Despite all the famous people who had it, who lived wonderfully full lives, etcetera, he couldn't bear to think of that grisliness. 'Does this mean I have to take down my disco ball?' he asked. The doctor looked lost. 'Yes,' Luke answered his own question, 'but only because they're hideous.'

He wasn't taking the medication now and hadn't had a spell in almost a year, but he'd been warned off any triggering substance. Maybe he'd been too cautious, too good. Anyway, alcohol wasn't on the list, thankfully.

Though nothing was broken or stolen and, in fact, thanks to the insane cleaning person the place was left spotless, the boardroom became out-of-bounds for parties and 'When Luke left' became an office slogan of sorts.

A different slogan was shortly to supersede it: 'What happened to Luke.'

First, however, he did The Hague, acquitting himself well,

though the case predictably was lost on technical grounds. For Luke, it was all a success. He'd seen process, been inside it. In a small side room off the Court he'd come across a brilliant lawyer, Rick Weenink, who was weeping. The man was in the textbooks, having been involved in preparing additional protocols to the Geneva Convention in the late seventies. He was fluent in several European languages. Behind his studies there was a stellar sporting career abandoned. Moreover, Weenink had a daughter—nineteen years old—whom every young lawyer back in Wellington was in love with. (Luke himself hadn't come across her; the witness was Charles Fuge, who'd offered, in his style—that is, without further explanation—the quote, 'When red-headed people are above a certain social grade, their hair is auburn.') Weenink sat with his head in his hands, sobbing. The Court's decision was still a month away. What was this distress about? It didn't seem credible that the Attorney-General's closing statement had such power, no matter that he'd used the Montesquieu quote—another of Fuge's finds—to good effect. The French, with their faces, gave nothing away on hearing their famous countryman pressed into service against them. 'Ever since the invention of gunpowder . . . I continually tremble lest men should, in the end, uncover some secret which would provide a short way of abolishing mankind, of annihilating peoples and nations in their entirety.' There'd been a battle over the 'lest'. Fuge's idea was to modernise. The AG's office came back that the AG wanted to retain the feel of the past. Fuge sent through his version regardless. It was ignored. This tiny setback seemed to lodge deeply with Fuge. In his address to the Court, when the AG gave the name of Montesquieu's work, Fuge hissed the correct pronunciation rather fiercely into Luke's ear.

Could Marbles' tears even be connected with the beautiful daughter?

Finally he looked up at Luke, wiping his eyes and smiling. 'I've always found court work very emotional,' he said. Then he stood up and walked out of the room.

This was astonishing. Weenink was a man with the searing

monotone of the best jurors. His nickname was Marbles not because he'd lost any but to indicate his temperature, his stony cool. Marbles was a gibbering wreck, as flaky as any actor.

Here, however, Luke was made to feel he'd committed an error; he'd told Fuge of his discovery. Fuge had cut him off, delivering a surprisingly solemn lecture on the necessity for loyalty. At first Luke had thought this was being offered ironically. 'Access to all kinds of information comes with responsibility to the sources of that information.'

'Of course,' said Luke.

'One of the more effective ways of maintaining this self-discipline is to no longer think of oneself as a civilian.'

'I see.'

'I think of everyone else as Civvy Street.'

'And yourself?'

'We're in the Service.'

'As in wartime?'

'Pretty much, yes.'

The idea—ridiculous in many ways—could not be attacked, even really in Luke's private thoughts, since there was no one to share these thoughts with. And he had to admit The Hague was, to a great extent, a kind of barracks. Within these confines, they did feel special, secretive, trusted, cut off. The Hague was, after all, The Hedge. They were crouching behind a hedge, waiting for the moment to strike. There was an enemy too—courteous and impeccable, but an enemy nonetheless.

At this point Fuge must have felt the need to acknowledge his junior's scepticism. 'Of course we don't carry weapons, and there's little hand-to-hand combat!' He gave an unconvincing laugh. 'The grenades we lob are metaphorical ones.' This coda did nothing to alleviate the seriousness of the speaker's intent. Fuge had issued an order. There was something implacable in him which, despite this direct attention, Luke suspected was not connected with his own person. He didn't doubt he was now on notice—but everyone seemed to be, with Charles.

The team went for a drink that evening, and at a certain

point Rick Weenink asked Luke where he got his suit. He was touched by all at the table—even Fuge, perhaps softened by the alcohol, gave him a considerate poke in the arm. Fuge was also in a good mood, having been put in the nice position of owning up to a piece of inspiration. Justice Carling had wanted to know who'd provided the Cicero quote in the AG's opening statement: '*Silent enim leges inter arma.*'

'One of Charles's, I believe,' said Weenink. 'Actually made me think of General Vladic.'

'Indeed,' said Carling. '"Laws are silent in time of war."' The recent fall of the 'safe area' of Srebrenica hung over the table for a moment. Seven thousand massacred. The understanding that this had happened on the continent where they were dining flickered briefly. 'Well done, anyway, Charles,' said Carling. 'Good old Cicero. Safe pair of hands.' This last statement amounted to his catch-phrase; its invocation again of Srebrenica seemed accidental. 'Grisly end, though. Head cut off and nailed to the Speaker's podium in the Senate. Herennius did the honours at Mark Antony's bidding.'

'Some people can't bear to see others with gifts they themselves lack,' said Fuge. This was uttered with such complete seriousness no one quite knew what to do with it.

'And fortunately most of us don't carry around sharp enough knives,' said Luke.

He'd relieved the tension. There was laughter, Fuge even joining in after a moment. Carling, the old man, had moisture in the corners of his eyes from the merriment. Luke felt they wanted him or that they wanted to tell him he was one of them.

'I'm sure they winced at the Montesquieu,' said Weenink.

'If only to hear their language mangled,' said Fuge.

'Not another of yours, surely?' said Carling. 'My God, man, what are you, a walking dictionary of quotations?' There was the possibility that the older man's admiration was a mixed substance now.

Fuge showed no sign of hearing anything but endorsement. 'Memorable statements stick,' he said.

'To concede something to our friends on the other side,' said Luke, 'I thought, as language alone, their description of our arguments as science fiction rather good. Quite witty.' He wasn't sure whether he'd gone too far. Beside him, Fuge, for one, was determined not to concede anything. He was looking off in the direction of the bar.

Weenink rescued him. 'Science fiction? Yes, I see what you mean.'

'Yes,' said Carling, a bit gloomy now. 'The AG is solid enough but not witty. Not in the job description really, is it? Think of the best of them.'

'Palmer,' said Weenink.

'Exactly.'

That evening Luke walked by himself through the Old City, past the churches and palaces and along the canals where he discovered Spinoza had lived and Descartes often visited. There were others too the city was claiming, Mozart and so on. A horse-drawn carriage went by, carrying two couples who raised their champagne flutes to him and called out in a language he couldn't identify. 'Cheers!' he said. The men attempted to stand and bow but they fell on to the women, everyone laughing and screaming.

He sat on a park bench beside an old-fashioned street lamp—old-fashioned or old?: that was always a problem in such settings; much that seemed historical was merely a reconstruction. He was aware that theorists purred over such phenomena. Generally he didn't, and certainly not now. There was a point at which he might have headed towards academia. His two years of postgraduate work consisted of some tutoring and a lot of note-taking, the only breakthrough being his willingness now to write in the margins of books—previously he'd it considered vandalism. He'd had a six-week fling with a lecturer a few years older than himself who'd declared him an honorary lesbian and herself on sabbatical. She read and smoked in bed. Her duvet cover had burn marks. Scattered throughout the house were submissions for the journal on whose editorial committee she sat. He organised these for her—even read a few of them and offered comments: the area was Public and International Law. His own research topic was the US Supreme Court's activities in Environmental Law. He also allowed a pass to be made at him by a History professor, whom he'd gone to for a view of nineteenth-century European nationalism—in the classic mode of the non-finisher, everything seemed connected. The man, in his fifties, rake-like, head like a bald eagle, often to be seen jogging out of lifts in a tiny pair of shorts, was an amateur runner who'd competed as a veteran in marathons around the world. 'To run beneath the Brandenburg Gates,' he said, 'was one of the great sexual moments of my life.' They had been talking about Germany. Luke didn't quite know what to do with the Professor's hand, which had moved from Luke's arm to rest on his leg. They were sitting in a small office, the door closed. Hanging from a hook on the back of the door was a pair of blue running shorts. The Professor was wearing trainers. An article on him that had appeared in the Staff News a few weeks before spoke of some serious injury—to his knee, perhaps—from which he'd recovered despite a dismal prognosis. He'd just been given an Excellence in Teaching Award. 'The Wall had just come down a few weeks before. One felt part of all that. Part of the emotion, part of the change. And running! You know running releases all sorts of things through the body.'

In the history of seduction, these sentiments hardly ranked high, but nor were they, Luke thought, the worst either of them had heard. The Professor was certainly a ham—quite a number of excellent teachers were—and possibly a creep, but at no time was there any question of an advantage being taken—more like an opportunity—and Luke had the choice now of whether to accept or decline. The proposition was straightforward; in a certain light, even flattering. This man was A-list, albeit in a smallish alphabet, and handsome in a hooded way. His richly musical baritone had been put to use in several unlikely contexts. He was the voice of an airline safety message and a number of TV commercials. As a result he was unpopular with that sizeable minority of colleagues who'd gone into the academy hoping to cure themselves of shyness or a speech defect and who'd done well while nevertheless retaining some aspect of the old deformity.

Unhorrified, Luke stood up, thanked the Professor for his time, and left the office.

Luke couldn't deny the appeal of the brand of dysfunction peculiar to academic life: highly intelligent individuals operating, at least on the personal level, at a complete loss. Perhaps Foreign Affairs would be no different. From his current position, however, the university appeared horribly arrested. In an attempt to give up cigarettes, his lecturer who smoked in bed had bought a large jar of lollipops. Whoever came around was offered one. The theory crowd, it was proved, had a decidedly sweet tooth.

On the park bench in The Hague, in The Hedge, he was completely powerless against a feeling of wonder and happiness. There was humility too, though his sneaking pleasure in it probably signalled something else: a sense of entitlement. There was no one else about, and yet just around the corner a few hundred thousand people lived and worked. Great minds had found this place. He couldn't help but feel something rather arranged in the moment. And, as if on cue, from the trees there came a scuffling sound. He watched as a deer stepped carefully out onto the sandy path. Luke was still. The animal bent its head to the path, straightened and saw him. Luke had read that The Hague was the greenest city in Holland, and that its forest, from which the city had grown almost eight hundred years before, was the only non man-made urban one in the country.

The previous day, they'd been taken to look at the ancient castle, whose grounds were still frequented by the game that had given the place its original purpose. This was what the nobility had built to rest in after the deer hunt. Their group, made up of the legal team together with their Dutch hosts, had walked into the trees, careful to remain quiet. They'd inched along, stopping at various points when someone believed he'd heard a sound.

Though they were assured it wasn't important, the hosts began to take it as a matter of pride that they should see a deer. The Dutch began to argue very quietly among themselves. The party was led further into the trees. 'Can you smell it?' they asked. Luke couldn't but joined in the nodding.

In the end, they surprised only a watercolourist with her easel who turned and shrieked at the group of suited men creeping around the forest. The Dutch said something to her which infuriated her further. It was Weenink who saved the day. He began to speak of his visit to the Mauritshuis, passing over *Girl with a Pearl Earring* and even *View of Delft*, asking the woman painter whether she knew much about Paulus Potter. This proved a hit. She'd studied Paulus Potter for years. 'Ah, his cows,' she said, glowing. It was Weenink's cue to step closer. He asked to see some of her work, would that be possible? At once she was retrieving paintings from her bag. Quickly a sale was arranged—the Dutch paying cash—and the judges were gifted some small paintings of the castle. These were given to Charles Fuge to carry; he passed them on to Luke, indicating the umbrella he held as his own burden.

Weenink asked after a painting which showed a deer drinking from a pool of water. It wasn't clear whether he meant anything satirical by this suggestion, since the painting had caught the thing they hadn't. Whatever the case, the woman said it wasn't for sale because it was unfinished—the deer had no reflection in the water. 'Very hard,' she said. Weenink murmured his assent.

Fuge came up and pointed bluntly at the painting. 'What if there was a wind,' he said. 'Rough up the pool's surface. Wouldn't have to worry about a reflection.' He finished by waving his hand over the work. Transparently, this wasn't so much an effort to enter sympathetically the difficulties of the artist as it was a piece of pragmatism to remove what in Fuge's eyes was a very small problem.

The painter turned slowly to face Fuge, all her hostility at having been interrupted returning. This time Weenink showed no interest in appeasement. He moved off, leaving Fuge to recover things. This in itself might have been a dressing-down of sorts. The main party was already too distant to see what was transpiring. Only Luke remained. Whether it was this fact that caused Fuge's next action or simply that he didn't know what to say, Luke wasn't sure. Fuge, displaying no signs of embarrassment, stared for a moment longer at the painting, then gave the woman the briefest unsmiling nod before turning on his heel, the swivel slightly military, his walk stiff and upright but no more so than usual.

On the way back they saw some cattle eating grass in a clearing, though their hosts didn't comment on it. The cows were a slap in the face. Weenink paused a moment at the back of the group and spoke to Luke. 'Paulus Potter,' he said.

Luke had to admit he didn't know the work, hadn't been to the gallery. Ahead, Charles Fuge had stopped and was turning to assess the nature of this *tête-à-tête*.

'Picture called *The Young Bull*. Wonderful. As famous in its day as Rembrandt's *Nightwatch*. Cattle under a tree, a few sheep. And the old farmer leaning against the tree trunk. Could be an uncle of mine.'

Weenink didn't wait for a response but walked on. Perhaps the story was connected with what had happened the day before, when Luke had found him crying, but in what way, exactly, he couldn't be sure. No matter how inconsequential the confession, Luke did feel a kind of elation in being singled out to hear it. Fuge's backward look could also be counted as contributing to this feeling. The overwhelming sense he had from Fuge's ticking off over loyalty was that Fuge had been annoyed not to have seen for himself Marbles in that state of discomposure. To carry on the military image, Luke had been in a position to which his rank did not entitle him: namely, he'd been able to get something on someone, a superior. His advantage was further underlined by the incident with the woman painter.

Now the deer had come to Luke, several miles from where it should have been. A private show.

The deer stood motionless but poised to leap away. On its

rump were two white markings. Its legs seemed almost too fine, as if the animal would fall over with only a quick nudge. It had the quality of an ornament. The ears appeared as two perfect triangles. What did you do with a deer: call it over like a cat? And if it came, what would follow? Basically he was scared of animals. He didn't get a chance to act. From a distance there was the sound of raised voices and the crunch of carriage wheels—the champagne crowd was coming back. Luke looked off, and when he turned around the deer was gone. He stood up and walked away quickly. It was beginning to rain and he was suddenly tired, rather teary and lonely too. Luke could expect these feelings, these emotional lurches. The lawyer known as Marbles had shown the way on this. Back in his hotel room, Luke wept into a large and soft white towel, distracted in the end only by the monogram pressed to his cheek.

He was a natural at the UN too, which that year was turning fifty. His 'mind' was good, he'd been told this—lawyers and diplomats tended to think of the mind as a separate part of the body, so to have a good mind was like having good legs or a good arse. Best of all, though, people seemed to like having Luke around. Someone said to him he had just the right amount of cruelty in him. 'Not too much and not too little.' At first Luke was surprised at this judgement, then later considered it more or less accurate. There was a brief period in which he started assessing everyone he knew along these lines. The danger was always that the pure at heart might appear deficient, a bit bland perhaps.

He was back from The Hague barely six weeks. It was mid-October, a warm Fall evening, and he was walking home from the office. His single apartment was where he slept and sometimes ate. He hadn't yet found out how to turn on the stereo or the television. The need hadn't arisen. If his life had a certain transience attached to it, this was fitting. It was standard to be at a distance from anything resembling the homely state that marked one's previous existence. To be travelling up seventeen floors seemed right too, not as an expression of the vertical nature of his career trajectory but simply because it seemed out of proportion to everything that had gone before it. He looked up. There was scarcely a sky. His building was a massive, charmless slab, hidden from view even though he was only a few minutes from it. There was the thing people said that Manhattan buildings loomed, forcing you to crouch—humans were made little—but there was the opposite effect too. The eye was raised. The sense of possibility was stretched.

That day he'd been at a productive informal meeting with the Nordics, following up the good stuff from the informal informal the week before—the language was still worth savouring: on first hearing this doubling of 'informal' he'd thought the speaker had a stutter. Some people, he'd observed, were put on this earth to do wonderful work and go unnoticed or at least to have their rewards deferred. They achieved invisibly, though if anyone did think of them he or she recognised at once their contribution. Their manner suggested diligence, loyalty and a touch of servitude. They were the good. Luke knew he was not one of them. He'd been on the front page of the *New York Times* in week one. A wide shot of the General Assembly applauding the US Secretary of State, and in the bottom right corner, surviving but only just the printer's ink—the rest of his country cut from the picture—it was him. He was a flier, a mover, a face. The photo was duly ordered, enlarged, framed and hung in the lobby. The hope that the print would show more of them was sadly groundless. Luke stood for the nation. In a few weeks, the SCM would take place. This Special Commemorative Meeting, centrepiece of the 50th Anniversary celebrations, would bring together all the world leaders. Clinton, Yeltsin, Castro, Arafat, Chirac, Mandela, Jim Bolger. The Australians might have nabbed the chairmanship of the committee preparing the big Draft Declaration which would be read out at the final session, but the New Zealanders had got the PM on the Day One podium, after Spain and before Arafat. The speech had crossed Luke's desk a number of times already. He could hear it in the PM's mouth, which always sounded as if he'd been interrupted eating; there was something—gristle perhaps—which needed to be passed into a serviette. Each night Luke looked up to see the Secretariat building lit up with its 'UN 50' message—a festive gesture not quite in keeping with either the organisation's tasks or its perennially embattled position, but cheering nonetheless.

Then, literally, he turned a corner. He saw something rather distant from all of this.

Luke became that thing without which nothing can happen, will happen, has happened; a figure of greater importance, he sometimes thought, than either perpetrator or victim—he was a witness to a crime. He was the key witness. There was another, but finally it came down to Luke's finger and where it pointed. When he started to tell an associate—his counterpart in the Australian delegation—about what was going on, he was interrupted: 'How very New York of you. A friend of mine got posted to Johannesburg and he couldn't relax until he was involved in a carjacking.'

But Luke was not relaxing. He was tightening. He felt sick. He was given counselling. He was well looked after. He thought of the woman from Treasury at his going-away party gripping his shoulders, attempting to see his future. Had she seen this? And he began to faint again.

When he was telling it for the—what?—thirtieth time maybe, not counting the times he'd told it to himself—in his head these moments were on a loop—he used the term 'street theatre'. The glibness of the phrase made him queasy at once. He vomited—it filled him with vomit—and again that night. And every night. He was sick quickly and efficiently, in the same way his mother had done it, sitting up in the hospital bed after her first operation, and more or less in mid-sentence—'Ah,' she said, 'ghastly'—then she went on with whatever she'd been saying. His own purges seemed to his counsellor a disorder which was not particularly striking. That was the counsellor's word too— purge—to indicate the necessary cleansing. He was getting rid of stuff he didn't need.

Except he wouldn't be cleansed. What was the story then? He

didn't quite know. There were details that were wrong now, he was sure. After thirty or three hundred times the thing became less rote, less fixed. The entire sequence seemed available for revision. He'd been walking home from the Mission, had just turned the corner into his street and, realising he needed something for dinner, he headed towards his local deli. From across the road he saw a delivery van pull up and a guy taking stuff into the deli—Luke's deli, where he bought his bread, his salami, his beer—and there was someone else, a homeless guy, tagging along, asking the grocery boy for a hand-out, bugging him clearly. He'd seen something like it every day. A spot of panhandling of perhaps slightly greater insistence than normal. The grocery boy, apart from a little two-step he was doing from time to time, hardly even aware of the homeless guy; there's a buzz in his ear but he's a busy person, back and forth with his bags into the deli. The street lights had just come on, Luke remembered that. Each had his part, and he was playing the audience (not yet having use of the other word)—this was where 'street theatre' had come from, obviously.

When he was closer, two figures were in a tangle on the pavement outside the store. He didn't at first put these two together as the delivery man and the homeless man. For some reason he wanted to believe something else. He thought they were drunks, dancing or fighting. One of them fell over, going down hard, and the other veered into Luke's path. Luke stepped away to avoid collision and decided he needed to keep moving on from the scene. The man, however, began walking alongside him, muttering and swearing at Luke. The detective who interviewed Luke first was interested in the conversation.

'Was he threatening you or something?'

'Not exactly. He was saying stuff like motherfucker.'

The detective leaned his ear towards Luke. 'What was he saying?'

Luke repeated the word. Still the detective couldn't make it out. Luke performed the word finally in the accent he'd heard, at which the detective sat back, smiling. 'Oh! Now I got you.'

Then he asked Luke to go back a minute. He was taking notes as Luke spoke.

'What colour jacket?'

'Brown,' said Luke. 'Or red. I couldn't be sure.'

The detective looked at his pen, then he wrote. 'Rust,' he said.

Another detective came in with a piece of paper, and the two men talked about this for a few moments. The phone rang. The interviewing detective nodded and rubbed his mouth. He had a moustache and was bald.

'So he's out of the picture,' he said into the phone.

At these words the other detective made a whistling noise, picked up the piece of paper and left the room. There was something in the gesture Luke recognised from his own time in an office: the wrong form.

The detective put down the phone.

'What's happened?' said Luke. 'What's happened with the person?'

'He's out of the picture.'

'I'm sorry, what do you mean?'

'Just a guy trying to make a buck.' He shook his head. His tone was different, softer. 'An honest guy, trying to make a buck for his wife and kids. He just died in the hospital.'

The door opened again and the other detective was back with a new form which he placed on the desk. 'We need to get Homicide now.'

They passed him a rubbish bin and Luke threw up in it.

'Out of the picture,' said the detective again. 'Trying to make a buck.'

The detective with the form nodded sadly. 'Hardly worth going to work in this city.'

Two tough detectives, trying to make sense of a killing—very NYC. In hindsight, Luke kept telling himself, this would be remarkable—their accents, the room, the window with a grille—except he lacked that capacity to go forward and imagine the time when he'd be telling it all in a happy past tense to someone like himself for whom this was a kind of fantasy. The police station looked Third World, filthy, rudimentary.

He had to tell it to the homicide detective again, a few other people in the room sometimes who asked him about things he'd already said. They changed the chairs sometimes. It was a different room, then it was the same room but something different done to it—a blind pulled up, a potted plant in the corner, a new rubbish bin lined with a plastic bag. He resented none of it, and knew and accepted—was even impressed by, surprised by—the rigour. Everyone who came into contact with the case mentioned the victim's status as a wage earner. Luke learned the man was Mexican and twenty-four years old, a family man.

He hadn't seen the stabbing. There was no pressure on Luke to have seen more than he had, yet he felt the disappointment of the men around him with the direction of his testimony. He felt it in himself also, that at the point the pair were locked together, staggering around the pavement, he'd failed to take it in fully. His only thought had been to get away.

Then as the guy had come alongside him, as the smell of him came alongside, and Luke was trying to accelerate away from him, he caught sight of something. A flash, like a silver watch-strap, a piece of jewellery? A knife? With that thought he raised his briefcase—the briefcase his father gave him on graduation—and he said to himself, You want to try that here, you're only going to kill my briefcase. At the same time, he placed alternatives. The silver buckle on a belt. What had happened back in front of the store? He'd seen two people, incapacitated in some familiar way, come together in a moment of aggression or misplaced affection on a New York street, and one of them, unbalanced, had fallen. That this was the delivery guy now crossed his mind. He'd seen a bag of oranges on the sidewalk. He turned then to look back at the figure lying on the street but not wanting to lose the homeless man for a second.

'What happened to the knife?'

'I don't know. He was gone. He ran off.'

Even at the point he considered or intuited something very bad had happened, and not a block from his government-leased apartment, not fifteen minutes' walk from the UN, where he'd just started really, Luke was also thinking about homelessness, and maintaining a decent attitude to the homeless man alongside him, who was looking into Luke's face to test exactly this, his social conscience, his sense of justice—he'd just been at the International Court of Justice, he'd been photographed applauding Secretary of State Warren Christopher as he attacked UN inefficiency—his understanding of the warped ways of this great democracy, the only country deliberately founded on a good idea . . . there'd been a seminar . . . Luke didn't drop coins in caps but he was aware of the need for . . . It was David Lange who came to mind. Luke wanted to be bigger and stronger right then. What would Lange have done? Talked the guy around probably. Been affable, firm, successful.

'He didn't show it to you? Threaten you?'

'I don't think so.'

'When he ran, did he drop anything, throw anything?'

'Not that I saw.'

They made arrangements for a car to take Luke and the other witness, whose name was Kevin, to the photo repository.

'Do you want some coffee?'

'No, thank you. Water.'

'Something to eat?'

'No, thank you. I'm pretty tired, you know.'

'You'll eat something and it'll make you feel better. That's brain food.'

'No.'

It was a sort of bulimia. He ate and ate—like a horse, like he could eat a horse because nothing tasted of anything—and then he retired suddenly to bring it all up. He was not to be left alone. He was not to be alone especially in the evenings. So he ate with whomever—James or Sandy or Denise, or a couple of times with his boss—always keeping the music up. Eat like a horse, then pump up the music. Do you mind, I like it at this volume. They thought the music was achieving something. Maybe he told them this; he probably had said something, closing his eyes and leaning back and appearing to be all right. He stayed in their apartments or they used the spare room in his. He guessed they had a roster. His boss, Kerry, was not on the roster, thank God.

   Kerry O'Keefe was a sort of amateur military historian, getting up a hobby for retirement; he'd been in London in the late sixties, Moscow in the early seventies, Fiji in the mid eighties, and from none of these placements emerged a good, well-told, succinct story. He'd been with history but hadn't noticed. He'd had a ring-side seat and hadn't seen a thing. He rambled and he wandered; it was an office contest not to be stuck with him. To Luke's slight shame, in the first weeks of his posting, he'd found in Strand Books a hardback copy of a recent Napoleon biography Kerry had been interested in and had given it to the boss. Complete censure from his colleagues was avoided only when it became clear that the giver had actually read the thing. Either Luke, the new boy, had carried smarminess to heights so eccentric there was a sort of admiration due, or he really was intellectually voracious, eating Napoleon for breakfast and so on. The truth, for Luke, was somewhere between. He would never have bought the book without Kerry's prior interest but, having done so, he consumed it without thought for any advantage it might bring except that of being better informed about a period of history he'd missed out on. Similarly, he'd checked out Paulus Potter, from the Dutch Golden Age, dead from tuberculosis at twenty-eight, who used to wander around farms at night, looking at the animals.

   As the hours of New York's night turned over into the hours of New Zealand's day, Luke thought of calling someone. His brother, Andy, as far as he knew, continued to live in rooms that had no phone. He could be contacted only by calling 'the big house', and then someone would have to walk the hundred or so metres to wherever he had his lodgings—in some prefab, in some shack out the back—and haul him over to the phone. It had been his brother's life for years. Luke didn't want to talk with Andy about what had happened in New York. He wanted to hear his brother mumbling about horses, about mounts he missed out on, about winners—he'd had a few. (Paulus Potter did a good line in horses.) He thought about his brother, who was small, and he felt his own slightness; that he was not fully grown. That he was not David Lange. He had left his coat in his apartment that day and was wearing only his suit, carrying the briefcase that was a graduation present. The violence—it was not at all clear someone had lost, was losing, his life, and then it was clear and it had always been so—made Luke small. Andy had run away from home age fourteen, disappearing completely for a month, before calling up to say he was a stablehand and no one was to come and get him. Their father made a few noises of protest but finally any objection faltered against the solid fact of Andy's success. He'd got a job and he was doing what he wanted to do. Luke was not as small as his brother, of course. Horses terrified him too. Yet he thought of Andy—in New York, at that very moment when it was happening—he thought of his brother riding a horse across a frost, up in the North Island somewhere, the saliva hanging from the horse's mouth, blowing back from the gallop and freezing on the mane or on his brother's arm.

He started getting into bed with these people who were looking after him. He crept through the apartment in a kind of sleepwalk, though he was perfectly aware of where he was and who he was and what he was doing. The sleepwalk was for them—so that they would accept him and pull back the sheets and take him in for the night.

In the third-floor bedroom of the large, government-leased, Upper East Side brownstone, he could lie between James and his girlfriend, Sia, holding whoever offered a back. They let him touch them, or at least nudge against them—did they have a choice? Occasionally he put a hand lightly on someone's shoulder. At a certain point in the night Sia would leave the bed because she was too hot, and Luke and James would wake up the next morning as if they were the couple.

It was James who liked to take visitors up on the roof at night to crouch and watch the woman across the street undressing. 'I have one rule on my roof,' he said. 'No masturbating!' The woman, who was in her thirties, never acknowledged her audience, but she was a regular performer, moving close to the window as she took off her clothes in a sort of dance. The lights would be on in her apartment so everything could be seen. Her bed was there and the fringed lamps and, further inside, a grandfather clock, which seemed an odd detail. Once Luke had taken in the show a few times, he looked more closely at the clock than the woman. He knew her routine, her thin body, her slightly bowed legs. She would touch her breasts and run her hands over her body before closing the curtains. James would then lead the quiet applause. Sia didn't object to anything in this ritual except the crouching. 'If you all have to watch, then stand up and watch. Show her you're watching and that you're interested in her.'

'But that would ruin everything,' said James. 'To be a voyeur it's necessary to hide.'

'Then you're pervs,' said Sia.

'Exactly!' said James.

'We're pervs!' someone said, and soon the phrase had been picked up by others. 'We're pervs!'

The usual crowd included friends of the Mission, New Zealanders and Americans as well as a variety of foreign nationals who'd strayed into James's orbit. Kiwis passing through New York, with only the slenderest connection to the household, were very welcome. There was a fridge in the second-floor dining room stocked with Steinlager. James was known as a good host. The way he opened his bed to the sleepwalking Luke was an extension of this reputation. At night, when it was just the two of them in the bed, Luke thought that, in some dreamy reflex, he might have once or twice kissed the other man's shoulder. He took it as a sign of James's kindness again that no mention was made of this.

Once, on the roof, crouching down with others to watch

the woman strip, Luke had glanced at James and discovered he wasn't looking at the woman at all; he was looking at Luke. After a moment he smiled and winked. He gave Luke a thumbs-up sign and looked back to the woman. 'My God,' someone whispered. There was giggling. 'I forgot to announce my rule of the roof,' said James, though before he could complete it, two others had spoken for him: 'No masturbating!'

This sort of staring was common. Everyone looked at Luke over this time. They wanted to see whether he was all right, or whether he was near collapse. Some of them, he guessed, might have wanted to see what he'd seen that evening on the street when he'd been walking home with his briefcase. He was special, it was true, and perhaps even a little like the woman in the window—notorious, predictable, trapped. Of course she, it seemed, had the power to change her situation. All she had to do was close her curtains a few minutes earlier each night. However, she did not.

Naturally, her psychology had been debated with great frequency in the brownstone. Exhibitionist, nudist, repressed, abused, sensualist, addictive, compulsive, acupuncturist—someone claimed she worked in this field at a place in the Village, which later proved wrong after one of the group made an appointment and researched it. This was another part of the game: to guess her profession. Her address alone put her near the top earnings bracket. 'Her daddy,' said Sia, 'refused to carry on paying for her dancing lessons. She wanted to train professionally but he said no. He's dead now, so with his money she's turned herself into a stripper. She's dancing on his grave.' Someone else carried on with this, suggesting she was showing the world the body Daddy couldn't have, and then a debate followed around incest or whatever inflammatory subject was available, at which point Luke usually went to bed, giving his apologies and being met with the dreaded noises of sympathy and concern. James always stood up. He was gallant that way, or, according to Sia, stuffy and conventional. He always took a few steps to the door, as if to see Luke off. He always said goodnight. Afterwards, if Luke waited a moment on the stairs, he could hear the hushed voices. They'd be discussing him. Questions were directed at James, though it was Sia's voice he heard above James's, not exactly disagreeing with the established benevolent line but modifying it perhaps. She was a bit sick of him, Luke guessed, the way he disturbed her nights, his claims on her boyfriend. Fair enough. He was bored himself with the situation.

Then there was Sandy. In finding Sandy's bed, Luke made a mistake, but a pretty nice one nonetheless, and not at all an obliteration of self, as suggested by the counsellor he was seeing. Sandy had already been in New York for more than two years; it was her job Luke was taking over when she went home the following year. This was an extended hand-over period. Sandy was his mentor. She was in her mid thirties, divorced. Foreign Affairs, she said, was toxic to any idea of continuity. They had a sort of sex, with her attempting what Luke guessed were not wholly spontaneous gestures of condolence and healing. When he tried to recall the details with anything approaching vivid particularity, he could not. He knew she'd never moved herself on top of him. He could not see her body really. He was aware of her thighs, positioning him expertly, her fingers that took his penis with a sort of palpable patience, fitting him inside her. She seemed to sigh at these moments, though not with pleasure. It was more like the noise a mother makes when bending to fit her child's shoe on again. He was sure she didn't know she was audible. There was no question that the sex meant anything beyond itself. Outside this setting she let it be known her penchant was for South American men, preferably musicians, who could get her on guest lists. Before she started she placed a box of tissues on the bed, and after he was done she handed him a few without looking at him, then she rolled over and immediately went to sleep. This was not faked. She snored lightly. He could have laughed.

For all he knew they might have had a roster for this. Tuesday: sleep with Luke. Get more tissues. He appreciated it though. He was moved. These were great friends to have, and none of them he'd known longer than two months. He was not in a fog in these beds. It was all clear, without being curative. It was a sort of highlight. On leaving the beds, he met once more with his anxieties.

In the police car driving to the photo repository, he'd sat in the back with Kevin, the black homeless man who was the other witness. Kevin kept touching the door of the car as if he might make a run for it. The detective who'd first interviewed Luke was driving. He was checking on them both in the mirror. Kevin turned to Luke and said, 'Listen, when you look at the photos, you might see someone you know.'

Luke told him he didn't understand.

'Who looks familiar, know what I'm saying.'

'Sorry, no.'

'All I'm saying is it won't me.'

From the front the detective said, 'You relax now, Kevin. We aren't looking at you for this.'

'Telling the other man,' said Kevin, 'that he might see a face and put the two together.'

The detective spoke to Luke. 'Kevin wants you to know he's in the book, he's in the photos.'

'I won't confuse it,' said Luke.

'I'm just a simple person made a wrong turn. My family is all back in Mississippi, where I'm trying to get.'

Kevin started talking about this until the detective cut him off:

'Both of you are a long way from home.' The statement carried the charge of negligence. If only they'd stayed at home.

The fight was over the bag of oranges. After the homeless guy had run off, Luke had walked back to the spot outside the grocery store—called back by Kevin, who'd seen it from across the street. 'Hey, you all right?' That was Kevin's voice. 'I was over there when it went down.' The store owner was standing by the body, and there was the bag of oranges. When the ambulance came a few minutes later and took the body away, there was already its outline in chalk and, beside that, a chalk outline of the bag of oranges, removed by someone.

Something had been telling him, Keep moving, keep moving, this is New York. The homeless guy keeping pace, looking straight at him. There was a knife, though the homeless man held it without fuss. There was a knife! Must have been. He was explaining something to Luke in a dribble of words, pointing the knife in the air, as if they were conversing over dinner and he was brandishing cutlery.

Luke brought his briefcase up to his side as a shield.

This information came through at the debrief following the photo repository visit, where Luke looked at hundreds of faces, mostly black or Hispanic. He didn't see the man they were looking for and he didn't see Kevin.

'He had the knife pointing up in the air while he was talking.'

'And then what happened?'

Then Luke fainted in the interview room. He went down and he woke up in the ambulance. He felt better almost immediately. He explained about the golf ball hitting him in the head. They gave him a scan—as they'd done back in Wellington—and found nothing. They gave him a cardiogram—which he'd also had at the time of the first fainting—and said there was no arrhythmia. They gave him the tilt test and measured his blood volume: it was normal. They said there were lots of people who fainted for no reason. There was no rhyme or reason and nothing sinister in the fainting of all these people. Syncope was a mystery. They said most likely it was stress related. Was he stressed?

He went back to his apartment, where he got a call from his boss who told him it was the Mission's view that, should he wish to take no further part in the police inquiry into the murder, he would have their full support. Luke said he didn't mind helping. As a foreign diplomat, Kerry continued, he could step away from it at any time. Luke knew that there'd already been official dissatisfaction expressed by the Mission as to the use made of their man. For a few hours following the event,

Luke had effectively left the Mission's radar, no one thinking to notify the authorities as to what was happening. Certainly Luke himself had not made a call, though he had told the police exactly who and what he was. Vaguely, the word immunity had floated through his brain, but didn't that apply only when he was the one in trouble? Luke's efforts up to this point, Kerry said, had been extraordinary, quite extraordinary. It was difficult to decide, down the phone, where the emphasis fell with this word, but Luke sensed he was being told off through praise. There was, however, one request that had come in and which Kerry said he would pass on, though he'd told the detective nothing could be promised. They were now at the very outer limits of tolerance for the immense disruption caused to one of their top juniors. The police wanted to take Luke to a few of the favourite haunts of transients. They would send a car at lunchtime the next day. It would take an hour. 'Say no,' said Kerry, 'and we'll get on with things. I can say no on your behalf. Legally we have no obligation here and I can assure you there'll be nothing prejudicial with regard to your own record in a refusal.'

'I can go in the car tomorrow.'

Kerry gave a sigh. 'You don't have to.'

'I'd like to, if they think it might help.' There was a long silence. 'If the Mission's view in such matters allows it.'

'The Mission's view in such matters, Luke, is to try not to become involved in murders. It's a damn nuisance. Wellington's breathing down my neck.'

'I'm sorry.'

'Not your fault. Of course it's been kept from the PM. The need for a singular focus in this coming month is paramount. Nothing blurred round the edges.'

'It's unlikely they'll find him.'

'Who?'

'The person who did it, the homeless man.'

'Oh, him. Well, let's hope not.' Then Kerry talked of the advisability of shipping Luke home. Quite normal procedure, he said.

'But I'm fine.'

'You'll be back. Nothing gets marked down against you here.' Kerry gave the laugh he always gave before being humorous. 'Of course the *New York Times* will have to find someone else to photograph.'

After the call ended, Luke turned on the music and, without injury, fainted once more. As he fell, he was aware of what else was tumbling down with him: Mandela, Fidel, Arafat, Bolger. The Pope was due. The United Nations was fifty but it looked like he'd miss the party.

Later, on sick leave, he called his sister, Catherine, in South Canterbury, asking whether she'd mind a visitor, a guest, even an overstayer—telling her nothing of all this.

Someone was missing

Someone was missing from the table and naturally that person—it was Hamish, the farmhand—occupied a greater space than those who were there, greater even than that of the stranger in whose honour the linen tablecloth had come out of the cupboard. Each family member, Luke saw, pressed his or her palms down on the stiff white folds. The farmhand's knife and fork and spoon were fiddled with. They were waiting to see if he would show up since Phil said the boy was coming from the far paddock by Moore's and had probably forgotten to close a gate. Maybe Mr Moore has him, said the children.

'To do what with him?' said Catherine. She poured water into the farmhand's glass. Katie put the salt in front of his place. These were invocations, designed to call Hamish home.

It was just after 6.30, still light outside. Luke had the impression dinner had already been delayed, though not by the farmhand's absence but by his own presence. His sister would have tried to put off the usual eating time.

'Look,' said Katie, pointing out the window.

'He's seen it,' said Simon.

'I have,' said Luke. Earlier he'd looked at the daylight moon through the boys' telescope. Jesus, he'd said aloud on finding it. Was it that he didn't quite believe telescopes worked, or that what the boys said would be there was there? Anyway, it was hardly auspicious that he'd been so unprepared for a fact as singular as the moon.

'If you poured a beer, he'd show up,' said Phil.

The boys said they would drink it.

'I reckon you would,' said Luke.

'Hardly,' said Katie.

Luke considered, but not seriously, a wink. In the old days, uncles winked, didn't they? Why wasn't there wine? He'd presented the duty free to Phil who'd thanked him, tried to give the bottles back to him and then promptly put them away in a cupboard. Luke felt as if he'd had a few glasses anyway. The two nephews, his niece, his sister, her husband, they all floated, wavered somewhat. He wasn't right, he knew. There was a bed waiting for him, if he didn't put his head down now on the table. 'It was the flight' was the repeating phrase. Yet he was enchanted too. Two weeks ago, he'd not imagined sitting here.

Katie, his niece, was wearing a black cape tied at her neck with a red ribbon. Luke had only seen her in photos. They were stills and this was the film. He'd held Timmy as a newborn the last time he'd visited. It was this gap in time that made him think of the old days. When he'd looked at them in photos, he'd forgotten there would be sound.

Hamish's plate was in the oven, covered by a second plate.

'Do you know where Luke's come from?' his sister tried on the table.

They did—two of them—and, thankfully, paused only to say the place before getting on with their own stories. 'I'm sorry for my country kids,' she told him. 'New York's a bit of a blank to them. If you'd said Christchurch they might have sat up.'

'Christchurch is enough for me,' said Phil. 'I can't have crowds.'

Catherine laughed and said, 'You've washed up in a backwater, I'm afraid, Luke.'

With the telescope he'd said to the boys they had a great tool for spying on people, looking into their houses. But of course there were no houses, and the whole voyeur concept was strange to them.

Katie, who was eight, said grace. 'Bless the food, bless the cooker, and bless Hamish, who is missing.'

'Amen,' they all said.

'Not sure about the Hamish bit,' said Catherine. 'And what about your uncle?'

The boys' spoons were already at their mouths.

'And bless all those who have made a journey to be with us.'

They said amen again, with the sound of teeth on metal that tapped on his nerves. He'd been in the plane for days, what did it matter this little sound, yet it did. It was that he could hear things again. A sheep cried.

It was a surprise his sister had turned Catholic again. He'd had nothing to do with it since leaving home, though rejection seemed too strong a word. He simply existed, tension free, in a world free of belief. Maybe children put these things—God, the afterlife, sin—back on the agenda as they clearly put other things he barely considered into the mix: mortgages, wills, retirement. One time in New York, Sia had announced that she would never have a baby because she just couldn't imagine having anything growing inside her. They'd laughed. It was the statement of a twelve-year-old. It communicated something, however, about them all.

No one else was reaching for it and he didn't feel he could touch the salt, move it from in front of the farmhand's place, otherwise the boy would never come home. It was a fairy tale they were stuck in, surrounded by prayers and moons.

'Make room for Hamish a bit,' said Phil.

'But he's not here!'

The sound came on. The kids really were without mercy in

their talk: friends, enemies, fights, secrets that weren't. Were they speaking more than normal? Catherine gave up translating for her childless brother. She was watching as he smiled at them all and nodded. He laughed when he saw laughter. She would think, Yes, he's trained in this. Diplomacy. She was drawn as she passed behind him with a plate to kiss him on the top of his head. The kids saw and were embarrassed but kept going.

He felt flattered to be so involved as to be almost invisible. And he saw in his sister's frequent admonishments to her kids—that they speak more slowly and not while they had their mouths full and not all at once—that she was proud of their greedy energy. She'd been a teacher, a good one who could have gone all the way, and she criticised not to close them down but to improve their contributions. She said, 'I don't think I've met anyone who drawed a picture.' And when someone said, 'Why does he get more?' Catherine said, 'He? He? Who him?' It was a pantomime. Usually his sister would be a bit harsher, he guessed, since surely a mother, even one who's been a teacher, finally lacks the stamina or was it the shackles of a teacher, and gives in, or shouts a few commands. Catherine held back, but it was in her, especially when a glass of water—it was the missing farmhand's—was tipped over and the water ran under the tablecloth. 'Oh!' she said sharply. Then, 'Never mind.'

'No,' said Phil, the father, over some squealing. 'It's only H_2O.'

Luke continued to catch his sister snatching looks, trying to gauge his reaction. Here is my family, she was saying, here is what I have done. Judge me. He did not and could not. He felt tender towards them. These were awesome accomplishments. If only she was without this slight defensiveness, it would be perfect. Perhaps if he were not present, it would be. If only the stupid thing with the iron hadn't happened. Hamish was missing from the table and that too melted the equation.

His glass was refilled. The surface of the farmhand's water shivered.

At the far end of the table, Phil asked Luke a few questions about recent travel—what on earth in the end was The Hague?—but Phil was one of those serious, absorbed eaters, a good-natured, open-hearted person who looked strangely unhappy when faced with food, no matter what the quality. (In the cruelty scale Phil was hopelessly light.) To ask him to carry his part in an extended conversation at the table was like requesting he return serve while holding his knife and fork. Besides, the children's volubility was a gift, excusing the adults from the burden of appearing lively. Phil was tired from his day's work. He yawned a lot, failing to cover his mouth. Catherine had had the afternoon with Luke, and her retreat now from further discussion of the brilliant beginning to his career and the delicate matter of its temporary pause was natural. He'd hardly coughed it all up in private. There was no chance he would let light in now.

She looked at her little brother as he paddled at his soup, taking some off the bottom of the spoon where it'd stuck. He was aware of being studied, and also of the sort of judgements likely. He was thin, with hips. They poked from new jeans. Even his casual had thought in it. He was squashed flat from tiredness but he'd borrowed an iron for his shirt. For her, something strange was not seeing his forearms. Phil's appeared huge. Why did her husband call water H_2O? Why did she mind it that he did—since Luke felt this was the case? Beneath the table, Phil's feet were in work-socks. She, for once, had worn sneakers, which had already been noticed by the kids who asked if she was going out. There was anxiety around this issue. They didn't believe her denial. Katie ducked under the table until she was told to sit up again. She said she was looking at her mother's feet, to see if they went anywhere. 'I'm really not going out!' She may as well have been in flippers. She was conscious of everything. Her brother had made it so. In his own defence, he had the thought that it was good to be reminded occasionally that one's life was odd.

Usually for dinner they ate the leftovers from lunch, but because it was a special occasion—the day of Luke's arrival on the farm—she'd started from scratch. Leek soup to begin. Lamb casserole ('One of ours from last year,' said Phil), then pud. Catherine was a chronically discouraged cook. Her diners had bland palates. 'Sometimes the kids accuse me of putting something they call "flavour" in. I think it was paprika. One day,' she told Luke, 'we'll dump the family and you and I can go into town for some real food, if they've got it.'

'Home cooking,' Luke said with enthusiasm. 'It's so great not to be eating out.'

'Those restaurants must be hell,' said Catherine.

He laughed. 'I've been suffering.'

'He's thin,' Phil said to Catherine, then resumed eating.

Catherine leaned forward. 'Tell me one great place you went, when someone famous walks in.'

'Where we had swordfish,' he said. 'In a tiny place in Little Italy, and Martin Scorsese was there.'

Catherine clapped her hands with delight. 'I don't know who that is but I can imagine.'

'From the movies, you know.'

'Yes,' she said, adjusting the elbows of her youngest son.

Luke tasted his soup again, a little irritated. Surely she was pretending not to know. She'd seen films. Just because she was the Catholic wife of a farmer didn't mean an end to everything.

'Little Italy,' said Phil. There seemed to be more to come. The boys both looked at their father, before everyone resumed eating.

The cupboards in Luke's apartment had contained more or less nothing, certainly no spices, no ingredients. There'd been bottled water. The stuff for making sushi—mats—though he never had. Suddenly he wasn't very hungry. There was a habit he'd developed of eating his way slowly towards an appetite. He could make himself come to terms with the soup. He'd got through large meals from exactly this position in New York restaurants. Gone in uninterested and with a shallow feeling in the throat; left fed and full. He wouldn't start talking about New York, however. He'd take his cure—his cue, he meant—

from these children who didn't care since it was so far away and nothing to do with their bursting little lives. Why little? New York was an indecency. What did it matter that he couldn't talk about Martin Scorsese?

Phil spoke to Luke, though Luke had no idea what he was talking about: 'Those guys from the factory won't know what's hit them with Mr Moore.'

They all knew Moore; he knew Scorsese. He hoped that was the end of it. The children, however, picked this Moore up.

'They said Mr Moore called the judge names.'

'No, he didn't. He was the one got called names.'

'He stormed out of court.'

'He swore at them and walked out. He's so tough.'

'No one swore at anyone,' said Catherine. 'Alec's lawyer decided that they should leave the court because they weren't achieving anything.'

The boys asked would he go to jail. Catherine told them no. 'He hasn't done anything wrong. It's just an argument about the land, and the court will decide what happens. There's been no crime.'

This was a blow. Then one of the boys said hopefully, 'They say he punched someone, a lawyer or someone, outside the court. That's a crime.'

'No one punched anyone.'

'He's done it before.'

'Beware!' said Katie.

'Of what?' said Luke.

The girl grinned back at him, then ducked her head.

Simon asked whether he could drink Hamish's water since he wasn't there. Both parents came in a thunder: 'No!' It was the loudest sound Phil had made. The noise was a sign that brought Luke around. Was he a complete idiot? If it were not for his own presence, there would be some kind of search party got up and they would not be eating lamb and passing the potatoes.

'Should we go and look for him, Phil?' said Luke.

'For who?' Phil looked up from his plate.

'Young men away from home, earning wages,' said Catherine, 'there's an idea we should put a brand on the ones that are ours.'

'They wander, then?' said Luke.

'Hamish loves his tea,' said Timmy.

'I can see why,' said Luke.

The boy spoke to his father. 'He irons his shirts.'

'Your uncle's a man of many parts,' said Phil.

Soon they were back on Moore. Catherine explained to Luke that their neighbour and friend, Alec Moore, had been involved in a long-running dispute with the cheese factory. They'd driven past the factory on the way home from the airport. It rose from the empty plains like a city, or a film set. A few years ago it had been less than half the size; now it employed more than five hundred workers, and it was still expanding. Tankers rolled in and out day and night, scaring everyone off the roads and into ditches. The factory had been swallowing up the surrounding farmland, buying out owners who'd farmed there for generations. Catherine and Phil, as yet, lived beyond the desirable orbit. Alec, sitting on a key property, was holding out. The factory had taken him to court, calling him unreasonable and obstructive.

Phil, grinning, looked up from his plate which was empty. 'Plenty have called him that. It's hardly a charge that'll hold. You may as well arrest Simon here for having food on his chin.' An outburst followed—there was no one apparently without mess somewhere on their faces or their clothes; the trick was to find it. Simon pointed to a spot on his uncle's trousers.

'Got me,' said Luke.

At one point there was a hush—pudding had arrived—and Luke said to Katie that he liked her cape. It was black with silver stars sewn on. Had his sister made the cape? It didn't look bought—the stars were lumpy, made of felt. Through the telescope the stars, the real ones, had no bulk.

'Beware!' said Timmy, snatching his sister's current word, then he blushed and everyone laughed.

It was almost dark by the time they'd finished their meal, the windows moony.

'But what did Hamish say?' said Catherine, with sudden exasperation, though there'd been no comment just then on the subject of Hamish the farmhand. The children had left the table.

'He didn't say anything to me,' said Phil. 'I reckon he'll have his head stuck under the bonnet somewhere. This is the person who for his fourteenth birthday got a model of an internal combustion engine.'

Catherine was stacking dishes. Phil stood up slowly and, yawning, said he would take the farm bike out to see what was keeping the boy. Catherine responded with a quick look, as though he'd said something ominous. He went across to her, and from some reflex—he wanted to reassure her—picked up a plate. Once he had it, he didn't know what to do with it. She took the plate from him, and said, 'I wish he'd look at our car. It still sounds strange to me.'

When she'd collected Luke from the airport, this subject had been covered in depth. Neither of them was interested in the engine of course. Next they'd begun to talk about their brother, whom Catherine hadn't seen in ages. Was he still riding? Had his femur healed properly? His pelvis? They tried to remember the sequence. Did he have a girlfriend? They could only guess at most of the answers. Andy was as murky as ever, Catherine said. If you got him on the phone, he only grunted, worried about the cost of the call. Luke had almost told it then, how he'd thought of Andy on his horses at the point he was being interviewed by the police in New York.

'Hamish will jump at the chance,' said Phil.

'I wouldn't mind coming too,' said Luke. 'Have a quick look over the place.'

'Good on you,' said Phil.

'There won't be much to see now,' said Catherine. She suggested he take it easy tonight and they'd give him the tour tomorrow, but he said he wanted to get out into the clean country air for a while. Again she told him he should leave it to Phil. There was then a short, unsatisfactory exchange about jet lag, ending in Catherine going off to see about the kids' bathtime. 'Of the three of them,' she said, 'it's Katie who's the most soap averse. The boys seem to like to be clean.'

They decided to take one farm bike; Luke could ride on the back. Phil apologised for this, but he asked was it okay in the failing light for him to drive since he knew the way a bit better, though if Luke did want a go he could. Luke said he had no desire at all to drive the bike and land them in a ditch somewhere. Phil asked again if he was sure. Maybe Luke could drive back. Phil had terrific manners, which could be annoying—things took a long time—but it was also his charm. He was loved as the gentle are. 'Please,' said Luke, 'I'll kill us both.'

Phil went inside the garage, reappearing a few moments later looking unhappy. 'We did have a helmet somewhere.'

Luke said he didn't need one.

'You could have a kid's one, which is somewhere.'

'No, really.'

Phil told him how much Catherine had been looking forward to his visit. 'Normally,' he said, 'we don't miss visitors.'

'It's a privilege to be one then,' said Luke.

'I'm not sure if what I said sounded right. We don't get the practice is what I mean.' They got on the bike and Phil started it. 'Stay as long as you like,' he shouted.

'Until I can't stand it,' said Luke.

'That's the story.'

The farm was mostly flat land. They had fifteen hundred acres, more than two-thirds of it crops, the remainder in pasture. As they drove through the paddocks they occasionally disturbed sheep; a few of them in their confusion were drawn to run in front of the bike. Phil never slowed down and the sheep always got out of the way at the last minute.

They checked out a group of sheds first, where Phil said the farmhand sometimes went on his off hours to fiddle around with an old dead motorbike. Hamish wasn't there. Then they crossed a line of trees and followed a slight dip towards a dry creek bed—another favourite spot—yet he wasn't there either. They skirted the edge of a windbreak, dodging old tree stumps and bouncing over branches. Phil stopped the bike and looked around.

'He wouldn't have gone into town or anything, would he?' said Luke.

Phil didn't answer, and Luke didn't repeat the question. Luke had noticed this before in farming people. If the question showed a basic ignorance then it wouldn't be answered. It was considered a kindness.

Finally they found Hamish in one of the far paddocks, standing up against a hay bale with the tractor in front of him.

'Here's the bloke,' said Phil. 'What did I tell you, head stuck in an engine.'

Hamish flicked his eyebrows upwards in greeting.

'This is Luke,' said Phil. 'Catherine's brother.'

'Heard you were on your way,' said Hamish.

'Are you coming in for some nosh, young Hamish?' said Phil.

'I'd like to, Mr Henry.'

They walked over to where Hamish stood, and only then did they see why the farmhand hadn't made it to the table. He was pinned to the hay bale by the foot-long spikes of the tractor's hay-fork which had passed through one of his legs. His pants were wet with blood below that knee.

'Okay,' said Phil.

In that moment, with such a sound, Luke understood his brother-in-law had, at least temporarily, saved everyone. Phil's gentleness was a kind of armour which no calamity could penetrate. The situation had the appearance—with the boy standing upright and not inconvenienced in any other way, and the spikes entering the leg—of some sort of magic trick, a bit of conjuring like the circus lady harmlessly sawn in half. Luke still wasn't quite sure what he was looking at. Phil hadn't changed his demeanour. Maybe it wasn't quite as bad as it looked.

Phil touched Hamish lightly on the shoulder. 'What have you been playing at, young Hamish?'

'She rolled back, Mr Henry.'

'Did she?' Phil was looking around, though this was mainly to give the boy the idea that there was something that could easily be done and that this event was rather routine. A hay-fork driven right through the leg, yes.

'I thought I had set the brake but I mustn't have.'

'Never mind.'

'Mr Henry?' said Hamish. 'I'm sorry but I don't want you to move me.'

Clearly they couldn't get in the tractor and reverse it—that would only bring Hamish with it. 'What I'm going to do, Hamish, is this.'

The boy instantly reaffirmed his position in regard to being touched or moved in any way.

Phil explained about going back to the house to get help. Luke would stay with him.

'I don't want him to stay,' said Hamish.

Luke didn't want to stay either. He volunteered to go back to the house, but then obviously this wouldn't work: he might get lost and he wouldn't be able to find what was needed. Phil had to point all this out, speaking to Luke as he had to the farmhand, showing no impatience. Then he said to Hamish, 'He will stay and I'll come back very soon. I'm going to get my hacksaw.' At this word Hamish flinched, but his eyes never left Phil's eyes. 'From way back on the spikes here, I can cut, you see.'

'I don't want you to cut.'

Luke didn't want him to cut either. It was as if they were both pinned in position, Luke alongside the farmhand. Immediately he regretted his trip. It had all been a mistake, a bad joke.

'It won't move your leg. Then we can get you away from the tractor. All right? No one's going to be moving anything in your leg. You knew exactly the right thing to do. Be still.'

Hamish nodded slowly. 'I remember at my uncle's a horse had a broken fence-rail in its belly. She didn't want it pulled either.' His speech was full of sobs. He could barely complete it. In the final analysis, something not altogether hopeful had obviously happened to the uncle's horse.

They went up close to the boy and smelled what at first Luke thought was the wound—but of course there hadn't been time for infection to set in; Phil had checked on him late in the afternoon. Still he could have been stuck here for two hours or more.

'I'm very hungry,' said the farmhand, with the presence of mind to attempt to distract his boss from his shame.

'Because you missed your dinner, Hamish, buggering around out here.' With these words he again prevented Hamish from wailing outright.

'I didn't manage to get to the toilet,' said Hamish.

'Who cares about that,' said Phil.

'I've got to change my trousers.'

'We'll get you a new pair.'

Luke walked back to the motorbike with Phil.

'Keep him talking is probably the thing,' said Phil.

'Where are you going?'

'To get help.'

'Can I come?'

'You need to stay here.'

Luke nodded. 'I see that.'

'Will you be all right?'

'I'm sure,' said Luke.

'It's hardly the welcome we meant.' Phil started up the bike. The engine noise was shattering.

Luke almost moved to get on the back of the bike. 'How long will you be?'

'I'll be quick.'

'Hurry now,' said Luke.

When Phil had gone it was Hamish who started to talk. He asked about dinner—what was it? What was for pudding? He always wanted coffee at night, he said, but at the house they never had it; they had tea later. Some nights he was dying for a cup of coffee, and not instant coffee either. This was an appealing subject for Luke, but he stopped himself from sounding the self-pitying note that lay there. Where had this farmhand learned to drink coffee? Already the question was being answered. He'd been to Argentina for rugby!

'You might want to take it easy now,' Luke told him. But Hamish continued to talk. He said he was glad he had Phil for a boss and not Alec. 'That poor bastard Christopher who works for Alec,' he said, 'when they went out rabbit shooting one night, reckons he nearly had the boss in his sights and it was only sheer will-power that made him turn away at the last minute. Of course he never would have. But it was in his head that he might.'

'How's the leg?' said Luke.

Hamish looked down at it. 'I'm fucked in it, aren't I? Do you think I'll ever play rugby again?'

'Of course.' The answer was glib, offensive.

'What would you know?' said the boy. 'They'll chop it off at the knee.'

'No, they won't,' said Luke. He could make none of the statements stick.

'It'll be hell to chase the chicks.' Hamish laughed. He was afraid; Luke could see the way his chin was moving of its own accord. 'Wouldn't mind a coffee. I'd drink any old shit.'

'What was Argentina like?'

'The chicks are amazing.'

'Yeah?'

'Dark eyebrows.'

'You like the eyebrows, eh?'

'What?' Hamish was lost again. He looked at Luke with hostility. 'Going out, were you?'

'No.'

'Dressed up.'

'Not really.'

Finally there was a silence—or at least the sound of the night and the paddocks. Scuffling noises, from birds. No doubt this was the sort of quiet Luke had come for—and which his counsellor and everyone at the Mission had recommended. It was Luke who broke it. Suddenly he felt the need to speak. Hamish's fear had provoked a kind of dread of his own. He thought the farmhand would die and no one would see it but him. He wasn't qualified in any way to see such a thing, and both of them knew it. Of course he was thinking too of New York, the homeless man. What was this—a pattern? For days after the golf ball hit him, with all its attendant inconveniences, its freight of predicted problems, he'd fumed his little 'why me?'s. He had a well-developed sense of injustice. A few minutes before he'd been in his sister's kitchen eating dinner, thinking about soup, and now he was out here in the dark, facing the death of a stranger, someone younger than himself, whose life was unknown to him, except for the details of his work, his rugby, his love of coffee, his interest in Argentine women, his desire to eat. It was a further irritation, Luke felt. This was all happening too soon, too crazily, after he'd arrived. He was just off the plane. The farmhand was ordinary; the evening was too; the tractor was the tractor that had been in service for years on his brother-in-law's farm. The farmhand would die slowly, killed by the tractor because a brake hadn't been put on and because the farmhand had been standing in this spot. There was a glass of water for the farmhand back at the house, and his dinner in the oven, covered by a plate. They had eaten while Hamish stood injured and bleeding. The bottle of wine was for the meal, for celebrating. Christ, they'd been out of the habit so long they'd forgotten that the guest's bottle of wine had a purpose and was first off the rank. Had he drunk two glasses of wine, he would have stayed in the house with Catherine and grown confessional. It was wrong of Phil, who knew the farmhand, to have left him alone with a stranger. Yet it was the only thing to do. It was wrong for the little birds to be playing in the grass on this still night, yet what option did they have? Luke didn't think 'Life is going on while life is ending', since how could such a thought be had except in a sort of retrospection; he was simply flooded with something—it was like annoyance—and he spoke rapidly and without preamble. 'In Hollywood movies that are made in Ireland, you know, they always put in crickets when it's night. And there are no crickets in Ireland! The Irish audiences think it's hilarious.'

'Is that right?' said Hamish.

'It's just the Hollywood sound for night. Crickets.'

'Have you been to Hollywood?'

'No.' Why not? He could have easily, on the way across, on the way back. He'd missed his chance. He wasn't much of a movie-goer. It was hard to sit still. In the restaurant in Little Italy, it had been someone else who'd pointed out Martin Scorsese.

'Where's the boss?'

Hamish dozed for a minute and, watching him, Luke also felt immensely tired. He might have nodded off. He needed to keep Hamish from unconsciousness. He spoke loudly, asking the farmhand what he thought of the cheese factory. He repeated the question. Finally Hamish mumbled something about his brother or his cousin working there, before dropping his head once more.

'Did you hear about Moore in court?' Luke demanded.

At this Hamish's head came up, but he didn't have anything to say.

Next, Luke woke with the sound of voices. Phil was back, with Catherine and the man they'd all been talking about, Alec Moore. Sheila, Alec's wife, was apparently looking after the kids. The ambulance had been called.

Alec shook Luke's hand, gripping his fingers since Luke was not quite ready for it. 'Pretty exciting down here, isn't it?' At once all the pieces of information he'd heard about this man were in his head. The portrait was incoherent. Alec was friendly and big, with immediate authority, and there was the feeling that a process had been launched, a mechanism for saving the farmhand that would not fail. Luke was glad to see his sister and Phil again—they seemed to be meeting for the first time, as if there'd been no airport reunion, no car ride to the farm, no afternoon and no dinner—and so Catherine hugged him and Phil gripped his arm and smiled with seriousness; but most of all he was glad to see this figure Alec, though he thought he didn't like him much, and that he was not liked by Alec either—how could that be? Still, this was the impression, as if somehow it was all down to Luke, this rural disaster.

Catherine held Hamish's hand and gave him sips from a water bottle. He wept openly with her before deciding he'd had enough, then he was silent and tense. Alec was fitting his hacksaw with a new blade while Phil went to work. His movements were slow at first, and he checked with Hamish after every few strokes to see if things were okay. Hamish had closed his eyes.

'Wind her up a bit now,' said Alec quietly.

Phil increased the tempo of his sawing.

They watched Phil cutting the spikes, sending little blue sparks up into the warm evening air as if he was operating a machine rather than a hand-tool, and then Alec said to Hamish, 'That's a perfectly good piece of equipment down the tubes, you know.'

When he was almost through the first spike, Alec said, 'Bring her down now,' and Phil slowed right down again. They didn't want the blade to jerk at the fork when it was through. Finally the blade severed the spike. Hamish cried out but it seemed to be only fright rather than pain.

'You're a great person, Hamish,' said Phil.

'He's a brave, brave man,' said Catherine.

'Can you stop now, eh?' said Hamish.

'Stop now and you'd look pretty silly chasing the girls with a tractor attached,' said Alec.

Hamish grinned. 'That's what I said to him.' He closed his eyes again.

'I'll have a go,' said Alec.

Hamish moaned, and tears came down his cheeks. 'Please, Jesus,' he said. 'Not that butcher. He could have been shot.'

Catherine put her hand to his forehead. 'He's feverish.'

Alec was already bending to the task. He worked to the same pattern as Phil. They'd never done this before, yet it appeared from watching as if every day there was someone to be rescued from an impaling. Once Alec had finished, the men swapped again. The sweat flew off them as they rocked back and forth, gently attacking the metal. The spikes were a couple of inches thick at the base and they broke several blades trying to get through them. Sometimes they cursed the business and were always answered by Hamish's sudden cries which made them push on and try not to say anything that would upset him further.

'Would you like me to have a go?' said Luke, confident of a refusal.

'No!' said Hamish.

'The young fellow's not so keen,' said Alec.

He would offer help. He would be turned down. Alec's gratuitousness instantly robbed him of the relief he'd anticipated.

'I'll have a go,' he said again uselessly. No one seemed to have heard.

'I told Luke nothing happened round here,' said Catherine.

Alec said, 'We do a good accident from time to time but mostly it's a dull life to look at.'

'He's already heard you were throwing punches outside court today,' said Phil.

'A myth can grow in a second. All it needs is total darkness. Not that I wouldn't have liked to sort someone.'

'We heard you walked out.'

Alec was grinning. 'It wasn't my idea. It was the lawyer, Margaret Leeds, a tiny woman, but the next thing I know is she's packing all her things in her briefcase and telling them we weren't here to be abused. It was a great feeling to be walking out with all the factory people open-mouthed. You should have seen it.'

'We were hoping to be there, but in the end we couldn't with Luke coming in,' said Phil.

'You don't want to waste your time on observing the legal process,' said Alec. 'To be in it is waste enough.'

'I could have got a taxi,' said Luke. This was ignored.

'It's great to have family around,' said Alec.

'Plus you better watch it, Alec, with your cracks about the legal process. Luke's a lawyer.'

'I've never practised,' said Luke.

'Finally, with the law you're not your own man,' said Alec. 'Is that a fair summation? You're on behalf of someone all the time in a case. The truth is left to itself.'

There was a lot to say in light of this provocation, but where to start? Anyway, it was hardly the time. Catherine asked Luke how he was feeling. 'This is awful,' she said. 'I can't believe it's happened.' For the second time since arriving, he was ready to tell everything. He was ready for tears and was saved by the farmhand's cries.

It was fully dark by the time the job was done, both men stripped to their singlets despite the cool temperature. Alec moved the tractor back, and they laid Hamish as carefully as they could on the ground. Such was the weight of the spikes that still remained in the leg, Phil had to hold them in position so they didn't yank down and cause the wounds to open more. Alec slowly raised the injured leg and asked Catherine to bring over a plastic bucket lying nearby. He then eased the bucket under the leg as a support.

Now his leg was free of the tractor, Hamish seemed to feel greater pain. He moaned and wanted to clutch his leg, but every time he brought his hands near the place he remembered he couldn't do it and fell back against the hay while Phil tried to steady the whole thing, talking to him not so much in words as sounds as if the poor boy were a distressed animal.

'I think we press somewhere,' said Catherine.

'Where?' said Phil.

'Is it behind the knee?' she said.

'Don't touch me!' said Hamish.

Alec produced a small spirits bottle from the same bag in which he'd carried his hacksaw and tipped some into the farmhand's mouth. Most of it came straight out and over Alec's hand and arm. 'All these young fellows dream about is a drink and when you pour them one they can't handle it.'

'That's not your secret stash, is it, Alec?' said Catherine.
'It lives in the medicine cabinet and must be years old.'
'No wonder it's being rejected.'
'We're fine now,' said Phil to the boy. He had one hand behind Hamish's knee.
'It's bleeding less,' said Catherine.
'It's a rosier picture than half an hour ago,' said Alec.

Catherine touched the boy's hair and said whatever she could. His face was wet with sweat, and he was shivering. They put the men's shirts over him to try to keep him warm.

'Could we carry him?' said Luke softly so as not to be heard by the farmhand.

'No!' said Hamish.

'The young fellow's not so keen on that,' said Alec. 'Let me know, Phil, when you need a spell.'

Alec walked around, feeling in the hay with his boot for the broken hacksaw blades and storing them in his leather pouch. Where Hamish had been standing the hay was blackened with his blood. 'I'd clean that up,' said Alec to the farmhand, 'only you'll probably want to come back and look at it and boast about it.'

'Your Christopher will want the proof,' said Phil.

'Is there a bit for him to see?' said Hamish.

'There's plenty,' said Alec.

'Oh, I might die!' cried Hamish.

'From what?' said Alec. 'It's only claret. There's more at the bottom of some rucks, where you've been yourself. You'll tell the story to your grandkids until they beg you to stop.'

The farmhand began asking for his pants. To distract him, Catherine started telling them about when their boy Timmy had lost his first tooth; there was a little dribble of blood on his T-shirt and he refused to put it in the wash. He used to keep his baby teeth in a jar on a shelf above his bed and once, when Katie was mad at him over something, she took the jar and threw the teeth down the toilet, flushing them away, except for one, which sank and rested on the toilet bottom and was used to pin the crime on the perpetrator. 'We always said that showed how a bad deed came back to bite you.'

Hamish showed no signs of having heard her. Alec only grunted. A line of sweat was running slowly down the side of Phil's face. He couldn't move because he was supporting the spikes. 'Get that for me, won't you,' he said. 'It's tickling, it's killing me.' Luke reached across and wiped it away. 'Thanks,' said Phil.

'He wields a great handkerchief, your brother,' said Alec to Catherine. 'So, you did law but didn't practise. I'm like that with golf, aren't I, Phil? I do it but I never practise.'

'You give the course a fright,' said Phil.

'Silly game,' said Catherine.

'Agreed,' said Alec, 'but no sillier than anything else.' He looked across at Luke. 'You should sit down, you don't look good.'

'I'm okay,' said Luke. But he did sit down. But he didn't want to. But he couldn't stand up. He was just off the plane.

'Apart from a night in Wellington, Luke's been travelling for twenty-four hours or more,' said Catherine.

'All to get here on time to see this great show,' said Alec.

'In Hollywood,' said Hamish suddenly. 'Set in Ireland.'

'What's that, lad?' said Alec.

'Ask *him*.' The farmhand managed to point at Luke.

'Me?'

'What's this?' said Alec.

'Ask him! He was saying.'

'Oh, it was nothing,' said Luke.

'The crickets!' Hamish laughed foolishly.

'He's delirious,' said Catherine.

The farmhand lapsed again into unconsciousness.

Finally they heard voices and saw the lights from torches coming across the paddock. Phil called out to them, and the torches turned in their direction, wavering and jiggling as they ran. There were two ambulance officers carrying a stretcher and a large bag, and, further behind them, another figure struggling with the pace. He would run a few metres, then walk, then run again. It was Dr Cyril, they said. 'Here's a first,' said Alec. 'He'll be breaking a sweat soon.'

'What's his name?' said one of the ambulance officers. Catherine told him, and the officer bent over Hamish and asked him how he was feeling. Hamish was conscious for a moment. He cried out, then he was gone again.

The ambulance men were setting up a drip for the farmhand when Dr Cyril arrived.

'You got the bronze,' said Alec.

'Who moved this lad?' said Dr Cyril. No one made a response. He was puffing breaths of solid tea into their faces. It was a blast of this that brought Hamish around briefly once more.

'Hello,' said Hamish calmly.

The doctor looked across at Luke. 'What's with that chap?'

Luke stood up. 'I'm fine.'

'This is my brother Luke,' said Catherine.

'Going out, was he?'

'No,' said Luke.

The doctor turned back to the patient.

'I thought the lad would be saved,' Alec whispered to them, 'but now it's touch and go.'

'Quiet, you,' said Catherine. 'The man's a pain but he knows enough.'

'I smell alcohol,' said the doctor.

'Dispensed purely for pain relief,' said Alec.

'You great idiot, the rule is nothing by mouth, especially alcohol. You may have delayed this boy's trip to theatre by several hours.'

'Nothing went in,' said Phil.

Once the drip was in, and a bandage tied around the spikes at the wound, Hamish was lifted onto the stretcher and they set off very slowly for the house, Phil still holding the protruding ends of the spikes. He was cold now too in his singlet, Luke could see, and so was Alec, but their shirts were trapped under the silver emergency blanket the ambulance officers had brought to cover up their patient. He offered them the jacket he was carrying, a nylon windbreaker. It wouldn't have fitted either man. He got no response. The doctor trotted alongside, offering advice to Phil which he never acknowledged. Nearer to the house, Catherine and Luke ran on ahead to make sure there wasn't a gallery of curious children to see them go past.

A woman met them in the garden. This was Sheila, Alec's wife, though for some reason it was hard to put them together. She was a few years younger than his sister, Luke thought. In her arms she held a baby—this belonged to another neighbour; Sheila had been babysitting.

'Thanks for coming,' said Catherine.

'Is he all right?' she said.

'Let's pull the curtains,' said Catherine. 'What are the kids doing?'

'I've got them all watching TV.'

'This is my brother Luke. This is Sheila. We decided we wanted to put on a good show for his arrival, so obviously Hamish was sacrificed.'

'A wonderful performance,' said Luke. 'Very realistic.'

'The doctor was especially good.'

'I'm not sure what you both mean,' said Sheila.

'Just talking nonsense, dear,' said Catherine. 'It was all horrible but it's better.'

'Look,' Sheila said, 'before you go in.' She pointed to the front of Luke's shirt which carried splotches of the farmhand's blood. Luke looked at it and then, for whatever reason, he burst into tears. Tiredness. It was the shirt he'd ironed. He wasn't thinking at all about the poor injured farmhand. Shameful tears really of self-condolence and exhaustion. Catherine, he saw, was puzzled or disappointed. She didn't move to him. There were things to be done.

Sheila put the baby down on the grass; for a moment it looked as if she was about to go over to Luke and hug him. However, Luke stopped crying at once and told them they had to hurry, the men would be here soon. The ambulance, with its lights on, stood under the trees beside the dog kennels. It seemed extraordinary in its whiteness and largeness, like an enormous new fridge or freezer, with a suggestion of meat. One door was open and there was a metallic gleam, as if cutlery were held inside it. Luke thought about climbing into the ambulance himself.

The dogs paced back and forth behind the wire, whining a little.

Sheila began to follow Catherine into the house; Luke was behind her. They were at the wash-house windows, about to pull the curtains, when they looked out into the dark and saw the baby still sitting up on the grass, quite content, not puzzled, but waiting to be reclaimed in the light from the ambulance.

'Oh, Sheila,' said Catherine, 'look what you've done. How stupid of you.'

The vehemence of the outburst surprised Luke. Stress had made his sister harsh—perhaps he could also look into a little crack here if he wanted, but he wouldn't, didn't want to. He was a baby himself. Would he weep again? It was likely.

'Sorry,' said Sheila.

'You're a stupid woman,' said Catherine.

'You're right.'

'No,' said Catherine. 'That's rubbish. I'll get him.' She went outside.

Sheila turned to Luke. 'Your sister has to put up with so much.' It was a statement that matched the evening in that it was too full for Luke. No thank you, I've eaten already. A furry soup. The furry stars. His view seemed briefly to telescope out and upwards, towards the moon.

They watched Catherine reach down and pick up the baby.

'Are you down for long?'

'I'm not sure.' The lights from the ambulance ballooned and dispersed.

'Are you all right?'

'Yes.' Then he fainted, feeling himself go.

We don't know anything about syncope

For a while the 'mystery guest'—as Luke had wrongly been called—failed to appear before lunchtime, when the metallic smell of boiled potatoes got him up. Of course they all knew who he was, and many had met him and found him a lot like his sister. He was friendly and quick. He had the same dark features as she did; he had her brown eyes. He was very familiar. The mystery then was delicate, and perhaps only his niece had found the words for it one time they'd met in the hallway: 'Are you sick? Or just pretending?' Catherine stood behind her daughter.

His answer was, 'Just pretending', to which Katie replied, 'Just pretending to answer me, I bet.'

Luke had laughed at this—he laughed easily, tactically. Even with an eight-year-old, he was surely giving the impression of playing for time.

Since Hamish's accident, Luke had been 'taking it easy', which meant long periods in his room. Dr Cyril had checked him out after the fainting episode and declared him—as expected—clear of any sinister elements. Probably, Luke had said, he'd been doing too much. Not necessarily, said Dr Cyril. He'd had a patient who presented with similar symptoms and it was found eventually that he'd been doing too little. 'What are you planning to get up to here?'

'I was planning to have a holiday,' said Luke.

'That doesn't sound right to me.'

'Well, it's why I came.'

'Is it?'

'Get away from it all.'

'What an extraordinary idea.'

'You don't think it's a nice place to come and . . .'—how was this phrase to be completed?—'you know, be free for a while.'

'At your age?'

'I'm not old, I know.'

'At your age, you shouldn't have cares. Plenty of time for that later. You should be up and at life like a terrier.'

'I have been.'

'Back here with your sister, getting away from it all.'

'I haven't stayed with her for ten years.'

'She hasn't mentioned you in three, probably.'

He stared at the doctor. What a prick.

'Listen, we don't know anything about syncope but we know you shouldn't change everything because occasionally you fall over when you feel pressured. That lad who had the spikes in his leg was lucky not to lose it, you know.'

'I know. But I'm sorry, I don't get your point.'

'Oh well,' the doctor sighed, 'if you're feeling tired, you should rest, it won't kill you, I suppose.'

'Actually my sister and Phil mentioned that if I wanted to, and had the time, I could take their chimney down. They're putting in a woodburner.'

'Excellent!'

'Then you approve?'

'There's no contest. Woodburners are far more efficient.'

Some of us are trying to sleep

Usually Luke appeared while Catherine was doing the dishes. He would hear the sounds and walk down the stairs, timing it so he could help with the drying. Today he'd decided to come down while everyone was still there.

'Did we wake you?' she said.

'Were we too loud for him?' said Alec.

'Could you keep it down?' said Luke, grinning. 'Some of us are trying to sleep.'

Phil laughed at this; Alec didn't. The mystery around Luke was probably a bit long-running for Alec. They'd met a few times since Hamish's accident. 'What's he paying at this hotel, and can I have a room myself?' he said.

'We only have reputable types,' said Catherine.

'Still, he'll be cheap to run, I imagine, missing meals,' said

Alec. 'And I hear he does his own ironing.'

Everyone knew a loose end drove Alec wild. Occasionally this fault was played upon. Small pieces of information were held back from him. He had to know it all and at once, but he didn't like to be heard asking. Catherine sometimes drew things out. 'To keep the man honest,' she explained, 'since of all of us he might be the biggest gossip there is—except he won't be caught at it.'

However, it wasn't required in this case.

Luke hadn't said anything much about New York; he was home after only a couple of months to 'sort himself'. It would have been intense in New York, she said. It had been full-on, he said. But the work was wonderful and the city was too. He mentioned the birthday lights on the Secretariat Building. He'd developed the habit of rubbing at his eyes while he spoke. Had he had fainting spells over there? she asked. In fact there had been a moment or two when he'd felt unsteady, but it was nothing like the good old days, he said, laughing. 'Did you get it checked out?' Of course he had—and there was nothing there, as usual. He simply needed some country air. 'You?' she said—it was her turn to laugh, 'who can't be five hundred yards from a café?'

'It is terrible,' he said. 'But I'm coping, aren't I?'

In the fifteen years she'd lived down here, he'd visited only twice. She'd come to him with the same miserable frequency, but then that was an understandable failure, with the farm and the children.

'Stay as long as you like,' she said.

'I'm so grateful to you and Phil.'

To those who asked, he spoke about a 'break' after being 'chained too long to a desk'. The complaint appeared to work. A desk was naturally a horror to these listeners, associated with tax returns and form-filling and other sorts of inactivity. Luke was suffering, he was told happily, from a shiny backside. Also, he was asked if he couldn't have a quiet word to the Prime Minister when he got back. He was asked if it was true that politicians threw a dart to decide things. 'Only on the important issues,' Luke said. Of course a lot of the farmers of the district listened to National Radio on their tractors all day. They were well informed, and their deference was mostly humour. He had an inkling of this. He also suspected, from early on, that Alec represented, in a way, the worst of them. Alec had their general knowledge but not their tolerance for vague personal statement and none of their tact. Catherine appeared delighted to see her brother come down from his room, but something also told him he'd chosen unluckily. Alec was stimulated; he was using his elbows to indicate some space should be made.

Catherine passed Luke the chair.

'Take the weight off,' said Alec, with obvious mischief.

She was already setting him a place beside Tony, a local who'd worked casually for them in the past and now had Hamish's position. Christopher, who'd been with Alec almost a year, sat across from them, next to his boss. These were 'the boys', about eighteen. Alec and Christopher were over to help with some fencing that bounded the properties.

Once it was accomplished, Catherine appeared to regret the seating: she'd put Luke in Alec's direct line. She went to move the setting but Phil told her everything was fine and they could squeeze in.

Luke handed Catherine the knife and fork. 'I won't be needing these.'

'It's tender meat,' said Phil.

'It melts in the mouth,' said Alec. 'The boys'—he pointed his knife at the farmhands but not so carefully that Luke might not think he was being got at again—'the boys haven't been brought up in a place where manners mean much, otherwise they might be saying thank you to the cook.'

Tony looked up from his plate and mumbled something. Christopher hadn't heard and continued to eat.

'You'll make her blush,' said Alec.

'I would too, to get a word like that round here,' said Catherine.

Phil felt the challenge and announced his wife was the most

splendid person, worthy of all the gratitude he could muster. 'I'd be completely lost without her.' Though the compliment had been propelled by banter, it finished on such a note as to make even Alec's snort seem a kind of tribute rather than a sound of derision. Only Tony, perhaps immune to the truth of feeling between his employers from having seen it every day, wasn't stopped by it. 'Any more meat?' he said.

There was a leg of lamb under a tea towel. Steam lifted off it, and from underneath the tea towel came a small trickle of fatty blood. Catherine took the tea towel away and carved off some more meat. She brought this to the table, offering it first to Luke, who shook his head. The boys went for it, having checked with Alec.

'I tried a salad one time and that almost provoked a mutiny,' she said. 'If lettuce appears, they'll put sugar on it.'

Alec turned to Luke. 'Are you jet-lagged still? Surely not. They say it was the problem with the fainting that time your first night.'

'I think I was a bit then,' said Luke.

'Down like a sack of spuds, Sheila saw it all, and all just to get a ride in the ambulance.'

'It was a great ride,' said Luke.

'Did they have the siren?' said Christopher.

'Here's another volunteer to get himself maimed,' said Alec.

'They didn't have the siren,' said Luke.

'There would have been no one on the road at night,' said Catherine.

'He was probably knocked sideways by that show we put on with Hamish,' said Phil. 'I felt woozy myself.'

'It was a great show,' said Alec. 'And finally Sheila leaving the baby out in the cold as a crowning touch.'

'How do you know about the baby?' said Catherine.

'From the horse's mouth.'

'No harm done anyway,' said Catherine.

'Have you heard from the lad himself?' said Alec.

'He's still back and forth from hospital,' said Phil.

'Those weren't small holes either. You could put your finger through.'

'Thank you, Mr Moore.'

'You were there yourself, Catherine.' Alec turned to the boys, who were listening hard. 'And then we get to the house and this new fellow's down in a heap. There's someone's baby sitting out in the cold, on the grass, in wee pyjamas. Me and him in our singlets. It was a three-ring circus with free entry!'

Christopher hit the table with his hand. 'I wish I could have been there.'

'No, boy,' said Alec sharply, 'you would have been useless.'

'I can't think why, Alec,' said Catherine, coming to stand behind Christopher. 'It was a team effort and we could have used another pair of hands.'

'Didn't need them,' said Alec. 'We had this new fellow to get out his handkerchief and wipe the sweat off of his lordship here.'

'I did my bit,' said Luke, laughing.

'And what will you do now?' said Alec. 'What plans?'

'He's on holiday, I think,' said Phil.

'You should try it, Alec,' said Catherine.

'We went to Wellington once and Sheila didn't know what to do with herself. She sat around like a burnt stump.'

'And what did you do?' said Catherine, who knew the story as everyone did, except Luke.

'Employed my mind,' he said, lifting another slice of lamb onto his plate. 'Or tried to.'

'He spent every day at Parliament!' said Catherine.

'Hideous,' said Alec. Evidently he had a few of the politicians' interjections off by heart. Phil was asking to hear one of them but Alec waved this away. It seemed he never spoke if encouraged in any direct way, except perhaps by Catherine. One time, Luke had heard him say to her, 'I can feel the psychologist in you, the way you see through us.' Catherine had a university degree and Alec had left school at fifteen to work on his father's farm. He spoke from a playfully pretended ignorance; she replied—

obviously not for the first time—that the psychology she'd studied offered no insights into people or their secrets. It was dry stuff, statistical. Besides, she'd been twenty-one when she'd finished, and remembered none of it.

Alec again addressed Luke with the familiar baiting tone, though friendlier now. 'You'd know it well, of course, that hallowed debating chamber.'

'Try to keep away from it,' said Luke.

'In your Ministry you'd be involved how with day-to-day Parliament?'

'Oh hardly at all.'

'He won't be drawn,' said Phil.

'Oh, I know, very cautious. Seeing this chap is as rare as seeing the Prime Minister in the flesh. He only ventures out when there's something gory to be seen.'

Christopher looked up and said, 'The mystery guest.'

Tony laughed at this.

'Our two wits,' said Alec, spearing another potato. 'Good spuds.'

Phil spoke admiringly. 'This is the bloke who's already had the lunch his wife packed for him. Eaten for morning tea.'

Alec acknowledged the compliment with his fork.

In the days following this occasion, Catherine would brief Luke on what made Alec tick. He was proud of his full leanness, his shape that was solid but which hadn't bulged. Food, in whatever quantity, was paltry to such a constitution. 'Bring it on,' he liked to say. But he could be a wearying dinner companion. A buffet was a kind of military campaign; each dish was to be outmanoeuvred. To the inquiry 'How was the meal?', Alec would likely give the answer, 'We made short work of the chops' or 'We saw off the cake.' He was bewildered by someone else's unfinished plate. Appetite was firmly attached to virtue, though the glue was discipline. He didn't like people who made pigs of themselves. His special suspicion, however, was reserved for anyone skinny—man or woman—and he worked until he found the buried cause of the condition. His greeting could often come in a single thrust: 'I hope you're not ill, are you?' Phil was safe announcing this first lunch his neighbour had eaten. In contrast, nothing could be said without fear of offence in relation to drinking. Alec did this in watchful moderation, responding to any joking with terrific prickliness. He hated to see a man drunk. He'd never been so himself, he said. And though the example could never be brought up in his presence, this strictness was easily connected back to his mother, who 'took to her bed' for years, sustaining herself on soup and gin. Alec had brought Sheila back from Omarama to help out and she became his mother's *de facto* nurse through the end.

Alec named Luke's Minister and asked what he thought of him, to which Luke replied that he'd only come across him a few times and he was decent enough.

Catherine said, 'Once he shaved off his beard it was strange, because now he looks a bit shifty to me, as if he's got something to hide, which presumably was the point of the beard. I don't understand it.'

Phil said that Tony was growing something, and Christopher took a predictable pleasure in this comment. Under such focus Tony brought his hand to his chin and blushed. 'At least I can,' he said. Alec found all this prattle pointless; he sighed and fidgeted, taking up the salt-shaker and weighing it in his hand as if he might throw it on somebody's roof, before setting it down again.

Pudding came out and no one talked much while that was eaten.

Luke had a piece of toast and a cup of tea, then he stood up. 'I'll see you guys again.'

'You take it easy,' said Alec. 'Go and have a lie-down if you like.'

'I think I've earned it,' said Luke. He carried his plate to the sink where Catherine was working; she never sat down with the men.

'I'm going into town later if you'd like to come along,' she said. 'See the sights.'

From the table Alec called out, 'For sights you'd want to keep driving him a long way off, Catherine.'

'I might come,' said Luke. 'I need to get those tools for the chimney.'

'There's no hurry,' said Catherine.

Phil spoke at the table to Alec. 'We've said he might take down the chimney for us and he was quite keen on that.'

'Quite keen?' said Alec. 'I see he keeps a builder's word too!'

'No hurry,' said Phil.

'I'm ready right now,' said Luke.

'Great stuff,' said Phil. 'He wants a mask and some good gloves, protect his hands.'

There was a snorting sound from the farmhands. Everyone looked at Luke's hands.

'Filthy, dusty work,' said Phil.

'I've got some old gardening gloves,' said Catherine.

'Not for bricks,' said Phil.

'Too small probably as well,' said Tony, which made Christopher laugh, then stop.

'I've had the man waiting with the woodburner,' said Alec.

'Sing out if we're holding anything up,' said Phil.

'There's nothing to hold up. He'll deliver as soon as you need it.'

'I'll start today,' said Luke.

'You'd better have some dinner then to build your strength,' said Alec.

'I'll have something later.'

Phil pushed his chair back from the table and said to Luke, 'It was good to see you down.'

'We were privileged,' said Alec, mockingly low.

Luke hovered just beyond the doorway, out of sight, one foot on the stairs leading up to his room. He heard Catherine say, 'He's had a rough time.' There was silence. Everyone—even the farmhands—would be waiting for her to add something to this diagnosis. What would 'rough' mean in a life like that? Yet even if she'd wanted to, there was probably not much to add. Her brother was all hints and jokes. He parried her with the same set of sounds he used with anyone he met. Was he sick or just pretending? Katie's question still held. 'Just pretending to answer me, I bet.' His niece spoke a little like the girls who appeared in the novels about witches that she read—'consumed', Catherine said. Luke had picked these books up and looked into them when Katie was at school. He couldn't read them. The simplest narratives seemed instantly to tangle. Even the newspaper tripped him up. Maybe it was the world he was sick of. Still, he went to the international page. He'd missed the Pope's address to the General Assembly. 'Freedom is the measure of man's dignity and greatness.' The Pontiff asked that the world overcome its fear of the future. 'The answer to the fear which darkens human existence at the end of the twentieth century is the common effort to build the civilisation of love, founded on the universal values of peace, solidarity, justice, and liberty.' He made a mental note to discuss the Pope with Catherine.

There was also a lot of backwards writing left on bits of paper around the house, which he had trouble reassembling. EID TSUM UOY SIHT DAER UOY FI. It looked like Vietnamese. A month back he'd sat beside Thailand, and Norway, and Guam. He'd had the world if not at his feet, then at least at his elbow and in his ear-piece. Would the gang be back at Smorgas talking cocktails, back on the rooftop hitting tennis balls?

Now when the coast was clear he drifted from room to room, opening drawers. There wasn't much in his defence if anyone caught him at it, though he never approached that old stand-by of the illicit wanderer: the knickers drawer. Catherine was his big sister, forty, and she and her kind husband, Phil, had opened their home to him.

Yet he had been caught, if only on his own turf. Simon had come in to look for something, forgetting the spare room was in use, and had seen his young uncle waiting by the window. It was midday on a Saturday and Luke wasn't dressed. 'You can see the mountains today,' Luke said, utterly failing to fake the emotion required of the true contemplative. Simon nodded and backed out. The sky was blue, long and flat, and grew pale when it reached the Alps. What would a thirteen-year-old want with a mountain view? What would a twenty-seven-year-old? The boy would have it all over now that his mother's brother was staring into space all day, and not wearing clothes.

In the kitchen it seemed there was nothing to be gained by Catherine pressing her brother's case with Alec. Clearly he believed she was being taken advantage of—which might have been true. Luke re-entered the room to get a glass of water. He thought it was oddly touching that this difficult and selfish man could adopt a cause that wasn't his. It suggested something no one seemed quite sure of, and on which no one could rely completely: Alec's friendship, his loyalty. Even Sheila, Alec's wife, seemed unable to find that assurance—and this bald fact provided the disquiet, the disturbance, to Catherine's—and to everyone's—relationship with him. Luke was aware that Alec was credited with 'a streak': it could lead anywhere.

Phil alone did not believe in any ambivalence. That became clear to Luke over the next few weeks. Phil listened to everything Catherine said about their neighbour and agreed with large amounts of it, but finally he could not say Alec was anything but honourable and good. He'd stood with Alec in storms—real ones and those brought down by idiots; Alec had battled the banks—'the good fight', he termed it—and the meat companies and now the cheese factory. There were a thousand tasks they'd shared. Phil had knowledge of his charity too: the money Alec sent his sister through her serial disasters, though he often said she had to find her own feet; the fund for the family of a shearer killed on the road one Christmas; the sudden jab with which he broke the nose of the fellow who was saying mirthfully that the same fatal accident was 'a hose job'. Pow! That he gave out money while living with fierce frugality either increased or detracted from its sense—people were never sure. Of course Sheila, who lived with the consequences of this redistribution, never complained, further obscuring the argument. All arrangements of money within marriages were, in the end, profound mysteries.

Alec was also physically courageous. He'd had an early career in flying, and Phil was afraid of heights. Indeed, Phil's faith in his friend went a long way to provoking it in Catherine, with the proviso that she could lose it at any moment. At the Church of Alec, she liked to say, her attendance was social rather than religious. She went there to see her neighbours and not for a revealed truth. There were enough in his thrall already.

Alec Moore was on the Regional Council, and was that body's most potent voice and the instigator of some notable scraps. He was a withering correspondent, though never to newspapers: that was the domain of crackpots. Instead he wrote, he said, to 'the actual names'. He played golf with the Mayor, using only three clubs and none without a smouldering sense of grievance. He took divots out as though swinging a spade. And though it threatened to turn his touch completely caustic, he sat on committees, sensing that to learn patience might finally offer a route his nature otherwise denied him. There was never a shortage of fools to suffer, he told Catherine and Phil, and this art was perhaps the politician's most valuable accessory.

'Is that something you'd be interested in, a politician?' said Catherine. It was widely known that he'd been offered things from time to time.

'Never,' said Alec. 'There's no place for farmers up there any more.'

His attempts to draw Luke on government matters weren't idle. Nothing was idle with Alec. He wanted everyone else's plot out in the open—a need for transparency that tended to throw a sheet over his own moves.

Right now, however, Luke's appeal had waned—he saw this. Alec had had enough of the subject of Catherine's Wellington brother who wouldn't work and wouldn't eat and wouldn't speak. He stood up and clapped his hands. At this signal the boys were on their feet. He told Catherine thanks again and that being there for a meal was always a special time, he remembered them all, he said—he was speaking with the flatness that in his case signalled emotion, sentimentality even—and then they went to the back door to find their boots.

Where the men had walked across the lino there were damp patches from their socks which quickly disappeared. For some reason Catherine watched this process; what was she thinking of?

Katie had told her—and Catherine had passed it on to Luke—that their uncle was a hex. He had arrived on the day of Hamish's accident; the two things were plainly connected. 'Maybe she's right,' said Luke. 'I'm bad news.'

'What else can we blame you for?' said Catherine.

'I don't know. Crop failure? Locusts?'

'So it was you with the locusts.' She laughed. 'Actually I always thought of you leading quite a charmed life.' This was said with a hint of criticism.

'I'm charmed here. In this house. With all of you. Just what I needed.'

She studied him dubiously. 'The country air.'

'Right,' he said. 'And hopefully I'll go before I'm an utter nuisance.'

'Don't go anywhere,' she said, annoyed.

Luke had decided he would stay downstairs, offer to help his sister. Phil let the others leave and then he kissed Catherine on the cheek. 'I was wondering on the chimney again. If it's too soon, we could wait a bit.'

'He said he was keen,' she said. They were speaking as if he wasn't there.

'I am,' said Luke. 'I worked one university holidays on a building site.'

This suddenly seemed a pitiful qualification.

'There's no hurry,' said Phil.

'Of course if he climbs a ladder I don't want him falling off it,' said Catherine.

'What did Cyril say?' said Phil.

'Who cares what that man says,' said Catherine. 'He was

positive, as far as I know. Told him to snap out of it basically. Is that right?'

Luke nodded.

'Tony could help,' said Phil, 'but not today or tomorrow. We'll be that long out there on the fence.'

'One good thing about Luke is it's getting old Alec worked up. That's always fun.' She spoke without real conviction.

'He's been a beast on this fence. The poor boys were looking to stay a while longer in the kitchen and have their tea and slip down in their chairs for a bit.'

'You go easy on them then.'

'Alec is old school, I guess. He thinks his duties under the Employment Contracts Act are pretty much covered by pushing the boys hard as he can and telling the poor sods every hour, You'll sleep well tonight!'

Catherine scowled. 'Awful man.'

'He loves it here though. All morning he's going on about it. What's Catherine got for our dinner and so on. Then the lamb. It appears Sheila won't do a roast.'

'Good on Sheila. But that doesn't sound right, much as I'd like to believe it.'

'He says she won't do it any more.'

'The pity he has for himself, is it any wonder there's none for anyone else?'

She was kissed again, thanked again, hugged too. Phil hovered. He had nothing to say. It seemed he simply didn't want to leave the house and that this was a sort of routine—to spend as long as possible with Catherine after the others had left. She gave him a little push towards the door; she meant it too. Go, leave. Finally he closed the door behind him.

Catherine turned to Luke and must have realised he'd been observing this little moment. 'I love this time,' she said. 'I can get on with things, the housework.' She grimaced playfully. 'Hardly what was prescribed for my generation!' At university she'd gone out at night with a women's group to spray-paint their politics around town.

'I can see the appeal,' said Luke.

'Yeah right!' She collected some mugs from the table. 'Sometimes I think, if I hadn't met Phil, if I'd met someone else, what would that be like? What would my life be like this instant? But I did meet Phil.'

'Phil's great,' said Luke.

'He is great. And so are the kids.'

'The kids are terrific.'

'They're funny kids.'

'You've done so well, Catherine.'

'Let's not go overboard.'

She went now to the window, but everyone was gone. They could hear Alec calling out and the farm bikes revving, and the dogs. It took several moments before he realised she was crying. These were muffled sobs—she'd put her hand to her nose.

'What's the matter?' She didn't turn to him but stayed at the window. 'Catherine?'

'Jesus Christ, I don't know!' She ducked past him, went to the kitchen bench and grabbed a handitowel which she pressed against her face. 'Maybe it's catching.'

'I don't understand.'

'The other morning, early, I was walking past your door, I heard *you* crying.'

'Really? I must have been asleep.'

'I waited at the door. It was still dark outside. I didn't know whether to go in or not. Then you stopped.'

'It must have been in my sleep I was doing it. I don't remember it.' This was true, though he'd noticed his pillow was often damp in the mornings. 'I hope I wasn't waking the house. Pretty embarrassing.'

She crumpled up the handitowel and threw it in the bin. She appeared completely recovered. 'At least you don't blub in the kitchen like any mad housewife.'

'No,' he said, 'I have my dignity.'

At this she struck him on the arm. 'Remember what Andy used to call you? Lucky. Poor old Andy.'

'Why? He's done all right, hasn't he? Done what he wanted.'
'I suppose.'
'We should see him, get him down here. I'd like to see him.'
'Good luck on that,' said Catherine. 'Good luck, Lucky.'
He didn't go into town that afternoon with Catherine. He wanted to walk instead—was there something he could deliver? He'd noted the traffic of used goods between the neighbouring farms. Baking tins, magazines, clothing. Stuff went around—and came around. There were always items on the back porch: preserves or chemicals or tennis racquets. Nothing was ever thrown out. She said he could take a set of sheets over to Sheila and Alec's place, if he wanted the walk. 'No one will be home. It's a shopping day.'

What are you doing?

He hadn't even intended to knock on the door. He'd thought he might just leave the sheets inside their front porch and continue on his walk. And yet no one really walked. For a start there was no footpath. Animals walked, but humans kept sensibly to their vehicles. They had things to do, places to be. Walking anywhere took too long. Each car that passed slowed right down to check out the walker. Who was it? Did they know him, this odd figure, walking, with clearly nothing to do? He got a few toots, a few offers of a ride. Maybe his car had broken down. He was a great sight, the walker. The sheep paused, the horses and cows too.
He'd heard someone moving about the house and he thought he might have already been seen from one of the windows. He was forced to knock.
He'd met Sheila only once after Hamish's accident, when she was visiting Catherine. She'd asked how he was feeling. 'It was my fault,' she said. 'Leaving the baby out like that. So ridiculous.' He told her it wasn't that at all. He'd been exhausted from the flight.

'I'm so sorry,' she said.

'But it had nothing to do with that,' interrupted Catherine.

Sheila was his sister's dearest friend, he knew, but she required a bit of work. She spoke in a rapid sort of whisper; it was hard to listen for long. The content wasn't missing, but it was made obscure by the quick motion of her head and by the way her hands tended to pass over her mouth as she formed the words. At the UN, Luke's opposite in the Chilean delegation had the habit of touching his ankle at certain moments while speaking, pulling at his white sock. Sometimes Luke was certain the motion invoked a metaphorical fugitive knife concealed there at his shin. The message was this: Listen to me or I'll plunge this blade deep into your chest. What was Sheila's message? Shyness, naturally, but was it also damage? Was this what he credited Alec with—creating a debilitated speaker, a person always in a rush to finish her sentences, to hand the conversation back before she ruined it too much? Yet Sheila was hardly 'wrecked', physically he meant. She was in her late thirties but she could have passed for ten years younger. Her skin was remarkably smooth, the envy of her friends. Alec was fifty and might have been mistaken for her father.

The door opened and immediately she was opening it wider, inviting him inside. She told him she was the only one home. At first he said no, he had a lot to do. 'What are you doing?' she said.

The question was rather startling in its simplicity and directness, also in its severity, though that wasn't quite right. It wasn't in the same league as Dr Cyril's rudeness. She really did want to know, it seemed. In looking for his answer and not finding it, a gap had been created and he heard himself filling it by agreeing to come inside for a few minutes.

He sat at the kitchen table while she got the tea things. 'I thought today was a shopping day.'

'I went earlier,' she said.

'I saw Alec over there,' he said.

She received this statement standing very still and inclining her head slightly towards him as if she was listening for a different sound, a sound behind the dominant one—a child calling out, perhaps, though they were all at school. He was talking to a mother. It forced him to add more, about Christopher and Tony eating their puddings in about three mouthfuls. She nodded slowly and brought the cups over, sitting down at the table and turning the pot. Her deliberateness was putting an insane meaningfulness into any banal thing he said. He decided to stop speaking. His shoes, he saw, were covered in mud. He slipped them off and immediately she had them, taking them to the back door. She carried them without distaste, as if they were her own. They were both in socks now.

'And what are you doing?' she repeated. Now he heard in her question a sort of automation. Her mind was somewhere else. It struck him that whereas he'd previously thought he was the one with the power to ignore and pass on, she too had exercised this right, and done so even more thoroughly than he had. Maybe she'd got all the information she needed from Catherine. But certainly she hadn't bothered personally with him before now. Perhaps he'd seemed too foreign to compel her attention, with his fainting, his long periods in bed and his inactivity and his dependence on his sister. An immature person and an unnatural one. Turned up with mud on his shoes and walked straight into her kitchen. This was undoubtedly how her husband felt too, and yet in Alec's case the censure was as easy to spot as to receive. The heavy sarcasm was trying but it was also reliable. You knew what was coming. In Sheila's case, the disapproval could head in any number of directions, including, he felt and hoped, towards its opposite. Hoped? It was true: all at once he didn't want to disappoint her. She'd carried his shoes.

'I'm doing bugger all,' he said. 'I'm on holiday.'

She stood again, to get the milk. At the fridge she said, 'I'm going away.'

The fridge door had closed at the same time, sucking some of the statement away, locking it within. He saw now how ancient the fridge looked, with its peeling chrome handle, a stain where the maker's decal must have been. He began to notice the house. It too was shabby and aged. The lino was lifting in places, the ceiling had several large water marks. What had she said? Going away? What did she mean? She sounded neither hesitant nor triumphant but as if she'd just thought of it—maybe she had. He couldn't guess at her flakiness. Yet there seemed a growing satisfaction with the idea. Her head made the tiniest nodding motion, as if in agreement, one part of her mind being convinced by the other part. She was asking about his tea now, and talking about Alec who liked it black and could drink it scalding from years of practice. A cup of tea, she told him, was for standing up. 'Some men won't drink it sitting.'

Was she getting at him? He was aware of everything womanly about himself: his gestures, his crossed legs, his lips. He had zero interest in camp, but once he'd seen himself on a video and discovered a precision he'd been unaware of. He looked thoughtful, studied. He looked like some sort of counsellor, used to drawing people out sympathetically. The thought had occurred to him during his sessions in New York after the murder that he might have made a more convincing counsellor than the man he visited, who was often surprisingly brusque. Luke had several disqualifying traits, however. He appeared amused, fastidious, even disapproving, despite the sympathy bit. Maybe he was like this but he didn't want to think it was so obvious. His smirk seemed full of judgement, though he felt this was not always the case. In the end, what could you do with your face except use it honestly, or at least try not to send the wrong signals.

'Where are you going?' he said.

She laughed. 'You look so worried, Luke!'

'Do I?'

'Yes, look at these lines here.'

She reached over and touched his forehead with the lightest pressure. Odd feeling. He wanted her to press harder, but that would have been too strange—to ask for it, not the touch itself—and she'd removed her fingers anyway.

Of course she was a fixture in the district, married to Alec. She could no more leave than one of the paddocks could pull up its roots and walk off. How could she leave? He was looking at her famous skin properly now. The Leader of the Opposition had such skin too. He'd had the chance to study her up close in a meeting room twenty-five floors up on 1 UN Plaza. The office girls had been talking about this complexion. There was a sort of Gothic effect, however, with Ms Clark. He thought of powder even when there was none. He thought of some essence drained off to arrive at this surface. Sheila had nothing of that. With her, he thought of the opposite: something essential held in, encased perhaps but living. 'Where are you going?' he tried again. 'A holiday?'

She waved a hand then, dismissing the notion of holidays.

His own secrets and wounds had been such a precious possession, he was surprised to feel someone else might have a greater claim, a better secret. At once he saw Sheila as offering not a pedestrian self-effacement but a genuine puzzle. And while in his own elusiveness—the sleeping in, the evasive personal history—he saw the deceit of a sort of premature retirement (it was the word his brother-in-law had used good-naturedly one day), in hers somehow he felt the integrity of action. She was going—was she?—leaving. She had un-retired herself. Where was Alec in all of this?

The newspaper was on the table, opened at the story of a small plane crash. His nephew had shown him the piece and asked for his opinion, as if Luke had some information that wasn't yet public, as if he were connected with it in the same way as he'd been connected with the farmhand's accident the day he arrived. A manager at the cheese factory had been killed. When Luke walked around, things dropped from the sky.

'Terrible,' Sheila murmured. 'We've had him in this house too. Sitting right here.'

'Trying to buy you out,' said Luke.

'He was very young, with a wife and two babies,' she said, unruffled. It wasn't for him to say what was going on with the farm and the factory, especially not at this moment.

The photo in the paper, he saw, was marked up in blue pen with lines and arrows. 'That's Alec explaining it to the boys,' Sheila said. She flipped the paper over suddenly as if she'd had enough of it. He felt consoled by this action. Or included. He too had had enough.

The sun had come into the kitchen where they were sitting. It struck Sheila's wrists, making angular white cuffs and causing her to extend her fingers. She had a presence, he decided, and she was a lovely person who functioned without malice and bitterness. This was her concluding power, clear of any considerations of what was hidden in her. These qualities were not hidden but intensely communicated. She was earnest and kind and good. He was finally seeing what Catherine saw. It was Sheila who'd moved instantly to comfort him on the night of his fainting. He'd not forgotten that.

He thought of Phil's reluctance to leave Catherine after lunch. He hoped suddenly that his own visit could stretch and stretch, aware at once he was enjoying not being at his sister's place. But it was more than that. There was terrific urgency in the scene, and an immense calm. He was doing the talking now, inventing topics to prolong his view of the light over her arms. It was nonsense what he was saying, and she gave him no encouragement; she seemed distracted now. He was twenty-seven years old. He didn't have children. He didn't have a job, or it was on hold. Free of the need to speak, she could sit perfectly still and give him back all his lacks and deficiencies. But she didn't move, so he went on with it. He was telling her about the UN, making her see he had a world that was his. He'd been working in the area of the relationship between security and non-compliance with international environmental treaty obligations—a bit tenuous at first glance, that relationship, but finally central to the UN Charter in which security was broadly defined. Non-military sources of instability were highly significant. He was babbling probably. Article 33 came out. The ICJ. The Hague. The French. He even mentioned the PM. He was twenty-seven but he'd lived. He was twenty-seven and she was not, but somehow because of him, absurdly, she had to stay where she was. He had no argument but only an internal plea, thankfully internal otherwise it would have been even more embarrassing—and the plea had no weight to it beyond this sudden and sourceless conviction. She must not go away yet, now that he'd come to be here. Without her permission—without his, it seemed—this unwilled conviction had joined their fates, though he didn't believe in fate. He believed in the continuum of techniques as outlined in the literature on conflict resolution. Power based, rights based, interest based. At the time of his return home, he was being advanced rather pleasingly inwards towards the outer circle of dispute settlement. The literature was receding nicely; the world was coming along and being bloody difficult. The skirmish with the French at The Hague was just the beginning. The deer had been a sort of token. You finished work at midnight. You flew to Nairobi or wherever. His colleagues had had such trips. You flew through the time zones. Japan, Europe. 'Originally,' he told her, 'I was thinking of the Law of the Sea, but then I thought they were sure to send you off on some fishing trawler to Iceland and I'm no good on boats.'

Sheila smiled a bit and looked off through the window, and, as if answering the look, men's voices came back to them from across the paddocks. A wind was bending the heads of the crop in a nearby field. The whole area looked as though it was leaning towards them. He wanted to say something about the effect but he didn't know the name of the crop. He was always asking Phil to identify crops for him but he could never remember the distinguishing features. They were all plants to him. The wheat and barley had just gone in, he knew that. Potatoes, he remembered Phil saying. Still he didn't have the language for it; 'country air' was an example. He would learn the crops. He would read the clouds. The telescope back at the house offered new visions.

Slowly she stood up. 'I should put the oven on,' she said.

He almost burst out laughing—not in cruelty but as a sort

of relief from the pressure he felt in his throat and chest. 'Yes!' he said. 'Yes!'

'What is the ICJ anyway?' she said.

He didn't remember how he got out of the house—his sister wasn't back from town—or how he made his way back to his room. Once there he lay down on his bed and fell instantly asleep, thinking of the words International Court of Justice.

When he woke up it was dark and Simon was standing beside the bed. 'It's dinner,' he said.

'It's always dinner round here,' said Luke.

Simon scowled, suspecting an irony just beyond him but not worth tracking down. 'Simon says,' said Luke.

The boy groaned. He was happier with this. 'Everyone says that.'

'Sorry, mate,' said Luke.

As he swung his legs out from under the blankets, his nephew was looking, or sneering. 'You woke with the bone, man,' he said. There was something permanently derogatory in Simon.

Luke covered himself with the blanket. Then he was reaching inside the top drawer of the dresser. He took the coins out—the American loose change he'd found in his suitcase—and dropped them into the boy's hand.

Simon looked at them. 'I can't spend these.'

'So do you want them or not?'

Simon closed his hand and left the room.

Luke didn't understand why he'd given his nephew the money. He didn't understand what was happening with Sheila, or with his idea of her.

He would look at these details and feelings in private, as it were. The physical labour of removing the chimney and cleaning the bricks could also have a meditative aspect to it. He knew he was guilty of the sedentary person's illusion of the soulfulness of manual work, yet the illusion held against reality. Work made his brother-in-law tired. He wanted that sort of tired. Phil was in bed by nine most nights, or snoozing in front of the TV. The top of a ladder was no place to do thinking. He could fall.

But why, he suddenly thought, couldn't Simon, that great satirist of the human condition, be pushed up the ladder?

Probably it was time to go back to his life soon. Wasn't he simply missing the world? Everyone had been gearing up for the Pope, and now the Pope had come and gone.

Home Help Wanted

He stood with Catherine in front of the community noticeboard outside the public library. The life of the district in all its vivid particulars was pinned here—for sale, for rent, to a good home; notices under notices under notices—and while it was the librarians' complaint that these pages were better read than the books in the library, it was easy to miss things—not that he was looking. He was only a visitor to the district, passing through. The particulars struck him as boring, though not particularly— his sister had clearly been hoping to serve up the place. She was reading out the 'funny' ones. Her original purpose had been to find out the start date for ballet lessons and to see whether any poor mother was flogging off cheap leotards. Katie had already bullied them into buying the shoes; she'd taken to wearing them around the farm and soon they would be ruined.

They'd just come from the hardware store where he'd bought a pair of safety goggles, some heavy-duty gloves and a packet of disposable paper masks. He swung the bag, aware of his own impatience. His chimney was waiting. His hands were blistered; his back hurt; he'd breathed in dust and soot, which had also got into his eyes and behind his ears, everywhere—and all from a half day's work. He'd started on it without any of the gear, and against his sister's wishes. He'd told her he was simply going up the ladder for a recce. Then he'd found himself knocking at a few bricks. Just as Phil had said, a few blows with the mallet and the mortar crumbled. It was wonderful. He was bursting—what was this sensation? He was employed, he guessed that must be it. His work ethic had always been strong. It had been a week since the lunch at which he'd said he would begin. He had a taste for dismantling now. Soon there would be several hundred bricks. A brick was something great, he'd discovered. A marvel. You felt like a little god, or at least an athlete, with one of them in each hand. Terrifically balanced and strong. In the simple act of carrying bricks, you could have been made of brick. And it was a quick job. He'd already finished dismantling the chimney above the roof-line and was now working within the attic space. Once a brick was dislodged, it was just a case of dropping each one down through the chimney, where it would land in the hearth. Most of the bricks at this height would break, which was fine with Phil. They'd save the ones further down, and these could be used elsewhere. A couple in the district—Eileen and David—wanted to build a path. At first Luke had trouble with this dropping, flinching each time he released a brick into the darkness. The hearth was sealed with heavy polythene and there was no danger below, but it still seemed a reckless act. He let bricks go carefully, unhappily, with a feeling of vertigo. Soon, however, he was enjoying this moment. Bombs away! Each brick gave a different sound, some landing with a dull, completed thud, like a fist into a mattress, others shattering like plates, ricocheting around and sending echoes back up to him, followed by a smoky dust. He varied his drop, sometimes tossing the brick against the side of the chimney so it bounced down, sometimes aiming dead centre so it passed noiselessly to the bottom where it cracked. All of this was remarkably satisfying. It didn't take much to imagine he was dropping the bricks on someone or something—even on some aspect of himself he was sick of. At the end of the day, he'd un-tape the polythene and clear out the mess. He was raring for more. He'd work faster with the gear.

He was ahead of his sister on the noticeboard. Without interest he lifted a sheet. Handwritten in fading red biro, on carelessly torn notepaper, and making its request in three words only—Home Help Wanted—the message, if it communicated anything, was that any applicant should expect to receive the same off-hand treatment as the notice itself. To that extent, once the author was known, it was honest and direct.

There were no other details except a phone number scribbled at the bottom of the page, and this was not without its problems: the sixes could be eights, was the one really a seven? The writer, fighting the pen, had gone over the middle word several times until the paper was punctured. It was to this word that the eye went. Help. And then the ambiguous phone number. Around it the usual suspects: a guitar for sale, no strings; a reconditioned two-stroke motor; and 'Cooking with Rice: a demonstration', where Catherine had paused, placing her finger there and, with gentle mockery, reciting. He smiled. In fact he always did have trouble cooking with rice. He'd been given the sushi set as a tease.

He watched his sister bend to read the home help one.

'That's Alec's handwriting,' she said finally.

'You reckon?'

'It is. That's their number.'

'You can't read the number.'

'It's Alec.' Catherine gave a laugh. 'Home Help Wanted.' She'd been thrown. Why did Sheila and Alec need home help? Why were they going about it in this way? She was turning the questions over for him, not that she thought he could help. If anyone needed anything, she said, they asked for it and it came. Or they didn't even need to ask; the help was just there and you couldn't say no to it even if you wanted to. Food appeared, or kids were whisked off for an afternoon, or someone's truck was waiting to haul a load. 'Rendering assistance is what we do best and you better watch out. We like a case, you know.'

That was him, of course—he was a case. He woke sometimes with a wet pillow and no knowledge of how it got like that.

On the way back from town he pondered why Sheila had told him and not her best friend—for this was surely the reference: Sheila was going away—and Catherine continued to work aloud the mystery of the ad. Sheila and Alec's kids played with their kids all the time, Catherine said. Nothing could happen in the circumstances of either family without prior knowledge. Home help for what? Sheila was devoted to the home; her life was all help. What was Alec thinking to write that? What was going on?

'Maybe she's pregnant,' said Luke. His sister failed to respond. 'Or perhaps they're splitting up?'

Catherine laughed sourly. 'Good one, Luke.'

'Why not? Alec's an oppressive bastard.' The unintentional strength of the opinion caught him, but he found he didn't want to alter anything in it. Alec was a sort of bully. He had the bully's charisma at least—and the bully's wife, perhaps: docile and hesitant.

'Don't be stupid,' said Catherine with sharpness. 'She'd never leave him.'

For the first time he felt she was telling him off, releasing a part of the resentment that had been building. At one time he might have been brilliant, but down here he knew nothing. He was an LLB, come from NYC, from the PM, from the UN, but who cared if he was like pig-shit when it came to guessing about people, her people.

She was correct, and she was also not correct. They drove in silence.

Still, he thought, if Sheila was the bully's wife, he'd missed these requisite qualities: dissatisfaction and the daily incentive to escape. He remembered her standing at the fridge: 'I'm going away.' He couldn't tell Catherine this now. He'd sound conceited, or callous for not sharing it earlier, for making his sister suffer the confusion.

At home Catherine wanted him to ring the number and pretend to be interested in the position. Luke was flummoxed. 'Why me?' he said.

'Because I can't, can I?' His sister was jumping almost, very agitated.

'Why can't you just ring Sheila and ask what's going on?'

'I can't confront her like that.'

'Why not?'

'It'd be too much, believe me. If you ring, Luke, and pretend, we'll find out a bit more and then we can decide our next move.'

He refused to be the dummy caller, but she made him listen on the other phone as she called. It wasn't Sheila who answered but Pip, their eldest daughter, who was fourteen. Catherine disguised her voice and said she was inquiring about the home help ad. Pip said her parents weren't home, could she call back later.

'Could you give me some details first?' said Catherine.

'Like what?' said Pip.

'How many children?'

'Three.'

'And are they nice? I'll only do it, you know, if the children are nice.'

Pip made an uncertain noise in reply.

'Well, are they nice or not?'

There was a silence. Pip, a clever girl, was deciding not whether the children were nice but whether the caller was. Then she spoke clearly and rapidly: no, the children were not nice, they were awful, real brats.

'Are they really?' said Catherine. 'Then I appreciate your honesty, Pip.'

Pip wondered aloud at being known.

'Oh, I know all you awful brats.'

Finally it was up. Pip let go a shout of recognition. 'It's you! It's you, isn't it, Catherine?'

'Maybe it is me, Miss Philippa.'

'Say sorry then.'

'Home help, huh?'

Pip said it was for when her mother went off to university.

Catherine paused. 'University.'

It was in Christchurch, Pip told her, which wasn't far but it was far enough.

'It's not really very far to Christchurch,' said Catherine.

'To study pictures, art.'

'Art,' said Catherine.

This unconvincing, echoing little procession of responses finally made its impression. 'Didn't she tell you? Why didn't she tell you?' There was a flare of exasperation and misery in the questions. It was justified.

'Of course she told me,' said Catherine.

'We don't want her to go,' said Pip. 'No one does.'

Here Luke almost joined in.

'I'm going to run away probably.'

'Rubbish, Pip. You'll stay and lead. You'll show the others. This is a wonderful chance for you all.'

Pip had begun to sob.

'And we'll be here, won't we?'

This last statement caused a wail.

'Hey,' said Catherine. 'Pip, listen, won't it be great, though? Think about it. What a great opportunity.'

'How?' said the miserable girl.

'How? To be free of your mother for a bit? Who wouldn't wish that?'

Pip sniffed. 'That's true, I guess. But why does she have to go now?'

'The university year is such a short year. What fun we'll all have.'

'Yes,' said Pip. 'Except Dad.'

Catherine made a non-committal grunt. Alec. The girl was right. All three of them on the line knew this. There would be no fun with Alec. How had Sheila done this thing? The astonishment of it all finally struck. Luke heard it in the great sigh his sister gave. He didn't think she was about to start crying herself but she wasn't speaking yet either. She was breathing through her mouth.

Pip said, 'Is there someone else on the line?'

Luke hung up.

Looking at nude paintings

A party was organised to celebrate Sheila's news. It was the way Catherine chose to punish her friend—not for going to university, which Catherine regarded as a triumph, but for not telling her first.

She phoned everyone, making a big thing of it. Alec pretended that he couldn't understand the fuss. 'She hasn't done anything yet,' he said. Sheila herself tended to agree with him. It had looked for a couple of days as if she wasn't going to be able to make it to her own party. There was so much to be done. Finally, everyone was there—half an hour before Sheila and Alec were due. Catherine and Phil's lounge had been cleared of most of its furniture. Streamers were hung. There were balloons. The women had worked on the food all day. A child was posted at the front gate to give the signal. Someone had the idea of turning out the lights, though the guests knew what they were in for. They waited in the house in darkness.

When the guests of honour walked through the door, the lights came on and everyone cheered. Alec looked like hell—damp and ferocious.

'We thought we had the wrong day,' said Sheila.

'No we did not,' said Alec. 'We saw the lights go out.'

Sheila couldn't stop apologising for bringing them all out on 'such a terrible night'. It was raining lightly; the grass creaked with it. Her own hair was slightly wet. She even tried to apologise to Phil and Catherine until they told her it was their house so the journey hadn't been that great. Though she laughed, this did not make her less unhappy. 'Catherine,' she said, taking her friend's arm, 'I'll stay and do the dishes.'

'You won't, you know,' said Catherine. She banged Luke on the shoulder. 'That's my brother's job.'

Luke thought Sheila looked horrified but also distracted, as if even her ordinary state of apprehension was impossible to maintain in this setting. Briefly, while hanging coats, they had been left alone.

'I think it's terrific news about the university,' Luke said to her.

She appeared to flinch at this. 'You're still here, Luke,' she said, looking around the room, disturbed by the demands she'd placed on the people gathered. They would hate her, wouldn't they? 'Among us, I mean.'

'I am,' he said. 'I like it here.'

Sheila seemed pained even before he'd made this statement. 'Do you?' she said.

He didn't know why he'd added this, since secretly he considered it was his going-away party too. Weeks had disappeared. Might he not be allowed back in time for a New York Christmas? Kerry, his boss, had taken him aside for a final heart-to-heart. There was one thing, he'd asked. What was it? Luke said. That when he was in New Zealand, he'd do something. What was it? Kerry paused. 'I ask that you bring me back some Buzz Bars in your luggage.' Then Kerry laughed and pressed Luke's shoulder between his fingers. The touch was valedictory and seemed to undo the Buzz Bar line. Luke was uncertain whether he'd ever see Kerry again.

There was a hot-looking flush in Sheila's cheeks, and pale circles about her eyes. Her hair was black, but he saw a few grey hairs, as sharply defined as silver tinsel, above her ears. He was searching for the person who'd sat opposite him in her own kitchen, with the light on her wrists, but that composition seemed remote now—had it ever been true? It seemed his talent these days to be wrong about things. Here he was surprised by her height—she was as tall as him. With Alec she didn't seem this tall, or she seemed to stoop and weave, moving behind and around him, never quite by his side.

They were standing beside the fireplace which was boarded up. The chimney was down. 'Now I'm doing something, you know. Making myself useful.' He gestured towards the fireplace with his foot. Sheila looked blankly down at it. 'Actually it could have been worse,' he said. 'It could have been a surprise party.'

She chose to ignore this. 'You're staying and I'm going,' she said. Again her eyes roved about and she seemed scarcely aware she was speaking. Luke had heard Alec call her 'dreamy'. She was the opposite of that. It was only her anxieties tuned so high that gave her this disengaged look.

There was someone else at the door; Catherine was opening it. 'Who could that be?' said Sheila.

It was Hamish, the farmhand, walking on crutches. Immediately he was swamped.

'Oh, look. I must go over.'

'Don't go yet,' he said. 'There's a crush.'

She turned back to Luke, studying him for the first time. 'And how are you feeling? With the fainting, I mean.'

'Listen, I can certainly help out Alec whenever he needs it.' He'd put his hand on her arm. 'I'm okay with kids. I could be your help, you know.'

He'd surprised them both. Sheila was the first to recover, patting his hand. Her smile was all force. The proposition was ridiculous and she suspected—he saw—in this 'kind offer' that he was somehow being dishonest. Was he? In announcing his willingness it seemed he'd almost overcome his own natural objections. He did want to help out. But this still left a residue of motive. Anyway, once she told him no, he would be free to leave. It would be over—whatever 'it' entailed.

'That's really sweet of you, Luke,' she said, 'but we've got a girl. A very nice girl . . .' Sheila had put her nose almost inside her champagne glass while she continued forming words. A few of them were lost. Some obliterating male voices came close by. '. . . even though she's youngish.'

'How old is she?' Luke didn't know how this mattered. A fact might bring her around, that was all. Sheila was beginning to look about the room; there were plenty of people she should talk to and thank and who would want to hug her. Clearly it was worrying her.

'Pardon?'

He repeated his question, but now Sheila seemed to have understood perfectly its pointlessness. She shook her shoulders as if to clear away this non-subject. Hamish had freed himself of his supporters. He was at the drinks table, with Christopher, and they both raised their glasses in Sheila's direction. The farmhand grinned at Luke. All was forgiven and forgotten.

'I'm so glad Hamish could come,' she said. 'Alec said he probably wouldn't, but I think he just said that to put Christopher off coming. He's very mean to those boys. I suppose he has high hopes of them all the time.'

'When Hamish had his accident, he almost leapt out of his skin at the thought of Alec helping him.'

'But he did help, and now look at him.'

'Yes, he did help. He sort of took charge.'

'That's Alec.'

'But now you've taken charge.'

'He completely forbade it, of course,' she said with sudden harshness. 'There was no way I was going to university while I still had duties here.'

'But the girl you've got.'

'Oh, she's just . . . no, no. No. Poor Alec.'

'He seems fine to me,' said Luke.

She laughed at this, as if he'd said something terribly naïve. It must have been obvious how easily she'd wounded him. 'Yes, of course he's fine. Oh, it's complicated, Luke. Life is.'

He was annoyed with himself for making her patronise him. He'd cured her of her panic, but into its place he'd moved something worse. He could feel himself dwindling in her eyes. She swallowed the rest of her champagne. She tipped her glass back again and nothing came out. He thought he would tell her then about New York and his role as a witness—the homeless guy waving his knife as if it was cutlery and so on. The line-up. That would make her see there was a real weight behind his generalisations. That would stop her seeing him as someone who went down in a heap at the merest touch. There'd been blood on his nicely ironed shirt and he'd fainted. The frequency with which it was repeated back to him about his jet lag and his tiredness being the cause of his collapse convinced him that no one believed it. Dr Cyril would have been busy on this front, though it hardly needed his indiscretion to circulate the alternate theories: that he was weak and squeamish and city-bound. That fainting—this falling out of his life—was a well-timed and convenient exercise in evasion. To faint, after all, was to miss that moment when things threatened to become too much. It was a form of malingering, the most dramatic expression of the wish not to face whatever one dreaded: the sight of a needle, the sight of blood, news of some tragedy, the prospect of ugliness, the possibility that there was such a thing as an ending. It would have been surprising had his counselling sessions in New York not covered this subject. But he couldn't faint to order and, anyway, he'd been hit in the head by a golf ball. There was no metaphysics there, only physics. And he'd seen someone murdered, which was physics plus. He'd remained upright and more or less alert throughout that. He'd not folded—not at once. He should tell Sheila his side of the story. He stopped himself, however. He wouldn't wield his experience in this way, as a sort of testament of worth. What horrible pride he carried. Anyway, let her find it somehow, he thought. Let her meet it by accident, as he had met it, while walking home from work. Besides, he'd not even had the decency to tell his sister—because why worry her, why bother her. Also it was Sheila's party, a celebration! He must have been mad to think of introducing all that.

'Then how did you get him to agree in the end?' he finally said, unable to remove the sulkiness from the question.

'How?' She was looking directly at him as she spoke. She seemed to understand the challenge—and met it. 'I said I'd kill myself if he didn't this time.'

The party closed in on them at once and Sheila was turned away from Luke by a hand. Someone was bringing her forward into the middle of the room. The official part of the evening was about to begin. A glass was tapped, cries of 'order, order' and laughter. He made his way towards the back, glad he wouldn't have to speak to anyone for a while. What Sheila had said made no sense. There was horror in the confession, but excitement too—for him at least. She'd spoken plainly and without emotion. She seemed to understand his juvenile need for a harsh truth. She had chosen the harshest, though not perhaps to encourage a bond but to break one, to end his interest in her. She wanted him to know she was operating at a distance far removed from his sphere. She had promised to kill herself if she couldn't go to university. Of course she had no idea that this declaration gave him a strange sort of hope. If she was in isolation, he thought himself perfectly capable of joining her there.

She was wearing a straight brown skirt and a plain red T-shirt, and sandals. Her long hair was tied back. She wore no make-up. She should have appeared drab, shapeless—and maybe she did, to others—but for Luke she was a charged figure; not exactly unself-conscious—she vibrated with a consciousness that seemed at times to cripple her—but still she remained excitingly exposed. He looked at her neck, at that beautiful place beneath the ear.

When the noise died down, they could hear the sounds of the television at the end of the house. More than a dozen kids were watching it, lying in sleeping bags and wriggling across one another. It had been Luke's task to look in on them occasionally. A couple of the older ones had taken a few sips from his beer. Has anyone chucked yet? Simon asked.

There was also some sort of plan. A few of the older kids were getting dressed up: the girls were applying lipstick; the boys had wigs. Something artistic was on the cards, though it had been kept from Luke. His sister was behind it.

Phil now stood beside Sheila, his hands clasped, welcoming everyone again to their house on this auspicious occasion. He explained that there were no rules to the formal bit; anyone who wanted to say a few words to Sheila, and to Alec of course, the poor bastard, all they had to do was take the 'speaking cup'—here he held up a tankard—and the floor was theirs.

'What's in it, Phil?' one of the men called out from the back of the room.

'Johnnie Walker!' called another.

'Nothing in it,' said Phil. 'It's a speaking cup, for the ignorant people at the back. Belonged to my grandfather who was in the Dunedin Debating Society.'

'The drinking society, Phil?'

Phil pushed on. 'There are, however, I'm happy to say, plenty of other receptacles for imbibing.'

There were cheers.

'Who'll start us off?' said Phil.

No one moved. There was some standard coughing.

'Oh dear,' said Sheila, then she brought her hand to her mouth. 'I could start myself, in that I'd like to say how wonderful it is to be sharing this party with Hamish. Not officially, I mean, but in spirit, because he has come back heroically from what we all know was a terrible injury, and here is. Where is he?' Hamish was found: he was drunk and happy in the corner of a sofa. 'There he is! So can we toast him?'

'I think he's toasted already!'

When the shouting had died down, still no one came forward to take the speaker's cup.

'Then I will myself,' said Phil. He held up the cup. 'Sheila, you're a dark horse and this is a big surprise but I just want to say, good on you. To improve your mind and to gain access to all sorts of knowledge and to push yourself is one of the truly great things. We could all be improved, I know that. You'll thrive up there and you'll come back to us a richer person than . . . we are! We'll all be picking your brains, of course. I know Cath here will. And Ella and so on. So study hard and watch those student parties!' This was applauded. 'And to Alec, mate, you've been Sheila's rock. Your support for her in this exciting move is just another sign that you're not as dumb and stubborn as you look. Good on you both! To Alec and Sheila, everyone.'

The room rang with the toast.

'Just want to second that,' said Trevor, who with his brother Barry—the district's 'most eligible bachelors', both in their sixties—owned the farm adjacent to Alec's and Sheila's.

Phil handed him the speaking cup. 'No, that's all really. Bon voyage!'

'She's only going to Christchurch,' said Alec. 'Be there in a couple of hours, Trevor. She's home on the weekends.'

'Alec hasn't got the speaking cup,' a voice shouted.

'I'm home on weekends,' said Sheila. Her echo was a sound they were all used to.

'You'll be putting the phone off the hook then, eh, Alec!'

'There'll be plenty to do, I tell you,' said Alec, speaking seriously over the laughter.

'Oh, Alec, don't be so gloomy, we'll look after you,' said Ella. For a moment it looked as though Ella might hug him, and Alec moved slightly away. She and Jeff farmed on the other side of the valley. Luke had heard their story. Ella put on plays in the community hall. The men all thought her 'bossy'. At various times she'd had every one of them on the little stage in false beards or in dresses. She'd seen them in their underpants. Alec, she always insisted, was a fine natural actor though he wouldn't let himself be cast in anything but the smallest walk-on role—a butler, perhaps, or Man in Shop. He was tall, however, and overcame these parts too easily. All eyes went to him, and his murmured 'You're welcome's were listened for and replayed in the viewer's mind as if they offered the dramatic key.

'We'll be all right, thanks, Ella,' said Alec. He loomed now, formidable in his moleskins and hand-knitted jersey. He was daring anyone to continue with the toasting.

David Tanner stood up and took the speaking cup, raising it in the air. David and Eileen ran a little pottery store at the back of their house; he fussed around the till while she made the stuff. They were the ones waiting on the bricks from the chimney. This pair had also shown signs of wanting an attachment to Luke. He'd been to their house on an errand and been fed over-strength gins. Aggressive artistic conversation had been the order of the day. There appeared to be a problem in Eileen's eyes with MoMA and with the Metropolitan Museum—in fact with most places Luke mentioned, though this did not stop the flow. At the point she seemed ready to throw him—and David too—out of the house, she poured more drinks.

Eileen, David had been saying to everyone at the party, was at home with a migraine, but she was through the worst of it and would pop up again tomorrow. It happened that Eileen had spoken to Luke earlier that day and said she wasn't feeling social but she would tell David she had a migraine so he could repeat the lie innocently. She didn't trust him to pull off a deception. Luke saw at once that David was one of those earnest men whom no one believes or much listens to and who are always suspected of improving life. In the harmless embellishment about Eileen 'popping up' the next day, he somehow undid her excuse. The whole room knew Eileen was most likely sitting at home suffering nothing more than her periodic aversion to present company. It was mutual. As a potter and a vegetarian, Eileen thought they—Catherine and Phil, their neighbours and friends—had their values in perfect reverse, being too kind to each other and too cruel to animals. She liked to give the impression that with Luke alone she could speak freely, when in truth she was incapable of anything but frankness, or rudeness, as many considered to be the case.

'To our friend and scholar, Sheila!' said David.

Everyone said 'Sheila' and it made quite a sound, a short and definitive shout which, as toasts tend to, died instantly, presenting a hole. Immediately afterwards no one knew what to say.

They were standing in a sort of circle, with Sheila in the middle, smiling awkwardly back at everyone. The arrangement made it seem that they could simply close in on her crushingly, a potential which her look suggested was worryingly real. Luke felt he should step forward, place himself between her and them. He could speak even. But what could he say? Something. He was a good impromptu speaker. He'd performed in a variety of settings. He almost did it—and at the last moment he caught Sheila's eye. She was warning him off, he felt, but without hostility. Had she understood him?

Finally, someone asked her what she was going to be learning about at the university.

'She's going to be looking at nude paintings,' someone said. The men laughed heartily.

'No,' said Sheila, 'art history.'

'Nude paintings. Where do you sign up for that?' said Jeff. 'Sounds good.'

'Yes, where'd you sign up for it, Sheila?'

A few more titters were raised and someone said something about 'live models' but the comedy had already become slightly resentful and Phil turned everyone's attention to the rain falling. 'Listen to that, eh,' he said. There was the faintest sound of it against the roof of the porch.

'It won't be enough,' said Jeff.

Phil was forced to agree, though it had hardly been his point. Luke supposed that vaguely his brother-in-law had been after the patter of rain to lift the mood or add to its poignancy. Phil was not artistic. Every Christmas, Catherine gave him a novel, but he hadn't ever followed one all the way through. They could be seen in a stack on his bedside table, the bookmarks emerging from them a bit like—it was Phil's own image and he was proud of it, repeating it whenever the topic came up—a row of tongues. Occasionally he read a page to send himself to sleep. Yet he was 'aware', if only of an absence in himself, and loved to encourage his wife, and Ella, the drama queen, to behave in whatever extravagant terms they saw fit. He was always offering their house for rehearsals or read-throughs. And he knew the words to a surprising number of old songs and could sing them in a good voice. Catherine had all her kids learning the piano.

'I'd rather it didn't rain at all if that's the extent of it and that way no one's hopes would be raised,' said Alec.

'Good old Alec,' said Ella with a laugh. Finally she did manage to touch him, at the elbow. It delivered to him a kind of shock which he bore. Sheila—Luke had been watching her throughout—also flinched at this approach, or at her husband's response to it. Ella then started speaking about Sheila's 'brave act', but she was shouted down—she hadn't picked up the speaking cup.

Catherine had been out of the room for a few moments. She returned now and gave a signal to Phil, who moved toward the window. 'Can I have everyone's attention, please?' she said. 'I've just been outside and it seems our reputation for great parties has spread. We've been having a little problem with gatecrashers. I've done my best to warn them off the property, but they're very persistent. They claim they know Sheila and that they belong at her going-away party. So we've decided that they can stay.'

Then she gave another signal and Phil pulled open the curtains. Instead of a view of the front garden out across the paddocks, the darkness lacquered the glass of the window and gave them back themselves: a group of mostly farmers and their wives, a few interlopers, standing as if to attention, the glasses in their hands figuring as sharp lights, their faces peering and, in some cases, confused, bashful even, before the mirror effect. Sheila saw herself and turned her head away. Luke saw Alec's back; he was pouring himself a glass of beer from one of the bottles lined up on the dining table.

'Turn out the lights!'

The lights went out and immediately they saw into the garden. Figures were moving about. Some were dressed in white sheets and went slowly and gracefully over the lawn, gliding among other figures who were sitting or lying in poses for the 'painters'—three of them, who stood behind easels, holding their brushes, touching their chins in thoughtfulness, adding dabs and strokes to their 'works'. There was to be identified a Van Gogh, with a bandaged ear; an Andy Warhol, with blond hair; and was that a female Rembrandt in the soft cap?

'Is that our Rebecca?' said Jeff.

'There's Amy!'

'Ben.'

The rain was visible only in the small arcs coming from the

outside house-lights; after that it fell in the dark—the grass carried a glitter of it. There was no sign in the faces of the models that anything was bothering them. They were quite still.

'Are they warm enough?'

'Aren't they beautiful.'

The parents inside the room pressed closer to the window.

Ella came to stand beside Catherine and put her arm around her waist, whispering into her ear. Luke watched his sister's head go back; she was laughing quietly. Together like this, the two women went to Sheila, who turned to them and smiled and touched Catherine's shoulder. Alec was also watching this trio, sipping his drink. Sheila, still smiling, looked over at her husband. He drank again. Then he called across to the women, 'Who are the ghosts?'

'They're not ghosts,' said Catherine.

'Are they spirits or something?' said Barry. 'Beautiful.'

'They're supposed to be Muses,' said Catherine.

'Ah, yes,' said David. 'I used to know their names.'

'They do look like ghosts though,' said Sheila.

'Phil, I thought it was the Ku Klux Klan out there for a minute,' said Jeff.

'You did not,' said Ella, his wife.

'You want to call them in now, Phil?' said Alec.

'Have we had enough?' said Barry. 'Oh, let me look for another moment.'

Ella stepped forward; the theatre was her place. 'Before you do, Phil?' she said. Then she raised her hands above her head and started clapping. Everyone joined in, including Alec, who tapped his fingers against his glass of beer.

At the sound of the applause the children on the lawn all turned to face the window and bowed. Then they ran inside, shouting and screaming. Several of the mothers went to find their performers and dry them off. The room was suddenly half empty.

Luke wanted to get to Sheila again but found himself on the men's side of the room, joined to a conversation about the recent plane crash near Omarama. Even though it was Jeff who'd personally known the factory manager who'd been killed, Alec was being deferred to—this was a flying matter at heart. Luke remembered the newspaper marked up with Alec's notes the day he'd called in on Sheila.

'There'll be an inspector with his piece to say.'

'It's in poor taste but you've heard they reckon it was you, Alec, pouring sugar in the tank.'

'I knew the man a bit,' said Alec.

'No love lost!'

'He was a mouthpiece, a kid really,' said Alec. 'All of them at the factory just take orders, that's the whole point. He was a poor sod to end up like that though.'

'He was a good young bloke, all differences aside. Two littlies.'

'But what will they say about the crash, Alec?'

'They'll find something.'

'It was a new plane almost, which is scary.'

As a young man, Alec had been a glider pilot, taking tourists up over the Southern Alps, starting from Omarama, and showing them the glaciers, Mount Cook if it was clear, and the Tasman Sea, before turning for home. He'd done this, Catherine had told Luke, to escape his father, who expected him to help on the farm and then, as the only son, to take it over. Eventually this is what he did, but first he needed to disappoint the people who knew him best. It was good to remember Alec had this rebellious colouring in his character and his friends liked to hear him speak about it. It was also utterly consistent—Alec had never had an interest in pleasing anyone who was waiting round for it.

'These buggers aren't trained is the problem,' said Alec.

'That's right,' said Jeff.

'That's a twenty-something-year-old kid up there with a couple of hundred hours' flying under his belt.' At this, Alec looked at Luke, and for a moment he stood in for all the murderous stupidity of that age. The report Luke had heard had spoken of engine failure but that seemed to be of no account at the party.

Luke said, 'How old were you, Alec, when you were flying?'

Alec was answering before the question was fully out, saying that he'd been trained to the hilt and had experienced all conditions, all situations, before he even thought of endangering another life. The men agreed with this, nodding and drinking and waiting to see what Youth could say in the face of this rebuttal. Youth drank also, then asked something neutral, deferential even. Luke had no intention of deferring to this man but he discovered he wanted to hear him speak and a sort of dim flattery seemed best. He said that he'd like to know what it was Alec saw up there and what it felt like.

There was a kind of general shuffling at this mention of feeling. Luke didn't care. The exhilaration of the art history window display had evaporated too quickly. He wanted something in its place. Sheila had evaporated. He wanted a connection with her, even if it was only through her husband. And he'd downed three glasses of wine.

Up in the glider in the space of a couple of hours, Alec said, you got a good sense of the variety of land mass.

He won't sell it in terms other than these, Luke thought. The dullest. 'Land mass?' he said. Though they were dead against him, Luke sensed among the men a sort of urging, as if they wanted Alec questioned. He had, in effect, their proxy.

Alec sighed. You could see how everything connected up across the width of the island, he went on, the plains and the valleys and the lakes and the peaks. In your mind's eye you made the glaciers meet the sea. Even with no geological knowledge, you understood a pattern, whereas if you were driving in your car, say—Alec didn't care for investment in roads, even though these roads had presumably brought him his clients—you just thought the mountains were in the way. 'Of course, if you catch the Norwest Wave,' he said, 'that's like nothing on earth. Climbing at a thousand feet a minute, takes your head off.'

It was the longest, most expressive speech Luke had heard

him give. He felt nicely reprimanded, and Alec's mates had clearly enjoyed observing both the challenge Alec had faced and the sight of this outsider being taught his lesson.

Alec, Luke knew, had no formal education beyond the fifth form. Everything he'd learned, he'd learned for himself. In this he was probably not much different from any of his mates standing with him. Phil was the only one who'd been to university. Their children would go to university, naturally; some were there already. Education was gold. Of course when Sheila wanted to go to university Alec forbade it. Luke wondered why it was that when she said she would kill herself Alec had had to believe her. He looked like someone who always called a bluff. He must have had to think she wasn't bluffing. He was also someone who never gambled against the odds.

Now Luke knew where things stood, he believed everyone could guess the truth. Alec and Sheila were the unhappiest people in the room. Yet Alec's grimness could easily be attributed to what was naturally morose in his character, just as everyone might read in Sheila's tentativeness her habit of taking her cue from Alec. They had merged, in a way, into the perfect working unit, which was probably why Sheila's 'sudden' desire to go off to university struck Alec as a betrayal. It was not simply that he was selfish; he was bewildered, hurt. The most severe injury, of course, was to his pride. Hadn't he provided the globe upon which they both could travel, this globe being the farm and the outlying districts? His objections might have been to the practical—who would look after the kids, who would cook the meals, who would run the house—but the unanswerable offence was to his imagination, which had failed to provide him with this possibility. She was going away to learn about something he had no knowledge of and which, if he saw a point in it, he could not yet bring into any relation with their life. Worse, he also suspected everyone was laughing at him, even those, such as Catherine and Ella, the drama lady, who did see a purpose in his wife's perversity and applauded it. In these people's eyes it would seem as if Alec had 'lost', and they would savour the defeat of the powerful. For once Alec had not had his way. There was no gloating but there was satisfaction. It took the form of a low-level, constant ribbing from even his most unquestioning allies. The men were talking again of clothes being taken off.

Hamish was now asleep on the sofa. Alec went and stood behind him. 'That was a great show we had with this young fellow.'

'He could have lost his leg, they reckon.'

'It was more than that he could have lost,' said Alec.

'All the blood he lost.'

'It was claret everywhere. If he'd slumped over, that would have been it.'

'If he passed out, you mean, Alec?'

'That's right. It was the surgeon told Catherine that.'

'My God.'

'But we got him back in one piece, get him back to the house with the ambulance, and what do we find?' Alec pointed at Luke. 'This fellow's the one that's passed out!'

'You were dead tired from everything, weren't you?'

'I was,' said Luke. 'If I'd had a tractor in my leg, I would have been all right.'

'That's true!'

'Very good, yes!'

'No,' said Alec, a little unhappily, 'but this is the fellow who's already in the ambulance. Ahead of Hamish.'

'I was sitting up by then,' said Luke.

'He's off to get himself a ride in the ambulance!'

'Shame they didn't have the siren going, but it was a great ride,' said Luke.

'Good on you!'

'No, and one more thing,' said Alec, more strongly, 'there was a baby, sitting out on the grass in the freezing cold in its wee pyjamas. We almost tripped over the thing!'

'How did that happen?'

'How did it happen? Sheila left it there.'

'Sheila?'

'Probably she was thinking about art and university. It was a three-ring circus and free entry. It was a great show. And now look at this fellow.' He gestured towards the sleeping Hamish. 'He comes out of hospital. He's been on medication for a month, and he has two bottles of beer and look at him.' Alec walked out from behind the sofa and gave Hamish a light kick in his good leg, which failed to make him stir. 'He could have lost everything if we hadn't have been there.'

'He was very lucky.'

When everyone had gone home except Alec and Sheila, Phil brought a bottle of whisky to the table and they sat around trying to find a suitable end to the event. Alec had drunk a couple of whiskies at the table already and he didn't stop Phil when he went to pour him another. 'Tell me when,' said Phil.

'It's a special occasion, they say,' said Alec grimly.

Catherine had made coffee for herself, Luke and Sheila, though just then Sheila wasn't in the room. She was settling one of the children who'd woken with a nightmare. Their kids were top-and-tailing with Catherine and Alec's kids.

The plane crash came up again; this time it was Phil. Alec repeated his diagnosis of the problem, though now he seemed a little tired of the subject and actually said, 'But Luke here has heard all this.' He stopped talking.

'What Luke hasn't heard,' said Phil, 'is about the midair fight you had over Greymouth.'

Alec seemed disinclined to tell it—'Ancient history,' he said—but Luke said he wanted to hear and Catherine joined him in demanding it.

'One time,' said Phil, 'a passenger, a Canadian lady, right Alec, tried to grab him around the throat when they were flying?'

Alec held up his hand to stop Phil.

'Then tell it, you miserable sod,' said Phil.

Alec told his story, beginning again with the passenger's nationality. This Canadian lady lost it, he said, just lost her nerve, and they had struggled together for a short time before Alec managed to free himself with 'a couple of blows'. He thought they were above Greymouth. 'It was all such a long time ago,' he said. 'Don't know why I'm telling it.'

'What happened then?' said Luke.

'Now you've got him hooked,' said Phil.

'You think I've that power?' said Alec. 'I'll continue, but only because Phil likes it for his bedtime to be told about the olden days.'

'It's true,' said Phil, laughing. 'But you've never put me to sleep yet.'

Alec went on. After the fight his passenger sat quietly until they were down again, and then she gave Alec a whole wad of money, perhaps four or five times what the ride cost. Before she walked back to her husband who was waiting in the little corrugated-iron shed which served as an office, she allowed Alec to wipe off with his handkerchief the small trickle of blood that had come from her nose. 'It wasn't broken or anything,' Alec told them, as if they were thinking that hitting a woman to save a couple of lives was still a bit much. And finally the woman had said, 'Would you please not mention a word to him.'

When Luke asked him whether he was scared during this attack over Greymouth, Alec went back in the story and started speaking about the Canadian woman's husband who hadn't wanted his wife to go up and who certainly didn't want to go up himself. The woman wouldn't listen and was already walking towards the glider.

'The husband called out, "What am I going to do down here?" "Come with me then," said the woman. "I won't come," he said. "Suit yourself," she said. "But won't you come anyway? Will we ever have another chance?" But the husband turned and went back inside the shed.'

Alec's skill at voices was a revelation for Luke. He hadn't taken him for much of a listener.

In his experience, Alec said, women were always braver about heights and about new experiences than men. He must have sensed he was close to paying a tribute to his wife; he closed up suddenly.

'You're a closet feminist, Alec,' said Catherine.

'Don't count me among that type,' said Alec. Still, he said, it was always the woman leading the man to the glider. She was always seated and ready before he was. And she always listened more carefully to the pilot than he did, with the result that it was the woman who often had to repeat things to the man.

'But the pilots are usually always men,' said Catherine.

Alec didn't seem to hear this, or chose to ignore it. 'So I looked at this money I had,' he said, 'and I went in to the boss and I said, "I've just had a near-miss and I'm taking the rest of the day off."'

'A near-miss,' said Phil. It was obviously a favourite part of the story.

'And he said, "When will you be back?" and I said, "It won't be before the morning and probably the afternoon to be quite frank." And I promise you I wasn't back in the morning either. I had a few quiet ones that night, I can tell you.'

This final detail of the drinking was the only piece that didn't fit—who could imagine Alec resorting to such a measure, even as a young man? The whisky he'd been taking now did not appear to have the effect of either stimulating or anaesthetising; he was dealing to it, that was all.

'I don't blame you,' said Phil.

Alec looked resentfully at his own glass. 'Because it only means something a while afterwards, an experience like that.'

'You were in shock,' said Luke.

Immediately Luke recognised this as an offensive detail. He'd thought the phrase bland and insulting when applied to himself in New York, despite the fact that all his symptoms were classically arranged. It was also the sort of thing David Tanner went around saying, a pointless editorialising such as that he'd supplied to Eileen's invented migraine.

David had latched on to Luke late in the evening. Together they'd tried to track down the names of the Muses. They got

Calliope, Thalia, Clio and Erato—weren't there nine in total? None, David believed, were connected with the visual arts but it would have been churlish to complain to Catherine that her tableau had this flaw. Agreed, said Luke. The man was a pillock but something in this pretentious talk—that it *was* pretentious—made Luke like him. David was incapable of censoring himself. It made him bearable. Then David had asked whether Luke had things to do now the chimney was finished. Not quite finished, Luke had said. Eileen had a proposal, David said. Would Luke like to lay a path at their place? Luke said he'd never laid a path before. 'I thought that might be the case,' said David, 'but Eileen is keen.' Luke promised nothing; he'd have to check with Phil and Catherine about their plans, and then he doubted if he'd be around for that long anyway. 'You might get the pros in,' he said. David nodded sadly. 'My words exactly. Still, Eileen loves an experiment. It's why she's an artist, I suppose.'

'But I'm not,' said Luke.

'No,' said David, with comradely feeling. 'Neither am I.'

Alec spoke to Phil: 'I've never tasted beer like that in my life. Before or since.' Again the observation sounded second hand—any of the men at the party might have spoken it but not Alec; he would have turned away in irritation had he heard it.

Now Luke wasn't sure that Alec meant what he'd said about any of it. He may not have liked these humiliated men, but surely he didn't completely blame them either. Didn't the story of the Canadian woman choking him when they were up over Greymouth suggest another aspect of female unpredictability? The men at least in their caution could be relied upon.

'Anyway,' Alec said, 'that was when I told the company, if you don't install a partition between the passengers and the pilot, someone's going to die. So they did install the partitions.'

'Marvellous,' said Phil.

Catherine turned to her husband and asked him whether he'd ever consider going up again in a glider. 'You won't catch me up there,' said Phil. 'I've never felt so green.'

'You did all right for the first time,' said Alec. 'The mistake was you never went up again.'

'Then maybe I will some day!'

The two men toasted each other and Phil drank. Alec quickly returned his glass to the table as if he'd suddenly been told he was drinking dishwater.

'I don't think I'd like it either,' said Catherine.

'There goes your theory about women being braver,' said Phil.

'No, but you both think the same and that's all right,' said Alec. He seemed to have surprised himself by arriving at this point and he stopped abruptly. To have offered, even by accident, this complimentary judgement on Catherine's marriage made him suddenly shy, and he rubbed at the table with his finger. 'Sheila went up a lot with me.' Now he'd introduced her, he wanted her there, as proof, and he looked around the room for a moment as if his wife might be hidden somewhere, crouched under the table, behind the door. That she wasn't present suggested neatly the bereft condition in which he would soon find himself once term time began. He'd met Sheila at the Omarama aerodrome where she worked part time for the contractor who did the cleaning; she was also live-in care for an old aunt of hers in the township. After that he'd taken her home to be his mother's help.

'That was love,' said Catherine.

Luke didn't imagine she'd ever used the word with Alec before, but perhaps she'd felt encouraged by his openness, which might have just been the cushion of circumstance, something soft on which his emotions had unusually landed on such an unusual night. Sheila was really going away to university. Alec's vulnerabilities were briefly displayed. Everyone was aware of the fleetingness of the show. Phil, also taken off guard, had no other response but to pretend he was hardly there. Luke understood he himself scarcely existed for Alec anyway, being so temporary an installation. Phil poured more whisky into his glass, though he'd not finished what was already there. Some spilled on the table. All looked at the puddle.

Reading was a sore point for Alec, whereas for her it was an excitement, a kind of turning point.

Sheila had called in on Catherine a few days before. It was the first time, apart from phone calls, the two friends had seen each other since the home help ad had been sighted. Luke figured he was invited to join them for a cup of tea because his sister feared an awkwardness—not her own but Sheila's. He came down from his ladder. By the time he was cleaned up, they were sorting out the business of why Catherine had to read an ad to find out Sheila was going away. It turned out that Alec had said he would phone Catherine and Phil to tell them about Sheila's plans—and he never had. He claimed that since the ad had always come second in his mind, he believed he'd already done the first thing.

'But why did you ask Alec to ring us?' said Catherine.

'He wanted to,' said Sheila.

'Didn't you want to as well?'

'Oh, Cath, please, it's a very stressful time. Of course I wanted to.'

'Never mind, it's a wonderful time too, isn't it?'

Sheila said she'd been thinking about university for ages, years in fact. She'd got the idea first, she supposed, from reading to her kids. Looking at the illustrations, she remembered a passion she'd had for books and pictures as a girl which had then been forgotten, squashed—not deliberately, she quickly added, but by circumstance and by choice, since she had chosen things and neglected other things as everyone does. 'Like you became a teacher,' she said to Catherine, 'and then—'

'And then I became a mother, yes,' said Catherine, giving the sigh that is a joke but also a form of shorthand for everything contained in that statement.

Sheila chose to cheer Catherine up instead of join in. 'But you've kept up with books and everything.' She'd found perhaps a new note for such an observation. Previously there would have been nothing so spontaneously admiring as this; she'd always approached the topic of books with great caution and the usual sort of aggression. She had had a single year more of schooling than Alec.

Once a week the mobile lending library van parked for an hour at the end of the road, and there were books kept for Catherine 'under the counter', titles she'd reserved on the recommendation mostly of Ella. Sheila had thought all this 'beyond' her, and whenever Ella and Catherine talked about something they were reading, Sheila, holding her hands over her ears, would laugh and say, 'I won't listen, I promise.' Now she was confessing her secret, life-altering pleasure.

'The kids all hate me of course,' she said.

'They'll come round,' said Catherine.

She took her friend's hand. 'Do you think I'm bad?'

Catherine gave Sheila's hands a light smack. 'I think you're very wicked.'

Then Sheila burst into tears. She was laughing too—they both were. Catherine was also crying. Luke wasn't even there as far as they were concerned. He left the room quietly. From his ladder, peering down inside the chimney—he was getting to grips with the bricks, making real progress—he could just make out their muffled voices.

Alec stood up from the table, swaying slightly. 'Time to be off, then,' he said.

'No hurry,' said Phil. 'The girls haven't had their coffee yet.'

'Sheila won't have coffee this late,' he said.

'Sheila asked for it,' said Catherine.

'Not this late.'

'It's not that late,' said Luke.

Alec looked at him as if finding him there for the first time. 'How's the noggin anyway, young Luke? Heard you and a golf ball had a disagreement.'

Luke was taken aback. Of course his sister would have said something to her friends about his accident, yet he was unprepared for Alec's calculated deployment of it. 'I'm fine. That was years ago.'

'What about those kids, eh?' said Catherine. 'Dressed up like that.'

The obviousness of the interruption was striking: perhaps she was simply too tired to do any better, or perhaps she wanted Alec's line of inquiry pursued—Luke wasn't sure. But he felt himself finally being given up, abandoned, to Alec.

Nevertheless she pressed on: 'Did you see Ben out there? He was Vincent Van Gogh.'

Alec, not to be derailed, had turned back to Phil. 'You could get killed on a golf course.'

'That's true, Alec,' said Phil, confused about the signals. He spoke to his wife, asking who someone was supposed to have been. Catherine replied that it was another painter she'd forgotten.

'You've been checked out anyway, I suppose,' sad Alec.

'He's been checked out,' said Catherine.

'Rembrandt,' said Luke.

'It was wise to pull you from overseas.' Alec held up one hand, halting Catherine's objection. 'I'm not using the correct term, no doubt. You'd be in some form of R'n'R.'

'I think he's on holiday, Alec,' she said.

'If he had these fainting problems in a foreign place, it would be precautionary and proper to ship him home for a while.'

Catherine tossed her head back in frustration. She glanced at her brother, urging him, it seemed, to speak. She was abandoning him for sure.

'Anyway, we're leaving.' Alec was stern now, irritated, not about the coffee perhaps, or even by Luke, but for the confidences he'd spilled—had there been any? That the question even hung between them was enough to cause him to retreat with his old sullenness amiably, busily intact.

'We've got the kids, Alec,' said Catherine. 'You can sleep in tomorrow.'

'He hasn't slept in since he was ten probably,' said Phil.

'That's right,' said Alec. 'Neither of us likes to lie about. We only need to wake once and that's all the signal we need.'

'The signal! You sound like you're waiting to go into battle, Alec,' said Catherine.

Sheila was at the door. 'What battle?' she said. She looked as though she'd come from some skirmish. Her eyes were adjusting to the brightness of the room. Of course she'd been lulled by her own reading to her youngest daughter under a dim light while the others slept. Her hair was messed up, as though hands had been pushed through it—perhaps her own, perhaps Georgia's. Sheila allowed herself to be attacked whether by fists or kisses. She was often the pillow her children sought out and fought over. She had her chair beside the fire, and it would be scaled and vicious assaults made at her from above, which she would greet and weakly try to fend off. 'Be careful,' she would say, though it was only her own safety in doubt. Catherine had seen her beaten up, in effect, tears in her eyes from some pummelling. Now the collar of her T-shirt was twisted. She was adjusting her skirt. Her immense tiredness gave her the look of the young. She would have preferred not to reappear and it was certain she wished this minute to be in her own house, in her own bed. Nevertheless, Luke held up the coffee cup to her.

She quickly looked at Alec, who had moved a few paces from the table. He brought his hands together in a soft clap. 'It's very late, isn't it,' she said. Her words were the unnecessary translation of his eloquent hands.

'You don't have to go,' said Catherine, not wishing to punish her but possibly to draw something out, to have said what hadn't yet been said and which perhaps could never be said.

Alec was perfectly capable of causing a scene now. He wrung his hands.

'Shall I just help with some tidying up and then we'll go,' said Sheila.

'You certainly won't,' said Phil.

Luke spoke. 'In New York a man was murdered right beside me.'

'What do you say?' said Alec.

Luke repeated it, adding some details.

Catherine sighed. Phil sucked in on his teeth, scratched his head. Sheila stopped.

Now it was out, Luke was filled with regret. There was no release. Nothing had moved 'off his chest'. His chest felt tighter than ever. The room heaved around him. Please no, he thought. He would not go down. Catherine had him by the arm, which helped. The touch brought him back strongly. Phil was mumbling something in sympathy.

'How awful,' said Catherine. She asked Luke quietly whether he was all right.

'You saw the true side of that place,' said Alec. He seemed impressed finally, or satisfied at least.

The language, as everyone knew it would, ran out. Only Sheila hadn't spoken. What would she say? She avoided his eye. She was gathering up a few glasses from the sideboard.

'Please leave all that this minute,' said Catherine.

Luke knew his sister's heart was always in play with Sheila. She wanted to kick her dear friend and shake her, just as she told him she did whenever she saw Sheila taking the brunt of an attack from her physical children. On Day One, his first day on the farm, when Sheila had famously left the baby out on the grass, his sister had yelled at her. Sheila was a special kind of non-adult perhaps. Catherine was also awestruck: Sheila had managed to decide something and arrange it, and here she was about to carry it out, all without her help, without anyone's help. She had called into question more lives than just her own.

But what did she have to say about his story? Still she wouldn't stop moving. She would not face him.

Catherine said to him, 'What happened afterwards?'

'It's probably not the time,' Luke said. 'It was horrible, but as Alec says the place can be like that.'

Luke doubted that Catherine knew about Sheila's threat to kill herself. Sheila wouldn't have told her about this, just as she hadn't told her about leaving for university in the first place. It was Luke's role to receive these secrets. For some reason she had chosen him twice now. Were they non-adults together? 'I'll do it,' said Luke, standing and reaching towards Sheila.

Sheila looked at the things in her hands before Alec took them from her and went through into the kitchen.

'Lovely party, Cath,' said Sheila. 'And Phil.'

It struck Luke then that she was not going to say a word to him about the murder. This refusal, while the others contributed what they could, meant she had different feelings. Her inarticulacy was powerful. Was it that she resented his not telling her earlier, at the point she had confided in him? Of course she might have simply lacked the resources, been incapable of a response. There was something fugitive in her.

'Nude painting, Sheila,' said Phil. The whisky had finally had its stupefying effect.

Alec called it out, the perfect idiocy, but companionable now, without harshness: 'She can't even draw.' It made Sheila smile and roll her eyes as though she was married to a man full of amusements.

The alcohol had unpleasantly reached Luke's head. He was close to speaking some terrible phrase of accusation. She had chosen him, it seemed, and not this man in the kitchen. Alec was old, a breaker of noses. Luke's soft hands required gloves, blistered easily.

Everyone was standing now but paused. He'd ruined the end of the evening, it was clear. They were wondering if they should wait for more from him, but they also wanted it to be over. Everyone was tired. Catherine would probably resent the fact that he'd told his story in public without first confiding in her. Or perhaps she wasn't thinking about him at all. He watched his sister hug Sheila and say well done. Then she repeated it as a sort of test to see whether any more meaning or urgency could be squeezed into it. Beside Sheila's great hesitancy and constant fear stood an equally persistent courage. And everyone understood she would now walk for fifteen minutes down a dark road with Alec into their empty home. A brief despairing look crossed Catherine's face. It had cost Sheila so much to come this far, an unaccountable store of energy and bravery had been raided, so that now the project which wasn't yet complete seemed suddenly doubtful and fragile and open to a new threat. Alec had said yes, and he had stood at a party in her honour, but no one was sure this wouldn't finally decide things in the opposite direction. That night Sheila might change her mind.

In leaving her children there at her friends' house, Sheila was rather stripped and purposeless. Her dream was to sleep with them always, have them close always. When everyone was following Plunket, pulling doors closed on screaming babies, waiting the four hours, Sheila had them with her. Phil kissed her. Then she let Luke give her a quick hug. She was close to tears. 'I'm so happy,' she said. They all seemed to have forgotten Luke's tale, or were acting as if they had. Perhaps they thought it indulgent of him to have clung to it for so long. Certainly he felt that way himself.

At the door, Alec turned and said, 'I suppose you've heard why she's doing this to me, haven't you? It's because of the glider I bought.'

'What glider?' said Phil, smiling. No doubt there was still some hope Alec was joking. Something left over from the story of the Canadian woman he'd had to punch.

'I hadn't told them,' said Sheila, 'and that's not why I'm going to university anyway.'

'I bought an old Wills Wing Falcon from a bloke in Omarama. More or less in pieces. It's a restoration job.'

Sheila said to Catherine, 'He borrowed the money.' In this statement there was an attempt at light-heartedness, but the last word—money—caught in her mouth and it came out more as air than anything, as if its speaker right then had been given a physical blow. She seemed winded.

Their notoriously strict budget came into view. Nothing was new in their house, which was Alec's parents' old house. Alec did the plumbing, the wiring, the maintenance—all on a farmer's holiday. Sheila worked a ringer washing machine, which she sometimes claimed to enjoy. She also spoke of the smell a drier gave to clothes and sheets. No money could be spent on the place, since it was always the plan to build a new house—and that never happened.

'So,' said Alec, grinning into their faces, 'it's tit for tat.'

He took a few steps into the dark. Sheila was already walking ahead, walking quickly. Soon they would hear the dogs, spooked in their wire-mesh kennels, and Alec's single word to silence them.

The hare

They were trying to prise the wooden fire-surround from the wall in one piece. A few of the small nails were impossible to get out, so they were using wide, flat chisels as wedges to free the surround. Phil and Luke were at opposite ends, each applying pressure. Only the hearth remained. Simon was sweeping the room while his little brother worked outside the open window, cleaning the bricks that would go to Eileen and David.

Phil had been talking about house fires. A few years before someone they knew had lost everything when a poorly installed flue had come into contact with some old sarking. Strong winds had the place gone in minutes. The owners escaped in their pyjamas.

'Tell him the rabbit story,' said Timmy. He'd come inside to show his father a bleeding finger, clearly concerned that by the time Catherine came home from town the blood would be gone. Luke remembered the story Catherine had told to distract the farmhand Hamish from his injuries—about Timmy wanting to preserve his blood-stained T-shirt when his first tooth came out.

'You mean the hare,' said Phil.

'Does he have to?' said Simon. 'We've heard it a million times.'

Timmy pointed out that Luke hadn't heard it, though this did nothing to persuade Simon, who slumped to the floor in irritation. He'd slumped where he could still hear the story.

'What happened?' said Luke.

Phil released his chisel, leaving it stuck in position. The surround had already cracked in a couple of places. 'The day Simon was born—' he began.

Simon cut him off. 'But it's nothing to do with that!'

'The day Simon was born,' said Timmy, teasingly.

'Which was a very warm day in February,' said Phil.

'Very warm,' said Timmy.

'I'll kick you,' said Simon.

'No, you won't,' said Phil. 'On that day, February 24th, at Trevor and Barry's place they were having a wee burn-off.'

'A wee fire,' said Timmy. 'A wee baby.'

'I'll kill you,' said Simon.

'No more, both of you, please,' said Phil. 'Trevor was there, and so was Alec. The farms are side by side. It was a paddock of barley, I seem to remember, they were burning off. There's a road between the farms. Alec was sitting in his truck, keeping an eye on things. Then he sees something flash by, something in the grass by the side of the road. He gets out of the truck and looks again at the spot. He takes two steps towards it, then the thing makes a run for it—a hare! But a hare on fire! Like a little ball of fire. Alec shouts at it and it runs straight between his legs!'

Timmy laughed. Even Simon was grinning.

'It goes between Alec's legs before he can do a thing, the whole back of it on fire. It runs straight into Alec's paddock, which is barley. Tinder-dry stuff. It'd been a hell of a summer.' He turned to Simon. 'Your poor mother carrying the lump of you around in that heat.'

'I didn't ask her,' said Simon, though he was enjoying it now too.

'None of us asks for it, do we?' said Phil. 'To be born.'

'What happened with the hare?' said Luke.

'The hare hasn't gone more than a few yards into the paddock, when whoosh, it's on fire!'

'The barley's on fire?'

'The whole thing takes only moments, according to Alec. He goes to the truck to get his gun to shoot the hare, and by that time the whole place is alight.'

'What about the hare, Dad?' said Timmy.

Simon made a fizzing sound. 'Barbecue,' he said.

Timmy clapped his hands in delight.

'Meanwhile,' said Phil, 'young Simon here has arrived. Almost two weeks late. So I start the ringing around and can't get anyone. They're all over at Alec and Sheila's for the fire, trying to save the rest of it. That hare caused thousands of dollars of loss.'

'Barbecue!' said Timmy.

'Of course, go back another five or six years of summers and we had a stock truck come through here started thirty fires in an afternoon. Sparks from the exhaust. It's a precarious lifestyle all right.' Phil kept a straight face, but he was satisfied with his own conclusion.

'Because I was born that day, what does that have to do with it?' said Simon.

'It was the reason I wasn't there, my man,' said Phil.

'So?'

'Usually I would have been there. I was in the volunteer fire brigade. Alec didn't let me forget it. He thought you were a very dim excuse to be missing the day the hare set his paddocks alight. He wanted to know what I was doing in connection to the birth, was I helping push?'

'What were you doing?' said Simon.

'I was there.'

'Doing what?'

'Your mother wanted me there.'

'For what?'

'To give her support.'

'How?'

'How? By being there is how.' The boy's persistence was working at his father's composure. There was the impression that if Luke hadn't been present, this conversation might have ended more quickly. 'And of course I was there for you, Simon, to see you into the world.'

'What about me?' said Timmy.

'I was there for you too, as you know. There are pictures to prove it.'

'The pictures are disgusting,' said Timmy. 'Blood.'

'Mr Moore wasn't there for his births,' said Simon.

'Different approaches,' said Phil.

'I won't be either,' said Simon.

'Is that right?' said Phil.

'I'll be busy at home, doing stuff.'

'How will you know when your child is born?'

'They'll call me.'

'Nice,' said Phil.

The boy was unwavering. 'If you'd been here, the fire might never have started. The hare wouldn't have run into Mr Moore's place. You would have been there too and the hare would never have run past two men. One man, yes, a hare will run past one man. Two? No. So it's not my fault, because I never chose to be born that day. But you chose to be there for my birth, you had the power. Nothing you did at the hospital helped me get born. There was a doctor for that and Mum was doing it anyway. She pushed me out.'

'Her vagina,' said Timmy.

'Jesus,' said Phil.

It was an unnatural word. To his credit, Simon pressed on. 'But on the farm, or in the fire brigade, you could have done something. So Mr Moore was right to feel angry at you.'

Phil looked at Luke. 'Is this lawyer potential?'

'Far too well argued for a lawyer,' said Luke.

They tried again with the fire-surround, using greater force. It was Catherine's hope that it would come off whole. Apparently Sheila had always admired it. There was certainly an elegance to the woodwork, and the mantelpiece was a nice weight. They could gift it and it would stand as the nominal beginning of a

'I don't know if she liked me much to begin with,' said Alec. He'd spoken without a trace of self-pity. He was a factual man, even drunk—if this was his condition—and wounded, which he seemed to be. It was unclear whether this was it, the complete statement of their early history together, and Alec would close down. Yet he added something: 'I couldn't have been very nice to her.'

'You were tall and handsome, according to her. And her aunt was a battle-axe and you saved her from all that.'

'I might have told her she had to go up with me.'

'You did it to me,' said Phil. 'I had no intention of going up.'

'But then she enjoyed it, and we went up all we could. I wonder why. We had some rides. She had the feel for it, I suppose.'

'You proposed up there,' said Catherine.

'I did not. There was nothing settled. I said she should come back to the farm with me, and she said, "You look like a farmer." Before that she thought I was a pilot. I could see she was disappointed. She hated her aunt, and so it came down to a choice: the aunt or me.'

'She tells it from her side with a bit more romance than that, Alec Moore,' said Catherine.

'I don't believe she was ahead of me. We were both as ignorant as urchins. I wouldn't have known how to propose and, if I had, she wouldn't have known what it was I meant by it.'

'The woman is always ahead of the man, no matter what he thinks,' said Catherine.

'These were two hopeless cases. You knew neither of them.'

The statement shut down the topic for him, yet there was more in it still.

'Amazing that Sheila could enjoy the gliding,' said Phil.

'But you're forgetting, Sheila's a very brave person,' said Catherine.

Sheila was somewhere in the dark house, putting a child to bed, reading someone a story. Alec was dyslexic to some degree and never read to the children beyond the early picture books.

new place. Phil wasn't so keen on the idea, which he was still on the provocative side', but he was still exercising great

Simon, having made his great speech, slumped again, down, soot in his blond hair.

'One thing, Mr Simon,' said Phil. 'When we brought you home, past the burnt paddocks, the trees still smoking, Alec had a tear in his eye.'

'It was the smoke, it stings,' said Simon.

'He had a tear from seeing you.'

'He did not.'

'Why?' said Timmy.

'Because he felt something.'

'It was the smoke.'

'What?'

'Emotion. He felt pleased for us. He especially liked the fact you were a boy. Naturally, he liked that.'

'Did he not cry, that means, when he saw Katie?' said Timmy.

'Oh but of course! Our beautiful Katie, he did!'

At that moment, as if called, the girl walked into the room. She let out a cry as the fire-surround came away from the wall. There were a few small cracks in the wood but it was otherwise in good shape.

Irredeemably English

David said the brick path should be snaking. It would curve through the garden. There was a pergola to pass under, and then a small clearing, finally arrival at the roses, a surprising number of them, the hidden patch where David put most of his energy and which bored Eileen since roses were irredeemably English, churchy. It was David's argument he'd won new life for the roses in concealment. He never won an argument, though. Luke thought pottery was English too, in its current crafts manifestation. It turned out Eileen loathed the pottery scene. Luke had won instant points by suggesting to her that there

ng a bit more like sculpture in her work than the
t from bush kilns. He meant it, though sculpture was
t for him. He'd tried, through Rilke's book on Rodin, but
remembered only the famous opening about fame being the
sum of all the misunderstandings around the famous person,
and perhaps something about things, the great calm of objects
which know no urge—he knew that bit. As a law student he was
once in a flat which had a poster of 'The Mask of the Man with
the Broken Nose'. It was kept in the toilet under a beer poster.
Inevitably this now brought to mind Alec's punching prowess.

Eileen told him not to call her an artist, however. If you made a teapot, if that was the warped kind of person you were, you may as well make one that poured: anything else was incompetence. She had long ago left that particular nightmare anyway. Teapots and cups and saucers. For eating and drinking she bought commercial stuff herself, as long as it didn't have any floral connotations. She could live with Arcoroc. The unidentifiable colour or non-colour, the suggestion of ashtray: such heartlessness was astringent. In her militant phase, she said, she'd gone around dropping cups and saucers in cafés, making it her task to defeat the genteel enemy. The old Railways crockery was a model—as was the word 'crockery'. So close to crock, Luke said. She laughed. He was working out quickly how to please her.

Eileen was strongly built. She got around in black leggings and baggy sweatshirts. David dyed her hair each month—jet black. Luke knew this because she told him. She asked David to hold out his hands for inspection. 'There,' she said. 'That's the evidence.' Under a few of his nails, and in the cuticles, there was a dark residue.

David had done the grunt work, levelling the ground, removing the dirt, creating the boxing. There were stakes and string everywhere. The bricks from Phil and Catherine's chimney were stacked in the driveway at the front of the house. Luke made trips with the wheelbarrow back and forth, bringing David the bricks. Finally, and fairly, David didn't trust Luke with laying them out. Luke was a labourer only, though David made a pretence of asking his advice. Eileen stayed away, alert obviously to the danger of falling into some domestic role she'd long since abandoned—asking the men whether they needed a drink or lunch, perhaps. David did all this too, bringing a tray out onto the lawn. Sometimes Eileen would join them. She would talk about the people of the district but always through their animals. She loathed the term 'livestock'. Catherine and Phil were apparently better than most at caring for their sheep. 'What I do,' said Eileen, 'is walk about. I go over their land, everywhere. They hate it, of course, and a few would like to shoot me no doubt. I always wear my orange jacket for exactly that reason. I've told David that in the resulting court case over my murder, he's to make sure the fact of my orange jacket is made clear.' She believed Alec's farm to be one of the worst. 'And he's also one of the best shots, I've heard. But his poor animals look exactly like his wife, from whom I've had about five clear and audible words of her own in the entire time we've been here.' When Luke challenged this, saying Sheila had grown out from under that shadow and was a new person, Eileen laughed. 'That woman's madder than me! Did you know they met when they were twelve?'

'She was seventeen,' said Luke. 'He was older.'

'She was his mother's nurse.'

'I know.'

'They come from the Gothic part of us. The type which ends colourfully, usually in a family slaying.'

David spoke up finally, asking that Eileen not talk like that, given Luke's friendship with Alec and Sheila, the connections with Phil and Catherine. She was taking things too far.

Eileen laughed again and said, 'It wasn't me who said the thing about visiting the house, was it?'

David blushed, muttered something.

'What thing?' said Luke.

'He said that each time he went to Alec and Sheila's place he had the thought that he'd be discovering bodies.'

'I didn't!' said David. 'How I phrased it was different, I'm sure.'

'The phrasing may be up for debate; what remains is the sentiment, one which I felt was accurate.' Eileen turned to Luke. 'I remember it because most of what he says is so waffly and hard to follow.' She walked off in the direction of her studio.

David wanted to talk about New York, where he'd been for three days ten years before. 'In Central Park when you first walk in, you think, I'm in Central Park! Then you calm down after a few minutes, but I never quite lost that feeling. For you it must have been different, to work there. I remember I saw this mother with her child and I thought, They're Americans! They probably live close. This is their neighbourhood park. The little girl ran towards the ducks, and this was amazing. Of course she's running towards the ducks, of course she would. She was wearing mittens. The ducks ran away, the American Central Park ducks. Am I making any sense? I don't know if naturally I'm a traveller. I find it difficult to pass on. Eileen says she won't go anywhere with me because I just stand and gawk. It's true. But that makes me sound like a terrifically sensitive observer, which I'm not. Just a very slow processor of information. How about you?'

The sandwiches were ham off the bone and mango chutney. The meat was kept—barely tolerated—in a separate fridge in the garage. There was a vegetarian option too, David pointed out. Lettuce and tomato with fresh basil. A jar of mayonnaise was there if needed. David had peeled a couple of oranges and cut them into segments. It was all neatly done, as was the path, which at current rate would take them weeks to finish. Luke sometimes felt this was David's plan. He appeared desperately lonely.

'Some of us used to go running in the Park,' said Luke. The idea—never developed far—had been to improve the rooftop tennis through a fitness regime. Kerry had got word of it and had actually come along once. After that, it fizzled.

David clapped his hands and grinned. 'I saw those people! Amazing.'

'I was never a runner before and the first time two things happen: you run too fast and, like everyone says, you feel everyone's watching you.'

'Only me,' said David. 'I'd be watching.'

From the workshop came a crashing sound which made Luke turn. David was unmoved. He put an orange segment in his mouth.

'In fiction or television,' David said, 'potters are usually insane.'

'Potty,' said Luke.

'They're almost like witches. Their kilns are fires and they might easily dance around them naked. If you think about it, the clay and so on, it's as if they've emerged from the bowels of the earth covered in primeval mud.'

'I've never seen Eileen covered in primeval mud.'

David looked at Luke, serious. 'She washes it off.'

A victory for tradition

Luke had tried to phone his brother Andy, and had learned that Andy was then driving down to the Christchurch Show with some horses. It was Cup Day. Andy was now a trainer, it turned out. Luke had the address of his brother's digs in Christchurch; he was staying at a good hotel in town. Catherine thought the story was faulty, or a smokescreen behind which their brother could move undetected. It all seemed too straightforward, too convenient, that he would actually come to them, just as they'd wished. Everyone went up for the Show—Andy would know that. Phil said it was an institution, a religion almost. 'All those who believe in Christchurch attend.' It had started in the 1850s. In the early days and until recently you could wrestle greased pigs and push cows over. A lot of fun had been taken out of it now of course, he said, though there'd been excellent additions such as the Ferris wheel and underwear parades. There was, from time to time, a wryness in Phil that was greatly appreciated by everyone, especially—Luke saw—by his wife. It indicated confidence. He appeared happy to be going to the city for this event, something he was utterly sure of, and which was of course cyclic.

'That's where we found him last year,' she said. 'Parked by the runway, with a crick in his neck! Put girls in their undies and you've got a hit show.'

Phil smiled. 'What was it Alec said? "All aspects of the natural world are worthy of attention."'

'Both of them with daughters too.'

'Guilty, I'm afraid. Guilty as charged. No defence, your honour.' Phil laughed.

The plan with Andy was to turn up and surprise him at the racecourse—if indeed he was there. 'Don't give him an excuse to bail on us,' said Catherine. For years she'd wanted to get him down to the farm for Christmas, and he'd always sounded keen on the phone, but whenever the time came to make the travel arrangements he'd found something that needed doing: a horse was sick or a meet was on, or someone else had to shift their holiday plans so Andy was required over Christmas. One time, three years before, Catherine, chancing on the information, had travelled to Balclutha where Andy had a horse running, and they'd had a meal together. Pies in a hotel, with a small and regrettable argument about who had the honour of shouting the other. The one who'd travelled furthest finally had to give in. Even this reunion involved a cancellation. They were to see each other the following morning, but Andy left a message at her motel saying he'd decided to head out on the road early to beat the rush. 'This was Sunday morning,' Catherine told Luke. 'When I got the message I went and stood out in the middle of the main road of Balclutha, and it was only boredom and cold that drove me inside again.'

'Maybe he doesn't like us much,' said Luke.

'He likes us okay but he doesn't need us particularly,' she said. 'He prefers the company of horses.'

'Fair enough. You know I've always liked the idea of having a brother who trains racehorses.'

'What do you think of having a sister who's a farmer's wife?'

'It's very exciting.'

Catherine snorted. 'The diplomatic life was made for you, Luke.'

'I mean it,' he said—and he did.

And she saw he did and her eyes watered, so she had to laugh and rub quickly at them. 'We're so pleased you're staying here with us.'

It was his turn to feel a little undone. 'I've been the life of the party,' he said.

Catherine walked a few steps away from him—to compose herself, he thought. She turned back. 'Andy misses us terribly.'

'In Christchurch let's grab him then. Let's insist and not take no for an answer and kidnap him if we have to. We're bigger than him after all.'

'We could throw him in a sack.' Catherine gripped his arm and smiled. 'What happened, what you saw in New York, the awful thing, is only a part of life. It's not the full picture.'

'I know.' He hadn't realised they were in this territory. The fact that he needed no time at all to organise an answer showed them the territory was somewhere he seldom left.

'I know you know, but it's worth saying.'

'Yes, you're right.'

There was another person involved in the trip south: Sheila had started university in the summer trimester. Luke wondered whether his sister had this on her mind too.

'Tomorrow, for instance, you'll see men who are the best in the world at chopping wood. Have you seen them in action? I used to not like watching. There's something about the logs being opened up, chewed into by the blows of the axe as if they were no harder than apples. The axe flying right close to their feet. Some people, and I was one of them, worry about the toes of the choppers because they're thinking about their own toes, they're thinking that they'd likely chop off their own toe if they swung an axe as sharp as that, as fast as that, while standing on a log.'

'That's how I'd feel, I think.'

'But then you see that these men are not you.'

'They know how to do it.'

'Exactly.'

'You think I've got things out of proportion.'

'The minute I hear you say that, it sounds like what I'm asking you to do is cheer up.'

'Seeing Andy will cheer me up.'

'Me too.'

'My guess is Andy will be portly. As a trainer he'll have resumed eating.'

'Andy with a little pot belly?'

'Can you see it?' said Luke

'I can,' said Catherine.

On the Saturday morning they met Alec and Sheila with their kids in the carnival area at the show. Luke followed Phil and Catherine in kissing Sheila on the cheek. He tried to inhale as he drew close to her skin but he couldn't get anything. The air was too full with hay smells and oil from the farm machinery and the rides. After negotiation, the kids were given money and instructions on which rides they were allowed to go on and who was in charge, then they disappeared into the crowd. Sheila was clearly less convinced than the others about the soundness of this strategy but finally she was outvoted—by kids and adults— and her only compensation was the length of the hug she gave Georgia, who seemed herself to be battling with the freedom she'd won, and Bill, the youngest, who couldn't wait to escape. Aware of the other girl's hesitancy, Katie had grabbed Georgia's hand and pulled her away with a shout of joy which Bill echoed. Luke saw Sheila blink under the force of this declaration of independence, and she remained standing in the same spot after the kids had gone, until Catherine came back for her.

It was Luke's ambition not to get stuck with the men but he

was soon walking ahead with them, as Sheila and Catherine stopped to look at a hat stall. Alec appeared solemn and satisfied. He repeated the statement Phil had made about the show being an institution, but without a touch of the irony his friend had thought to provide for Luke. Alec's institution was the real deal, a victory for tradition, a vindication of a way of life. These weren't the words he used, but Luke thought they were the meaning behind the words. He'd been coming since he was a boy. He didn't think they'd missed a year. The two men talked for a bit about experiences from previous shows. The escaped emu, the big storm, the terrific heat one year, a rash of fainting—here Alec drew the inevitable comparison with what he called Luke's 'problem'. 'How are you feeling today?' he asked. 'Once those clouds burn off, there'll be some heat in the sun.' Luke acted out a few wobbly steps for them, and brought his hand to his head. The other two went on with their reminiscing. At least they didn't bother to explain everything in detail to the third party, and for this the third party was thankful. They simply announced some key phrases—'that emu was out of its mind'—and passed on to the next memory. Alec paused to say a few words to a man he knew who was sitting under an umbrella at a stall selling soft toys. He picked up a lamb and said, 'This one needs shearing.'

Luke broke in, 'So long as it's not crutching.'

The man behind the stall didn't laugh, but he stood up. He shook Alec's hand, then Phil's and finally Luke's. 'If you see my wife anywhere, tell her it's my break and to get back here.'

'We've all lost our wives,' said Phil.

'It's part of the greatness of the show in some ways,' said the man.

They moved off. And now she'd been indirectly invoked, Luke said, 'Have you seen Sheila's flat yet?'

'A pokey hole,' said Alec.

'Then she's really a student,' said Phil.

'You'd know the life, Phil,' said Alec. 'I only know the reputation.'

'I told her at least she'll have no trouble getting into pubs,' said Phil. 'She told me she wasn't planning on visiting any.'

'She can't stand the places,' said Alec. 'She hates smoke for a start.' He turned to Luke. 'Where did you go? Not here.'

'Victoria,' said Luke.

'Mine will stay in the South Island.'

'Says who?' said Phil.

'If I'm paying I'd be looking to have a fair bit of input on the decision,' said Alec.

'Philippa seems to have a strong will,' said Luke. It was a clear provocation.

Alec eyed him up before answering. 'As we speak, she's a long way off the university route. Her ambitions are in advance of everything else. A shock will be needed soon for that one to come right.'

'She's a capable girl though, Alec,' said Phil.

'I'm not doubting potential. It's application, isn't it? In fact I'm sure most who get to universities waste even that chance.'

Luke began to speak, saying that he didn't think Sheila would waste her chance, but Alec had already turned away to greet an acquaintance. Luke walked on, past more stalls selling jewellery, food, paintings of barns and rivers. He could hear a loudspeaker announcing the start of something but he couldn't make out what. He stopped and tried to find Sheila and his sister in the crowd. They were gone from the hat stall and he couldn't see them. He made his way back in that direction. He'd lost them. The sun had come out and he felt it unpleasantly against the back of his neck. His sunglasses and his hat were in the car. He stepped into the nearest tent, where they were selling homebrew kits and offering beer tastings. A girl dressed as a maid, in black and white pinafore with a bow tie, asked him to lean forward, and she placed a small plastic cup on a string around his neck. 'Tasting charge is five dollars, sir. For that you can try everything. Sales are available at the far end, by the exit sign. Enjoy!'

She stood in front of him, smiling, until he realised he owed her five dollars. 'I don't know if I want to drink,' he said.

'Oh.' She looked lost now, a little hurt, as if no one had said that to her yet, at least not a male.

'But what the hell,' said Luke, and he gave her the money.

The tent wasn't busy—perhaps too early in the day—though there were a few men moving along the trestle tables, holding out their cups and drinking. Luke accepted a dark ale, which he sipped, connoisseur style. The stuff was good and strong. 'Liquorichy,' he said to the man, sounding at once as though he was pissed. He had a lager, then some wheat beer. He stepped further along, and someone reached out and had his cup and was pouring again. The action brought Luke's head close to the other man's head, though they both looked into the cup as it was filled. It was a Pilsener apparently, and Luke downed it at once. He asked for another. 'Messy boy,' said the man, pouring.

On his shirt where the cup was, Luke noticed a beer stain. The man picked up a serviette and mopped at it for Luke. 'Thank you.' He would stink of beer, yet the concern was half-hearted. He felt great, not drunk—the cup was small—but still elevated, as if he were taller and lighter. He'd always liked the honeyish smell of grass in a marquee.

'On your own?' said the man.

Luke guessed he was in his late thirties, early forties. Germanic. Dyed blond hair. Blue eyes. He immediately put him in a uniform. Boots, buckles, the works. The name of a brewery was tight across his T-shirt. He wore an apron around his waist.

'Yes.'

'I'm Grant.' He put his hand out and they shook.

Luke told him his name. 'Is this you all day then, Grant? Pouring drinks, mopping up.'

'I'm off at two.'

'I'm from out of town. My first time here.'

'Thought you didn't look like a Show person. Have another, Luke.' He took Luke's cup and pulled him close. Again they both looked into the cup as it was filling.

'What does a Show person look like?'

'Oh, I don't want to stereotype anyone.'
Luke drank his beer. 'What happens at two?'
'I get off.'
'Shame, I've got another appointment.'
'Take my card.'
Luke accepted the card. Sales Manager.

They became aware of something happening in a corner of the tent where a small group had gathered. There was rhythmical clapping.

'Oh fuck,' said Grant.
'What is it?'
'The entertainment.'

Luke drank the beer, smiled at Grant and moved over to the group.

A man dressed in the riding boots and the silks of a jockey was slowly lowering himself to the ground by bending over backwards. On his forehead sat a pint of beer. The man's eyes were fixed on the glass. His body was amazingly supple, like that of a boy gymnast. The whiteness of his pants contributed to this impression. The crowd clapped as he went down, and there were gasps as the beer inside the glass moved from side to side with each motion the man made. He now reached behind himself and placed first one hand, then the other, on the ground, steadying the glass at this point and causing the crowd to go silent.

Grant was still behind the trestle table, serving other customers now.

Luke noticed a young woman at the front of the group who had put the knuckle of her index finger inside her mouth. She was turning away from the man and miming a sort of disgust with his act, then turning back quickly to check on his progress. He knew immediately this was the man's girl.

'Come on, Corky!' someone shouted.

The girl, panicked, looked to see who'd spoken, and gave her nervous smile before going back to the trial. The man seemed stuck. He was painfully positioned with a fully arched back and balanced on his extended fingers. The heels of his boots couldn't touch the ground. His head remained level and the beer in the glass made only the smallest movements.

'Corky, you can do it!' said another.

'Come on, Corky!'

'You can do it!'

Then Corky, from under the pint glass, which seemed larger than ever, said through a tight mouth, 'I'm buggered if I can.'

The crowd laughed, and stopped. They were aware perhaps of the suffering girl, who whimpered and bit at her hand. Luke thought of Andy, his one-time jockey brother. It wasn't Andy on the ground but it might have been. When Andy was nine or ten he used to walk around on his hands and ask people to put coins on the soles of his feet. If the coins remained there after he'd crossed the room, Andy would win them. He made a few dollars in this way, and then no one would pay. They wanted him to do other things, harder things. It was too easy, they said, though none of them could do it.

Luke heard himself call out, 'Come *on*, Corky!' People turned in his direction. 'Come on!' The second shout from him was even louder. He began a slow handclap. 'Cor-kee! Cor-kee! Cor-kee!' The clapping and the chanting were picked up. Soon the entire audience was one animal. Luke looked again in Grant's direction. He was looking back now. Luke held up the business card and Grant gave him a wave.

Corky seemed to sigh. His chest rose and fell. The audience went quiet again. Corky moved his hands and somehow that allowed his body to descend, and he got his backside down first, then he stretched his legs out, and finally he lay down, bringing his head to the ground in one perfect, smooth motion. He was flat out, with the beer glass on his head, like a man who'd fallen asleep and then had a trick played on him by his friends. Not a drop had been spilled. The tiniest pause of contemplative appreciation, of shock, held them back, then everyone applauded. The man remained in position, except he'd closed his eyes. His small chest rose and fell in short, shuddering movements.

Several men leaned over the body, taking one last look into the beer, as if to check that it was real. They threw notes down on Corky before leaving. They'd lost the bet. Luke could see a couple of fifties there as well as twenties.

The miserable girl who'd joined in at first with the acclaim stopped clapping and took a few steps towards the man. She stared down at him, waiting perhaps for him to open his eyes, but this didn't happen. He was torturing her again, it seemed. Was it her role to gather the money? She hovered uselessly and then she shaped as though she would kick him, or kick the glass. Her foot went back. But she didn't do it. She pushed through the people and ran from the tent. At which point Corky opened his eyes, took the glass from his forehead and popped up. He was sixty or even older. The girl might have been his daughter. He picked up the money and raised his glass to the few who remained watching. Then he downed the pint in one go. 'You got me through it,' he said to Luke.

'Can I get you another?' said Luke.

'Drinking while not on the job, you mean? Not allowed.'

Luke handed him a five-dollar note. 'For later then.'

'You're a good man.'

'When did you give up riding?'

'Not as long ago as you think. How did you know?'

'My brother's in the game.'

'I'm not out of it yet. You never are.' He looked at the five dollars. 'Buy one of these fag beers, you won't get change from this. Now if you'll excuse me, good sir, I need to piss. Your brother would be a good pisser too, I'd bet.'

Corky walked out of the tent. Luke followed a moment later. As he was leaving he glanced back at Grant, who held up two fingers. Two o'clock. Luke then found a tree to sit under, away from the crowds, and fell asleep. He woke revived. The sun had dried his shirt.

He discovered the others, now reunited with their children, in front of the wood-chopping, which had just finished. The grass nearby was littered with large white splinters which two teenage boys in white coats were collecting in buckets. Simon, his nephew, was watching these boys longingly, wishing no doubt that he could one day have such a coat and such a task.

'You missed it,' said Catherine.

'There's so much to fit in,' he said.

Sheila was bent down, talking to Georgia, who was crying. There wasn't an opening. The plan was that Alec would drive home to the farm that same afternoon, leaving the kids with Sheila for the night. He'd then drive back to collect them the following evening. Where in this plan, Luke wondered, could a space be made for him to see Sheila? On the trip up, he'd had ideas about visiting her at her flat, which she shared with another older woman, a nurse. Sheila could show him around campus, take him to her favourite café; they could walk around bookshops together—the fantasy was quite worked up. The nurse was away for the weekend, which gave the kids a bedroom. He could drop in on them all, though surely that would be too strange. Sheila had spoken to Catherine of looking forward to a night alone with the children. If he turned up, there'd be confusion on her part and resentment on the part of her kids. No one would know how to behave, least of all him. Besides, there'd been no sign from her. He appeared to exist within the generalised orbit of her warmth and delight at seeing old friends. If he was the newest of these old friends, there was nothing to be read into the sudden promotion. He was part of Catherine and Phil's family, and Sheila was immensely pleased to have them all with her. He couldn't honestly find a stronger description than this. And, as always within Alec's orbit, her kindness had a wary, apologetic tinge, as if she had to remain vigilant against any flare-ups. The court had set another date for the hearing between them and the dairy factory. Alec had been preparing by acting with deliberate mildness—a sure sign he was ready to explode.

Luke made a move in the direction of Sheila, who was still comforting Georgia. Catherine stepped in front of him, pointing at her watch. It was already time to go to the racecourse to find Andy. Luke thought again of the old jockey in the beer tent and the possibility that he represented some sort of premonition—but in what way? Was that Andy's future, to perform tricks in a beer tent?

Among the many possible versions of The Day They Found Andy—and these included bluffing their way past security guards, calling to Andy from in front of the birdcage when his horse was walked, using binoculars, and so on—the one which they'd discarded straight off turned out to be what actually happened. They bumped into him, or rather he saw them first and came over. He'd been on his way to the toilets. He wasn't furtive at all. He seemed pleased, delighted. He hugged them both. He was laughing and making them laugh before anything had been said. He was better prepared, and the thought occurred to Luke that his brother, knowing he'd strayed into their territory, had considered an assault by them likely and had therefore steeled himself for it.

They simply looked at each other and laughed, in the middle of Riccarton Racecourse. They were euphoric, which was a surprise, since they weren't sentimental about family, but once it hit the feeling seemed obvious. Yes, no one is like us! The deep pleasure they felt in standing together, in being with one another, and knowing they were the same, despite the differences: this was remarkable and ordinary. Luke thought of their mother—sadly, guiltily, too—and as if on cue Andy said something about her, that it was a pity she wasn't there, that she liked an event—Luke didn't quite catch it since Catherine rushed in, agreeing. 'Dad too,' she said, which was patently untrue, since he never liked crowds. But they nodded at this. It might have happened with two of them, though it took three—it required the triangle—for the feelings to be this conclusive and expansive. Catherine had tears in her eyes. Her two brothers might easily have followed in kind had Andy not spoken then. 'What happened to you?' he said to Luke.

Luke wasn't sure what he meant, or whether Andy knew himself. 'I know, I know.' Andy was feeling Luke's shirt. 'What about you!' Andy was dressed in a suit and tie. A few blades of grass stuck to his polished shoes. This was where they all looked.

'I'm at church, aren't I?' said Andy. He moved his foot so that one shoe was resting on top of the other. He wanted the grass gone, or the shoes themselves.

'Amen,' said Catherine. They all laughed again.

'But where are the kids?' Andy said to her.

'I've done a runner.'

'Good on you.'

Catherine said, 'Why aren't you pacing around, getting nervous and smoking? Don't you have a race soon?'

'What day is it?' said Andy.

'He's very cool about it,' said Luke.

'Hold out your hand flat, hold it in the air,' said Catherine.

Andy showed them his steady hand. The tips of his fingers were stained from cigarettes.

'Pretty cool guy,' said Luke.

'What's to worry about? I mean, it's not the United Nations, you know.' Andy gave him a little punch on the shoulder. 'Eh? Is it?'

'No, this is far more important,' said Luke. 'The New Zealand Cup.'

Andy gave him another punch. 'Did you know something? Nine out of ten of those bastards have stomach ulcers.'

'Which bastards?' said Catherine. 'The jockeys?'

'The horses,' said Andy. 'The reason I'm calm is we were just scratched.'

'Oh damn!' said Catherine.

'No, it means we can sit back and take it in.' Andy took out a packet of smokes from his jacket and offered them around. 'I'm giving up myself,' he said when they turned him down. His lighter wouldn't work: 'Useless thing.' He got a light from the cigarette of a man nearby. He turned back and held his own lighter up, showing it to them. It was silver and tapered, and he seemed to be offering it as a conversation piece, as evidence of something. It was Catherine who picked up on the cue; she asked whose lighter it was.

'It's Barbara's,' said Andy shyly, pocketing it and turning away from them. 'Shall we sit with the money?'

He took them through into the Members' Stand, where they told him about their plans to surprise him, and he said he wondered why they didn't just call him and arrange something.

'Just like Balclutha, you mean?' said Catherine.

Andy looked puzzled.

'Have you forgotten how you abandoned me?'

'I have. In Balclutha, you say?' Andy turned and looked over his own shoulder, as if in an effort to retrieve the town. He shook his head gravely and was quiet.

'You were riding then,' said Luke. 'Maybe you blanked out from lack of nourishment. When did you give it up?'

'This season. It's a young man's game.'

'Rubbish! You're not even thirty!' said Luke.

'The body's about a hundred. I have a long list of strange complaints from being in the saddle, things only professional cyclists get, and a few top rowers. I can't actually sit for very long.'

They'd taken seats halfway up the stand. The crowd was growing.

'We were wondering about the break you had—your leg, right?' said Luke.

'Oh, that was a long time ago. I don't care about fractures—they're easy meat for the doctors. Sitting is the bugger. Nerves.'

'Why are we sitting then? We could walk,' said Catherine, 'if walking's easier. Shall we go down and look at the horses?'

'Balclutha,' said Andy. He was unsettled for the first time.

'Forget it, Andy,' said Catherine.

'Like you have,' he said, with a touch of sharpness.

Luke was aware that just as rapidly as the euphoria of their reunion had arrived, so some new—or old—sense of futility had crept in. Their time apart, Luke thought, seemed to have lessened their interest in each other. They were siblings, not lovers, and the vitality of that relationship lay not in any bold engagement with another's motives or fate but rather in sometimes earnest, sometimes floating explorations of the facts, the motives having long since been fixed. A sister, as much as a brother, was a machine of prophecy—one which was nearly always right. It was as though the cloud that had come over suddenly and cast the entire stand into a chill shadow had also lowered the temperature of their enthusiasm. They didn't regret meeting up like this, but it felt to Luke that the moment was already passing into its own retelling, where it would be improved.

Catherine shifted her hands over her knees and shivered. 'Who's Barbara then?' she said. 'Since you're dying to tell us.'

Andy grinned. 'Not who but here,' he said, and he pointed to a well-dressed blonde woman of about fifty who was making her way up the steps towards them. She saw Andy and gave a little wave. 'She's the owner.'

'The owner of the lighter?' said Luke.

'Of the horse,' said Andy.

'And anything else?' said Catherine.

Andy turned to Luke. 'You've been putting up with this for how long?'

Barbara was introduced and she sat beside Catherine; Andy was between his brother and sister. She stared at the three of them, smiling and calculating. 'I see something but you're hardly peas in a pod.' She pointed at Andy and Catherine. 'You two with the skin that should never have left Ireland.'

'We used to tease Luke that he was adopted, that we found him in the street actually,' said Catherine. 'Wearing no clothes.'

Luke thought this was Andy but he didn't correct her. 'I had an abusive childhood, you see,' he said.

'Andy's told me nothing,' said Barbara.

'Must have been ashamed,' said Andy.

They were announcing the next race. The voice from the loudspeakers listed the horses. Andy checked his watch. He repeated the names of a couple of the horses and asked Luke who he'd bet on. Luke hadn't bet on anyone.

'We were sorry to hear about the scratching,' said Catherine.

'We weren't contenders this year, Andy says.' Barbara had spoken with affectionate sarcasm. She fingered the pearls at her neck and adjusted the turned-up collar of her cream blouse. Her trousers were pure white, brilliantly pressed.

'We weren't,' said Andy. He bent down and brushed the grass from his shoes.

The last horses were entering the stalls.

'In the end you're in the trainer's hands,' said Barbara. 'Is anyone else cold?'

They took a table near the window of the Members' Bar. From here they could watch the races. Luke went up to the bar to buy the drinks and Catherine went to the toilet. He turned back to the window to see the finish of a race, and when he glanced over at their table he saw that Barbara and Andy had leaned close together, and that while almost everyone else in the room was watching the race, they were talking and looking at each other. Then he saw Barbara reach across and straighten one of Andy's lapels. Luke waited a bit longer at the bar, watching his brother and the owner of the horse he trained. But now the couple had retreated to their former positions, and someone they knew had sat down at the table, kissing Barbara on the cheek and shaking Andy's hand. Catherine appeared at Luke's elbow.

'What do you make of Barbara?' she said.

'She's a handsome woman.'

'I don't think we'll be able to kidnap Andy.'

'I don't know if he wants kidnapping.'

'Who won the race?'

'Someone.'

When they got back to the table, Andy and Barbara were alone again and Andy told them they could have won sixty-five dollars if they'd listened to him.

'Is that what you won?' said Luke.

Barbara said, 'Andy doesn't bet.'

'Why not?' said Catherine.

'Bad habit,' said Andy.

'I have one rule for betting on horses,' said Luke, who'd not placed a bet in his life. 'Never go for a phonetic spelling. Eezadream or Arfachance. Those god-awful jokey ones.'

Barbara moved back from the table, appearing to consider this carefully, and it struck Luke that he'd spoken without knowing what her horse was called.

Andy was grinning again. 'What about Enda Me?' He spelled it out.

'Enda Me,' said Luke. He was cautious now, though the alcohol from the beer tent and the stuff he was on to made that more difficult than usual. 'It's a better joke, isn't it? It's not bad at all. Enda Me. It's turning it round, so the punter's involved. They bet this money and the horse doesn't come through. I like it.'

'That's yours? Enda Me?' said Catherine. 'How did you decide on it?'

'For twenty years,' said Barbara, 'I suffered from endometriosis.'

There was silence at the table, until Andy reached for his glass of beer.

'Of course I'm joking,' said Barbara.

'Oh,' said Catherine.

'Not about the condition, which I certainly had, but about the name of the horse. When we bought him that was his name.'

'The thing to remember, Barb's a warped person,' said Andy. 'How's the farm?'

'It's going all right,' said Catherine.

'Where's your farm?' said Barbara.

Catherine told her.

'I was married to a farmer,' said Barbara. 'His real passion, though, was speedboats. That's the story behind the horse. I got him from the divorce settlement.'

'We know a farmer who's building a glider, a plane, right in his living room,' said Luke. 'The wings are detachable.'

'I give the relationship six months,' said Barbara.

'Interesting,' said Luke. He was beginning to like Barb.

'It'll never happen,' said Catherine.

Did she mean the glider or the end of that relationship—Luke couldn't say. Andy was asking about New York. 'We've heard nothing about it,' he said. 'That's where it was, right? Barb, my little brother is fresh from the United Nations, being our nation's mouthpiece.'

'Amazing,' said Barbara. She scooped a piece of ice from her gin and tonic and put it in her mouth.

'If you can get him to talk, I'll be grateful to you,' said Catherine.

'*You*,' said Andy to his sister. '*You* haven't managed it?'

'What's he hiding?' said Barbara.

'Maybe he's just like his brother,' said Catherine. 'Prefers the mystery.'

'We're men of mystery!' said Andy, clapping a hand on his brother's back.

'Cheers!' said Luke, and they all raised their glasses and drank.

Another race was about to start. Luke stood up and went to the window. Andy was soon beside him. 'Who do you like here?' said Luke.

'A couple of the bastards could walk all the way and still win.'

'Then there's no contest.'

'Only they won't be allowed to.'

'It's fixed then?'

'No, no. Everyone's on their own schedules, I suppose. Some days you don't want a win because it might be worth more on another day. Today was a genuine scratch, but we're hardly crying into our beer.'

The gates closed and then they opened and a roar went up.

'Do you live with Barbara?'

'We're in the same house.'

'You're together.'

'Don't laugh at me.'

'I'm not.'

'Don't pity me, Luke.'

'Why would I?'

'The first day I met Barb, she told me about the endometriosis. It was like you meet someone and they tell you they have a dog called Spot or something. I went straight home and looked it up in the dictionary. That's the kind of person she is, straight up, but weird. You never know what she'll say. She invited me to a drinks party at her house, full of wealthy people behaving nicely, and by the end of the evening she was in bare feet doing the limbo. I was holding a broom, and she and her friends were trying to pass underneath it. They had the stereo playing very loud. Elvis. A Hunk of Burning Love. None of them could make it under the broom but they kept saying, "Lower! Lower! Lower!" My God, it was a great night. A lot of people won't say a word about my height though they're thinking all the time, Who's that short-arse? Barb is different. She set the work computer's password as "dwarf". Endometriosis. I said to her, "Listen now I know what you've got, I can tell you, I live in more or less constant pain from nerve damage in my pelvis from riding fucking horses all my life." And after that, we were set.'

'You were just a pair of pelvises in love.'

'We were! And how about you, Luke? Where's the yank girlfriend?'

'Forgot to get one of those on the way through Duty Free.'

'Don't tell me there's nothing happening. I hate to say it, but you're a good-looking fellow.'

'Andy, I never knew you cared.'

'It's great to see you, bloody great.'

The horses had turned for home and all around them punters were on their feet. They were jostled at the window by friendly elbows, handbags. Women were on their tiptoes. One guy, very tall and very fat, went to put his glass on Andy's head. 'Excuse me,' he told Andy when his hand touched Andy's hair.

'While I'm down here, what if I jerk you off as well?' said Andy.

The man moved away, startled.

'It's why they call it the Members' Bar,' said Luke. But Andy appeared not to have heard. He was watching the horses approach the finish, moving his lips soundlessly. Just above one eyebrow and around his cheekbones, Luke noticed, there were patches of flaky red skin. At Andy's ear, near his sideburns, were the stretch-marks he'd noticed on his own face, and in a similar pattern—as if a mask was being worn, or something had happened to change the fit of the skin. He imagined them both as old men, old shrinking brothers, who saw each other once every few years at the prompting not of conscience but of circumstance—a wedding or anniversary, a funeral.

'Can we meet up tomorrow?' said Luke.

'Tomorrow?'

'Yeah, let's do it.'

'It'd be fun.' Andy's face showed little of this emotion.

'Absolutely.'

'Only we're off at the crack of dawn. There's another meet.'

'What about tonight then?'

'There's a thing, a Cup thing. Big fancy dinner,' he said sadly.

'Go to that and we'll meet up afterwards.'

'Oh,' Andy said, perking up. 'That's when I'll be in bed.' This seemed to be, as far as Andy was concerned, the winning hand.

'Don't be,' said Luke.

'I don't have to be, but I get up at four.'

'Get up at six or seven. Come out with us, Andy.'

Andy rubbed his chin, unhappy. 'Wonder if I could get out of this dinner.'

'I reckon,' said Luke.

'Barb's going.'

'Both get out of it.'

'She's got the tickets already. Cost a packet.'

'I'll pay her, I'll pay you both to come out with me and Catherine and Phil.'

'You'll pay us?'

'Reimburse you for the tickets. I'm loaded.'

'That right? From New York?'

'It's the US dollar. They were giving me a daily allowance on top of my salary.'

'Creaming it, were you?'

'Hell, yes!'

Now the topic was changed, Andy was animated again. 'You going back?'

'I'm going back to get me more of that cash!'

'Seriously, what are you back here for? I thought you were gone for years. Three years. What's the story, Lucky?'

That name—Andy was now its sole user. 'I'm on a break,' said Luke.

'They give you breaks every few months? Like in the army, in combat or something?'

'We're in there fighting for our country.'

'They pull you from the front line and tell you to go and stay with your sister?'

'To recuperate, to recharge.'

'From the hostilities?'

'Right.' This recalled the words of Charles Fuge at The Hague, when he'd told Luke off for reporting on Rick Weenink's tears.

Andy looked over at the table where Barb was talking to Catherine, then he looked back at his brother. 'Luke, you're really full of it.'

'So you'll come out with us.'

He smiled. 'They won't miss me at the dinner, will they?'

'Good. There's so much to talk about.'

From his motel room, Luke called the number on Grant's card. Sales manager for a brewery.

'I'm in bed, I'm zonked,' said Grant. 'What about tonight?'

Luke explained that he was meeting family. Could he come round now?

'Now? You're keen.'

'I am,' said Luke. 'I'm not lukewarm.'

'Lukewarm? I get it. You're Luke hot.'
'Grant me that.'
'Okay, will you fucking stop it already.'
'Give me the address then, prick.'

He took a taxi to Grant's apartment, which turned out to be an inner-city place, above shops. From the kitchen window, upon lifting the venetian blinds, he could see the Avon through the traffic. 'Do you go for punts?' said Luke.

'I love your smut,' said Grant.

'That wasn't smut, that was a straight question.'

'Straight? You? Calling me a prick on the phone.'

Grant hadn't bothered to get dressed. He was in a pair of boxers. Luke found this a disappointment. He liked an effort. Looking around, he saw none. Basically this Grant was a slob. The cleanest lines belonged to the blinds which were shut in every room. A grey and pongy murk was everywhere. 'Sorry about that.' He did regret it.

'Behave, cunt.'

'Oh dear,' said Luke.

Grant gave him a shove. Luke almost lost his balance. They were moving around the dining table.

'Oh dearie me,' said Luke. 'Look, Grant, I think there's been a mistake.'

It was not unusual in such circumstances to be reading from different scripts. He'd not been wrong about the uniform. Grant the Nazi. There was still a chance to get back on the same page—a gentler page. Why had he spoken like that on the phone to this shithead? Why was he here at all?

'Come around here, waking me up after a hard day's work.'

'That might have been a mistake, yes.'

'Damn right it was.' Grant tried to push him again. This time Luke was ready and stepped out of the way. Grant fell forward, banging his leg against a dining chair. 'Fuck!'

'Are you all right?'

'My fucking shin!' He sat down on the floor.

'That would have hurt.'

'It did. It really hurt.'

'Hey, Grant, listen, I've got to go actually.'

'Ouch. Look at this bump already.'

'Thanks for everything.'

'You're going right now? You just got here.'

'I've got stuff to do.'

'Well, at least blow me.'

'It's a great offer but I'll have to pass.'

'Or I'll blow you.'

'You're a real gentleman, Grant. Sorry.'

Grant tried to hobble to his feet but the pain surprised him and he slumped once more. 'Anyway, you've got my card.'

'I do.'

'You know where I am.'

'Every time I see the Avon, I'll think of you.'

Andy couldn't get out of the dinner. He rang their motel just as they were heading out to meet him. Barb was getting some sort of gong at the dinner. He had to be there. He was sorry. He said he'd be through again soon and they'd make a date.

'The intention was always to skip out on us,' said Catherine.

'To be fair, he had a prior engagement,' said Luke.

'Then why not just say no? Just tell us, "I can't."'

'He tried. It was only my hounding him got us a tiny opening.'

'Fact is, Andy said he could get out of the dinner.'

'But Barbara's getting something.'

'He couldn't say no to you because he can't. He's constitutionally incapable of a straight answer. It's Balclutha again. Did you see that today? I don't know, maybe he really had forgotten that particular renege, but another part of him, deep down, was disturbed. That I'd remembered: that was puzzling to Andy. That things have consequences. Now, if two or even three other people had approached him with offers for this evening, he would have given them all hope. He would have been outwardly encouraging in every direction, just as he was with you, and he would have been inwardly certain he was going to disappoint every single one of them. Believe me. It's how Andy is wired up. It's his flaw, and it's harder to spot as such because it's also his great appeal. The man who always says yes. Basically this is someone who hasn't developed past a certain point.'

The portrait was harsh, but Luke's disappointment was so great he couldn't find any clear objection to it. They were already dressed to go out; the babysitter was arriving soon. Now all he felt—and surely his sister felt the same—was enormous tiredness from the day. He certainly didn't want to spend the evening with her; probably this was mutual. That single topic—Andy—would be between them. With another—Sheila—equally present, equally treacherous. A third—Grant the Sales Manager—was non-existent for one of them and getting that way for the other.

'Let's not let that spoil the night, eh,' said Phil.

Luke saw his chance. 'You know what?' he said. 'I'll stay and look after the kids. You guys go and enjoy yourselves. I insist. How often do you get the chance?' He'd got in just before his sister, who nevertheless attempted a similar offer but was easily beaten. There was no sense in him and Phil heading out on the town together. It was clear that Phil would have settled for the motel TV, but he'd been removed from the decision-making process.

When I had my first child

During the term, Sheila was home on weekends, though only her family got to see her properly during these visits. This time was precious. Was she banned from seeing others and getting out? No, Catherine didn't think so. At least no order had been given out loud—it wouldn't need to be. Catherine spoke on the phone to her friend, and saw her at netball, broke into their domestic arrangement once or twice, reporting back to Luke when he asked. Sheila was working hard to appear unchanged. She cheerfully admitted as much. The books she carried from university she quickly dumped in the bedroom. Boring books. Good old Mum. Bad paintings. Bad art history. The entire history of art banished to the bedroom. Silly old stuff. Soon she was wearing her apron, taking charge. All her things were scattered everywhere—this had to be expected when others stood in your place. 'Anyone seen the wooden spoon?' 'Anyone know where the lemon squeezer is?' She re-gathered what was hers. The clattering in the kitchen drawer—that was recognisably her. Above the TV, or above piano practice, or above some dispute. The kitchen floor was laid with stone tiles. Whatever dropped was not redeemed. Was she clumsier now? The clattering and the dropping of things came above Alec's reading her out something from the paper. So much noise! She'd not noticed this before. It must have been normal. 'Listen to this.' They were all used to this reading Alec. And it was nothing, the stuff he read. It was zero. It was to do with him, always. Prices. Yields. Weather. It affected them all of course. It was important. 'Are you listening to this?' It must have been normal. The way they didn't make much of her return, it showed how well they were coping.

On the phone Sheila was always leaving the conversation to answer one of her children, to tie someone's laces, to hold someone who was crying. Someone was always crying. She looked ragged, elated. She was having a wonderful time. The university was amazing. Her teachers were incredible. She forgot to eat, then she ate terrible food—takeaways, Peanut Slabs, Coke. She was addicted to Coke which she bought from the machines that were everywhere. She was probably falling behind terribly. Everyone else in her classes probably thought her a real pain, with her slowness and her stupid questions: once she'd started asking questions—that was in week two—she found she couldn't stop. Catherine told her she shouldn't stop ever, that education was all about asking questions. But, Sheila said, you had to be careful. There'd been an article in the student paper about mature students and how they drove other students crazy because they started every statement in tutorials with the phrase 'When I had my first child'. Stuff them, said Catherine. No, but there was a letter the next week defending mature students, Sheila said, because if you had one in your class you could kick back a little since the mature student had always done the reading and always had something to say. Sheila laughed. 'And I realised that was me!' Lazy bums, said Catherine. Then Sheila had to go because there was someone crying. 'The children,' she said over the noise, 'have been so, so good. And Alec. I'm so lucky. And thank you for all the help you've been giving them. I wouldn't be able to do this silly thing if it wasn't for everyone helping.'

'What have we done?' said Catherine.

'To help darling Alec is no easy thing.'

'We simply turn up. It's better if he hasn't any warning.'

'Oh, I don't know, Catherine. He might not like that.'

'Of course he doesn't like it!'

The sound of the crying was in Catherine's ear now too, and she ended the call herself.

These are your lambs

Alec and Sheila's house was set among overgrown trees that hid it from the road, hid it from everything. The shaggy branches almost touched the windows. In the night they gave a creepy touch to any dreams. For years Sheila had hated the trees and confessed she sometimes took a saw to them when Alec was out on the farm, dragging the branches far off so he wouldn't see at once. Then she gave up. What they hid deserved to be hid perhaps, and she let them grow. 'We live in a shoe,' she told people, repeating something Alec's mother used to say, 'but it fits.'

Catherine had never liked the house. The coldness in it remained trapped even through most of summer. The window-sills were rotting. Sheila washed the curtains regularly and made up new ones, but they still sucked in the damp and mould. It was the same with the bathroom; around the basin and the bath a grey tide crept up the walls. It was a tide because she beat it down and it came back. Rust ran down from the taps. Tiny chips of enamel ended up in the towels and facecloths. The first time Sheila had picked these bits out she believed she was losing the coating from her teeth.

Everything was spotless—due to Sheila's work—but all of it was ruined. She fought and fought—and lost and lost.

In the bedroom where Catherine's kids had sometimes slept, the wallpaper was stained with the shapes of bent figures, leaping animals. A big freezer sat at the end of a long dark corridor of loose boards. To be asked to get the ice cream or the chops was a nightmare. You ran and never looked or stopped. Even the boys set up a loud whistle to protect them on the errand. Rats had been seen, standing on their hind legs, eating pears.

The car bounced around. The driveway was unmetalled and rutted. Puddles stayed for months. 'Slow down,' said Luke. He was holding the still-warm pot on his knee and the soup was sloshing around. 'Sure, sure,' she said. They'd had a minor argument over the soup already. Luke thought it wrong for summer, but Catherine's idea was that it would go in the freezer and when the weather got cold they'd have a ready meal. Luke then understood that his own objection had little to do with the practicalities of this plan, which after all were foolproof. He was really responding to the idea that Sheila would still be away at this time. He simply didn't want to face it that she'd be gone for months and months, and it became clear to him that he, as much as Alec, wanted Sheila to fail. Or simply wanted her around for the duration of his stay. This, too, was astonishingly selfish on his part. Alec, at least, had the kids ranged on his side of the argument.

He thought then of Eileen's report on the house and its inhabitants, and of David's feeling about its violent potential.

Sheila had always wanted Alec to build the new place, as he'd promised when they were married—it was a theme their friends liked to keep current also—but to Alec the old house was a victory over everything that shifted and disappeared, the place his father had built—wrongly, since it faced south, as was pointed out often though to no effect. 'I see my father's hand in everything,' he said. 'I see him working on the veranda posts, on Mum's cupboards. He broke his back to make her this place. For the times it was normal. Now it seems like heroism.' It was agreed that 'for the times' the house was a great achievement, but times change, they said, and Alec's challenge was a new one, though in a direct line from his father's. The new house would maintain the connection with the old through a fresh exertion. At this point in the argument, Alec would smile and say that it was truly touching that people had this concern for his family history, but such sentiments had to be paid for and currently he was short a few hundred thousand.

One year, however, when prices were strong, he'd actually had a site surveyed and some plans drawn up. It was on a slight rise, instead of the current hollow, and the architect had delivered on paper a release from the damp and the dark. Alec had left Sheila alone with the architect while they planned the kitchen—'What do I know about that?'—and she'd had another session with him on the garden. She didn't believe it but it was going to come true. The great event was about to happen, and Sheila conferred with everyone on the sort of things that would be best: new cupboards, new bench, new oven, new windows. Catherine drove with her to Christchurch and researched bathroom fittings, furniture for the sun room. Specifications and quotes were written down in a small notebook, and this travelled with Sheila wherever she went. She didn't visit a house without reference to the notebook. It became a little joke: 'Watch out, she's writing down the size of your bath.' She enjoyed the notion that she'd become a bore on the subject; it showed the new house had moved from the realm of the fantastic—vague and wishful—into the dull and detailed universe where things really happened. All her plans and ideas were passed on to the architect, who was real. He had letterhead.

Still, she trembled with doubt.

Once the plans were received, Alec said they should sit on them for a while. Too many disasters had resulted from people rushing in with their heads full of architects' nonsense. He'll never build, Sheila told Catherine. He's spent the money on the architect, said Catherine, he won't want that gone to waste.

A couple of months went by and it was winter—bad time to build, you pay every time it rains—then Alec said he wasn't happy with a few things but the architect was on holiday. Then it got hot—in summer you don't want to be putting timber framing up—and finally Alec said he doubted they could afford that style of house, and to think of something more modest was really to aim for a slightly better model of what they had now, and he would rather build big next time, do it properly. They would wait. Where was the land going anyway? They owned it, it was theirs.

Sheila had wept in front of Catherine when she told her friend of this decision. 'I knew it,' she said. 'I knew he would never go through with it. When he put the plans in the drawer the first time, he closed the drawer in such a way I saw he was saying no. Maybe when he left me alone with the architect he'd already made up his mind. Why give me all that power if not to snatch it back in the final instant? It's pure Alec.'

'I think he's waiting for you to fight for it,' said Catherine. 'He's stubborn, as you say, but he likes to be challenged.' She was almost going to say 'he respects that', but she felt she'd already become patronising towards her friend.

With unexpected bitterness, Sheila said, 'He likes to be challenged by you. He expects it, looks forward to it. From me he requires something different. Above all he likes things as they were, which in the end is why he won't build. It's quite simple really, and actually I like it in him. He's a very strong man.'

'Meanwhile you live in a house which isn't suitable.'

'To tell you the truth, I hardly notice it these days.'

Now the cheese factory wanted some of Alec's and Sheila's land and were prepared to pay a premium for it. They needed it for whey distribution. Cheese, Alec liked to say, was a culture: 'All it knows to do is grow.' He wouldn't sell, and would never sell to the greedies who already owned too much of the district. In public meetings he'd stated his opposition. Meanwhile he'd watched several of his neighbours sell off paddocks to the factory. A few, it was said, were in receipt of fantastic sums. The prices, Alec observed, were good if it was only the land that was counted in the sale. 'What these fellows have given up amounts to a great deal more.'

They parked around the back of the house. Bill, the only boy, aged seven, appeared at the door. He was wearing his best clothes: dark trousers, white shirt, a tie. Behind him stood his eldest sister, Philippa, who wore an old T-shirt and jeans.

'Very smart, Bill,' said Catherine.

The boy pulled at the tie. It was more like a decorative noose. He slid away inside again, still tugging at it. Apparently, the help—a girl of eighteen called Maeve—had had to go into town for a couple of nights to help with her sister, who'd just had a baby.

'She's been at it again,' said Philippa. 'She puts the tie on him, then she kisses him on both cheeks, looking right in his eyes. She's practising.'

'Practising what?' said Catherine.

'Marriage. She calls him her little groom.'

Luke was holding the pot of soup. It was heavy, with the awkward wrestling weight of liquid. 'Shall I put this inside?'

'What is it?' said Philippa.

'Soup,' said Catherine. The girl's lip curled in distaste. 'But there's baking in the tin. How are you getting on with Maeve?'

'She's got thick ankles,' said Philippa.

'That must cause all sorts of problems around the house.'

'She's always taking off, going out to the boys with more tea and sandwiches when she knows Dad isn't around. Meanwhile we go starving.'

'The soup will fix that.'

'When Dad's out, she gets in the Falcon to get the milk or the mail from the road. She won't walk fifty metres unless it's to the woolshed or somewhere the boys are.'

'Where is your father?'

'He's inside with Georgia. There was an accident today.'

They found Alec in the living room, reading the newspaper. On the arm of his chair was a glass of lime cordial, his usual. Georgia sat at the piano, picking at the keys with a fingernail. Her knee was bandaged. Luke saw her take one sandal off, lift the lid of the piano stool and slip it inside. He felt she'd done this just to be observed by him though not by her father, as if she was saying something about Alec's powers, their limits. Was she showing Luke what they could get away with now?

Alec stood up. 'Didn't know we qualified for meals on wheels, but we'll not turn down charity.'

'We heard there were starving children in the house,' said Catherine.

'The poor mites, as you can see, they're fading fast.'

Georgia was a broad, bulky girl; where the bandage pressed down, the brown skin of her leg rose up in mounds. Alec was not above offering a comment on her size. She was Sheila's main worry. Alec went across to her. 'We've been in the wars.'

'What happened, Georgia?' said Catherine.

'Fell off my bike.'

'Ouch,' said Luke.

'Tell them how many then,' said Alec.

'Seven stitches.'

'There was nothing of use in the medicine box,' said Alec.

This was directed against the absent Sheila, of course; Catherine ignored it and spoke to Georgia. 'Is it still sore?'

In response the girl burst into tears and rushed at Alec, who comforted her with one hand. In the other, his glass coolly perspired and wept. Finally she calmed down, then she moved over and licked her father's glass. Her tongue was briefly magnified. 'You see,' he said, 'they're parched too.' He turned to Luke. 'I hear you're a brickie now.'

'I'm trying.'

'It's a brave person to take on Eileen as a boss. The joke is she throws pots.'

'That's an old one, Alec,' said Catherine.

'He wouldn't have heard it.'

'I haven't had to duck anything yet,' said Luke.

'It's David who's the target. She seldom misses. We all have something of hers in our cupboard and no one knows a use for it.'

'Nonsense, I have a vase I use all the time.'

'Are you sure it is a vase, Catherine?' Alec laughed. 'There's usually just the one topic between us. She thinks my dogs are too skinny. I tell her she'd be skinny too if she clocked up the distance those beggars have to each week. Then she thinks I'm having a go at her weight, of course. You can't win, and I don't bother.' He turned to Luke. 'Do you know about the wee fridge with the meat in it?'

Philippa made a pot of tea for them and set out the cups and saucers on the kitchen table. She arranged Catherine's biscuits on a plate, and filled a milk jug which she placed on its own little mat. She was performing it all in the way she'd seen her mother do countless times before, and with just a hint of parody.

'They're growing up, aren't they, Alec?' said Catherine.

'There's no choice in the matter. The girl is gone.'

'She'll be back in a day or two though.'

Alec began idly to turn the pot. He pressed against it with the palm of his hand, keeping it there—and was scalded. He shook the hand and inspected it as if it wasn't his.

'Why did you do that, you great fool?' said Catherine. 'Put it under running water.'

'Get me some ice,' he told Philippa.

'Let's see,' said Catherine.

'Are you burnt, Dad?' said Georgia.

Bill was in the room at the mention of the word. He wanted to see too. Alec had his handkerchief out, ready for the ice. 'Show's over,' he said. He waved the handkerchief at Luke. 'I should have asked you.' The reference remained obscure for a moment until Luke recalled the evening of the farmhand's accident when he'd mopped at his brother-in-law's sweat.

Philippa dropped some ice into her father's handkerchief and Alec wrapped it around his hand. 'What did they pay you for the bricks anyway, if you don't mind me asking?'

'I can't remember,' said Catherine. She asked again about his hand and whether running water was better than ice.

He waved her questions off with irritation, then he regained something of the host's humour. 'Pour the tea, someone, when you're ready. I'm parched. They always treat the accident victim with liquids. The dying man is given a sip.'

'Are you dying, Daddy?' said Bill.

'Not at this moment, I don't think so.' He put his free hand on Bill's shoulder and turned him to face Luke. 'Have you seen this? Could he get a job in Wellington dressed like that?'

'I'm sure he could.'

Bill twisted out of his father's hold, grabbed a biscuit and left the room. Once she'd poured the tea, Philippa was also gone. Only Georgia remained, close to her father, delicately running her fingers across the bandage on his leg.

'She won't be back,' said Alec. 'I've talked to her parents.'

'Who will you get then?'

'Someone older, who knows? It's a thankless task.'

'Rubbish,' said Catherine. 'They're an excellent lot.'

'Did I say it was them I meant?'

'Then I agree with that. If it's looking after you, I'd say they should get extra.'

Alec laughed and took a biscuit. 'Great biscuits, Catherine. Are you getting all this home cooking over there, Luke? You're a lucky devil. Now Phil said you gave them those bricks for free.'

'Why did you ask then?'

'Has Eileen ever given you anything for free?'

'It's not a contest.'

'You'll be laying the path for free too, won't you?'

Luke looked from Alec to his sister and back again.

'I thought so,' said Alec.

'But I've never laid a path before. It's more like they're lending me their property to practise on.'

'Practise for what? I didn't know it was something you had in your future, to be a brickie.'

'It's probably a more useful skill than the ones I have. Besides, I'm only the wheel man. It's David who's doing all the design work.'

'Sometimes,' said Alec, 'it's hard to see the seriousness in either of you. How's the woodburner?'

Catherine said they'd only lit the fire to see it going, the weather had been so warm.

'The business with the fire-surround, I don't know what the idea is.'

They'd delivered it a few days before, when Alec wasn't there. 'You might have a use for it.'

Alec winced and flexed his sore hand. He looked around as if expecting someone to enter.

'What happened with the girl, with Maeve?' said Catherine.

'It was her youth, we could call it,' said Alec. 'The other night when she put our dinner on the table, I looked up and said, "What's all that?" Her shirt was covered in splotches of blood. I had to look twice.'

'What blood?' said Catherine.

'Wait on. "Oh," she said, "sorry, I didn't notice." So I said, "Either this meat was still alive when you diced it, or . . . I don't know or." "No, from when I went to see them doing the dipping, it must have been." "From the dipping?" I said. "Yes," she said. She couldn't keep the pride from her face. "I was helping them a bit." I said, "Helping them a bit with the dipping?" "They were showing me," she said. "Showing you how to dip?" I said. "Yes," she said, "they were very nice about it. When you were off in town." "But it's not usually a job involving blood," I said. For which she had no answer. "I'll go and change," she said. So I just said to her, "You've cooked the tea like that, why change now?" "Oh, okay," she said. Poor girl. She couldn't decide whether to sit down. She didn't know whether she was being told off. She was smiling at us, from a crouched position. "It's weaning soon," she said. God knows why. "The poor wee lambs."'

'Had you told her to help on the farm?'

'I had not. So I said, "One thing. These are your lambs."'

'You weren't making it easy on her.'

'"These are your lambs." And she said, "Sorry?" "These," I said, and I pointed to the children. "That's your flock there." She sat down. And then I banged the table. It was more of a smack. Bang! She's on her feet, runs from the room.'

'Can you blame her?' said Catherine.

'In hindsight, no. At the time, I was surprised she was gone, or that someone—it was hardly credible it'd been me—had made such a noise. I remember looking round at the children. What happened? What's all this? What's the matter? It was a thing to see their faces, the poor wee devils. When I'd banged the table, they all must have jumped. And then I didn't know what to say to them. So I said something. I can't remember.'

'You said'—it was Georgia speaking from under the table where she'd slipped to—'you said, "What would Mum say about all of this?"'

'I don't believe those were the exact words.'

'They were!'

'Anyway, finish up your tea and I'll show you the plane.'

On the drive home, Catherine said to Luke, 'The more I see of him, the more I think what a terrific actor Alec would have been. Ella has always said so.'

'You think he's faking it?'

'I don't know if faking is the right word. It's hard not to be convinced by him, but you also feel that you are being convinced, that something is working on you, almost against your will or your better judgement or something, and maybe that's what makes me think of an actor. All that time and he never mentioned Sheila by name.'

'But it was all about her.'

'Of course,' said Catherine. 'It was a hallmark of his

performance, to build everything around her absence. Still, I'm a bit worried for the kids.'

'He wanted you to be.'

'It worked!'

The Married Couple

The problems of young single women with blood on their clothes produced the Married Couple, who were to live at the house everyone called Poppa's. Alec had bought Poppa's years ago for next to nothing. It sat on the edge of his farm and was used by shearers mostly. It had never been a farmhouse or lived in by one of the families of the district but had been dropped down by someone, an outsider, who'd had a bright idea which had never worked out—something to do with fishing cruises. The area was coastal only at a stretch: the sea was just twenty kilometres away, yet it never penetrated. Small hills and a prevailing wind stopped it. There was a still-operational diesel bowser behind the house.

The Married Couple, as Alec was pleased to call them, were Doreen and John. John would work with Alec, while Doreen was the home help. It was hard to get people in the run-in to Christmas, so this pair were regarded very favourably just for turning up when they did.

They were childless, in their mid-thirties, and had been travelling the country for a few years, picking up live-in jobs. They were saving to buy their own place, a place which would be the exact opposite of Poppa's. At the same time they were seeing where they liked, what parts of the country suited them best: compare and contrast. 'Amazing,' said Doreen, 'that most people settle for what they know.' Alec might have taken this as a criticism, except he thought the woman was at heart a fool, one of the deluded, he said to Catherine, rootless and lost, her face always pressed against the window of life. Travel was a kind of idleness. They'd chanced on the ad outside the library where,

Doreen told him, they'd been looking to see if there was Bingo on. 'No Bingo,' said John. Often he spoke in these two-word sentences. Get home. Hot weather. Doreen's job was to use all the other words, so it didn't much matter. 'No,' said Doreen, 'but . . . bingo! Your ad, see.' Yes, said Alec. His mother had played Bingo. He hated the enterprise, and could never call it a game.

Doreen rode her bike over to the house in the mornings, then Alec gave her a lift back to Poppa's place after dinner. She was a large woman, an unlikely choice, and one that made people think Alec was again making a point about his situation. Most people thought Alec had revived the bicycle and presented it to Doreen just so the sight of a fat woman on a bike could be burned into the district. The offence he took at the Wide Load jokes was purely decorative. Doreen was not lazy and sometimes even went out of her way with the children. Once she made Bill a pirate costume out of tea towels, and she helped Georgia look something up in the atlas.

John was tall, taciturn, not very motivated, though Alec claimed to be getting his money's worth. He took an age to get his smoke rolled, and drank hot water, never tea. When he went into town, he bought cans only: tuna, tomatoes, beans. He was called Iron John. Did he smoke dope? It was entirely possible.

Luke had met him once in town and asked how he liked working for Alec.

'Great man,' said John. He'd phrased this almost as a question: was Alec a great man?

'Hard on you?' said Luke.

'Hard man?' The question emerged more fully this time. John was smiling and nodding, weighing up the proposition. Luke waited for the outcome. John, however, believed the meeting was over. He left Luke with a friendly flick of the head.

The second time Sheila came home for the weekend, Alec invited John and Doreen over for dinner. There was no sign he enjoyed their company, and he never used their names; it was always the Married Couple, which was how Doreen had first spoken of herself and John. What about our special time together? Sheila asked. All it meant was she'd have to roll a few more spuds into the roasting dish, Alec said. (She'd agreed to roasts again.) The pair turned up and Alec more or less ignored them the entire evening. On Sheila's next weekend home he asked them again and at the last minute they couldn't come. Suddenly a call: 'Terribly sorry, we can't make it because someone's just arrived.' 'Who could that be?' said Alec. The next time—since it had become a mania of Alec's—Doreen came by herself. 'Must have been working the poor joker too hard, eh,' said Alec. 'Yes,' said Doreen. After the meal she helped Sheila with the dishes, despite Sheila telling her that she was the guest and she should go and sit down. 'Sit down?' she said. 'John sits down and he falls asleep!' To go and sit down also meant to take up again with Alec in the next room.

When Alec was out on the farm, Doreen, in the time-honoured tradition obviously, would drive the old Falcon to the front gate to get the milk or the mail, or she'd make one of the kids run and get it.

'Why don't you?' Philippa said. 'It's your job.'

'It is not my job! My job is in the home. The home is this. I don't have to walk out the door if I don't want to. I don't have to do anything that's not in the home.'

'What about the washing?' Philippa said. 'To hang out our clothes. Then you have to leave the home.'

She thought about this for a moment. 'Where's your mother?'

'You know where she is.'

'Safely out of this lot,' said Doreen.

Philippa walked to the door, opened it and took a step outside. She was going to run straight to Catherine and Phil's with the tale. 'Maybe you ate her,' she said.

'And you're a skinny witch!' the help shouted back. That was the only thin thing about her, her skin.

This was not how it finished. Alec wasn't prepared to end the Married Couple's tenure on the hearsay of a child. He needed the proof himself and got it the day after Doreen called in sick.

It was a Sunday. He walked round the back of Poppa's place—on suspicion of nothing, he pointed out, but only to say hello and see how things were. There was John, filling up his ute from the bowser. Usually there was a lock on the pump. It was a marvellous performance to watch, Alec said, this fellow rolling his smoke while the ute was filling; he might have been whistling a tune too had he been the sort. In truth, Alec said, he was a dour bloke of limited initiative who had to be handed a written list of tasks at the start of each week. He had a curious memory, forgetting the obvious and dredging up something small. When Alec spoke about this after the Married Couple's reign, it was offered that John was indeed a dopehead, a smoker of more than just tobacco. This seemed a genuine surprise to Alec, who asked whether there might have been a plantation somewhere on his property tended by Iron John and which could get them all into trouble. John was boring to work with and the written list took him mostly off by himself. He might have thought this ideal.

At Poppa's, the thief looked up and gave Alec a nod.

'Filling her up, John?'

'I am.'

'That's right.'

'Save me some time from the trip into town.'

'Not all it saves you, John. That's my diesel, isn't it?'

Alec bent down and picked up the padlock. Shorn through! John said he couldn't find the key. Alec told him the key was on his key-ring; did he want to open other things he had, maybe the shed where he kept his chainsaw, his farm bike? What's mine is yours, John, Alec told him with what would have been a razored sincerity.

The grass was burnt black from the diesel. The bloke smelled of diesel. He put the smoke to his lips, sealing the paper with a certain lasciviousness it must have been, Luke thought, to make Alec mention the bloke's tongue as 'thin'. In that moment a door inside the house closed. He could hear a woman's voice, humming in contentment. This was the sick Doreen.

'I was going to pay you for it,' said John.

'We'll settle it in your final wages,' said Alec.

The bloke took out his matches. 'He would have lighted it too,' Alec said. 'I might have let him, too, had I not thought of the bowser and the house and my own eyebrows and the bike I'd spent a few hours on lying not far off. I reminded him of all of this, and he looked around as if I'd said we were living on the moon and to be careful of the craters.' He stepped with great steps away from the ute and diesel and from the house and from me, Alec said, as he had probably stepped away from most of his life, in slow motion, with Doreen in tow—or her pulling, he wasn't sure. 'They were visitors from another planet where one good turn never goes unpunished.'

It surprised Luke to learn that Alec had been regularly hit by such disappointments, losing a good deal of farm equipment to light-fingered employees over the years. His trust was given utterly. He was unusual in this way; living in such certainty of his own morals had not given him a suspicious nature. Nor had his losses soured his faith. Everyone was estimated very highly. When this error became apparent, Alec might crash for a day or two, incapable of pursuing the offender, wishing the bloke gone for good. He could never mention the name again, and if anyone brought it up they got nothing from Alec except beadiness, blankness. Apart from this, he was Alec again, careless where he didn't think care belonged, notably in the business of those he was paying. Money truly didn't mean much, except as a subject. This was what the cheese factory failed to understand. Alec loved to talk prices as much as the next farmer but he had no feeling for accumulation. Did this mean, strangely, he had no feeling for the future? The rate he was chewing through the home help made the case stronger. The three children were frequently scattered about the district in the beds of friends. Alec, following up on a loose invitation, went as far as going to dinner at Eileen and David's place, throwing them into a panic. He behaved, in the end, and by Eileen's account, beautifully, even buying one of her most expensive pieces. Naturally this act was also scrutinised for any meaning it might carry regarding the purchaser's state of mind. Was Alec losing it? He started getting many visitors, many of them carrying dinners, offers of assistance. People wanted to help; they also wanted to know whether he was going nuts.

Finally, Sheila had to come home, missing a week of varsity, then another. It was almost Christmas anyway. The university had a break. Was this the end of it? Catherine thought so. 'Such a shame,' she said.

Phil agreed, saying she'd had a good run and she could always pick things up when the kids were a bit older. She'd seen what was what and later on it'd all be easier.

Luke was shocked that it had all been decided, as it seemed to have been. This pair was speaking with the authority of the district.

'Apparently,' said Phil, 'she got an A for everything she handed in, except one.'

'Sheila's a smart cookie,' said Catherine.

'And that one she didn't get an A for, she paced around with it, asking everyone for an opinion as to why. Even came to me with it! She had a B+ too.' Phil laughed. 'I thought it might have been a D the way she was worrying at it. Did you see it, Luke?'

Luke hadn't seen it and he felt a pang for not being involved. 'I don't think she should give up now,' he said. He realised he'd spoken with some determination.

'As Phil said, she can come back to it,' said Catherine.

'What a waste, though. I don't see the problem. Why can't everyone just manage for a while?'

Catherine smiled at him, a little condescendingly, though her voice was mild. 'It's proving difficult, I suppose, with the children.'

'They're doing fine,' said Luke. 'They have all the support they need. My God, the way everyone's got in behind it, what more can that man want?'

'If she went back to uni at a later date,' said Phil, mollifying, 'she could probably still use those As, I'm sure.'

'No, she couldn't,' said Luke. Phil ducked his head at this firm negative. The compliant gesture irritated Luke further. 'She could only credit completed courses, not individual essays within courses. Everyone knows that, Phil. You went through, you know that.'

For Catherine, this was too much. 'Obviously, they are not doing fine,' she said. 'They're miserable. And so is Sheila, despite the As.'

'How do you know that?'

'Because I know Sheila.'

This delivered a sting. He paused before he replied, gathering again as much calmness as he could. 'She's doing what she wants to do. And what you all supported her in doing. I don't see what's changed since we all toasted her and wished her the greatest success. Remember what you said, Phil? To push yourself is one of the truly great things. We could all be improved etcetera.'

'It was an experiment, what she did,' said Catherine.

'Which should be allowed to continue.'

Catherine sighed sympathetically. Here was the summing up which would close off the argument for good. 'She was heading into the unknown. It was brave and wonderful. And now she knows what's there, she can see, as everyone else can see, that right now, university study, away from the family home, is perhaps not the best idea.'

'Despite the As,' said Luke.

'Despite the fantastic marks, yes,' said Catherine.

'So you're not allowed to advance yourself? You've got to stay in your box?' He hadn't intended the attack to be any broader than the subject under discussion. His sister's face betrayed the hit.

Catherine drew a breath. 'She helped make that box. That box, as you call it, is her home, her children.'

'Alec.'

'Yes! Alec!' She was red in the face now. She attempted to recover her poise. 'Good old Alec.'

'Good old Alec,' said Luke. 'She told him she'd kill herself if he didn't let her go this time.'

Phil looked up. 'What?'

'Who said that?'

'She told me. Sheila told me it was the only way he'd agree.'

'When did she tell you?'

'At the going-away party.'

'Rubbish.'

'She told me.'

He saw that his sister was disgusted with him, repelled by his petulance, and also that she believed him utterly, knew he'd not made it up. Of course she wouldn't say so. Phil too seemed convinced without further statement. They knew her better than he did. Immediately Luke regretted his outburst. He'd betrayed Sheila too. They were silent for a moment.

'It's not the first time,' said Catherine quietly.

'Sorry?'

'Sheila's had a rough time in the past,' said Phil.

'With Alec?' said Luke. He'd not found his way on to this new path yet. Where had they gone? It felt as though they were now in protective mode, keeping something from him.

'With everything,' said Catherine.

'Been a bit fragile,' said Phil.

'I think she's really tough,' said Luke, already aware that such a statement, though he believed in it, carried the depleted charge of a hope uttered aloud against some large, hidden obstacle. He had the feeling a fact was about to roll over him and pin him just as quickly and simply as the tractor had pinned Hamish, their farmhand. 'What do you mean?' he asked.

'She's had some periods in care,' said Catherine. The word was being quoted at him. Care. What was that? 'Alec used to drive her up to a place near Nelson so she could get herself together again.'

'When was this?'

'After each child was born, and at other times.'

'Postnatal depression,' said Luke, delivering it like an expert.

We have your diagnosis. Rest is what you need, and some quiet.

'There was an element of that. But it went further.'

'She'd had things go wrong years back, apparently,' said Phil.

'What things?'

'We weren't supposed to know at first,' said Catherine. 'Alec didn't want it about, and Sheila wasn't exactly advertising the thing. We had no idea he was driving her there the first few times. They talked of a relative who was sick. Then there was a crisis one time, and we were called in to help. That was seven, eight years ago. Poor Sheila. Bipolar was a phrase being used, though that shifted. The diagnosis, if you were looking for the medical definition, it wasn't ever quite fixed as far as we know. When Alec told us, he said Sheila had laughed on hearing it. Bipolar. Thought it made her sound like an explorer. "I'm at the south polar today. Next month I'll be at the north polar."'

Luke found he wasn't surprised. It didn't much help with his disorientation. 'She's functioning now though.'

'She's a lot better than she's been at certain points, for sure.'

'Knocks your confidence though,' said Phil.

'Varsity has helped her confidence,' said Luke.

'A point of achievement is when she often crashes,' said Catherine.

'Is she crashing? It's Alec who's crashing, I think.'

They were talking quietly, as if in danger of being overheard. All the children were in bed.

'She is strong,' said Catherine. 'She's amazing. But it's something on Alec's mind. He told me once he doesn't stop thinking about it for longer than an hour or two. He said he considered it an injury, something chronic. Both of them were injured in this way.'

The idea of Alec's sensitivity—his injury—was almost too much. He couldn't quite believe in it.

'You look tired, Luke,' said Catherine softly.

This might have been an infuriating statement, yet he

discovered he was grateful for it. Suddenly he felt completely flattened, out-manoeuvered, emptied—emptied evidently of all those ideas he'd held about Sheila. 'I am a bit.'

'Must be because of getting back into your proper work,' said Phil. 'Not used to it yet.'

'A different set of muscles, you reckon?' said Luke. He'd phoned Wellington. No, they didn't want him back immediately but there was some short-term contract stuff available. The next day a courier van had delivered a parcel. For the past week he'd been doing a literature review, working at Katie's little desk in her bedroom while she was at school.

They stood, the three of them, facing each other. For the first time since arriving, he kissed his sister goodnight. She appeared stunned by it. What could there be for Phil? The instinct, as much on his part as Phil's, was to shake hands, but they both recognised the situation required something more than that. Their arms twitched forward in anticipation. Instead of the handshake or an embrace, they gripped each other oddly by the elbow. The lights went out in the house within minutes of this contact, everyone in bed.

Is it late?

The following day, by chance, he met Sheila at the public library where he'd driven Katie. He had in his hand a book—*Charlotte's Web*, which he'd chosen for Katie because he remembered it from his childhood. He'd just shaken off David Tanner, who'd been borrowing some architecture magazines and wanted to engage with him. The brick path was completed. There'd been talk of Luke's availability for other projects—an extension to Eileen's workshop was in the offing. The children's section had been his escape.

Sheila saw the book and told Luke it always gave her the shivers. Because of the death of the spider? he asked. But she hadn't read the book; it was all tied up in ancient days, with

Alec's mother in fact. She needed only the most gentle of prods to tell it. He said he knew she and Alec had met in Omarama when he was flying. And as he spoke he was wondering why he had gone down this autobiographical route when it had that destination. Leave Alec out of it. Luke couldn't stop thinking about Sheila as a mad person.

They were sitting alongside each other in child-size armchairs made of tough vinyl. Christmas tinsel hung on the walls. Sheila was down to a library whisper. It helped for once. She spoke in some of her new phrases as if testing them out. She wasn't tentative though. She was theoretical, almost Socratic. He saw at once she'd be a killer student, listening hard to the patterns a tutor made—not the bullying sort of tutor, but someone who appeared to be on an adventure or in a maze which you were helping him or her out of. Terrible if you were tired and just wanted to know stuff. He envied the tutor—whom he saw as a young postgrad bloke—and his relationship to the female students in the class. Of course that had been him not too long ago.

When she'd come back with Alec from Omarama, Alec introduced her to his mother Elizabeth as someone who could help rather than as someone he wanted to spend the rest of his life with. Though it was never spoken about, Sheila assumed they would never marry until Alec's mother had died. Elizabeth was bedridden. 'People went to bed in those days. It was a different thing. An acceptable sort of sanctuary, a little holiday spot. You could go to bed, for years.' Did she mean him in some way? And surely she was wrong anyway. People taking to their beds in the seventies? An operation carried out at the hospital in Christchurch was said to have laid Elizabeth low. Had something gone wrong in the operation? She didn't know. 'I was hardly more than a girl and this, like so many other questions from that time, remains unanswered. Woeful. I was caught up in a woeful period for the self. I'm sure we both felt it, that we were divided by something. History probably. The history in her bedroom, Elizabeth's bedroom. So after nearly a year's service—I call it service, but I was living there in a little room out the back, part of the household in every way and Elizabeth knew why Alec had brought me there—I was allowed in to her bedroom, to my horror, to clean—all that! It was suddenly down to me. Before then I did everything else, the cooking and so on, but nothing much in her bedroom, except carrying trays in and out. She'd been firm on that. I wasn't to move anything or disturb anything. Someone else came once or twice a week to wash her—an older woman, older than Elizabeth. Then for some reason she couldn't come any more.'

Luke offered that it was the bedroom of an alcoholic, which made her glance his way discouragingly—no, that wasn't a useful direction in this maze. She'd been speaking while facing the child-high chalkboard above which a sign read 'Tell Us A Story'. There was no chalk, only a duster. One good reason, he thought, for retreating to one's bed was the provision of booze, though this didn't seem the thing to say either. Had Sheila taken over as supplier from Alec?

Sheila took the book from him.

'I remember the first time I had to clean in the bedroom, Elizabeth leaned forward to get something, and I offered to plump her pillows and she said, "All right but don't hit them too hard." I bent towards the pillows and I saw a spider web. It ran pretty much the length of her bedstead, against the wall. There were insects caught in it too. I didn't have my cloth in my hand so I didn't know what to do, and she was already lying back against the pillows. There was probably an instant when I could have scooped at it with my hand, but I was squeamish. I hesitated and it was too late. I couldn't tell her then. You see, I was very young. I don't think I spoke much at all back then. And this is what I felt: that this woman, who seemed old to me, though she couldn't have been more than mid-fifties—she was in a web. She was caught in the web I'd seen. When my daughter, it was Philippa, read *Charlotte's Web*, I felt quite nervous and a bit clumsy. I didn't feel quite right until she returned it to the library. This is probably the same copy.'

The analysis was a stretch, he thought. Still, imagining for a moment they might have a discussion about the book, he told her he couldn't remember much from it. She seemed not to take this in. Truly he had no feel for the maze—or the web. He hated the image of Alec driving her to the psych place near Nelson. The hours in the car, driving his crazy wife, leaving behind their children whom the crazy wife could no longer cope with. Especially he disliked the expanded notion of Alec this presented, the enormous patience it must have taken for the farmer to leave everything and try to get help for this person he'd married and who had now, in effect, gone missing. But she was back. She was amazing. He looked closely at her. In the eyes, where the drugs might show, there was only alertness, intelligence, inquiry. Another point registered: that Catherine and Phil might have been looking for something to warn him off her, and that the story of her problems, which he did not doubt, was in fact old and over with. People came back—psychiatry was an efficacious business, and if it wasn't psychiatry that did it, time was there as healer. How long had it been since the 'crisis'? Seven or eight years. Sheila was back, had been for a while. He would come back. This was part of her fascination for him, although up to this point a buried one—that she'd survived.

'A web had formed around Elizabeth, I thought. I'd seen it. I had this shameful sense of something spun from an abdomen. Damp elastic ropes ran from her bed to all her things. The things wrapped in this web. In the garden even now I still hate most that accident, walking through a spider web. Elizabeth! I think. The garden, for a moment, seems full of these . . . secret selves.'

What was she reading from, her diary? She'd been told to keep some kind of journal, he was sure. This was memoirising. He was oddly elated. It was not for him but he'd made it happen, or if not that then it was happening in his presence, which couldn't be discounted. It was something to be the cause of something. Did she also know that she'd caused him to want her, to long for her skin, her wrists? He had an erection and he moved the book she'd handed back to him onto his lap. Had E. B. White ever been used for this purpose?

She was working through an inventory. Alec's mother's hand-mirror with the paua inlay, her blue crystal bottles on the window-sill, a special lamp with a brass mount. 'My goodness, her shoes! The leather had stiffened until each shoe was set hard, a little shoe-shaped box. I cleaned everything, and Elizabeth from her bed watched me like a—I was going to say hawk but her features were all softened by then, and puffy. She was softened too—I mean her personality. Sometimes she'd ask me to sit on her bed, then she'd ask me about my own family, where I was from, what my mother did. She was basically a lonely person, fallen out with her sister, with everyone. I tried to clean the room but all she wanted was a feather, a dry cloth at most. Gentle, she'd say. Gentle. There was a substance made of dust but stickier than dust—a kind of adhesive—on everything. My cleaning didn't make much of an impression. A soil really on everything: is that why I think of gardens? She asked me to bring her a face-cloth, some warm soapy water in a bowl—but not too soapy—and a towel. Then I had to leave the room, even though I'd offered to help. "Come back later," she said. "Don't hang around either, you can go into town, have a bun." She'd give me a couple of dollars from her purse. I never went into town. I stayed in my little room. I waited for an hour or so, then I went back into her room and took the bowl out. She'd usually be asleep. Not sure if she actually used the water. She looked unchanged, the same dryness around her mouth, moist around her eyes. Everything was masked with perfume. There were bottles on her bedside table. I think it was only a few weeks later that she died. And when she died, we had to face the bedroom, me and her son.'

Why say 'son'? Because somewhere she'd written this for her tutor or lecturer, someone who'd claimed an interest. He tried to think of the great artists who'd kept diaries. A lot of them had, but he couldn't even think of one great artist except Van Gogh, old hat. Paul Klee? He couldn't get going at all. He was thinking back to the children's display at Sheila's going-away party.

'Where we finally discovered what was hidden or trapped.

I don't mean the spider web. Spiders get in everywhere, no big deal really. I mean we could see her stuff properly. The person dies and, sorry if this sounds awful, sense prevails. Alec was full of energy suddenly. He never dallied in the bedroom before. He wouldn't stay for longer than a few minutes and always spoke to his mother as if he was only managing the farm, had been hired, and she knew best, controlled everything from her bed. He'd put everything as a question or a possibility. "I was thinking we should put in some more fencing . . ." And she would nod or say, "Go head with that." She was gone now, and he went in and said, "This place is a dump." I was shocked but I also thought, Good, now we're getting somewhere.'

'You could get married.'

'Right. Life could start.'

'Where was his father in all of this?'

Alec's father had died of a heart attack the year before Sheila got there. He wasn't part of this memoir. 'So the day arrived and I told Alec to have a few moments by himself. Go into his mother's room and just have a quiet moment. "What for?" he said. "I don't know," I said, "you just might like some time by yourself." "You think I'm going to clean up the bottles under the bed?" he said. "Hide the evidence?" He was angry with me. We'd never talked about the bottles. No one had ever mentioned the word alcoholism. It was too obvious. We weren't hiding anything. It was just never mentioned. But he did go in to the room by himself. When I went in, I found him sitting on her bed, lost, like a little boy. Waiting. At first I thought he was waiting for me. But that wasn't it. When I walked in, I might have been a stranger, an intruder—such hostility, the look on his face. Unrecognition. Grief, of course. Mixed with bitterness and resentment. All aimed at Elizabeth, but also at anyone getting within the radius of that room. There was a ring of heat you could almost feel. When I spoke he came out of it. The heat left. Very quickly he was himself again. And after that we began the sorting. But first he pulled the bed away from the wall and said, "Look at that." There were empty gin bottles in cardboard boxes, maybe four boxes. "Look at that. It's a lot of G and Ts," I said. That broke the ice a bit, excusing the pun, and we got on with things. A lot of the stuff we just threw out—some of it no doubt was worth something. Alec was pretty cavalier.

'Then I suggested we clean a few of the pieces. Why store them dirty? Elizabeth had had an eye. I remember picking up the hand-mirror and rubbing at its back. Alec took if off me and he started having a go. It was really shining by the time he was done. He gave it back to me to polish the glass. I said, "Why don't you finish it?" "No," he said, "I don't want to see myself in it." Then we got to work on the antique bottles—not the gin bottles. She had a collection of crystal bottles. We did a few and they came up very nicely. I'd noticed the interesting shapes before then but they actually contained . . . it was Alec who said it, a sea of light. His mother's words maybe? Maybe he remembered this original effect from when he was a boy. He was very moved by these things. You saw up close and noticed the details. I remember on the lamp that was over in one corner, that she never had on, the shade was in the form of mint-coloured leaves that actually were rather intricately veined. I got in there, right down into them with a matchstick, and really went to town. Only the shoes . . . well, Alec gave them to the dogs for toys. By that stage he was no longer moved. Both of us were probably a bit sick of it all, ready for a joke or two. There hadn't been much fun up to then in the house. At Omarama there'd been fun, when he was flying. He'd had a sense of mischief. He loved to tease.'

'You went up with him in the glider.'

'Yes, and he'd pretend to be lost or the plane was in trouble. He'd always try to scare me, and sometimes he succeeded. I remember there were boys at my school who, to show you they were interested, would steal your school bag and run over it on their bikes. Alec was a bit like that. But at home all that had disappeared. Anyway, the shoes. The dogs promptly buried the shoes in our garden and never returned to them. A few days later Alec must have had second thoughts. He dug them up and put them in a box in the garage. When I used to tell people that, usually they all laughed. The dogs burying them, then Alec digging them up. Then I stopped telling people. One time, it was the last time obviously, I told someone about the dogs and Elizabeth's shoes, Alec was there and he got up and left the room without speaking. I think that was the moment I understood I was responsible for Alec's happiness. Not of course totally responsible but my actions could have that effect. I had that power. Up to then I must have believed myself to be . . . negligible.' She looked around herself, almost as if someone had called to her. 'Is it late?'

It took Luke a moment to even register the question. Within it was a frightening reminder. The days and weeks of Christmas were upon them, when people disappeared inside their families as if into a box and a lid closed. He reached across and took her wrist. She looked at him, not at all alarmed, but alert, quickened. When he saw this, he was glad. If there'd been pity and sympathy, he would have let go at once and walked off. He would have felt 'understood'. It would have been over. She didn't understand him, though, in this way. She was tense, thinking of herself perhaps—probably of Alec and his happiness, of her feelings which could hardly have been simple since she looked a bit awkward too, and anxious. They were sitting in the public library. She had a history. Was it irresponsible as well as reckless then to make this move? Yet it hadn't been a move he'd planned in any way. Then she put her own hand over his, for just a moment. He felt the pressure most not on his hand where she was touching him but along his forearm and up his shoulder. Everything was connected of course. Quickly, he looked at their hands, as if seeking proof. Yes, her fingers were there. He was excited, scared. Scared not of what might follow but that she'd interpret the moment as nothing more than Luke wishing, through kindness, to affirm her value, to say that she was indeed not negligible but vital.

Sheila stood up suddenly. The light outside the library had dipped. Katie arrived and snatched the book, looking at the first illustration which showed the father sharpening his axe. She then put it down, saying, 'I don't like farm stories.'

He found he wasn't in any kind of reverie but rather the opposite. Ideas zipped about. 'She likes witch stories,' said Luke. 'Transformation.'

And as if nothing had happened for her, though perhaps what had happened gave her extra fuel, a kind of speediness to match his own acceleration, immediately Sheila was away on this word. It was what she'd learned: to riff. Her thesis was that children enjoyed changing but it was always necessary to change back. In *The Wizard of Oz* only the adults, the brainless, heartless, fearful adults, want to change, she said. All Dorothy wants to do is to get back to Kansas. 'As now I do!' Sheila made herself laugh.

He followed her to the issues desk, dismayed and lifted. 'What about you, though?' he said. 'You've changed. You followed the yellow brick road, or at least the red brick one, university.'

'I've changed back too,' she said. 'Otherwise I wouldn't be recognised.'

'Are you giving up university?'

'Who says?' She looked unhappy now, annoyed with him. 'You'll leave soon anyway.'

Finally, in this accusation, he saw some firm hope. 'I won't,' he said.

She stared at him, weighing this declaration. Then she had her books and she turned away towards the doors.

'When can we meet?' he said. He was trying not to allow his voice any urgency because of Katie, who was just behind them.

She said she had to go before somewhere shut. She was speaking of Christmas too, buying something. He took in none of it except the noise of avoidance or refusal. The mental sharpness was gone—his own for sure, but also hers, since her eyes were flicking around and she was back to that anxious look she possessed or that possessed her. Alec might have been just around the corner. Had she said she was off to buy him a gift? What could he get; what more did that man want from her?

Things were a mess now. They were already outside in the street. The library spell was broken. The lovely bookishness gone. Here was the town—her town—and these were her people; this was her rubbish bin attached to her lamp-post, these three concrete steps were hers, and in stepping down them she was moving an incalculable distance from him. She was going to buy Christmas presents for her family. The notion was crushing for Luke. It was how she'd managed to get out of the house alone. Behind them was the community noticeboard where Alec had pinned the home help notice.

Sheila was looking up and down the street, as if she might dash across. She took a step towards the kerb. There were no cars but she hesitated. It struck him that she might have been waiting for traffic, one of the milk tankers perhaps. He moved to her side and took her arm. 'We can drive you,' he said.

Katie heard this. 'She's got her own car.'

Sheila stopped and turned to face Katie. They had both forgotten the girl. Then Sheila bent down and hugged her hard. Katie's observation was quite brilliant, something neither of them might have thought of without a great deal of effort. His niece had saved them this trial. Sheila held the girl for several moments, gripping her completely until they almost toppled. Katie stepped away, surprised. Sheila smiled, apologised, said something about helping with the weaning. He took the excuse of not having heard properly and stepped closer to her, touching her shoulder so that they were turned away from the girl.

'The shed on Phil and Catherine's place, by the windbreak,' he said. 'Do you know it?' She nodded. 'I'll be there at eleven tonight.'

She laughed harshly. 'I can't,' she said.

'Will you come?'

'How?'

'Anyway, I'll be there.'

'Yes,' she said. Then she ran across the road.

Had she looked first before crossing? You could hear the traffic anyway, even if she hadn't done a thorough check. Still there'd been enough of the headlong about it to make Katie gasp.

All evening he felt strange, removed from the household in a new way, and therefore cautious about seeming so. He made sure he asked Phil what he'd been doing. Phil said he'd been dipping that day. He was shattered. Luke watched Phil fall asleep in his chair within minutes of eating dinner. They'd eaten off their knees while watching the TV news. The Queen was urging an early divorce for Charles and Diana. Rabin's assassination would not derail the Israeli–PLO peace process. Bosnia, Serbia and Croatia had signed the Dayton Accord in Paris, ending the war. Not much of this penetrated. Catherine snatched the remote from Katie and turned it off, sending the kids scurrying. Something was wrong but Luke didn't want to know what. Still he asked. He knew this: they'd had a higher than normal rate of stillborn twins. Also the spring crops were behind. Catherine said that the Wattie's man had been out again to revisit the contract. They had peas and potatoes and neither was performing as well as last year. They had a bit too much light land. Catherine might have been waiting for some follow-up question here, but it never came. Light land? Well, Luke sort of understood. In his weeks around the place, and despite intentions, he'd failed to grow any great curiosity about this life. They might have been practising satanic rituals out there in the paddocks for all he knew. Later he heard his sister telling the boys off. It was time to retreat.

He lay on his bed, viciously alert, and was promptly asleep. He got stuck on a formulation that he knew was probably not accurate: that the farm girl in *Charlotte's Web* saves the pig from her father's axe and delivers him finally to a devastating grief: the death of his friend and saviour, the spider. The Christian interpretation was screaming at him, or rather in his head the phrase 'the Christian interpretation is screaming at you' was screaming at him. The book was back in the library, however, and in his dream, as in reality, the library was closed. Tough. He looked at his watch. There was an hour to go before he walked down to the shed. He could go early, of course. The house was already asleep. He closed his eyes again. Would she come? In one scenario she was there before him, waiting, smiling, wearing a Swanni and smoking. But she didn't smoke. In the dream he knew this and said as much to her. Annoyed, she threw the cigarette away. In another moment, he stood outside the shed for hours. Dawn was coming. Sheep walked past him as if he wasn't there—and of course he wasn't. He said as much to the sheep. Finally she appeared under the pines and he laughed and waved to her. She failed to move, however. Something was holding her back. He went to her, ignoring the gestures she now made that he should keep back. He stumbled over tree roots but kept going. He fell heavily to his knees and he imagined she would no longer be there once he looked up. Yet she continued to stand in the same spot, one arm he now saw trailing behind a tree. She was holding something, or someone. Mixed in with this moment were half-waking thoughts and near-feverish questions about the moment he'd held Sheila's wrist and she had touched him. Maybe her response had been consoling and friendly rather than intimate or urgent? If he hadn't touched her first, would anything have happened? And what had happened really? Two friends hold hands in the public library. Then how to explain the terror of her leave-taking? He was convinced now she'd simply run blindly away from him, rejecting his proposal, run straight across the road, and that Katie's gasp had been the right response, even rather moderate in the circumstances. He might have screamed and reached for Sheila and caught her, stopped her. He was wrong to have let her go. Finally, he reached the place under the pines where she was standing. 'Darling,' he said, breathless. He'd not said the word to her before. She seemed to hesitate, then she moved her arm and a child stepped forward from the shadows: her daughter, Georgia, still carrying the bandage on her knee from the day they'd visited with the soup. A noise further back, a scuffling, made them all turn—Luke, Sheila, the girl. Who was there in the shadows of the pines? Something or someone awful was the general idea. At this point Luke sat up in bed, completely awake. It was time.

He took no special care in walking out of the house, thinking it better not to be furtive in case he was discovered. He was up to nothing except taking a stroll because he couldn't sleep. He moved calmly, half expecting a voice to call to him, perhaps Simon's. Or Katie's—the girl was clever, watchful. Had she seen something at the library? All the lights were out except the hallway one. The moment he closed the door behind him, however, he felt a surge of emotion which almost made him take off in a run. He headed out quickly along a path which took him past an old water tank where the kids came to poke at the frogs. This was the long way but he wanted to avoid the dogs' cages. The night was cool and poorly lit. He'd not thought to bring a torch, and now he wondered whether he'd even make it to the shed. For some steps he went ahead half blind, feeling with his feet for obstacles. The dim shapes of fenceposts gradually became a useable pattern, and he adjusted his step whenever the ground showed the darker patch of a hole or a rise. Soon he was out in more open ground and the sky was also revealing itself in patterns of purplish light. He paused and looked back in the direction of the house, which showed in its roofline. Phil had told him he'd been bothered for days by this view until he realised what was changed: the chimney had gone. Nearby there was a sound as though someone was ripping up dresses: an animal was eating grass. He pressed on.

The shed was a corrugated-iron structure the size of a double garage, with a roller-door on one side and a smaller entrance on the other. There was no electricity, but the white concrete floor gave some illumination. Phil used the place for storage and as a workshop for repairing the tractor and the farm bikes. Odd pieces of farm machinery lay about, and there were empty oil drums stacked in a corner. It was the first place they'd looked for Hamish on the night of Luke's arrival. In front of a large window there were a couple of broken armchairs and an old sofa. These were sometimes used by farmhands on smoko if they were working the surrounding paddocks. In the gloom, Luke accidentally kicked over a beer bottle.

He sat in one of the armchairs, from where he could see through the window out across the land. The shed was built on a slight rise. But where would she sit when she came? She would probably take the other chair, and this didn't seem promising. He moved to the sofa, though this gave him a view of sky only, and he could feel the springs through the threadbare material. There was still ten minutes to go. He stood up and walked over to the oil drums. Something flew out of the drum he peered into, brushing the arm he threw up in front of his face. It banged against the far wall, then was silent, or perhaps it had made it out the door. Luke listened but he couldn't hear anything. Was it a bird or a bat? Were there bats? He'd never heard anyone mention them. Surely Katie would have. They were her sort of unnerving creature. He stamped his feet and walked towards where he thought the thing had landed. He called out and clapped his hands. 'Ya! Get out! Out! Get out, you fucking devil!' He kicked out. Yet he seemed to be alone once more and he felt stupid for all the noise he'd made, and for his fear. Even the frogs by the water tank, where Catherine's kids had taken him for a show, were not quite the comedians he pretended they were. He read resentment in their grins. In entering the green water, they plopped obstinately like turds. When they surfaced again, it was as knots of muscle, like the insides of a knee floating up, the most prominent parts of something larger that had drowned some time ago, and he understood perfectly the boys' ambition to sink the evidence once more with sticks. For fairytale Katie, his niece, the frogs were naturally in another sort of disguise entirely. 'Beware!' she said.

He left the shed and stood on the concrete pad in front of the roller-door. This was one of those moments he wished he was a smoker. In the end you smoked your own thoughts. You sucked in and blew out what was on your mind—this accounted for the strange look of gratitude seen on the face of a person with a cigarette. Birds called to him. They didn't know that in a high school quiz he'd identified the cry of the North Island brown kiwi as a porpoise. He thought it still aquatic and plangent.

At five minutes past eleven he decided he wouldn't look at his watch again. When he looked again, it was to confirm that time was passing more or less how he imagined it was. In fact he'd been virtuous and it was later than he thought. As a reward to himself for this stoicism, he checked his watch again just three minutes after that. Soon it would be 11.30. He was back inside now, in the armchair, with his feet propped up on a wooden crate, dozing and listening to the wind gusting through the trees. With his eyes closed, he discovered there were none of the fantasies of meeting Sheila left. He appeared instead in the UN, where he carried a briefcase through several security points, and at each point, despite his pleas, they refused to put the briefcase through the scanner. The briefcase contained the literature review he'd been working on. They all told him he was fine and to proceed. He sat up hopefully on this word and looked out into the night, which was lighter. He could see towards the horizon, the silhouette of poles, some stars. She was not coming.

In the morning he waited until Catherine was outside and then called Sheila, but there was no answer. He didn't know when she was leaving for university again or if in fact she was ever going back there. Hadn't there been talk of one final trip north to pack up her things from the flat, say goodbye to her flatmate, the nurse? Why hadn't he asked her about her plans when they'd sat together in the library? He was in a panic.

He'd promised to paint the ceiling above the new woodburner. It would be his last job. It was almost as if there'd never been a brick chimney in that corner. He wanted to finish it. However, he didn't want to risk being around his sister when he was in this state. Catherine, if she still had the patience for it, would ask him what was wrong and he was not at all convinced he wouldn't tell her. She'd already said he was looking tired again. He was tempted now to say something even without prompting.

He felt a new recklessness. These were the crucial hours, he believed. Futures depended on what happened, and for too long he'd behaved coyly, dishonestly. Finally, though, he didn't tell Catherine was what going on. He made an excuse about being needed urgently at Eileen and David's place. He'd had a rotten sleep, that was all. Perhaps she believed he was still smarting from the previous evening's argument.

Having invented the idea, and still unsure of his next move, he found himself with David, talking about the extension. He couldn't concentrate. In their living room, he picked up a book on New Zealand painters. It was perfectly possible to think painting was over as some people, maybe even most people, believed classical music was over, David said. But it was hard to argue against human effort, wasn't it? Luke went to the toilet, and under the noise of the kiln he had a good cry. It was now in the power of a platitude to tip him over. The work in the book, though, had done its job too, if the job of art, he thought, was to make us blubber.

When he emerged, Eileen had come out of her workshop and there was a discussion about viewing art. Desperately he wanted to escape. Eileen argued against the contemplative spirit in which this activity was bathed—or shrouded was a better word, she said, since it got at the veil, the gauze, the sorry pious state one had to be in to truly 'get it'. When she looked at a picture it was always a speedy process. She was in favour of running around galleries and museums, physically moving fast. The slow wander was deadly. Everyone was yawning after ten minutes. Yawning in front of Picasso, yawning in front of Brancusi, yawning in front of x, y and z, the great artists of all time. 'The stuff I like,' she said, 'it speeds me up, my heart rate, my blood's pumping. It's not a conversation I want to have. I hardly want to look. It's electricity. I don't mean the shock of the new or anything, actually, truth is, I pretty much like the shock of the old. I mean the good stuff gets me going, end of story. And nor do I buy that rubbish about short attention spans, the media age ruining us all for proper appreciation of the finer things. Point being the connection happens at once or not at all.' David naturally had things to say about the role of critics in such a terse and, as he called it, velocitous depiction of the art experience. He'd been smiling throughout at Luke, nodding to indicate this was old ground and Luke should wait for his material. A few sentences in, however, Eileen left them again and he soon petered out. Luke got it then. He finally got why they liked having him around, and perhaps why he'd let it happen: he was their means of communicating with each other. He was their child.

Eileen's rant had only increased the tempo of his thoughts. He was feeling dizzy but not, he thought, faintful. He excused himself and set off for Alec and Sheila's farm. Naturally the two cars that passed him stopped to offer a lift—he knew them both. They'd been at Sheila's going-away party. He thanked them and turned them down. His route took him near the cheese factory. Even from a kilometre off, he could hear the tankers' engines. The sour smell was something you almost stepped inside. He was conscious of a sort of border in the air. There was little wind to carry it off. Crossing into the pungency, he walked faster, nearly breaking into a run at certain points. The factory itself was soundless. Nothing moved in its compound. Behind the chain-link fence the car park was full of vehicles, but it was also deserted. He had the impression of being watched from the small windows of the main building. High up on one of the circular tanks a set of neon letters, not switched on, said Merry Christmas. No doubt the UN Secretariat Building would be sporting a similar message.

Luke looked up and saw a small plane, flying in low. It seemed to be heading straight for some trees on the far side of the cheese factory, and for a moment he thought of Alec. Could he do this? Was he about to smash his plane into the factory in some magnificent gesture of refusal? It would be the refusal to see the truth, of course. Luke realised he was ducking, though the plane was several hundred metres away. The plane engine made the only sound in the world. But Alec flew gliders.

How could it be Alec? Still, the tension didn't leave him. He straightened and watched as the plane missed the trees, then turned and came in over a nearby paddock, its engine sounding sick now, staggering. Clouds of something shot from the plane's wings. He could see the figure inside the plane—not Alec. He was spraying potatoes for blight—Luke knew this at once, and felt crushed and also proud for knowing even this much about the plane's reasons. Phil had had the crop-duster in the previous week. He'd had to go up with the pilot on a recce. Basically, Phil said, there was nothing to the plane. If you looked down at your feet, you saw the land through gaps in the fuselage, the tree tops streaming past. Air rushed in and froze your ankles. He hated it.

At Alec and Sheila's place, Luke found himself taking off his shoes before knocking on the door and entering. He called out, but no one was home. The kids would be at school and Alec out on the farm. Time to turn around and go home. Put on his shoes and leave. He had no business in these lives. Sheila had not come to him the previous night. He'd misjudged the entire thing. There was a single outcome from any further involvement with this household: disaster.

He could see from the doorway that on the kitchen table, which was otherwise clear, sat a piece of notepad paper. So? The paper had nothing to do with him. It was a shopping list, or a reminder for someone. One of the kids had to do something. He crept in his socks closer to the table. He leaned over the paper. There was a Christchurch address written on it. Instinctively, he put the paper in his pocket.

The strong pine smell brought him to the living room where a large Christmas tree sat in a pot, surrounded by tidy stacks of presents. In a sort of terror, he saw the place had recently been cleaned. There was not a single pine needle on the carpet. The presents gave him a sharp pain which he felt in his neck—a pain in the neck, he thought. He sat down on the piano stool. The piano lid was closed, the surface of it polished. He got up and looked inside the piano stool. There was a neat stack of piano books but no sign of the sandal he'd seen Georgia put there the last time he'd visited.

Back in the kitchen—he'd meant to return the note to the table—he lifted up a tea towel under which sat a tray of biscuits. There was a note beside the biscuits giving freezing instructions. He went in a state of automation to the freezer. What was he looking for? Evidence of some sort, though by now he had enough. She was gone; what else needed to be found? She'd fled finally. She'd known he would come looking for her, so her last act had been to leave the address for him. The freezer was full of ice-cream containers, each of which had a meal inside, identified by name and date. She'd stopped short of writing a day of the week on each lid but Luke still found it depressing. This degree of care and foresight so late in the day. A feeling of envy had him. Why was she thinking of them, devoting her hours to the place that had made her unhappy? Of course he knew why, and this largeness of hers caused a wonder in him to spring up again. Her kindness was a miracle. Another thought: was it only kindness she was showing him? No, he believed they'd left that sphere. He was also excited, stirred terrifically. Christmas was only four days off. Certainly she'd made sure they would have gifts but, he thought, they would not have her. Why else make these sorts of preparations? Her failure to show the previous night was on account of this fastidiousness. She didn't want to ruin their chances—Luke's and hers—by some idiotic night-time rendezvous. She'd gone to Christchurch as an adult and she expected him to follow her. He had the piece of paper in his pocket. He would leave the next morning to be with her. Or perhaps he needed to go now, as soon as possible. Catherine and Phil would understand—not the fact he was going to be with Sheila, he wouldn't tell them that, but something about spending Christmas with friends, work colleagues. Relief all round. He had presents for the kids. They were already wrapped. He was prepared. He needed to get back in the swing of work, his proper work, as Phil had rightly called it. He wasn't much of a Christmas person. Here they might object, finding in his stoicism a good dose of self-pity. Why couldn't he wait until after Christmas? Spend the day on the farm and then go. No, his friends in Christchurch were also lost souls—family-less, un-Christian, without the spirit of giving. They were great people, and there was a plan—a trip somewhere? Perhaps a lake. Hide out until the good cheer had died down. He'd have the details—his sister would want the details. He'd speak sincerely, since this was how he felt. The farm had been wonderful and now he was better, rested, clear headed, steady on his feet, physically stronger—all those bricks, all that home cooking—he was feeling rather good, and his world was waiting.

He had her address in Christchurch.

He recognised the purple plastic container they'd decanted the soup into the day Alec had shown them the glider. Instead of leading them towards the garage or to one of the sheds at the back of the house, Alec had opened the door to an internal room which proved to be the dining room, or rather a room that had once been used for 'best' and which was now given over completely to the glider, which sat half assembled on a large tarpaulin, surrounded by piles of mechanical equipment: levers, lengths of wire, dials. The dining chairs had been pushed back against the walls. A chandelier hung from the centre of the ceiling. The window-seat in the far corner was covered with a sheet, and here were more bits and a toolkit apron opened out to show its pockets filled with rows of spanners. Catherine had laughed in shock. Alec bent down and touched a section of one unattached wing which lay on the floor. 'She's a major project all right,' he said.

'I suppose this means you won't be having too many big dinner parties for a while,' said Luke.

'I work nights on it,' said Alec.

'Until what time?'

'I don't know. I don't notice. Two or three.'

'And up again at six, I suppose,' said Catherine.

'It was in a much worse state than I first thought.'

'You'll be in a much worse state too if you keep up with those hours, Alec.'

'No, Catherine,' he said. 'For me this is relaxation. Putting something together. It's much better than the sleep I get anyway.'

'Because you're going to bed overstimulated,' said Catherine.

At this point Alec had turned to Luke. 'Maybe I should be getting tips from this fellow about sleep.'

The room in which this conversation had taken place was only a couple of metres away now from where Luke stood in the kitchen, but he knew he wouldn't go in there. He was about to close the freezer door when he saw a container pushed to the back. He reached in and brought it out. It was sealed with brown tape and marked with the word 'Alec'. This gave him another physical pain, in his side now, like a stitch. Quickly he put the container back and closed the freezer door. He needed to walk away. Whatever had given him the right to enter the house, to examine the contents of the piano stool, to wonder morosely at the extent of Sheila's attachment to her children and to this man, was now finished with. His self-pity had been tweaked as far as it would go.

Then he opened the freezer again, operating through a plain curiosity, he told himself. What could be inside the container? Cakes perhaps, or some specialty involving liqueurs. Medicine? Or some Christmas treat. The tape was to stop small prying hands. He took the container to the table, got a knife, sat down and began cutting the tape. This was wrong. He paused in his cutting, looking at the container. The knife was blunt and the tape was hard to get through. He could put it back and no one would know. He started sawing at the tape again, more in experiment than anything else, wondering how long this would take. He was putting more effort in, and pulling at the tape, which was starting to unwrap. Sweat ran down inside his shirt.

He was through now. Sheila must have used yards of the stuff. There was tape sticking to his elbow and to his shoe. He gathered all of this up in a ball and looked at the container.

He took off the lid. Something was wrapped in foil. He considered replacing the lid and taping it back up, but with what? He lifted the package onto the table. It felt a bit like a kebab, food definitely. Was this Alec's weakness, Middle Eastern fare? Then why the tape? He overcame a moment of squeamishness. There was bad news here, he was sure. A sense of doom gripped him. Sheila was mad, he had to remember. The mad could do anything. But she was cured too. She was well—and functioning. She was full of spirit, courage, decent medication. It wasn't mad to leave Alec. This signalled her health.

Carefully, he unwrapped the foil.

It took only the briefest of looks—the quickest sighting of fur—and at once he shot back in his chair. He might have made a small sound too. Luke stood up, moved away a few paces. He was flushed with a rapid heat, and he stumbled slightly. When he'd lifted it out, the package was soft, bendable. It wasn't fully frozen. Sheila must have put it there quite recently, at around the same time she'd baked the biscuits and named the meals. That morning. He approached the thing again, feeling unsteady, unwell. He knew the signs by now. He needed to sit down, drink some water, breathe. He didn't need to see anything else. Still he peered at the thing. Dangerous to lean like this. Soon it would happen. He was watching himself almost, as if he were two— one about to go down in a heap; another looking on, shaking his head, wondering at the stupidity of this person ignoring the warning. Laid out on the foil was the body of a large rat.

He might have been on the floor for several minutes. He didn't think it was longer. The light was the same in the room as when he'd left it—he had left it, but where had he gone? A deep shame fell on him. His legs were tangled in the chair he'd knocked over. Bitterly and freely he wept for himself, lying on the kitchen floor. Then he stood up. He was better. He actually thought to himself, 'I am better.'

The argument against vintage

Before he'd made the journey back to New Zealand—before it had really been thought necessary—they'd been downtown in a cab on Madison Avenue waiting at a light. There'd been a reception hosted by the Chileans, with whom, as everyone pointed out, they shared a latitude. The catch-phrase—tossed off by Luke, picked up by the seniors—was 'From Latitude to Attitude'. This to signal closer ties between the countries. He was back to his best. No more sleepovers, sleepwalking, loud music. He was eating properly. The sun was out, he remembered. The talk in the cab was about sunglasses; the verdict on someone's was they were definitely not even last year's. These had been expensive Raybans, sold—wait for it—as timeless. No one was wearing gold rims any more. Sandy was arguing against vintage, especially the bowling shirts with other people's names on the pockets. She hated them. Or blue-collar stuff worn by bankers on weekends to clubs. 'Everyone works at Tony's Garage. These are boys who wouldn't know where to look for the engine.' Something about the sunshine in the cab—and the cocktails—made it all perky and interesting. Luke confessed that in his first week in the city he'd bought a couple of said items, one involving, he thought, a Chinese laundry service, purchased for the cool dragon on the back. The girls yelled. James said actually he did look the tiniest bit Chinese, especially squinting, without his sunglasses. 'I'm terrified to buy a pair now,' he said. He'd worn the shirt under things. When would he come out?

He looked out at the street. He saw the homeless man. He saw a man. Back in the cab—it seemed like 'back' in the cab, as if he'd left it, gone away and returned—someone asked if he was all right.

The man, in profile, was waiting to cross. Luke looked again, leaning forward.

He felt something and looked at his own legs, which were pumping up and down. He was shaking. People spoke to him.

Sandy put both hands on his legs and pressed hard against them. 'What is it, Luke? What is it?'

He managed to point.

His throat produced something.

'Him? Is that the guy? You sure? Right there? Is that the guy, Luke?' He'd looked at hundreds of photos with the detectives. He had a gallery permanently in his head, a grisly slide-show of faces that might have come from another era, any era—a Walker Evans show or the Middle Ages.

James spoke to the driver, 'Stop the cab!'

'We're stopped,' said the driver.

'Don't go anywhere.'

At that moment, the homeless man halted in the middle of the street, right in front of their cab, as if one cue, as if he'd forgotten something or had changed his mind about crossing. As if he was waiting for Luke to give him a big old hug. Good to see you again, my friend! People passed on either side of him but he remained rooted.

'Know this guy?' said the driver.

Luke peered through the windscreen. Certainly this was the man. Luke tried nodding. It was the only thing he could do.

'Yes? You're sure?' That must have been James speaking again.

Then the cabbie sounded his horn, and the man moved off again, quite quickly. Often the homeless had an athleticism. This man might have been only in his thirties and he was light on his feet.

Someone had a door open. The driver called out. The lights were green. He was ordering them back in the cab.

James closed the door again. 'Where's a phone?'

'Get out and follow him!' said Sandy.

'I'm trying!' said James.

There was an argument with the driver. He couldn't stop anywhere. They were shouting at him to stop the car. All the time, Luke's legs were bouncing up and down under their own steam. He'd lost control. He had the strange sensation he was running already, that he was out on the street and pushing through people to get to his man, or to get away from his man, since this was the effect—he felt pursued himself. Sandy had her head out the window, trying to see where the man went. 'I can't see him!' she said.

'Hurry,' Luke whispered. His voice was nothing. In the noise no one heard him. 'Get that fucker,' he rasped.

Finally the cab pulled over. James left, running.

James didn't catch him; a cop did. At the point James was about to give up, he found the man being talked to by an officer on the street for no other reason than he was missing a shoe and banging into people.

That evening Luke was behind a glass screen, looking at seven men in a line-up. They were all dressed similarly, in torn and dirty clothes. They were unshaven, ragged. He'd seen their faces in hundreds of photos at the repository. Maybe one or two had been under the bridge or in the parks that lunchtime when Luke had taken the tour.

The police told him they'd meet him outside the Mission. This was the previous week. He'd imagined a suited detective, a discreet handshake, being led to an unmarked car. Instead they were waiting pulled up on the pavement in a squad car with a blue flashing light on its roof, and Luke had made the long walk past the lunchtime crowd, watched by many.

'You blend in,' said Luke, when he got in the car. There were two detectives: the guy from the first interview and a homicide cop.

'What do we do?' said the homicide cop.

Luke repeated himself.

The detectives looked at each other and shrugged.

'You should hear him say motherfucker.'

'Say it.'

'Motherfucker,' said Luke.

'There you go.'

'What do we do, we blund in?'

'Blend,' said Luke. 'Blend.'
'Spell it.'
Luke spelled it.
The interview detective, the bald one, slapped the steering wheel. 'From New Zealand.'
'Tell me,' said the homicide cop, 'in New Zealand, do you get the homeless?'
They talked about this until they came to their stop, which was under a bridge by the river, where the homicide cop got out and told Luke to stand by the car and not move from there. The driver stayed in his seat.
At first there seemed to be nothing to the place, certainly nobody around. The land was scrubby, marked by broken chain-link fences, oil drums, weeds and stones. This was the detritus which he knew, from countless movies, would somehow survive the apocalypse. There was constant traffic noise on the bridge overhead and the huge concrete stanchions carried vibrations into the ground. Luke stood by the car, feeling a buzzing through his shoes, and watched the detective pick his way through what appeared to be piles of rubbish, discarded clothing. The detective, plain clothed, wearing a black coat, walked with his hand on one hip, indicating that he was armed. He stopped and nudged one of the piles with his foot. The pile moved and slowly assumed the shape of a man standing, hunched. From Luke's distance it appeared as though this figure had been conjured by the detective's contact with the inanimate material at his feet. He might have been made of mud and stone. Then a face was formed—and it turned in Luke's direction. Luke shook his head: no, this wasn't the person. The figure then slipped once more to the ground, became again a brown heap, and was still. The detective repeated the procedure a few feet along. Luke looked and replied with a shake of his head. Maybe they summoned into being thirty or so men from under the bridge without finding a match.
A couple in the line-up were hunched and scowling—and might have been plucked from this location; others were upright

and defiant. Luke couldn't pick the actors among them—if this was procedure. Maybe all of them were from the streets. None was too tall or too short. They formed a sort of club. He saw the one immediately, which was a worry. He looked and almost pointed but managed to hold back. He didn't trust himself on such a swift decision. The implications were rather large, naturally. The man now had a lawyer, who stood off to one side, holding a briefcase in his arms, watching Luke.

'Will Kevin do the same?' Luke said to the detective beside him. It was the bald one with the moustache. Detective Pergolesi. Strange he'd never managed the name before. Pugnowksi, he called him in the versions he gave others, or Pultesi, Linguini, anything.

'Can't find Kevin.'

'You can't find him?'

The detective spoke quietly in the room. 'Looks like he's moved on, gone.'

'To Mississippi?' The moment he spoke, Luke knew he'd shown himself to be out of his depth. He turned back to the window and looked again at each of the men, attempting to rid his mind of the one lodged there. The one who'd stood in front of the cab was third in line. Accidental? Or some gesture towards fairness? Then again, would anybody pick the first in line, or the last? Maybe they always put the guilty somewhere in the middle to ensure the witness felt satisfied he'd had to sort through the lot to arrive at the identification. He suspected he was being made a fool of somehow, although Pergolesi had been a model policeman in all respects. Luke walked the length of the glass wall, then back again, studying the faces. The man on the end looked down at his feet and a policeman entered the frame, gesturing that he stare ahead once more. Had this little incident been scripted also?

A couple of the homicide detectives who'd sat with Luke in the interviews were with him in the room. They'd been pleased with Luke when he'd come in, and had asked him questions about his work, the place he lived, and they'd volunteered little bits of personal information about themselves. Pergolesi hung back a little, he noticed, allowing these colleagues their room. The mood was different, as if Luke had met them all at a picnic, away from their professional lives. He knew one of them had a son who had a broken arm from basketball. In the viewing room, they'd moved away respectfully, and he could hear their lowered voices, chatting about something, laughing quietly even, separate from Pergolesi. This was to make him feel less weight, as if the decision was routine, foregone. Not much was riding on it, except once they were done everybody could go home. It was after ten. Everybody except the one. A guy anyway without a home. One of the detectives had made the joke already. What they'd be giving this guy was a warm bed and a decent meal. Everyone was a winner. Luke just had to raise his finger and it was all over.

'I wish Kevin was here,' he told Pergolesi in a whisper.
'He was never as close as you.'
'Did the store-owner get a look?'
'He was in his store.'
'I only really saw him from the side.'
'What side?'
'He was on my left, I guess. So his right side?'

Pergolesi leaned forward and pressed a button. 'Turn side-on everybody, side-on so your right side is facing the window. If you don't know your right side, wait and you'll be positioned.'

The men shuffled around, some moving in the wrong direction, others wandering from the line altogether.

One of the homicide detectives came forward and pressed the button. 'Your right side, where your dick hangs in your pants.' There was laughter from the other detectives.

'I dress differently,' said Pergolesi.
'That's the Italian in you.'
'And the strength of my endowment.'

Luke waited while the line-up was composed once more, then he took a few steps along the glass until he was standing directly in front of number three. His breathing was too fast and he reached out and held the rail in front of him. The man stared off blankly, moving his jaw as if chewing, though the motion had the automation of some tic. Luke hadn't seen this before. In walking alongside Luke following the murder, the man's mouth had been still. Luke would have recalled the tic. Once you had it in your sights, the jaw was alive and seemed to move almost independently of the man. He was the one who'd stopped in front of the cab, but was he also that other one from the evening of the killing?

'Take your time,' said someone behind him.

He felt something strike the back of his neck, as if he'd been beaten there or stung. He moved his hand to the place. He stepped back from the window and spoke clearly. 'I don't think I see him.'

The detectives were with him now, close. 'What do you say?' They surrounded him, blocking the lawyer's way. Pergolesi had stepped back.

'I'm sorry, I don't see the man.'

The lawyer had stepped forward, alert and opening his briefcase. 'Thank you, gentlemen,' he said. 'Thank you.'

One of them made a whistling sound through his teeth. 'Take your time though.'

'He's not here.' Luke remained looking at the glass, concentrating not on the men in the line-up but on the surface of the glass itself, which caught light and was buffed with wipe marks, finger marks, small patches of human oil. He imagined noses had been pressed to the glass, hands, the faces of victims and witnesses set in fury or satisfaction or horror or even tenderness and forgiveness. He did not feel a softening of feeling for the person who'd ended the life of the delivery man, though something in him had collapsed—perhaps it was only certainty. He just couldn't be sure. He'd never been more sure of that.

He was offered water. He declined. They told him to take a break, but he shook his head. The teeth-whistling sounded once more, shaped more fully into damp exasperation. In fact the man wanted to spit on him, that was clear. The lawyer had begun to fill in a form, placing the paper on the back of his briefcase and writing quickly. He'd seen his opening; his job was not to let it close.

Finally Luke turned to the detectives. 'I'm just not sure.' This had nothing of his previous refusal. He sounded to himself lame, wooden. He was flinching inside, aware of their frustration and anger.

The detective closest to him breathed a word over Luke that might have been anything.

The lawyer came towards Luke, as if to protect him, though Luke didn't want him near. He was saying something about coercion.

'Look again, please,' said the detective with the son who'd broken his arm at basketball. He sounded wounded.

But Luke was looking and he couldn't be sure. He repeated the statement more firmly.

'We brought in the guy you saw on the street.'

'Yes,' said Luke. 'I see him.'

'Then he's the guy, right?'

'No. I couldn't say actually. I'm not sure. I'm sorry.'

'Then we've got nothing.'

There was another flurry from the lawyer. He was moving in such a way that Luke felt himself being ushered from the room, swept up. He felt the edge of the lawyer's briefcase against his side. He felt the air pressure changing, doors opening. Through some distant corridor there was light. Behind him he could hear the detectives talking loudly, Pergolesi's voice trying to come in over the top. He considered he'd let Pergolesi down. He kept moving. He was almost there. More doors were opening. The footsteps were his own and those belonging to others, though he couldn't tell the difference. Finally he stepped outside. He was free.

part two

Basic Geography

He'd last seen them, *sans enfants*, in Paris three years before. They'd been in France for the wedding of a former student billet. The invitation had surprised them into accepting. It was their first real break from the farm. Luke had come over from Moscow, where he was First Secretary. They spent the day together before Catherine and Phil left for the wedding, which was in the south. At the Gare de Lyon, he bought their tickets, showed them to their carriage, made sure they were safely seated, then waved them off. He had less French than his sister, but she was linguistically paralysed, unable even to utter TGV in a sensible way. Phil couldn't understand the absence of seatbelts, given the world speed record. Terror had them both. It was wonderful to see.

It was a year since Luke's Moscow posting had finished and in that time, back in New Zealand, he'd spoken to Catherine on the phone three or four times. She emailed photos, strictly of the children, never of herself or of Phil, unless they happened to be caught in shot with the kids. He'd intended to go down to the farm during the previous summer but somehow had never made it. Baden had booked a place in the Wairarapa. A disappointed Catherine accused Luke of being like his brother, of whom— as usual—nothing much was heard from year to year, except at Christmas when a card came. He was living in Australia, though not in contact with their father. The card, Catherine was sure, had been bought by someone else—a woman—then pushed under Andy's nose, a pen produced, a text suggested and, once completed, posted by that person. The method could hardly be faulted since Catherine herself probably had the same role in her set-up, as Luke did in his own. He'd bought Baden's father's birthday present—a silk tie—and had it wrapped. It was unclear in Andy's case whether the person who did these jobs was Barbara, the woman they'd met at Riccarton. She never made an appearance in Andy's message and they presumed her gone. When Luke googled her horse's name, nothing relevant showed up, only a horse called Thinga Me Bob, which wasn't as good as Enda Me. For Catherine, Barbara's disappearance wasn't surprising. She said she'd never seen a future in it. 'All that weird business with the name of her horse,' she said. Luke saw her point but he also felt Andy and Barbara might just as easily have made a go of it. There were stranger pairings than that one. As time went on, of course, it became easier to add Barbara to the list of characters, unusual in some way, met once or twice in extraordinary circumstances and never seen again. Photo albums were sprinkled with these figures, the memory even more heavily populated.

From his position at the airport gate he caught sight of his niece Katie, whom he'd not seen in a decade. She was the same—same dark brow, same sharp chin—but she was also different, moved differently. He had an advantage in knowing the facts, but he believed he would have picked her for a dancer anyway, even a student dancer since she was still self-consciously in the role. Katie was erect, straight backed, and walked in quick steps as if about to topple forward. The two years of full-time training she'd come to Wellington for would presumably make all this natural. She was on a scholarship. Her goal was international stardom. He had the newspaper clipping, scanned in by Catherine and emailed to him, in which she admitted the ambition. By all accounts—and certainly nothing was exaggerated in her mother's reports since Catherine loathed a skite—this wasn't an idle hope. The girlhood phase, whose beginnings Luke had witnessed many years before, was nothing of the sort. The leotard had been found, as had the ballet lessons, and thousands of kilometres had been eaten up in getting the girl to where she stood now, on the cusp, though everyone understood it was a crowded cusp. Some would have to retreat or fall off.

'I want it quite badly,' Katie said in the paper. She was posed in her bedroom, which was filled with cups and ribbons and framed certificates. The reporter tried to get her to rank her most important wins, which she couldn't. She hated competitions. Then she'd talked about Nijinsky—here the paper paused helpfully with dates for the Russian 'God Of Dance'— whose diary Katie had used as the basis for some 'found poetry' she was writing. (The paper did not pause here.) The poem appeared alongside the article. It consisted entirely of unresolved contradictory statements such as 'I am life and you are death/I am not life and you are not death' and 'I am a woodpecker/I am a knock knock, but you are not a knock.' Surely one of the most extraordinary things published in that paper. Katie said that Nijinksy was schizophrenic and a prodigy; she said she was neither. She could drive a tractor and crutch sheep. She was a country girl from the back of nowhere, she said. She was 'scared stiff' of the scholarship and she didn't know if she could take two whole years of study and training. Then, as if spliced in from a different part of the interview but presumably following directly on, she was quoted, 'I've never met anyone like me. My advantage is that I'm a creature that's not been seen before.'

The creature stood before him, her heels resolutely on the ground. She was making rapid turning movements with her head. There was something reprimanding about all this. Instantly, you wanted to be in better shape yourself. Her parents appeared to have flagged the contest. Phil and Catherine came along, looking weary. The smiles and cries when they spotted Luke had to be summoned, though the emotion was genuine. Catherine's eyes watered.

A few moments before, as the flight was disembarking, he'd seen along the passageway to where an argument flared and ended in Catherine speaking to her daughter with what could only have been her firmest tone. The dancer's head whipped back, wounded. The body position, fixed by her training, suggested pride and maybe insolence.

Up close, Katie's make-up was too apparent, which seemed another dancer's mark. She let herself be kissed, bending forward perfectly at the waist and offering her uncle a cheek. The cheek felt hot and dry. She was carrying two bags from the plane. Immediately she surrendered the larger one to Luke, who'd gestured only vaguely towards it. He murmured something about light packing. Catherine assured him there was plenty more where that came from. She carried an oval plastic container—an improvised cake-box—and her handbag, and responded to her brother's inquiry by handing him the container and telling him not to open it. Luke peered at it. On the inside of the lid there was condensation—freshly baked this morning.

'You think we're hicks to travel with food,' said Catherine.

'We are hicks,' said Katie. The voice was familiar—mocking and amused. He felt a moment's sympathy for the local reporter who'd gone to her bedroom and got battered with Nijinksy. Eighteen years of this—no wonder both parents had accompanied her. Mutual support. They wanted to make sure she arrived, and that she stayed. There was wonderful discipline in his niece's achievements to this point, but there was also a temperament that could lay to waste the final dream. At sixteen she'd given up dancing for good, resuming months later once her teacher had made a personal plea and given an undertaking to devote herself solely to Katie's advancement. Other students were laid off.

'For hicks we get around,' said Phil, who carried nothing. He stood with his arms crossed, the way competitive swimmers do when waiting their turn. 'Remember Paris, Luke?'

'We'll always have Paris,' said Luke.

They stood for a time while Phil asked about the airport, which he described as 'quite tidy' compared to earlier models. Luke had to invite them to start moving off. Something was certainly wrong. They walked consistently a few steps behind him, and no matter how he varied his pace they wouldn't quite come alongside. A bad flight? But they'd already eliminated this as a cause. Clear views of the mountains, perfect landing. Where was the wind? There was some conversation about the boys: Simon at Lincoln, Tim at boarding school. The parents flanked their daughter, who looked down at her feet as though learning a step. She might have been famous or an invalid—or a prisoner in transit. Were they afraid she'd make a dash for it? He could smell the cake—banana and chocolate, the cake of babies.

By the carousel a man in a wheelchair was bent protectively over the large suitcase on his lap, refusing to allow anyone from the group who'd met him to take it. 'Thank you, I'm fine.' It struck Luke that this was normal. Persuading the travellers you had come to collect from the airport that they needed your help was often difficult. The wheelchair, Luke believed, was not decisive. Wrestling matches could break out. But here he was in possession of his niece's bag, and the cake which would sustain her through the first dark days of separation from her family and the lonely beginning hours of hostel life. This gave him an intimation of the coming weekend: that they were fragile, suffering, that he'd be on call. Well, he owed them.

He didn't discount the idea that there was also some of the old playacting in their condition. Catherine always put the differences in their life choices and outcomes squarely in view. Behind the obviousness of these comparisons lurked a subtle critique not only of him but of herself too.

Suddenly the women were pointing helplessly to their suitcases, which were moving. It was his job to grab their stuff. Phil had met someone he knew, and stood off to the side, talking to a man who also looked like a farmer: ruddy cheeks, big hands, moleskins. Katie seemed on the point of becoming distraught about a sleeping bag. Luke fetched a trolley. They pointed a couple more times as things went past, and he made his lunges. They were very grateful—at least Catherine was; the daughter seemed incapable of the effort. Not that he begrudged her or them—his power here was novel and, even if it was unearned, he was prepared to exercise it. Phil wandered back. Then they all watched as Luke loaded the trolley up. He did it badly the first time and they watched as he re-arranged the cases. Again, they admired him for this. His sister hugged his arm. Her husband told him he was an expert. They'd been in the air a little over an hour, though it may as well have been days. They followed him when he said follow me. They walked behind him, in strangely small steps, out into the late Wellington sunshine, the concrete light of the parking lot. They halted when he halted, waiting just a little behind him while he remembered where he'd put the car. They set off again, in their careful formation. Was the girl about to collapse? Finally they watched as he loaded their luggage into his boot.

It was decided Katie should be given the front seat, to look out on her new home, they said, and to study the streets and get an idea from Luke of the basic geography; Catherine and Phil would take the back. Father and daughter got into the car, Phil holding the door open for Katie.

Catherine was at Luke's side as he returned the trolley to its place. 'Little fight at Dunedin, then big sobs on the plane,' she told him. 'Katie says she doesn't want to come here.'

'Is it too late?' said Luke.

'Don't you start.'

'No, I mean if things got desperate.'

'She's just anxious about the move. We all are. Our little girl. She's hardly been to the North Island except once to New Plymouth, and to Auckland a couple of times, all for ballet. Phil's bracing himself for the traffic and the people. Drive slowly.'

She seemed serious. They walked back towards the car. 'She'll be fine,' Luke told her. 'Phil, I'm not so sure about.'

It was a mistake to go back to his apartment. He'd bought in smoked fish, cheeses and pastries for lunch but no one was eating much. He should have driven them straight to the hostel so that things could be settled.

Katie spent most of the time looking at her cellphone. She'd promised her parents not to text anyone before they'd got to the hostel and seen her room and made up her bed and stuck her pictures on the walls. They'd made some sort of deal with her. Once things were in place, and she could get an idea about how her life would be, and also the lives of her fellow students—because Katie was unique but also one of many going through the same upheaval—then she could use the phone, communicate her confusion, her doubts, her rage—and, who knew, even her excitement and happiness. If she broke her side of the bargain, apparently she would lose some promised gift. Over lunch the phone, turned off, sat on the table in front of its owner, as if by the power of her stare Katie was making it ring, making it talk and text. Occasionally his niece did smile or grimace, as if she had heard something or was reading a message. She was still a witch then. Her sweatshirt, he saw, had a cat's claw on it and said *Purrfect*. They'd all taken their shoes off at the front door, and Luke had found himself doing the same.

'What would you be doing on a typical Friday night?' said Catherine.

He caught a look from his niece, suggesting that this was a painful reminder of what she was missing out on. Well, he was missing out too. 'Pretty much this,' said Luke.

'Where's Baden again? Hong Kong?' said Catherine.

His sister was exercising a skill; she could make even the simplest query ring with prurience. Besides, it was not a name you got used to, especially once the middle name was known: Powell. As people pointed out lewdly, a wholesome name. Baden's father had had a set of experiences in the Scout movement which were wholly positive. The name couldn't be shortened. One friend called him 'B', and there was Bade. Neither of these worked for Luke or really for Baden, who preferred the full punishment his parents had delivered him. For those inquiring after his 'real Chinese name', Baden sometimes said he was known as Yum Char. He didn't have another name. Baden's brother was called Derek.

'Singapore,' Luke said. 'There's a big fair.'

'What does he do again?' said Phil.

The special tone for conversations such as this had arrived at once. These were not bigots or prudes he was having lunch with, but they were heteros—curious and humorous. In short, the answer to his brother-in-law was probably this: Fucks men. 'Physiotherapist,' said Luke.

'Ah.' Phil nodded. Fucks men.

'But his product is to do with disabled people,' said Catherine.

'Shower chair,' said Luke.

'To help in the shower, which puts him in Singapore at the fair.'

'I see,' said Phil.

Katie groaned and raised her head again. The notion of people with disabilities taking showers was too much for her. 'I've got my neck.'

Catherine touched her daughter's neck. 'Bad?'

Katie grunted.

'If Baden was here he could give you a rub,' said Phil.

Because Phil was innocent, the statement gained in wickedness—at least for Luke, who thought he heard a snigger or a snort from someone. 'When Baden leaves work, Baden is definitely off duty,' he said. 'I've tried to interest him in my own ailments but he just looks at me and asks whether I've seen anyone about it.'

Catherine nodded. 'Alma, who cuts my hair, she never takes her scissors when visiting friends or family. People just can't help themselves.'

'I wasn't asking,' said Katie. 'It was Dad said it.'

'When I visit people, I never get asked to farm for them,' said Phil. He'd not spoken in jest; the observation was factual.

'What ailments?' said Catherine. 'You said your ailments.' From fucking Chinese men?

'Oh, no, just strains and pains.' Maybe they thought sex with a physio was rather more demanding than with other less physically knowledgeable partners. Baden, in fact, was heavier, less athletic, less interested in his own profession's qualities and virtues than the movie version might require. He even owned a pair of black 'Chinese' slippers—two, in fact; one pair he kept at Luke's place. They were tucked away in the wardrobe—Luke had done the clean-up, just as he'd hidden a few other things. Some books, magazines, DVDs. Hardly a stash. Friends had a locked filing cabinet, otherwise empty, where all this stuff could be thrown at a moment's notice. They had a plan much like an evacuation procedure. Though the imagination no doubt supplied worse, there were items one's mother didn't need to see.

His sister, Luke thought, might be hoping for something. She was looking around, taking it all in. Phil went to the little balcony from where a tiny portion of the harbour could be seen. Catherine was asking whether Baden lived nearby. The purpose of the inquiry was to prompt Luke to talk about the prospects of co-habitation. He answered truthfully that they both liked their own spaces—about ten minutes apart by car—and there were no plans to change things. 'I'd be too intolerant now,' he said.

'We can all change, Luke.' Much as she would have been interested, for all sorts of reasons, in such an experiment—her brother living with someone—it didn't sound as though she believed what she'd said. Basically she was conceding that his self-assessment was correct.

What he held back was his sense that things between himself and Baden were slowly, amiably petering out. They'd not slept together for almost three months, an omission lately on both their minds, articulated so far only in ways which were thoroughly acceptable and now part of a routine. 'Oh, dear,' Baden had said, on leaving Luke's apartment, 'I forgot to ravish you blind again.'

Katie stood up and walked over to the shelves where he kept what Baden called, not unjustly, the knick-knacks.

'Foreign booty,' said Luke.

Katie picked up a small Balinese statue. 'You get given this stuff?'

'Some,' said Luke. 'People are very generous when they think you're important.'

'You are important,' said Phil, from the balcony. 'Right? Four years in Canberra.'

'Three in Moscow,' said Catherine.

'You guys keep clippings or something?' said Luke.

Before he had a chance to say something about the piece, Katie put the statue back. 'They talk about you a lot.'

'We do not,' said Catherine.

'I'm flattered.'

Phil had declared himself interested in the beams that ran the length of the apartment's ceiling, and Luke was pointing something out to him. The building had once housed a shoe factory. When he looked back, he caught Katie gesturing to her mother. She was tapping her watch, miming strangulation, or boredom. The act startled him. She'd hardly bothered to conceal it. He was torn between thorough dislike and a longing to reach out to his niece, to offer her something which would change her view of him. What was impressive was not just that she was gifted but that she recognised fully the extent of her gift—a surprisingly rare, and surprisingly unpalatable, combination. He'd always thought this was the reason she'd given up at sixteen for those months—because she was afraid of her talent, or afraid it didn't run deep enough and that she was kidding herself. In two years on her scholarship she'd probably cause profound irritation among her class, and perhaps profound love—the two would play off against each other always. Come the end-of-term concerts, her fellow students would see how completely she was saving them. In searching for an opening, he thought of what he might say to her about dance. He knew no dancers, however. He didn't attend the shows, happy for once to endorse his partner's philistinism. From time to time Baden had treated a few of the top ones. They were all 'dying swans' to Baden. Every movement was 'about' The Disease. Baden liked rugby, which was 'about' rugby. The names of the dancers escaped Luke, and anyway he didn't feel like reintroducing Baden into the room. No one had met him.

Catherine was looking at the framed photos. He'd forgotten to hide the photos. Photos were invisible like this, showing themselves, regrettably, only once the visitor held them. They talked for a little about Canberra—a photo Baden didn't like since it pre-dated him—where Luke had had a surprisingly good time. Access to Sydney had helped considerably, though Canberra itself, since it was full of government people and foreigners looking for ways to spend their salaries, offered plenty. Lacking status, despite its various formal assertions of institutional and cultural importance, the city had developed a nice line in self-deprecating, ad hoc events. He was always being invited on the day to parties and last-minute picnics. Impromptu concerts and games—of touch rugby, tennis, cricket—were the currency of his group. Australia was more easily physical than New Zealand. More public spaces perhaps? A greater range of private ones—definitely. The unspoken rule was a more or less complete lack of organisation. Nothing was entered in diaries—those were for work, for country. Someone had an idea, an urge. A call was made, or an email sent, and people turned up or didn't. This 'personal' Canberra was nowhere near dissolute but it had represented for Luke at least a watershed. He had fallen in love twice on the posting, and had discovered that this provided a certain impetus; whether it gave him the skill to do it again or had helped create in him a desire more apparent to others than in the past, he couldn't tell. He was wild that he hadn't got here sooner, despite being assured several times that miles on the clock was seldom the recommendation being sought. Baden's gloss was 'You were practising for me'—and in a sense Baden was right. Both 'prototype' relationships, undertaken within 'the Service' and across national lines, crashed and burned, with spectacular vindictiveness the result in the first case, and in the second a low-grade sense of injustice—these characterised Luke's response, not his lovers'. They, the lovers, appeared to have little trouble moving on, a process assisted by the normal rotational career paths they were all on. He'd known this was to happen in both instances and yet still took it personally.

He gave his guests the clean, sexless version of the place, aware as he was doing so that they knew perfectly well he'd come out in Canberra—achieved not by grand declaration but a simple statement concerning some holiday plan—and that the boring photo which showed Luke and colleagues on the marble staircase of Old Parliament House was almost taunting in its politeness. Men in suits, a red carpet-runner pinned in place by gold metal strips, the wide steps leading up. Katie had drifted out of his range again. 'Is it time?' he said, turning to his niece.

'No, we're not on a schedule,' said Catherine, pointing to the people in the photo, wanting names. 'Someone's just a little impatient.'

Katie had suggested earlier that she might be disadvantaged by turning up late, since the good rooms at the hostel would be snapped up. The assurance that her room was already booked, as all the rooms would be, did nothing to lighten her anxiety.

Luke, ignoring his sister's request, called them to attention by slapping his hands together once. 'Right. I want to see this room. Let's go.'

Catherine tried to clear away dishes but Luke stopped her. She moved towards the smoked fish, and again Luke intervened. 'Leave everything! The cat can eat it.'

'Have you got a cat?' said Phil. He'd spoken with unchecked disapproval—further sign he, in particular, was struggling.

'It doesn't like visitors, but once we're gone she'll have her lunch.'

Katie was near the door, gathering her things—she looked at last as though she had a purpose. She took a step back towards the table. It was the opposite of a failure of nerve; now things were on the move again, her mood was better and she was showing that it was also in her repertoire to play nice. 'Will it eat from the table?'

'I don't care,' said Luke.

'He doesn't care.' She gave him an admiring look before turning back to the door. She was carrying her cake.

*

He didn't wait for the tears. He left the three of them sitting on Katie's small, single, new bed while the bravery was still on show. When they'd walked towards the hostel, a group of male students sitting on the roof of their flat opposite had called down, 'We'll fuck your daughters!' They'd all heard it but no one spoke. Inside Katie's room, Catherine had gone to the window and opened the curtain. The students were positioned directly across the road. They cheered again on seeing into the room. Katie laughed bravely. The curtains were drawn once more and the light turned on—a fluorescent panel over the desk. Phil said he'd sort those boys out and Katie told him not to do anything, they were fine, they'd go away sooner or later and he was not to do anything to ruin her first day.

The drawers of her built-in desk were opened and admired. Catherine hung a few things in the cupboard, while Phil began knocking his knuckles against the wall to test solidity until Katie told him to stop.

'Maybe we should check in to our hotel,' said Phil, who was jobless.

'Why?' said Katie. She looked suddenly desperate.

'No rush, Phil,' said Catherine.

'No rush, sweetie,' said Phil, sitting down on the bed. His legs swung out and hit the opposing wall.

'What do you think of my room?' said Katie.

'Cosy,' said Catherine.

'Very cosy,' said Phil.

'Do you think it's too small?'

'No.'

'Of course you won't be here a lot,' said Luke.

'Where will I be?'

'Out. Exploring.'

'Studying,' said Catherine, moving swiftly to swamp the noises of dissatisfaction now coming from Phil, aimed at Luke's idea that his daughter might venture from this cramped cell.

Katie considered these options unhappily and then she was looking rapidly from side to side, as if she'd lost something.

'What is it, sweetie?' said Phil.

Her hand came to her mouth in fright.

'What?' said Catherine.

'Where's my bathroom?'

Everyone looked around the room. For a moment the whole enterprise was endangered.

'Oh my God,' said Luke, 'someone's stolen the bathroom!'

Katie looked at her uncle and then she laughed—everyone laughed. They'd passed the communal bathroom back down the corridor, where a small metal sign had been stuck to the wall: No showers after 10 p.m. As if to suggest alternative means of night-time cleaning, this sign was adjacent to a large fire extinguisher. Luke reminded them about it, then he said goodbye.

'Love your inner-city pad,' he told Katie. The girl grinned back at him manfully.

Catherine followed him out into the corridor, thanking him for picking them up at the airport and for the meal. She moved him further away from the door of Katie's room.

'I have something for you.' She pulled a large envelope from her bag. 'It's a little bit professional—in the line of your work, I mean.'

'My work? Diplomatic?'

'Legal.'

He took the envelope. 'I'm not a practising lawyer, you know.'

'I know. It's also a bit personal.'

'Very intriguing, Catherine.'

'Open it at home. Tell me what you think. I should go back into that broom closet. Maybe we should get her moved.'

'They'll all be the same.'

'To the other side of the building. Away from those drunken yobbos.'

'She'll have a great time here.'

Catherine seemed on the point of being offended by this banal reassurance, then she nodded gravely, hoping to say a word to him but finally incapable of it.

Affidavit

He opened the envelope in his car. It contained an affidavit signed by many names he recognised from his time on the farm. Ella and Jeff, Trevor, Barry, David Tanner, a couple of others. The names alone summoned the unhappiness and confusion of the period but also the affection he felt for the place. He hadn't thought about it all for years. The first signatures belonged to Catherine and Phil. The document had been written 'in support of Sheila Howarth (formerly Moore) against her former husband Alec Moore, in relation to their divorce settlement.'

Two or three times it had happened that people he'd been at high school with had left messages on his phone. He remembered these classmates, though they'd hardly been great buddies and there'd been no contact for almost twenty years, and for one instant he felt excited at the prospect of making contact again. He was curious and also touched that these voices had given in to the impulse he himself had ignored. What would it be like to sit down with such a person? It was the weakness organisers of school reunions played on, and he knew if he'd answered the phone rather than listened to a message he'd have almost certainly have yes. Then almost at once this feeling vanished, his finger moved and he'd deleted the messages. Immediately a weight lifted. He re-entered the present with new vigour. He experienced something similar now: the quickening of surprise, then its extinction. He put the document back in the envelope and drove home. The difference in the drive was that this weight couldn't be wished away. Catherine was in town, and the world suggested by the envelope was not a matter of nostalgia—its whiff was living. Besides, he discovered he wanted to know everything.

The affidavit was arranged in numbered paragraphs and had been witnessed and signed by a Justice of the Peace. Its statements were in the stilted style of amateurs aiming for legal prose. Things were 'declared to be so'. The word 'upon' was used in place of 'when'. Clearly, in the common belief that this might compromise the eloquence of the facts, effort had been made to ensure no hint of feeling crept into the document. It was painful to read, the facts emerging with difficulty from language so strained that sometimes the sentence would break down completely, ending abruptly with an orphaned semi-colon—this piece of punctuation, he guessed, elevated by the authors to the grammarian heights of legal literature. In considering this aspect of the affidavit, however, he knew he was being obtuse, unkind. The central point could not be missed. Sheila was fighting for her life, or at least for a fair deal against the man who'd been her life for all those years. She was rid of him—this was the first fact he had to consider, and behind it lay, no doubt, an astonishing series of events.

He recalled his sister's ridicule of himself when he'd suggested things might change between her friend and that man. But it had happened, and he felt satisfaction. At one stage Sheila's achievement in breaking from Alec might have been sufficient. She might have run and run, putting as much distance as possible between herself and him. But this action of the affidavit tied her again to him, brought her back into his orbit. It showed perhaps that she was strong enough, healthy enough, for this connection. That was one reading; the other put Sheila in a less favourable light. The action might signal her continued dependence on Alec, a dependence she hoped to foster through exactly this sort of move. The courts provided a natural home for many such relationships, ones that relied for their fuel on third parties. On the other side, and equally dismal, was the prospect that through his contention—labelled malicious in the affidavit—that his wife should not be entitled to half the proceeds of the farm sale because she'd been unwell through much of the time and unable to make the normal contributions, Alec, too, might have been showing he still required Sheila's engagement with his life. A Law lecturer had once given them the line that there was nothing so intimate as a fight.

He needed, of course, the full story. What had happened?

The affidavit placed Sheila at the centre of the family's world, itemising nine aspects of her contribution while stating that this represented only a fraction of her indispensability with regard to all operations, social and economic. The phrasing finally couldn't obscure this content, which accumulated persuasively across twenty-seven years of marriage, beginning with Sheila's care for Alec's incapacitated mother, through the early and difficult years of child-bearing (reference here to her recuperative powers and courage), into crises on the farm—he learned that she'd taken on hard-labour sewing jobs at various times in a factory near town—and then on to 'years of profitability' when three healthy, well-balanced children, under their mother's selfless love and guidance, became young adults. On this final point the affidavit wandered a little from its own strictness. There was a sentence suggesting that the eldest daughter's apparent support of her father's side in this dispute was another unfortunate example of his ability to control the people around him. 'In using his own child as a weapon against the child's mother, he has expressed the same cruel side of his personality we believe to be behind his desire to deprive of her rightful compensation our long-time friend and neighbour.'

Here was a surprise. To take only the bit that he knew, Philippa had been the most affected by her mother's decision to go to university. Luke remembered the phone call on the day they'd found the home help notice—the girl's tears—and then her resentment at being in the care of strangers. A sense of grievance might readily grow up. Yet that was so long ago and Pip herself had shown signs of being rather stroppy and uncooperative—in no obvious way her daddy's girl, and a more natural ally for her mother's 'disobedience' than, say, the fragile Georgia or even proud little Bill. (He'd have to keep reminding himself that everyone was older by ten years and few of these characterisations might hold.)

One more thing he understood from the affidavit was that the farm was gone. The picture of Alec set loose, without a family and presumably with a pile of money in his pocket from the sale to the cheese factory—whatever Sheila claimed wouldn't make the amount less than a pile: this was a puzzle. Was the glider, that thing which had revoltingly invaded their living room, depositing its parts all over, still a concern? It seemed more likely that selfish projects would fall away once the impediments to their pursuit were removed. Maybe Alec would turn to drink, the selfishness without a project.

The next morning Catherine phoned to set up a lunch date. He told her he'd read the affidavit and she asked his opinion of it.

'I'm astonished,' he said.

'Meaning?'

'Meaning I'm amazed at what's happened.'

She appeared surprised by this reaction. He took this as implying he might have kept up a little better than he had. 'I suppose a lot has happened.'

They agreed to talk about it later. When he pressed her further she told him he'd have the opportunity to see first hand how far they'd travelled. Alec had promised to be at the lunch with his new partner, and Sheila would be there with hers. His sister's purpose was clearly to wrong-foot him. The affidavit had just been to soften him up. Blows were now to be expected. In the face of his noises of incomprehension, Catherine explained calmly that the lunch was in honour of Georgia, the younger daughter, who'd completed a cooking diploma, graduating top of her class. Luke thought back for a moment on this figure, the plump brown girl licking her father's glass, sitting at the piano, putting her sandal mysteriously inside the stool, speaking from beneath the table where she'd crawled. She was not unlike Katie, his niece, in her desire to suggest a mystery about herself, but she was distinct in her need to stay close to the family. She hadn't seemed interested in disappearing for hours, as Katie had. The separated parents, Catherine explained on the phone, were acting on Georgia's demands that everyone come together in Wellington, on neutral ground, and behave nicely, if only for the duration of a dinner. Agreement had not been not immediate.

When Catherine had heard about Georgia's wish, she took over. She persuaded Georgia not to cook and she negotiated it down to a lunch, promising to be at the table along with Phil, to buffer the occasion. It was all perfectly timed, since they needed to take Katie up to Wellington.

'But I can't come,' said Luke.

'Do you want to come?'

'What would my role be?'

'Alec often asks about you.'

He decided this was a lie. 'I was always his favourite.'

Perhaps she was talking in a difficult circumstance or had had enough. Anyway, Catherine didn't respond to his humour. 'I can say you're busy.'

'No, I'd love to come.'

He'd wanted to arrive last at the lunch, to drop blamelessly into whatever atmosphere had already been established, so as not to feel his presence had changed the dynamic. In fact the position he imagined best for himself would be at a neighbouring table. Of course, in the very act of waiting for him the participants might assume some sort of unnatural pose. His lateness might itself cause a shift, or suspend the action. Yet given the nature of the event—participants in bitter divorce settlement—this was hardly likely. He would arrive, apologise and take the last chair, avoiding too that awkward choreography as people jostled—while pretending not to—for the most favourable spot. Catherine might have a plan for this moment, but it seemed any prior arrangements would fail. The couples would surely couple. Lines would be drawn. His seat would almost certainly be in no-man's-land, near the respective daughters.

He allowed them twenty-five minutes, and when he entered the restaurant he saw across in the far corner, at one of the large round tables by the window, only Alec, sitting beside a woman, both of them facing out to sea. There was a moment when Luke might have turned and left, but then Alec, glancing towards the entrance, had him and had half-risen from the table. He signalled with his arm. Luke waved back and moved towards them. The woman too was now on her feet.

'I thought we had the wrong place,' said Alec, shaking Luke's hand.

'The others aren't here?' said Luke.

Alec introduced him to Denise, who said, laughing, 'We thought we had the wrong place.'

Luke heard at once in this repetition Sheila's own habit. Had Alec found another one? It was common to like a single style. He looked at the table settings. The table was too large for him to sit on the far side, but if he left places between himself and them, how many was right? Denise was on to it.

'We wondered if there was a seating plan.'

A mutter came from Alec to the effect that people could sit where they wanted.

'I suppose they can,' she said brightly. 'Ancient rulers would always have their enemies sit closest to them, to keep an eye on them.'

Alec was gruff. 'What's all that?'

'I'll sit next to you.' Luke took the seat beside Denise. 'But I'm not your enemy, am I?'

'As long as you keep passing the bottle of wine, I'm sure we'll be friends.'

'Is there one?'

'We've been waiting.'

'What time did they tell you?' said Alec.

'Maybe they got lost,' said Luke. He asked where they were staying. Denise named the hotel and spoke about it, answering Luke's questions with a good deal of confidence and humour. There'd been some misunderstanding between Alec and the room-service boy which Denise enjoyed recounting and which, Luke saw, Alec himself, though the story had him as a yokel farmer, took pleasure in. She dealt to his interruptions swiftly, and finally he gave up trying to take over. He'd placed his cellphone on the table in front of him and, in a reprise of Katie's action at lunch the previous day, was now gloomily watching it. Despite this act, Alec seemed physically in good shape—certainly a little fuller in the stomach and in the face, but this suited him, softened him.

'No message from them,' he said once Denise had finished.

A waiter came to the table with more water. Denise picked up the wine list and handed it to Luke.

'Red or white?' said Luke.

'White,' said Denise. 'Alec can't have red because of his gout.'

'An interesting fact for everyone,' said Alec.

Luke suggested a bottle.

'Where is it on the list?' said Denise. She got out a pair of reading glasses and looked at the list, then she motioned to the waiter that they needed a few more moments to decide. 'Have you had this?' she said to Luke, pointing down the list.

'It sounds good. You didn't like the other?'

'You chose the second cheapest wine on the list. Most people do the same. No one likes to appear cheap. The second cheapest wine is always a worse bargain than the cheapest wine. It's where restaurants make their biggest profit. Better to choose the cheapest wine or simply buy what you like from further down.'

Alec leaned over as the waiter reappeared. 'Denise has been in the industry.'

'Hotels mainly,' she said.

'She's managed big places. She knows all the tricks.'

'I know where the bodies are buried.'

Alec grinned, relishing a favourite line. 'She knows where the bodies are buried.'

Further conversation was ended because Alec stopped dead. He'd seen someone come in and was getting to his feet. He grabbed his phone and put it in his pocket, searching the table for anything else that might be there which shouldn't. He straightened the cuffs of his jacket, visibly composing himself. For now, Luke and Denise did not exist. Denise saw this as well because she exchanged a look with Luke, as if to say, We might have to rely on each for the remainder of our time at this table.

His snapshot judgement of her as a second Sheila was quickly banished. He found her conspiratorial ease, as well as her ironic acceptance of her position, completely winning. The idea that she had seen Alec's type in her hotels was reassuring on many levels. He had just enough time to ask her how they'd met. It was unfair of him, since he saw she too was now preparing herself. She murmured something about friends in common and stood up for the reception. Phil came in front, calling out to them.

The wine was arriving at the same time as the group, a happy fact allowing the first minutes to pass in conversation about what everyone might like to drink.

'It's on me anyway,' said Alec. There were protests, but Alec repeated the offer as a command to the waiter, who took it fairly well. 'The alcohol is on me.'

The waiter gathered up the orders while seats were taken. Sheila ended up on the far side of the table from Luke, two places from Alec. Phil got the seat beside Alec and the next one was occupied by Georgia. After Sheila came her partner, Joe, then Katie, then Catherine.

'We thought we had the wrong place for a while,' said Alec.

'My fault,' said Catherine.

'No it was us,' said Sheila.

'Anyway,' said Phil, 'we made it.'

'I had my cellphone too,' said Alec. He made a movement towards his pocket, then decided against presenting the proof.

'I was going to call,' said Georgia.

'Anyway,' said Catherine, 'I'm starving.'

'It was only Luke coming in that stopped us walking out, trying to find the right place.'

'You knew this was the right place,' said Sheila.

'It was fine,' said Denise.

Sheila glanced at Denise and smiled briefly. The expectation was that she would say something strategically kind to her, but the impulse, clear to most at the table, withered. Sheila herself looked alarmed at this failure and motioned to Joe that he pour her some water. It was up to Denise to add a few words to her first observation. Nothing came from her either.

Catherine stepped in. 'I was saying to Georgia, hasn't she lost weight.'

Alec stared at his daughter. Then, as if snapping out of some reverie, he lifted his glass and said, 'I'd like to say something.'

'Please don't, Dad,' said Georgia.

'To acknowledge the achievement.'

'Yes,' said Phil.

Sheila spoke across the table to Catherine. 'Why are we still talking about weight?'

Alec continued the encomium. 'The hard work.'

'The partying,' said Katie, grinning at Georgia, who bared her teeth in mock aggression.

'Definitely not an issue,' said Catherine, leaning across the table towards Sheila. 'Just that she said about it herself and I think she's done really well. Around food all day.'

'The sacrifices made,' said Alec.

'Hear hear,' said Phil, who lifted his empty glass, wanting to help Alec finish the toast.

Alec, however, was not done. 'And all achieved through a time of challenges for the family, of course.'

'Please, Dad.'

Sheila was studying the menu. She whispered something to Joe—a gesture which drew attention to him, surely her prime intention. He was in his early fifties, handsome, compact, his full, greying hair in neatly razored ends across his forehead. He wore a black, round-necked T-shirt underneath a dark jacket. A man who sometimes wore shoes without socks. Luke readily put him at art openings but also walking a dog along the beach near his bach.

'Challenges,' Alec continued, 'which have taken their toll.' With this statement he'd begun to drift towards dangerous territory. He was silent a moment, weighing those dangers. He looked prepared to wade in.

Phil intervened with a shout. 'To Georgie!'

'Yes!' said Joe, raising his glass. 'Good on you, Georgie girl.'

Alec looked across at Joe, gauging this remark. He showed no sign of fury, but that itself meant nothing. He might have been ready to leap over the table and grab him by the throat. Alec was wearing a jacket and tie. Joe's T-shirt would have been enough to send him over the edge. Denise, with what Luke took to be terrific timing, put her hand firmly on Alec's arm and said to Georgia, 'Did the job work out?' She'd been on a shortlist for one of the big city hotels.

'She hasn't heard yet,' said Sheila.

'What's the delay?' said Alec. 'They've seen the best applicant.'

'Hundreds wanted it,' said Sheila.

'A tough world,' said Denise.

'The top graduate, what's so tough?'

'Up against experienced people, Alec,' said Sheila.

'Internal applicants, who knows?'

'A stitch-up, do you think? Then it's a waste of everyone's time.'

Joe cleared his throat. 'Standard way of testing the market.'

Alec stared across the table. 'This is the top graduate.'

'Not questioning that, Alec,' said Sheila.

'Well,' said Georgia, 'I hate to interrupt but they rang just before.'

'Oh, darling, don't worry.' Sheila reached over and squeezed her daughter's hand. 'First attempt and everything.'

'I got it! I got the job!' Georgia burst into tears; she laughed through them, but they continued to come. The emotion was miraculous in that it changed utterly the bitter mood of the table while expressing a part of that same mood. Everyone was teary, to some extent. Luke doubted these outpourings had a shared focus, but that simply made it more marvellous. People's communal readiness for grief was itself a powerful influence. Phil's eyes had watered. Katie wiped at hers. Luke didn't need to see his sister's to know she was affected. Joe and Sheila had turned to face each other, away from the group, in a moment of mutual consolation. Alec was looking down at the table.

The waiter was coming with bottles, moving towards Alec. He paused and was unsure whether to go away again. It was Denise, showing her management skills, who gestured him forward and returned the table to other topics. Out the window she'd seen a boat which she wanted to know about. Was this the Eastbourne ferry?

It was probably an invitation for Luke to speak, but when Georgia began explaining the harbour to them—she'd been on a number of cruises and even cooked at sea—he gladly settled back. Post tears she was buoyant. Her mother appeared more at ease, listening to Georgia with clear and deep joy on her face. Luke looked properly at Sheila now. It was the same face, the same beautiful skin, reminiscent of though distinct from the PM's skin, as when Luke had first met her. The slight pursing around the mouth present when they'd sat down at the table and throughout the opening volleys—and which he'd hastily assigned to age—was only nerves and had disappeared. Alec, of course, was the distortion, pulling her out of shape. Once he was discarded, as now when Georgia was speaking, she regained that openness. He'd expected to be disappointed in her appearance or perhaps to have his vision corrected. He'd convinced himself he'd been wrong about whatever had attracted him to her. This had been the last woman he'd wanted, or convinced himself he wanted. To see her again would solve it. His not very advanced theory was that her sadness had been the clincher back then. He'd tried to make it a match for his own. And it was a standard of whatever dramatic genre you could name—TV hospitals, police shows—that in empathy there operated an erotics. He'd wanted to fuck his own doctor plenty of times—a man with family photos on his surgery wall. Baden had fended off passes from the biggest, ugliest rugby players, as well as one of the prettier ones. Of course Baden worked with massage, with unguents and devices, the target lying down, feeling the touch. Luke had touched only her hand—and only that once. He looked for these hands. With one hand Sheila was moving her cutlery around, the other was beneath the table, perhaps resting on Joe's leg—they were close enough and they communicated something of that lovers' world of mild, and mildly exciting, deception. Easy enough in that state to believe the world could be fooled.

'Joe's a vet.' It was Catherine who'd spoken, loud enough for Joe to hear. Phil was now talking to Alec and Denise. 'That's how they met.'

'She brought her dog in,' said Joe.

'Life's a bitch,' said Katie.

'Katie!' said Catherine.

'I should get a T-shirt with that for work,' said Joe.

'I hate that saying,' said Sheila.

'I hate "Shit happens",' said Luke. 'And anything with the verbs do or be in it.'

'Just do it,' said Katie.

'Be happy,' said Georgia.

'That one's all right,' said Catherine. 'Be happy, nothing wrong with that.' She started to sing the song. The wine, or perhaps just the occasion, appeared to have had an instant effect.

'See?' said Katie to Luke. 'Shit happens.'

'So you're a diplomat, Luke?' said Joe.

Luke was aware of Sheila's stare trained on him fully for the first time. She was looking from almost behind Joe's shoulder, where she appeared nestled protectively.

'You should see his stuff,' said Katie. 'He gets given all these cool things, from all the countries he goes to.' She'd finished her glass of wine ahead of them all. It appeared she was no drinker. Her mother moved a glass of water in front of her. Perhaps the dancing had been a distraction from the bingeing which was *de rigueur* for her age.

'What's the strangest thing you've been given?' said Joe.

The question drew giggling from both Katie and Georgia.

The image, from his coin-collecting days, appeared. A Rarotongan dollar—he wasn't entirely sure he'd got the right island—which showed a god and his curling phallus. He'd taken the coin to school, where eventually it went missing. He knew the thief but couldn't bring the charge since this would involve great publicity for the well-endowed god, and for Luke. 'I'm afraid I'll just disappoint the audience here if I answer that.'

'But tell us,' said Joe. 'Then we can go round the table.'

'What for?' said Catherine.

Denise overheard. 'What are we doing?'

'Joe wants us to go round the table,' said Georgia.

'Oh dear,' said Denise.

'What would the others have to say?' said Luke.

'Strangest thing,' said Joe. 'Anything. Strangest thing that happened to you on the way home. Strangest thing anyone's ever said to you. I don't know. There are no rules.'

'Except the rule we have to go round the table,' said Luke.

Joe gave him a look which was, briefly, less friendly than what followed. 'I think it'd be fun.' He shrugged and drank some wine.

'Oh, Joe,' said Sheila, 'I don't know. But are you off again soon, Luke? Another trip?'

'I'm not due again for a while.'

'When we last saw Luke, he was pretending to be a bricklayer,' said Sheila.

'Really?' said Joe, without much interest. He'd turned to Katie and Georgia, who were still hoping to revive his strangest thing idea. Joe had less enthusiasm for it. Catherine joined that conversation, mainly in the negative.

Sheila leaned across the table. 'Or a farm labourer. This was after he'd been at the United Nations.' She was speaking still for Joe's benefit, though he was only half listening.

'I thought I'd aim for something honest,' said Luke. 'How are Eileen and David?'

In response she waved her fingers in the air as if indicating something vanishing.

'Gone?' said Luke.

'Moved to Dunedin.'

'He was from there.'

'You remember.'

Joe got himself away from the two girls and also leaned over in Luke's direction. He was again elbow to elbow with Sheila. 'Why were you being a labourer?'

There was a moment when neither Luke nor Sheila could be bothered to answer. The question was then lost in the din of lunch orders which were now being taken. Luke's firm impression was that Joe had meant only to interject himself between them. The need was instantly wearying. He couldn't say whether this was the fleeting effect on Sheila herself. When Luke looked around, everyone was reading their menus except Alec, who was watching Luke and had perhaps been doing so for some time. Alec felt he'd been so completely caught in the act that he was forced to say something. 'Lucky you walked in. We would have gone in search of the right place.' He raised his glass in salute; his wine had barely been touched.

Luke had to leave the lunch early, before coffee. He had some work to finish, a genuine excuse and quite hard to pull off. Even the briefcase he carried appeared a little convenient. Someone asked that he open it and show them. The demand, supported principally by the girls, was cut off by Joe who said that one never asked a public servant to reveal the contents of his briefcase and that there was probably a law against it.

Luke tapped the briefcase, which was badly worn except for the handle, recently replaced, and a new shoulder strap. 'Top secret,' he said. He'd had the case all his working life.

'It's not to do with that pillock O'Keefe, is it?' said Joe.

The name, perfectly picked, didn't alter Luke's demeanour. He was fortunate to have already been smiling. He was carrying the draft report from the Secretary's office. Kerry O'Keefe was news: the previously anonymous ambassador who, after a career of well-executed postings—scandal free, at least as far as the public was concerned—had evidently found it in himself to speak his mind. That the contents of his mind included a complete disenchantment with the direction of his own country, its narrow-mindedness, its political leadership, its propensity to advance women through the legal profession—O'Keefe had recently been taken to the cleaners by a newish ex-wife who was a lawyer—this was, to use the PM's first response—at least as far as the public was concerned—regrettable. Nor was this quite in character for the Kerry O'Keefe who'd been Luke's boss at the Mission. O'Keefe had given the interview to a lifestyle magazine over a nice lunch. Maybe he was sozzled at the time, but O'Keefe was a teetotaller—an attractive quality at the Mission since it meant he often bowed out early in the evening. Luke's task was to look into the viability of the stress argument. Ex-wife aside—which would hardly gain him sympathy points—so far O'Keefe seemed the least stressed person on the planet. The transcript of the Ministry's own post-interview interview revealed a man unused to acts of contrition, blind to the damage he'd caused, keen to press on in his current role now 'the air had been cleared'. One suggestion was that O'Keefe was mad. 'At least he didn't say anything stupid about the Maoris,' a colleague told Luke.

Alec had heard the name. 'He'll be crucified, poor sod.'

'He's provided his own cross and the nails,' said Joe.

'There'd be a lot of us up there beside him if certain people had their way.'

Phil, next to Alec, murmured in a conciliatory way. Luke didn't catch what was said. It had an immediate effect. Alec nodded and said that he supposed if you occupied an official position there were obligations. This drew general agreement. Everyone was agreeing that Alec had made an effort and was showing, for him, terrific restraint in not moving round the table and punching Joe in the face.

'The son,' Catherine said, 'is a lovely person.'

'Who?' said Luke.

'O'Keefe's son. Phil was saying that we know the family a little.'

'Went through university with Peter, my younger brother,' said Phil.

'A great Southland Catholic family,' said Catherine.

'Kerry was my boss at the UN when I was in New York.'

'Really?' said Catherine. 'I didn't know that.'

Luke began to say something about Kerry's interest in military history.

Alec may not have been listening. 'I knew a Ronny O'Keefe, if it's the same,' he said. 'He was from somewhere down there. Don't know if he was a Doolie. Could I talk about the man's nose? If I could, it was turned up. Quite badly.'

This drew laughter from the girls, which Alec enjoyed. He told them it'd earned Ronny the nickname Piggy. 'Piggy O'Keefe.'

Even Sheila smirked as Alec put his finger against his own nose and pushed up.

'Still,' said Joe. 'This other one should probably have retired. What was your impression, Luke, when you knew him?'

'Maybe you're right,' said Luke.

'Those O'Keefes are a different lot,' said Sheila. 'Ronny had a sister.'

Alec pointed a finger at her. 'The sister! Who was from . . .' He was urging her to complete the statement. Sheila named the place at once, and Alec clapped his hands in agreement. He said another name to her. In response she began tracing the connections while Alec looked on, pleased. He chipped in with a few questions that they managed to answer together. Joe had begun to talk to Denise but it couldn't be sustained because Alec and Sheila were dominating the table. The sense of shared ground, shared history was palpable. Sheila was enjoying solving the family lines. It was one of those moments when the present seemed inert, and only the past, yeast like, was alive and, through the heat of story, doubling in size. The cooperative act, impressive in some ways, was naturally rather strange too and, given the situation of the affidavit, startlingly inappropriate. Surely this was clear to everyone except the speakers, the reconstructing partners.

'I wish I could stay,' said Luke, standing.

Catherine, wanting to redirect things, and let Luke go,

announced her own scepticism good-naturedly. 'I have two brothers,' she said, 'and their best trick is disappearing.'

'I remember the trick,' said Alec. Finally the genealogical double-act had finished.

'He picked us up from the airport,' said Phil.

Alec grunted. 'He's had enough of us already.'

'Not true,' said Luke. He asked then what they were all doing after lunch. Their faith in his enthusiasm for the gathering was partially reinstated when he agreed to meet those who were going rock climbing at the place on the waterfront later on, after they'd finished shopping. He'd gone a few times with Baden, remaining firmly on the ground, admiring that body he knew well perform fresh tasks above him, though the views offered were hardly flattering. He said he would belay if needed, which Katie said was very boring; couldn't they get him climbing. 'Oh no, I'd belay all day.'

'Sounds like a song,' said Catherine. *'I'd belay all day. Oh please come and stay*!' She laughed heartily at her own rendition and drank more wine. Then she leaned forward and, in an odd gesture, stroked Luke's briefcase.

He recalled that the other document in the briefcase was the affidavit, which he'd hoped to return to his sister at the lunch.

Cubed

The rock climbers were—somewhat alarmingly—Alec, Georgia, Katie and Sheila. Catherine and Phil had gone back to their hotel for a rest and because there was a cricket match Phil wanted to watch on TV. Denise was visiting a friend. Joe had driven out to a Lower Hutt address to inspect a pair of second-hand mountain bikes. At this news Alec, summoning generosity almost as he went along, spoke of the excellent developments in bikes. 'We should all probably be getting around on them,' he said.

Sheila pointedly ignored this and walked quickly to the counter so she could pay before Alec got there. Luke wasn't sure how much of the dispersal of bodies was tactical, but he was intrigued with the configuration and surprised to find himself the sole neutral buffer between the warring parties, if that was what they were. He presumed Georgia was on her mother's side, just as Katie would be, which left Alec alone. In that light it was remarkable though not wholly unexpected he'd come along at all. It brought to mind other against-the-odds battles such as the one with the cheese factory—he still hadn't heard what had happened there.

Their number was not perfect, of course. They stepped into their harnesses, received the instructions of the staff member, and began to pair off. Sheila went with her daughter. Alec suggested Luke should belay Georgia since he'd done it before and, despite Luke's encouragement, he wouldn't hear of going ahead of an expert.

'I'm here to learn,' said Alec. This was uttered as straight as possible.

It was only twenty or so minutes before closing time and they had the place to themselves. Georgia struggled. Having chosen an intermediate climb, spurred by Katie's declaration that the beginner wall was for babies, she couldn't get started properly. She swung a metre or so off the ground and Luke had to let her down each time. Sometimes she landed humiliatingly on her backside. In good spirits, from the alcohol at lunch or just the occasion itself, she would laugh and resume efforts. From high up by the roof, Katie called down. Georgia swore at her.

Alec offered to give her a push up but she refused this. They watched Katie abseil smoothly down, springing lightly away from the wall using her toes. She landed without sound and was detaching herself from the rope.

'Ballet cow,' said Georgia.

'Chef,' said Katie.

Alec moved in against the wall, ready to push. Georgia, unaware of him, put one leg on the wall and swung the other one out, catching Alec full in the chest. He staggered back, a little winded, then laughing. Georgia said sorry but that it was his fault because she hadn't seen him and she didn't need his help anyway.

'Pull her up with that rope,' Alec told Luke quietly. He was rubbing at the spot where he'd taken the blow. Luke explained he couldn't; even lifting a small child in this way took huge effort. Alec took hold of a portion of the rope himself as Georgia tried once more to go up.

Sheila had removed herself from the neighbouring climbing straps. 'No, Alec,' she said. He was holding the wrong bit.

A staff member, a guy in his early twenties whose name-badge said Jeff, had wandered over and now offered to help.

'Not making too much progress here,' said Alec.

'I'll get it,' said Georgia. 'Give me time.'

Katie was with her, showing her where to put her feet.

'She'll get it,' said Sheila.

Jeff retreated.

Georgia slipped again and dangled in the air. On tiptoes she couldn't quite reach the ground. 'Put me down!'

Luke released the clip.

'Earthbound,' said Alec, with some satisfaction.

'Alec, please,' said Sheila.

Georgia turned to them, her eyes filled with tears. Alec was immediately contrite, soft-spoken. 'Dear,' he said, 'why don't we move over to the other wall? Get the hang of it and come back to this.'

Georgia turned back to the wall, reached out for a grip and moved one foothold higher than it had been before. It looked as though she might do herself an injury. Katie's flexibility was natural, her movements elastic. Georgia's were painful. She grunted and pulled herself to the next hold, then quickly onto the one above.

'Push from the legs,' said Katie.

Georgia quickly made further progress, resting just above their heads. She was powerfully built in the calves and was now launching herself from the footholds, using her hands more lightly to guide the climb. She didn't have her friend's grace but there was strength; and, in the way the climbing lengthened her body, creating diagonals from planted toe to reaching finger, a surprising litheness could be seen. Alec and Sheila watched in silence as their daughter went up, reaching the roof with a few last large strides. She stopped. Everyone—not simply the climber—seemed out of breath. Then they were calling out to her in pleasure. Both parents were laughing. Georgia ten metres above their heads on a rope seemed such a fantastic thing. Katie whooped. She'd climbed up there!

Sheila made an automatic motion towards Alec, as if she was about to hug him—some contact was not only possible but necessary. It couldn't happen, of course. Alec was late to see this initial movement from Sheila. His denseness here was a reminder that even when they'd been together he was never the one to initiate such contact. Now he looked full of regret. In the moment's aftermath there was a brief collision of hands, for which Sheila apologised. They then moved apart. Katie, already bored with Georgia's triumph, wanted to try a different wall.

Luke called up to Georgia, who'd remained motionless, staring at the wall, her head near the ceiling. 'I'm going to let you down now, Georgia.' The girl gave no sign she'd heard. He repeated it more loudly. He told her to hold the rope in front of her, lean back as if she was sitting, and gently push off from the wall as she came down. He'd let it out slowly and she could tell him to stop at any point. Still Georgia failed to respond. Alec now called up to her. She remained in the same position. Sheila came back to where they were standing and also tried, but without success.

Sheila spoke to Alec in a low, accusing voice. 'Why won't she come down?'

'She won't come down,' he said. 'Is it my fault?'

'Maybe if you hadn't said anything.'

'Me? About what?'

'Earthbound.'

'It was a joke, and she was. She couldn't get up. Now she's up.'

'Now she won't come down.'

'That's what we can see, Sheila.'

None of this exchange would have been audible to Georgia. The speakers seemed unaware that anyone could have heard what was said. Luke ensured he was studying the ropes and carribiners. He could hardly walk away. He was attached to the floor and to their daughter.

Sheila spoke more loudly. 'If I was her, I wouldn't come down either.'

'Thank God she's got more sense than you.'

'Probably that's true. It took me a long time to get sense.'

Alec turned at this point, smiling, to Luke. He knew this at least had been audible and appeared grateful it had only been Luke who'd heard, rather than Katie who was scouting other climbs. 'Excuse us, Luke. A wee family squabble.'

Jeff, the staffer, came over and looked up at Georgia. 'She cubed?'

'Sorry?' said Luke.

'Cubed, frozen. Stuck.'

'Yes, she's cubed.'

Alec approached Jeff. 'He could just let the rope out. She'd come down.'

'Are you crazy!' said Sheila.

There was a moan from above them. 'Don't let the rope out!'

'Terrifying the poor girl,' said Sheila.

'Please calm down, Sheila,' said Alec. 'It's you who's doing the terrifying.'

Sheila stood close to Luke, ready to act, addressing Jeff. 'He's not to let the rope out.'

'I won't,' said Luke.

Jeff was unfazed. 'This is real normal,' he said. 'I'll go up. Talk to her. She can come down with me.'

'Don't come up here!' Georgia yelled out.

Katie walked over, attached herself to the harness and went to the wall. 'Belay,' she said quietly. Jeff hooked himself up, and Katie began climbing.

'Who is that?' shouted Georgia.

'Shut up,' said Katie.

'Fuck you,' said Georgia.

'Fuck yourself, idiot.'

'Who the hell got me up here?'

'You did, dumbshit.' Katie paused, then continued up, like a cat. She reached the same height and stepped easily across to Georgia. She put an arm around her friend. They touched heads. She was whispering in Georgia's ear. Then she gave Luke the thumbs-up. He released the clip and let the first inch of rope through his grip. Georgia, still quite stiff, jerked down and stopped. Katie made another gesture: speed it up. Luke began letting the rope out smoothly and Georgia, without using her feet against the wall, hanging awkwardly, shapelessly, descended. She might have been a bag of tools let down from a building site. Her elbows bumped against the grips as she came down; her feet were not employed but also collided at times with the wall. Katie was being let down beside her. When they landed, Sheila grabbed her daughter, who slumped sobbing into her arms. Alec went towards Katie who told him to wait until she was unhooked, then he gave her a quick hug. He moved away again, hoping to get to Georgia, who was still smothered.

'Nice work,' said Jeff.

'Nice arse,' said Katie, patting herself on the backside.

'That too,' said Jeff.

'The belayer sees it all,' said Luke.

'I'm Jeff.'

Katie shook the hand he offered, and gestured towards his name-badge. 'I can read.'

'She's Katie,' said Luke. 'What Katie Did. Katie is a great, great dancer. As well as a saver of lives. A saver of cubes.'

'This is my uncle.'

Jeff shook hands with Luke. 'I've got to close up, I'm afraid.'

'Enough excitement for one day,' said Katie.

Luke and Katie sat together while the others got out of their harnesses. He'd gone from the office back to the apartment before heading out again. His briefcase was at home, but the envelope containing the affidavit was in his jacket pocket and his fingers touched it, prompting the question he now asked Katie: whether she saw much of Philippa, Sheila and Alec's oldest daughter, apparently the one ally her father had.

'Not much.'

'What does she do?'

'The books for her dad. She's a sort of accountant-businessy person.'

'For the farm, you mean? I thought it was sold.'

'It was. No, for Alec's business. You know, the gadget thing he invented. You haven't heard of this? He came up with a little piece of equipment that helps gliders somehow. Don't ask me what it is. Navigation? Now he travels the world. Pip's employed by the company he formed, the company consisting of Alec. I mean, who else could cope? Pip seems to. Ask him. Ask him what his gadget does.'

Alec was approaching, still obviously working on Georgia, while Sheila was talking to Jeff by the counter.

'Sorry,' said Georgia sheepishly.

'It happens a lot,' said Luke. 'The guy was telling me. You got up, didn't you? More than I'd try. Would you go up there, Alec?'

Alec looked across at the wall. 'I reckon I could.' Perhaps he deemed any attempt to make his daughter feel better about herself no longer necessary. 'And make it down.'

Sheila came over. 'Do you know what it's called? They have a name for what happened to you, Georgie.'

'Why is she "Georgie" now?' said Alec. To mitigate the direct challenge this represented to Joe, the only other person who'd used the name, he'd asked the question of Luke.

'Cubed!' said Sheila.

They walked back along the waterfront towards Sheila's hotel. Luke's job obviously was to accompany Alec on this walk. It was clear no one else was up for it, the girls accelerating away from them. Actually Alec had grown morose, and as with most egotistical people this made him in some ways better company. The self-enchantment weakened, and so, his main subject obscured, he didn't find much to say. His gout was giving him trouble. The wine at lunch was a mistake. He seemed worn down by his effort throughout the day to behave well. This proved a good time to learn facts. Luke asked a question and he got a plain answer. He found out about the invention and the company. Alec had declared the need for this device, which was indeed a navigational aid, and had had a few ideas as to its creation, but he'd given the job of proper development and of course manufacture to others—'clever fellows'—who were co-partners and co-owners of the patent. In this detail, Katie's account had been off. Alec's job was sales worldwide, though the device pretty much sold itself. He'd been to South America two months ago, and before that to the UK. At the suggestion this might be an exciting sort of life, Alec agreed with such a lack of enthusiasm it made Luke laugh. Alec stared, deciding whether to revive or not. There were ghostly signs of amusement in his face. Though Sheila was walking well in front of them, with no chance of hearing this account, there was yet the need to send out the message that things weren't great in his set-up.

'Does Denise travel with you?'

'Sometimes.'

'She'd be handy in the hotels.'

'Do you know she worked as a manager in hotels?' He'd forgotten Luke had heard this at the lunch; it was possible Alec had forgotten Luke had been at the lunch. 'She knows all their tricks. She knows where the bodies are buried.' Here he paused, smiling to himself and looking out over the water to the monastery on the hill, before returning to his glum pacing. St Gerard's might have triggered the next comment. 'Ronny O'Keefe must have been a Doolie.'

They walked in silence.

'You never gave much away,' said Alec.

Did he mean about Kerry O'Keefe, the ambassador, or

generally? Luke didn't feel this was said in expectation that he defend himself. It had instead quite a private turn, as if Alec was almost talking to and about himself. The girls ahead had to leap out of the way of a 'crocodile' bike driven by a group of Japanese tourists.

'Great to have Katie up here for Georgia,' said Alec.

'They're good friends,' said Luke.

'Grew up together.'

Inevitably it was the farm which came into view for the first time. Alec's pace grew brisker. Luke quickened his stride to keep up. They were gaining on the party ahead, almost running. The entire feel had changed and Luke imagined something difficult if not outright awful happening once they were reunited. Alec seemed blind and driven. Fortunately, the name of his hotel appeared above the buildings across the road. Luke pointed it out. 'If you take that street, you'll be there.' This stopped Alec, who studied the name with scepticism. Was this a trick? Luke called out to Sheila, who turned. He indicated the hotel.

Alec was resigned to the parting. He looked at his watch and told Luke that Denise would be there. 'Evening, team,' he shouted, giving a wave.

Georgia ran back to her father and hugged him. 'Thanks for coming, Dad.'

'Honour to be here, dear. Absolutely.'

They arranged to see each other the following day, then Georgia skipped back to Katie and Sheila. Luke took a few steps away from Alec, raising his hand as a goodbye.

'How do you put up with it?' said Alec. 'Can't stand the travelling myself. Who do you travel with? I guess you're often with a crowd, which would be more fun. Of course Catherine herself is a Doolie; I forget. Contact with religion was one thing they asked about Sheila. Nothing there though. The kids know their prayers. I see the lad Hamish from time to time. He's a share-cropper. Married with kids. Still limps. Do you faint still?'

Luke was lost for a reply.

'I hate hotels.' Alec moved towards Luke and shook his hand. 'Enjoyed it.'

Luke watched him walk across the grass towards the crossing. There was no one else around. Alec had his hands in his pockets, his head down, moving purposefully. There was something of the farmer in this isolated, concentrated figure. The park might have been his paddock. The city, though it was all around, seemed to dwindle to irrelevancy.

Alec had separated at exactly the right time, since ahead on the walkway a cyclist burst through the group, then wheeled around and came back for the same again. Luke, a few metres behind the girls, saw what they hadn't. They were still shouting at the person, screaming, when he headed once more straight for them. Under the helmet it was Joe, grinning, riding one of the bikes he'd bought.

When Luke reached them, the girls had wrestled the bike off Joe, who was laughing hard. Sheila, also laughing, was telling him off, pushing at him and slapping him on the helmet. 'Did you see?' she said to Luke. 'He almost ran us over!'

'I almost got them!' said Joe.

Sheila glanced over Luke's shoulder, an action which had only one meaning: to check on Alec's progress. Luke looked too, and so did Joe. That gloomy, hunched figure was just disappearing from view.

'Did I miss him?' said Joe. 'Good old Alec. I could ride over and give him a dub.'

'Don't, Joe,' said Sheila.

Georgia toppled noisily off the bike some metres away and Joe, a bit more serious now his purchase was under threat, went over.

'It's their first real public meeting,' said Sheila. 'Alec has said some horrible things about Joe. For the first year he called him the rodent.'

The echo here was faint and, once he tried to bring it further forward, scrambled. He'd never forgotten handling the package from the freezer marked for Alec. She'd called Alec the same thing, in effect, that he'd called Joe, though there was no obvious connection for her in these two events. He'd wondered on the fate of the package. There was a good chance she would have removed it and disposed of it before Alec got anywhere near the back of the freezer. 'They were civil,' he said.

'It's wonderful to see you again, Luke.' She touched his sleeve. 'Beautiful clothes, I remember that.'

'You look very happy.'

'Joe's a vet. But you know that, don't you.' She laughed nervously.

'Does he do farms?'

'He has a practice in Fendalton. Mainly he does cats.'

'I have a cat.'

'Do you?'

They watched Joe bending to test the gears on the bike. The girls had grown bored and had wandered further ahead.

'Ours died,' said Sheila.

'I'm sorry.'

'Joe euthanased it.'

'I see.'

'What are we talking about!' She touched his sleeve again. 'So you're with someone? Catherine told me.'

'Baden.'

'He sounds nice.'

'From the name?'

'No, from what I've heard, maybe from Catherine.'

'She's never met him.'

'Oh, well, I don't know. Maybe he's horrible!'

'No, he's nice. Thank you.'

'What do you think of these girls, growing up, getting jobs?'

'Amazing.'

'Do you think life goes fast? Joe says it goes at different speeds, sometimes at a crawl, sometimes like lightning.'

'I guess that's true.'

'Oh, it's hard to argue with Joe. He's so sensible.' She sighed, but it was theatrical, letting him know she wasn't criticising Joe; that she was loyal to him perhaps and it was a loyalty built in understanding, not worship. 'Let's look at the water.' Sheila walked over to the edge of the concrete. The water was greenish and the rocks were coated in yellow algae. Something silvery glinted further out. 'What is that?'

'A shopping trolley,' said Luke.

'People are disgusting.'

'I know.'

'Why would you do such a thing?'

He was about to move on when he realised she was upset. She was even perhaps disappointed with Luke, in the blithe way he'd told her about the trolley in the first place. She put one foot down onto a rock. 'We should get it out.'

'I know. Maybe there's someone to phone. I'll ring when I get home.'

'No, we should do it now. Get it out.'

'We can't.'

'Pull it out.'

She was serious. 'Sheila, it's too far in. It's too deep.'

She continued to stare at the submerged trolley. It wasn't beyond the bounds that she'd dive in. 'Why would anyone do that?'

'Sheer stupidity.'

'Joe has to see a lot of cases of cruelty to animals.'

The leap brought to mind Alec's earlier procession of referent-less statements. 'There was a case in the paper recently,' he said.

She cut him off. 'I don't want the details. There's too much prurience around those stories.' Immediately aware that she'd been rude, she stepped away from the edge and spoke gently. 'I'm afraid, Luke, I've become one of those people who like to be positive. I don't read the paper even. I don't keep up.'

'You're not missing much.'

'I don't watch TV.'

'Who does?'

'I don't know what people are talking about most of the time.'

The issue was what in fact she did do, unless Joe kept her. The Fendalton surgery sounded promising. 'I take photographs,' she said, as if answering his thoughts.

For some reason this vaguely disappointed him. He felt the same when people told him they were writing a screenplay. 'I was going to ask about the art, the art history, I mean.'

'Some people would take a photograph of that.' She gestured towards the sunken shopping trolley. 'That would be life. That would be an accurate vision of life as it's lived. Wellington Harbour 2005. You can imagine a whole series: rubbish underwater. A drowned doll, or beer bottles. An electric heater. You can see the effects you could get—from the surface patterns of the water, from the colours, blah, blah. Silver of the metal trolley. And the commentary: consumer society, lack of caring, etcetera. I see work like that, I just think, Get the trolley out of the precious harbour. Now. It's just not interesting, it's irresponsible, I think. Pollution. Get it out.'

'But maybe the photographer is sending us that message, that we should act.'

'Don't care. Put down your camera and get the thing out.' She'd spoken with force. Now she shook her head and smiled, as if trying to regain her lightness. 'You're right, you're right. We're witnesses, yes, all that. The problem for me is that I've already taken the photo before I've taken it. You see? I've done it all, figured it all out. I can imagine more or less exactly how a series like that would come off.'

'What do you photograph then?'

She thought about this for a moment. 'I hardly take any photographs. What am I talking about? I can't believe I'm telling you this. *Photographer.*'

Joe was wheeling the bike towards them, scowling.

'Joe, what's happened?' said Sheila.

'Jammed. Unrideable. When Georgie fell off, the whole gear thing got whacked out of line.'

Sheila suggested getting it fixed when they got home. For Joe this was a defeat. He wanted them both to go riding the following day, around the bays. 'Couldn't we take turns on the good bike?' she said. 'You could go for a ride and then I could.'

He bent dejectedly over the bike again. 'I told them to be careful.'

Sheila turned to Luke. 'Do you know anything about bikes?'

Luke said he didn't but that there was a bike shop not far away. Unfortunately, it would probably be closed soon. Sheila asked what the time was. Surely they could try? Luke repeated the statement that he thought they'd be closed.

'I don't mind trying anyway,' said Joe.

'Even if it's closed, you can get the opening times from the window and Joe will know where to bring it in the morning.'

Soon Luke found himself, at a fast clip, accompanying Joe and the bike to the shop—Joe needed directions—while Sheila went after the girls. In the hurry no one said goodbye. Sheila's haste in leaving suggested irritation, perhaps with Joe's reaction to the bike problem, or with them both.

Joe walked the bike along the footpath. He was speaking about how much he wanted to get Sheila into biking. 'She hasn't got a sport. I'm not suggesting she get competitive. There are wonderful biking trails all over the place. Have you got a bike?'

'My partner does.'

'Gays are big bikers.'

'We're known for it.'

'Sorry, I didn't mean to stereotype you.'

'No, there's definitely a type. It's just not me, or Baden really. His bike hangs on the wall, minus the front wheel. More like art. Sheila was telling me about her photography.'

'Exactly. She could go for a bike ride and take her camera along. Get some snaps.'

'I didn't think she did snaps exactly.'

'You're right to pull me up on that.' He looked sulkily at the bike. 'This is a weekend I could have done without. I can't bear to see the effect he has on her.'

'Alec? He's kept his cool pretty much.'

'You realise he's threatened physical violence against me? It's three years they've been separated. He can never say my name. Notice? You know what he called me?'

'Yes.'

'I'm here for Sheila, and Georgie of course.' They were near the bike shop. It had been established that Luke would have to leave once they got there. 'Your sister and Phil have been amazing. Did they show you the affidavit?'

He appreciated Joe's bluntness. 'I have it in my pocket.'

'I helped with the language.'

They paused at the shop entrance. 'I'm not sure what my role is,' said Luke.

'Cast a legal eye.'

'I'm not really that sort of lawyer. Those skills have atrophied into general—I don't know what.'

'Plus we were hoping you'd draft your own affidavit, supporting Sheila.'

'A separate one?'

'Sheila doesn't know about this approach to you. If you wanted to use ours as a sort of template, otherwise I'm sure you could come up with a nice piece.'

'Do you think it's needed?'

'It can't do any harm, can it.'

'Of course I've hardly known Sheila for that long.'

'Not continuously, no. But at a significant moment you were around. Isn't that true?'

The word significant was wrapped in many layers. He was fairly certain Joe would know little of what had happened between Sheila and him. 'It was ten years ago.'

'Sheila went off to university.'

'Alec didn't like it much.'

'Your sister says Sheila was always coming back to save the family from crises. It's one of Alec's arguments she did what she pleased, never gave a thought to what effect she was having on the household.'

'That's untrue.'

'Would you be the witness here for just that period? It was Catherine and Phil's impression you got on well when you were staying with them. Had you been sick? Sheila even had time to see that things were good with you, to make friends. Am I making too much up? She's talked about you.'

'Really?'

'It was a crucial time, as far as I can tell.'

'Yes, but it's hard to remember exactly. Probably I wasn't in the best shape. Tell me, did Sheila carry on at university?'

'How could she, after Bill.'

'Bill, their son?'

'Meningitis. You never heard? Poor boy. Lost a leg. Terrible. That's what I mean about a crucial time. So much happened.'

'What about Bill?'

'He's a great kid, unstoppable. The reason he's not here, he's on a kayaking holiday. Terrific upper body strength. But it's been hard. An event like this one today always brings it up. Sheila spent the morning in tears. It was a great effort to make it to the lunch. If I'd had the casting vote, we wouldn't have turned up. But for the girls, we had to come. Listen, Luke, your affidavit, it won't win us the case but it'll be another small pressure towards the right result.'

He said goodbye and pushed his bike into the shop through the sliding doors, which immediately opened once again. Joe's back wheel came back out. He stood in the doorway. 'I said something a bit sharp to Georgie for breaking the bike. Stupid of me, especially on her day.' It was unclear why he was telling Luke this. The parallel with Alec's own elongated leave-taking was apparent. The proverb that all truths are spoken on the doorstep seemed part of it, except that what was said lacked, so far, any finality or even clarity. Luke hadn't moved. 'I don't have children of my own. I've had very little to do with them all round.'

Luke managed to say that he was hardly an expert himself. The news of Bill had shaken him strangely.

'No.' Joe, sufficiently distracted by his own failings to notice anything odd in Luke, put two fingers on the seat of his bike. Its leather lozenge was dimpled on top. An object belonging to the class of things that, once seen, have to be touched. Luke rested his hand there briefly as support. 'Bill's sixteen. Tough age.' Joe shook his head. 'Tough year.'

Thankfully, whatever might have followed these confidences never had the chance to develop. A shop assistant had approached Joe and was holding his bike's handlebars, encouraging the bike indoors. There was a call from Joe through the closing doors about catching up tomorrow which Luke answered with a movement of his head. He hoped this hadn't committed him to anything. He remembered a vague promise made over lunch to rendezvous with Phil, who wanted to see inside Luke's work or 'get some taste of power'. O'Keefe resurfaced nastily. The report was a mess. He hurried home to start on it, thinking of the boy Bill.

A phone call from Phil later that evening gave Luke the opportunity to learn more. The meningitis had been picked up early, in fact, with both parents at home, a few days after Christmas. Luke had dreaded a different scenario in which some stranger, the home help—if they'd managed to find anyone new—failed to pick up the seriousness of the condition. Then an avalanche of recriminations would fall, and carry on falling. It would be the mother's fault for not being present. Or it would be the father's fault for not providing adequate care. But this hadn't happened. Alec and Sheila had responded at once and in accord with each other. They'd got the child to the hospital without delay, and the doctors had acted as fast as possible against the disease. The amputation was inevitable by then, and life saving.

Naturally Bill's survival was the main thing, and it brought about a relatively harmonious period in the house. The retreat of pettiness following some major crisis—and its inexorable return—was a pattern Luke knew intimately. Baden had had pneumonia the year before and had been in a coma for three days. In that time, Luke had sworn off every small grudge.

Sheila gave up university for good—and this despite the urgings from Alec that she carry on. He thought it would be a waste to give up then. With Bill spared, he was in a magnanimous phase. Luke's memory was that by this stage Sheila had already decided—or been persuaded—to come home. She now devoted herself happily to her son's care, and Alec made a great effort to help her. Later, once it was clear that Bill's rehabilitation would be a drawn-out affair, with difficulties as great on Day Three Hundred as had been there on Day Three, it got—in Phil's word—'trickier'. This was a period Phil had neither the desire to dwell on, nor narrative skill to draw out. He went on to say that Bill was a very handy basketballer, with his father's height and some of his determination.

In finishing the call, before he handed the phone to Catherine, Phil asked whether it was all right if Alec came with them tomorrow since he had nothing to do.

'For a fight to the death,' said Luke, 'I must say you're all behaving rather strangely.'

'You mean the affidavit?' said Phil.

'I've been enlisted by Joe on your side, asked to plunge my dagger in, and now we have to go and play with Alec because he's lonely.'

'He's still a friend.'

'And clearly considers you one too.'

'That's right,' said Phil. 'Alec has done bad things, but I know him and will always know him.'

Catherine, when she got the phone, described how she was walking into the bedroom and closing the door since Phil didn't like to hear the sort of things she might say about Alec. He asked about Pip, telling her what he'd already found out from Katie at the indoor climbing place. 'Pip went flatting in Christchurch,' said Catherine. 'This was a couple of years ago. Sheila had a little flat of her own—her and Bill. She'd moved out. It was over. She'd met Joe. Alec was insane. He was on the farm by himself. He spent most of the time with us, in fact. Came over for meals all the time. On weekends, he'd go up to Christchurch. He'd turn up at Pip's flat, uninvited, and sit there on the sofa. Her flatmates had no idea how to take him. Sometimes they'd give him a beer and he'd drink seven of them too, no problem. This is Alec. Absolutely no effect. Or he'd look at the TV, watch anything, apparently. Then he'd say, Let's go, and Pip had to go with him. He'd drive the car across to Sheila's usually. And on the way he'd start weeping. Bawling his eyes out and driving at the same time. They'd arrive outside Sheila's flat and he wouldn't go in. Refused. He sat in the car. "If the rodent's there, I'll kill him." That's what he used to say. Pip had to go in and tell Sheila he was there. Sheila would come out to the car. He wouldn't go in the house. Sometimes Bill would come out too, but he didn't like the whole scenario and mostly stayed inside. Sheila would come out and they'd speak through the car window. He wouldn't get out of the car. And they'd have a row. Ending with Alec telling Pip to get back in the car, which she would, and they'd drive off again. That was what Alec did for Saturday night, for months. Sometimes he forgot he was driving Pip to her flat and he'd head out in the direction of the farm. He'd be driving along, top speed, one hand, banging the steering wheel, talking about Sheila and how she'd ruined everything, spoiled everything. Along these real dark, narrow country roads. He knew them bend for bend, but Pip was still scared. He was terrifying her. These were the drives he described to us as refreshing. They cleaned the cobwebs out, he said. He'd always liked to drive. He'd always liked speed, from flying too, I guess. On the worst nights he'd leave Sheila's at a hell of a speed, tear off into the night in the car, and he'd say to Pip, "I've got my gun, my .22, in the back. I swear I'll put it in my mouth." Barrelling along these roads at over a hundred. The following evening he'd be over at our place for a nice dinner.'

'To carry on cooking for him after all that,' said Luke. 'You were afraid of him.'

'No. Afraid of what he might do. And perhaps a little of what you say.'

'Joe's asked me for my affidavit.'
'Will you do one? It wasn't my idea. It was David Tanner's.'
'David?'
'When we got in touch with him, he seemed to think you could contribute. I told him it was a long time ago.'
'Ten years.'
'That was a memorable Christmas.'

She'd drawn this last statement out, giving it an ironic, unsettling tone. It was one of Catherine's sly thrusts. Levering. They'd never spoken properly about the manner of his exit a few days before that 'memorable' Christmas. On the day itself he'd phoned them. Under instruction, the kids had come on to thank him for his presents. He was back in Wellington by that stage. He'd spoken quickly to Phil and Catherine, making unspecific sounds about himself when they asked. It was Christmas; no one pushed too hard. He wouldn't be returning to New York, but in a few months there was a chance of another posting, perhaps the Pacific. This, in the end, didn't turn out. He went instead to Vienna for six months, from where he sent his sister's children chocolate, and—as a thank you gift—for Catherine and Phil an expensive quilt done in an Austrian folk style. The quilt was beautiful, he thought, showing figures from folk tales, a married couple—he remembered—asleep in their beds, with the moon in the bedroom window.

Before he spoke, she repeated the information about David Tanner being the one who'd suggested approaching him. Again the invitation was there for Luke to throw light. Again the sense he got was that his sister was already seeing—if only a little—by this same light. She knew something. Luke had no idea about any connection with David. 'Wonder why,' he said.

'He said something about how you used to meet up with Sheila in the public library.'

'I saw her there, I think, once. We talked about *Charlotte's Web*, the book. She told me about Alec's mother. She was on a high from university.'

'And you were a little in love with her.'

The question, so long in coming, was not in the end a surprise. 'Probably,' he said.

His sister was waiting for an elucidation of the facts, but what were they and how to phrase his feelings? The phone, not for the first time, was a useful tool. Whose turn was it to speak? Finally Catherine said, 'Isn't Joe great?'

'Yes,' said Luke.

They talked for a while about the bikes, then she returned to the topic, though now, thankfully, the heat was missing. 'And you met Sheila at the library in town?'

'Katie was there,' he said. 'I'd taken Katie in to get some books and we met Sheila there. Was that the time David Tanner meant?' The way he'd drafted his niece into the explanation, however accurately, was still shameful. She had the ring of an alibi, but only perhaps to a guilty person. David's evidence was puzzling. It would have been in character for him to linger and maybe to seek out Luke again in the library, and in doing this he could have come across him with Sheila, sitting in the kid-sized chairs. Was there enough in that discovery to think they met regularly like this? A lot depended on when he'd spied them. Surely he wouldn't have hesitated to break into their conversation if he'd not been restrained by something. 'I was just hearing about poor Bill,' said Luke.

'Could have been a lot worse,' said Catherine.

They talked some more about meningitis before saying goodnight.

Be My Baby

It looked as though O'Keefe was about to be recalled to Wellington. The news came in by email the following morning, Sunday. Luke's report, which he'd worked on for three hours, was outdated. His boss had called a meeting for that afternoon. Luke left all this, answering instead the one from Baden, who'd made progress with several Asian buyers and who'd sent the email after a hard night on the town. Baden was no writer, a condition fully embraced by the run-on, punctuation-free text. The gist of it was that drinking with people in wheelchairs was a very dangerous thing. The wheelchair was a great cover. A few of their party had slumped unconscious and been deemed perfectly okay by bar owners. They'd ended up pushing 'comatose crips' in and out of some very fancy places. There was travelogue stuff that Luke skimmed. The final observations were about the bed, and the pillows—Baden had forgotten to bring his own, a grave error and a running joke between them. He kept a special pillow—goose down—at Luke's. Even in his boozed state, Baden had the gift—he himself had wondered whether it was a Chinese one—for being minimalist about matters of affection. He signed off as B. Luke was addressed as L. No one else on his email list, he assured Luke, had this degree of informality. Luke used 'Dear' and 'Love', which Baden found impersonal. It was true also that in Luke's case there were others he addressed in this way. They'd experimented for a time with x's, lower-case letters, words such as 'kisses' and even 'smooches', but finally each returned to what felt most comfortable. Luke wrote a quick reply, leaving out O'Keefe, putting in the fact he'd been rock climbing, and ending with an effusive dedication to Baden's pillow who 'pined each night for that lovely head'.

He put on *Dancer with Bruised Knees*, a CD of odd and special meaning for them. Baden, who paid little attention to music as a thing in itself and certainly none to lyrics (he was the wife in this respect), caught perhaps in the beginning by the sound of French, started to listen. He asked who it was. When Luke told him two women, Canadians, Baden said, 'Dyke folk.' No, two sisters, the McGarrigles, and, as far as Luke knew, straight. Songs about drinking wine, reading in bed, Southern boys. If you looked at the lyric sheet the French ones were curious truncated fairy tales about sex. The CD had become a favourite. Baden loved, and liked for a time to repeat, the lines, from 'Be My Baby': 'I don't know why I live at home/I don't know why I sleep alone.' Luke left his breakfast to send another email telling Baden he was listening to the record. There was nothing on the Net about O'Keefe's recall. He skimmed a couple of local blogs that mentioned the affair, more or less along the lines of Joe's judgement. O'Keefe was an embarrassing fool, an unreconstructed misogynist, a rambling idiot in a good position to do the country harm. Looked reasonable. One blogger, probably flying a kite, wondered about O'Keefe's career up to this point. Had there been a pattern to this behaviour? O'Keefe had started in Jakarta in 1965. How had the Ministry covered for this plonker for all this time? Luke had a fair idea. Much like the Catholic Church and its resident paedophiles, the built-in mobility of the job made it easier for miscreants to avoid trouble. 'Shit and Shift' was one phrase he'd heard. Still, he wasn't aware of anything around the time of the Mission in '95 which smelled like mud in connection with Kerry. Following the anniversary year, and Bolger's appearance at the General Assembly, Kerry had got a gong in the Honours List. The real disasters, of course, tended to find themselves stuck in Wellington, suffering rejection after rejection until the penny dropped. They would never leave these shores again. They stopped applying. Such figures moved through the office corridors, resigned, sometimes resentful, but seldom—to invoke Baden's email—crippled. They were flexible, after all—the central requirement in the eyes of some for the life. As far as possible, adjusting their ambition, they made Wellington itself their foreign posting, and enjoyed foisting on new recruits a sense of impenetrable protocol and whimsical punishment. There were parts of the Ministry's Head Office on Lambton Quay for which, it was said, one needed shots. It was these members, slightly shabby, older, who also gave the place its family feeling. No other government agency had this. Like great-uncles or aunts, they were of almost zero interest and somehow great significance. In addition, by stint of their long and disreputable service, they knew things. He called one now at home, confident he would be on the same page as Luke, if not a little ahead. This was Roger Angland, a sort of ally.

'Kerry O'Keefe,' said Roger, drawing out the alliteration with relish. The blogger had riffed for a paragraph on the diplomat's namesake, the Australian cricketer, suggesting a similar skill with spin would now be required. 'You know we shared a spot. This was before you were born, in the seventies.'

'I'm thirty-eight,' said Luke.

'You're a mere child.'

'I had a sense you might know him.'

'Oh, he's not one of us, you understand. But I'm forgetting your own time with him.' Roger, mid-sixties, lived with his ancient mother. He'd told Luke he wasn't queer but that living with one's mother was more or less the same thing, so he accepted—more or less—whatever designation came his way.

'The wife cleaned him out,' said Luke. 'His outburst was revenge, surely.'

'Kerry? No, no. Well, a part of it might have been that. Selling the paintings and all that, I suppose. Fucking disruptive.'

Roger's swearing always carried more power than anyone else's. 'What else?' said Luke. 'Some self-destructive bent? Doesn't seem the type. At least he didn't when I knew him.'

'Self-destruction? Hurt the thing Kerry loves best?' Roger gave a laugh and began coughing. Someone in the background made a disapproving noise—the mother? His hand went over the receiver and Luke heard the muffled sounds of an argument. He came back on. 'Where were we?'

'How to account for O'Keefe.'

'Kerry O'Keefe. Why, by the way, are we doing this on a Sunday?'

Luke explained about the recall, the meeting, his abandoned report. 'I've got family visiting.'

'Poor thing,' said Roger. 'The recall is perfect bullshit.'

'Why?'

'He'll never come back. They'd have to send armed men. They'd have to change the locks.'

'They could do that, couldn't they?'

'They won't. How long has he got to go? Three, four months?'

'He'll sit it out?'

'He'll try.'

'But why do it in the first place, give the interview? What use was it? He could have saved the blood-letting for his badly proofed, shockingly illustrated, self-published memoirs, surely?' The reference was to the spate of such books, much enjoyed by those in the Ministry who'd finally been rewarded by seeing vain, power-hungry men summing up their lives in literature of a circulation around two hundred copies, of which one hundred and sixty odd remained with the author for discretionary distribution. Roger was able to quote at will from some of these works. At the launch for one of them, a question had come up as to how the book had been written: longhand first or straight to screen? Roger, speaking loudly enough to be heard by everyone but the target, had announced that the author, at all times of composition, had worn a condom.

'I recall O'Keefe was more or less illiterate. No disqualification, of course. But he'll not be wanting the pen to come out yet. Not with the next chapter about to open.'

Luke thought back to the bullet-point documents he'd had to deal with in New York. 'Containing what?'

'I thought you might have guessed by now. He's going over to the other side, if you follow. The dark side.'

'Bestiality?'

'The National Party.'

'O'Keefe's becoming a Nat? How do you know that?'

'He's not told me. He's not told anyone probably. He probably thinks he's still thinking about it himself. Kerry's not quick. He's not a deliberate person. But his accidents are better than most people's plans. Charmed almost.' Roger's own fall was indicated in this summary, which had grown a bit winsome. What had happened to end Roger's hopes was always left vague.

'What's your evidence? I mean, I'm sure you're right. It makes sense. Speak out now, seems like it's a natural progression to take one's dissatisfactions somewhere. He won't have this sort of coverage again. But how did you guess, Roger? Intuition?'

'A woman's intuition, you mean? Not this time. The flight itineraries of several key people. Remember that's in my patch. I'm more or less a travel agent. Anyway, with hindsight, everyone seemed keen on visiting our man, dropping in. The approach was made over the last few months. It would hardly have felt like an approach, more like a pleasant, unspecified sort of attention. A breeze moving one's hair. Near retirement one's thoughts do drift towards . . .'

'Posterity?'

'Death.' Roger coughed, not bothering to turn away; it came down the line harshly, as though someone had trodden on his foot. 'Listen, when you want a man to convert, you don't take him to church, you take him to the movies. Have fun at your meeting.'

That's who we need here

Parliament was closed and he didn't want to take them to his office, where he was likely to run into colleagues preparing for the afternoon meeting with the Secretary. He was still unsure what to do with Roger's information. Instead they went to Te Papa, which was Denise's suggestion, since neither Phil nor Alec had been before. Denise had visited the museum a few times but always in relation to work. She'd gone from hotel management to tourism. Luke was glad she'd agreed to come with them, since she filled with ease and skill the guiding role he feared he'd have to shoulder.

The day was overcast, windy, unpromising, and the museum had gathered up a good deal of this discontent. Parents who looked more than halfway through their day at 10 a.m. followed their young children through the rooms, which were alternately night-like then brightly lit. Large parts of Te Papa had always reminded him of a bar entered during the day; it had an indefinable malevolence perhaps to do with the dark marble floors, the appearance of hosts, often with brochures to get rid of. It was a reflex among his set to bag the place. As someone had dryly pointed out, Te Papa wasn't for them, it was for all New Zealanders. Overseas guests of the Ministry, speaking off record, provided frequent endorsements and wished for a similar institution back home. International artists and thinkers confessed tears when looking at the display connected with immigration: it was apparently the dream of a few of them—and not only those from disaster zones—to come and live; to join, in effect, the wall of faces and stories. On inquiry, they'd played all the interactive games.

For Phil and Alec, the entranceway and the staircase leading up to the first floor provided a genuine thrill. They were right. Luke lifted his head and got a brief shock of delight. The true story of the psychiatric patient who'd jumped from one of the upper levels, landing near where they stood, and which he'd told a few times from this same spot, did not get an outing. They were drawn to the large stone ball turning in its water bath and, just as the kids were doing, both men put their hands on it. Luke had never understood the ball—something to do with sponsors—but it was clear that in twenty or thirty years' time this novelty would be what the kids remembered from the museum, just as he remembered the cold turnstile from the Basin Reserve and not the test matches.

Denise led them to the escalator, but Alec peeled off and took the stairs. He raced up them, and was waiting at the top. Alec's idea was to start from the fifth floor and work down. He seemed very excited and energetic. He left them again at the lift, taking off up the stairs.

'Is he in training for something?' said Phil.

'The hotel is full of mirrors,' said Denise. 'Last night we could watch ourselves eat in one. Personally I find it a wee bit much. I wasn't impressed by what I saw.'

'In Alec?'

'In myself! I know my age, it's just the reminders I don't like.'

Phil told her she looked great. Denise thanked him, adjusting her silk scarf. She was dressed neatly in a light blue trouser suit. The doors of the lift opened and they stepped out, leaving behind the question as to why Alec had been bothered by the mirrors, if indeed he had. He was already reading the text at the start of the art exhibition. Certainly he was determined to appear keen. They moved picture by picture around the first room, as a group; Phil and Alec taking turns to read aloud the descriptions pinned beside each work, and inviting Luke, against his own disclaimer that he was the wrong person, to translate where necessary. The procedure was thoroughly earnest at first, with everyone listening hard to whatever Luke said, which was mostly very little. The heavy pausing in front of each work brought to mind Eileen's comment that art should operate as an electric shock. After a while, Denise drifted off to look at a different part of the show, and Phil stopped reading the texts and began looking ahead in a glazed way to the paintings coming up. Alec stuck to it and made Luke stay with him, but now there was surely something satirical in his questioning and he began offering his own verdicts, with frequent recourse to the phrase, 'That's different, isn't it.' This was uttered too with a degree of playfulness, as if Alec knew exactly the type of ignorance Luke expected of him and had decided to supply it. Yet when Luke answered by saying, 'Yes, very different,' Alec refused to let him get away with it. The game could be played only by him. He was complaining of the heat but wouldn't take off his jersey. Luke could see sweat glistening on his temples.

Alec now began to linger over technical phrases in the descriptions, showing signs of dissatisfaction with Luke's guesses. Finally Luke said to him, 'Sheila is the person we want here.'

Alec bent to read another of the small panels stuck to the wall. 'I should have the glasses. Did you notice we all need glasses now? Did you see her at lunch, Sheila has glasses! She looked a hundred, peering through her specs. I'd not seen those before.' He studied the writing, then straightened without reading the words aloud. 'Joe's a strange fish.'

'All day with pets,' said Luke.

'You've got it.'

Phil was further on, staring longingly out of the exhibition space. Alec turned and followed Luke's gaze. Phil looked like a boy desperate to go to the toilet but unwilling to put up his hand. He glanced back in their direction, and the contained misery on his face made both Alec and Luke laugh.

Denise came over. 'What's so funny?' She put her fingers to Alec's face. 'Are you hot? You look hot.' She told him to take off his jersey.

'I'm fine,' he said.

She began to pull at his sleeves, but he moved away.

'Shall we go find something else?' said Luke.

Denise took them to the marae. At the entrance, Alec stopped them. 'This,' he said solemnly, 'is a special place. Denise is not allowed to speak here.'

'Oh, Alec,' said Denise, grinning.

'Shush,' said Alec. 'You're supposed to be behind us, woman, so we men can protect you. Though maybe you could hang back with Luke, eh. No, just kidding, Luke.'

They stood in front of the large piece of pounamu, which was wet and showing patches of green coming through the yellowy surface from where it had been rubbed by thousands of visitors. A sign identified this as the centring stone. Luke stroked it and Denise and Phil followed his lead. Alec had already moved off. He was looking through the closed glass doors out over the harbour. 'How do we get out there?' he said. Perhaps he hadn't meant to express this thought, since he quickly turned around and declared the marae most impressive.

There was a Maori host standing by the stage area, and Alec walked up to her and began asking about the carvings.

'Forgive my cheek, if that's what it is, but are you a Maori?'

'I am. I'm Ati Awa, the local people.' The host was in her early twenties. Her light brown skin was covered in dark freckles.

Alec nodded at Phil. 'It's getting hard to tell these days.'

'Okay,' said Denise, looking to move everyone on. 'Next stop, Bush City.'

Alec stayed where he was. 'The Maori All Blacks are an interesting crew.' He was grinning again at Phil.

'Don't watch rugby, sir,' said the host.

'They've got a great record,' said Phil, also beginning to walk away.

'See, I played rugby with Maoris,' said Alec. 'Good blokes. These were real, old-fashioned Maoris, I suppose you'd say. Rough as guts.'

'I don't follow it.'

'Boil-ups, you name it. The old ways.'

'I see.'

The low-level goading continued. Alec was describing a hangi he'd once had at a rugby club. They'd dug up some of the pitch. There was no sense to what was going on. The only way Luke could connect the encounter with anything else was to see this as a continuation of the role-playing Alec had started while looking at the paintings. Here, he seemed to assert, is a redneck; this may or may not be me. He looked flushed in the face, uncomfortably hot. The agitation didn't show in his voice, however; it was even, light. 'This was down south, South Island.'

'Yes,' said the host.

'Do you know the tribes down there?'

The host leaned towards Alec and spoke in a low, untroubled voice. 'Oh, they're all cannibals down there, sir.'

The effect on Alec was hard to describe. At first he reacted as if he'd misheard what had been said, turning his ear again to the host. But the host had moved way and was now talking to another group. Then he seemed to register it, and, on seeing Luke had been witness to it all, was determined to show a kind of pleasure in the rebuff. He winked at Luke. This didn't come across as at all wholehearted. He continued to sweat. Denise called for Alec to come along.

'We better get outside before it rains,' said Luke.

'Did you hear that?' said Alec.

'I did. Very quick, wasn't she?'

'Very quick.' He glanced around disapprovingly. 'Lots of official functions here, I suppose.'

'Yes.'

'I was asked to throw my hat in the ring.'

'Sorry?'

'For Parliament. A few times they asked me.'

'Tempted?' Of course he'd heard about this ten years before. It brought to mind O'Keefe again. Anyway, Luke's question was lost as the doors opened and they stepped outside. It was cool and the flags on the yachts in the marina snapped in the wind. Alec was quiet. They walked over the little swing-bridge which didn't swing. Some boys, about thirteen or fourteen years old, ran past the path and leapt into the fossil pit. They began digging in the sand as though they were dogs, bent over so their heads were close to the ground, hands furiously paddling the sand behind them. They were spraying sand over two girls, slightly younger than the boys, who'd been carefully digging for the fake fossils that were buried there. The girls might have been enjoying it—this was hard to tell. They were screaming but also laughing.

Alec stepped into the pit and spoke to the boys. 'Quit it,' he said.

The boys looked up briefly, then returned to the spraying.

'You boys get out now,' said Alec.

The boys stopped. There were four of them. The oldest-looking one, a broad-shouldered kid wearing a hooded sweatshirt, brushed his hands on his pants. 'We're digging.'

'No you're not. You're ruining these girls' fun.'

'No,' said one of the girls, 'they're not, not really.'

The boys gave a cheer.

Denise told Alec to step out of the pit.

'Come out, Alec,' mimicked the big kid. He had some sort of a moustache.

'You.' Alec took a step towards the boy. Alec was taller by several inches and Luke saw that in the ten years his chest had grown heavier. He presented the slab of his body full-on. 'You be quiet.'

Phil came forward. 'No harm done, boys. Just be a bit careful, eh.'

'Watch yourself,' said Alec.

The big kid, a bit shaken, spoke to Phil. 'Tell him to get out.'

'All right, Alec,' said Phil.

Alec didn't move. He raised his finger, pointing at each boy in turn. 'This is a museum, all right. Show some respect, or I'll come back and bury you in this sand so deep you'll be the fossils.' He waited a moment, then he smiled at them, returning to something like normality, or at least his version of it. 'All right, boys. Take it easy, eh.' He approached the two girls. 'How are you doing? Found anything yet?' He'd put such gentleness in his voice they cowered.

One of the other boys, astonished into politeness, said, 'We can't find anything. I don't think there are fossils in here.'

'Oh, there are,' said Alec. 'Just have to keep looking.' He stepped back onto the path. 'Don't give up. One of the great lessons, that is. Don't give up.'

They walked around the corner, leaving the pit in silence. Denise was furious and wouldn't speak to Alec, who'd regained completely his poise and good humour. He stopped at a water fountain for a drink. 'Thirsty work,' he said. He put water on his face. Finally he took off his jersey. There were sweat rings under the arms of his shirt. He tugged at the material, loosening it. 'Certainly in my day,' he said, 'we never had such a place. What a marvellous place to bring kids.'

'Especially to get yelled at and threatened by older men,' said Denise, disappearing into the blackness of the 'cave', the simulated environment of glow-worms, here tiny electric light bulbs. Phil followed her in, appearing to want the peace.

'Where'd they go?' Alec peered inside.

'Go in,' said Luke. 'It's cool in there.'

'I can feel the coolness from here,' said Alec. For whatever reason, he was reluctant to enter the cave. Luke explained that it was an easy, atmospheric, two-minute circuit. Water dripped from the ceiling and there was a tunnel for kids to crawl through. They could hear voices from inside. Alec hovered. He grimaced and rubbed at his chest.

'All right?' said Luke.

'Indigestion,' said Alec. 'I can usually walk it off.'

'Why don't we sit down for a bit?'

Alec ignored this. He moved out of the way of a group emerging: two Indian men and presumably their wives, the women in saris, the shimmering red and gold material appearing from the shadows. There was an argument going on as to whether the glow-worms were real or not. Alec gave Luke another wink, whether in reference to the argument or the saris it wasn't clear. 'My father took me to see glow-worms,' he said. The anecdote, however, ended there. He rubbed the back of his neck. 'Don't much care for confined spaces.'

Luke thought for a moment. 'What about the flying? In the little cockpit.'

'But you've got all the air around you. No, there's no problem there.'

He saw his opening. 'Did you ever finish that glider you were making?'

'Ha!' This seemed to indicate the story wasn't worth telling. Luke was about to probe when Alec again winced in apparent pain and brought his fist to his chest. 'Hotel food,' he said.

'Come and sit down,' said Luke. As part of his preparations for the Moscow posting he'd done two things: attended Russian language classes for six months and completed First Aid training. Alec was as good a candidate as any for a heart attack.

Alec had returned to the glow-worm story after all. 'He took me at night to see them. I was eleven or twelve, I suppose.'

'This is your father?' Hadn't this person succumbed to a heart attack?

'Right. It was very exciting. The glow-worms probably meant very little to me, but being with Dad was good. We drove a couple of miles. You had to go to a park just outside town, then down a long path. It was quite dark. Dad was telling me how much I was going to enjoy the glow-worms. That was a bit unusual. Didn't say much on the best of days, my dad. But this trip was going to be something. I tripped on a tree root and he caught me before I fell. Then he held my hand for a bit until he let go. When we got near the place, he told me to be quiet. I thought, Quiet? Can glow-worms *hear*? But it was because he'd heard something, someone. "Listen!" We stopped and listened. We could hear voices. Two men were there, ahead of us, right by the glow-worms. We could just see them in the dark, swaying about, laughing. I think I asked who it was. "Shut up," he said. We got a bit closer and then Dad stopped again. The men had their trousers around their ankles and they were turned towards the bank where the glow-worms were. I tell you, it was a horrible event. They were urinating, spraying up on the glow-worms. Dad said something under his breath. Then he grabbed my arm and turned me away, shoving me off back the way we'd come. "Move it," he said. "Move." He didn't say another word all the way home and I knew not to say anything to anyone either. My God, he was let down a few times all right.'

A voice then came from the opposite direction on the path. Alec's head jerked around—Luke was sure he'd made this move in response to the voice—then he was gone, presumably into the cave, Luke didn't see it. It was from where the Indian party had gone, but it didn't belong to them. The slight hectoring quality was familiar. Luke at first misplaced it. He was thinking of O'Keefe still, and he imagined someone difficult, or with difficult questions on this issue, rounding the bend and catching Luke unprotected as it were. He hoped Denise and Phil would come out of the cave and conceal him. He considered ducking inside as well, but now he was sure he'd been spotted.

'There's Luke! Isn't it? Yes!' Joe and Sheila came down the path. Joe, looking pleased to see him, clasped his arm. 'What are you doing here? Loitering with intent.'

'Why aren't you at Parliament or wherever?' said Sheila. She seemed less pleased, looking around for the others obviously.

'It's Sunday,' said Luke.

Joe pointed into the cave. 'Is this where the glow-worms are? I really like glow-worms.'

Luke was about to tell him they weren't real but stopped himself.

'I'm not going in there,' said Sheila. 'I think we should keep moving.'

'Nonsense. Are you coming?'

'I'll wait with Luke.'

'Couldn't get the bike fixed. Not such a nice day either and Sheila hasn't been before. Well, if I'm not back in half an hour, send a search party.' Joe went in.

'Are the others in there too?' said Sheila.

Luke named them. 'Alec wasn't so keen. I don't think he's feeling all that well.'

'He's claustrophobic,' she said flatly. She peered after Joe. 'Oh, well, he's in there now.'

'He'll be fine,' said Luke.

'Of course he'll be fine.'

It wasn't at all clear whom they were talking about.

'Don't you like caves?' said Sheila.

'Been before.'

'Did you ever read *A Passage to India*? My book group did it.'

'I saw the film.' Surely she was thinking of the women in saris.

'Do you remember the Marabar caves? The Indian doctor who gets accused. Aziz. Poor Aziz. Or poor Miss Quested. What do you think happened? Was it all in her mind?'

Though the subject had arisen suddenly, these conversational jumps were not effected in a loopy way. Sheila was slightly sped up, but playful rather than intense, and she'd lost her anxiety. It was a contrast with the time they'd talked at the public library, where she'd been in monologue mode. 'I can't really remember well enough. I do remember Alec Guinness, in blackface, as a ludicrous Brahmin.'

The sound of raised voices came from the cave.

'A Marabar cave can hear no sound but its own,' said Sheila, in mock solemnity. 'The book group got quite hung up on that line. Yes, Luke, don't look at me like that, a few of us insist on reading the book.'

'I wasn't looking at you like that.'

'Oh really? Anyway, it's the line when Miss Quested has gone missing and Aziz wants to shout for help, but the caves, you know, the guide says it's useless. I like the bit where Aziz calls the silly guide gently to him, then slaps him across the face. Life might go a bit better if all of us could do that from time to time. I mean be on the receiving end as well as the giving end. Don't you think?'

The sound grew louder. These, it seemed, were voices of alarm, in competition with placating ones. He didn't think immediately of Alec. Lots of people fooled around in the cave, using the cover of dark to misbehave, to scare each other. He'd been in a few times and crashed into couples. A friend who'd worked for the museum had some good stories. A child sleeping overnight in the tunnel. Others interrupted. Luke thought at once of Joe and Alec bumped up against each other in the darkness. That would be ugly. Sheila had been right. Joe should have been stopped, or at least warned. They might have passed harmlessly on to the fossil pit.

Luke and Sheila both took a few steps inside the cave. He was close to her for the first time. He longed to ask her about that night he'd spent waiting for her out in the cold on his sister's farm. Why hadn't she come? Why had she agreed to it if she had no intention of coming? All the reasons and scenarios he'd played out in his head over the years—years in which he'd been utterly okay, sometimes fabulously happy, mostly content and, with the enhanced opportunity that had come his way to see into global deprivation, deeply gratified with his personal lot—all his own speculations now felt paltry against proximity to the truth. She was next to him. He could make out her ear, which had a transparent shine.

'It's Alec,' she said. 'Alec!' She called out his name in the blackness. It was hard to see anything for a few moments. She took his hand and stepped forward. They could hear the disagreeing voices better now. 'Where are you, Alec?'

'This way!' someone yelled—Joe perhaps. The acoustics changed the timbre.

Sheila didn't sound like Sheila. Her resonant call was full of assertion. 'Alec?'

'He's here.' That was Phil, with a strange rising inflection.

In the gloom they could now make out the slight gleam of a hand-rail. A drip of cold water fell down Luke's neck. They moved round the bend and saw the shapes of people ahead of them. They were bent down to something.

'Lift him up!' Denise's voice was thin and teary.

'I don't know if we should move him.'

'Who's there?'

'It's us, Denise. Luke and Sheila. What's happened?'

'Alec's fallen.'

'What's happened?'

'Alec's collapsed.'

'Is he hurt?' said Sheila. They were right beside Denise, talking at her face which they could only glimpse in brief spills of light.

'I don't know!'

Luke found himself at Alec's head. He could see better now. The person at the patient's head takes charge—he remembered that from his training. 'Call 111,' he said. No one moved. 'Joe, use your mobile to call 111. You'll have to do it outside to get reception. Ring from the entrance. Then you're going to stand there, keeping people out. Tell someone to alert Te Papa staff about what's happened.'

'Right,' said Joe. He left.

For a moment Luke considered the oddness here. He'd just sent a trained medical professional off to get an ambulance—sent him away from the scene. The others were waiting for their orders. 'Can everyone take off their jackets, coats, anything. We need to keep him warm.' He put his ear against Alec's cheek and watched his chest. He should have done this first. There was nothing. 'Undo his shirt, Phil, quickly.'

'What am I doing?' said Phil.

'I'll do it,' said Sheila. She began pulling at the buttons, her hands trembling.

'What's happening?' said Denise.

'He's not breathing,' said Luke. 'I'm going to do CPR.'

'Oh my God!' said Denise.

Luke put his fingers behind Alec's ears, tilting his head back. He opened Alec's mouth by pressing with his thumbs on Alec's chin. He leaned in to check the airwaves, but Alec's head jerked back suddenly and there was a convulsive sound. The tongue must have been blocking the passage; the head tilt had worked. Alec was gagging as if he were about to vomit.

'Recovery position,' said Luke. He extended one of Alec's arms behind his head, folded the other over his body, lifted one leg until it was bent at the knee, then pulled him carefully over. Again, this worked. He positioned Alec's head on the extended arm. Alec was perfectly in position. He had stopped choking but he was panting heavily, and beginning to shiver. The cave was cold. They folded the jackets over him. 'Has anyone got a hat?' Luke looked at the two women. 'Give me your scarf,' he said to Sheila. He wrapped this around Alec's head. Then he asked Denise to sit at Alec's head and talk to him.

'Can he hear me?'

'Ask him.'

'Alec. Love, can you hear me? Alec, it's me, it's Denise. Alec?'

Alec groaned and moved his hand.

'Oh, Alec!'

'Thank God,' said Sheila.

A few moments later Alec could utter a few words. His first statement was, 'Sorry about this, team.'

'Are you hurt anywhere?' said Luke.

Alec turned his head slightly to look at Luke. 'I hope you have it.'

'What?'

'The handkerchief.'

For a second Luke didn't get the reference. Of course it was to the night Hamish, the farmhand, had been injured.

'This bloke,' said Alec, letting his head fall back against his arm again, 'is a wonder with the handkerchief.'

'He is a wonder,' said Denise.

'Yes,' said Sheila.

When the medics were taking Alec out on a stretcher—despite the patient's own protestations that he could walk—Joe was alongside Luke in the cave.

'Look,' said Joe, nodding towards an alcove, 'the wingless female who emits light from the tip of her abdomen. The glow-worms.'

Luke thought, confusedly for a moment, of Elizabeth, Alec's mother, trapped in her bedroom, in the web—as Sheila had described it years before in the public library. Had Sheila told Joe this story also?

They emerged from the cave momentarily blinded. Sheila was walking beside the medics, talking to Alec. Denise, sobbing, was being consoled by Phil, who seemed in shock himself. Denise looked up at this moment and, as if remembering her place, walked quickly—almost ran—to the ambulance and climbed in. With a look of defiance, she stared out at the approaching party. One of the medics asked her to step out again; she could get back in once the patient was secured. Still she sat there. It was unclear whether she'd even heard the request. Finally Sheila came forward and reached out her hand to Denise, who took it at once, stepping down from the ambulance. When Alec had been put inside, she got in again.

Someone had to go with her, with Alec. Denise was no longer distraught, but she was still some way off being able to speak intelligibly on Alec's behalf at the hospital. It was unthinkable that she go by herself—but finding her companion was not simple. Phil said he needed to contact Catherine and the girls, who were back at Katie's hostel. He was trying to work Joe's phone. Phil was the big surprise, Luke thought. He'd had the stuffing knocked out of him. Seeing his old friend, the mighty Alec, go down in such a public way had affected him deeply. In a sense, however, Phil had been absent throughout the weekend, fretting about his daughter's big move, discomfited by the big city. The small crowd of onlookers must have seemed like a nightmare, confirming all his fears about the sort of thing that happened in Wellington. That left Luke himself, or Sheila, to go in the ambulance. Joe was ruled out. The ambulance's engine was idling and the paramedic had begun to close the back doors. Denise was desperate. Luke hesitated. He had the O'Keefe meeting. This was the ex-husband of his sister's friend, currently trying to cheat that friend of what was rightfully hers. He moved at the same time as Sheila towards the door.

'I'll go,' she said, pulling herself inside.

'I'd like to come,' he said.

Receiving no signal either way, Luke climbed in and the doors closed. He glimpsed Joe through the back window of the ambulance, looking bereft.

When Georgia had accidentally kicked her father in the chest at rock-climbing, although she'd caused no external bruising, the force of the impact had been sufficient to cause internal bruising to his sternum. This was the pain Alec had felt and which he'd called indigestion. This, as it transpired, was also why Alec had been inspecting himself in the full-length mirror of their hotel bathroom, causing Denise to conclude he was pondering the ravages of ageing—since he neglected to tell her at that moment about the chest pain. She knew him to have the sort of vanity, more common in males, which shows itself in avoiding all contact with mirrors, and therefore she blamed herself for not following up this inspection more carefully. 'I should have asked him,' she told Luke and Sheila while they were waiting for Alec to collect his things and leave the hospital.

When they'd arrived at Te Papa and Alec had done his mad running up stairs routine, Denise had thought again this was to do with a kind of conceitedness, some bravado associated with stamina. 'I'm sorry to say this, Sheila, but last night he kept going on about Joe and the bikes he was buying. That really got to him. About how there were always bikes lying around the farm and you never once showed an interest in getting on one. He said he always supported bikes as a means of transport, those were his words.'

'Sounds like Alec,' said Sheila. 'Bikes these days are somewhat different from the ones we had.'

'I told him that.'

Luke saw again the image of overweight Doreen, from the Married Couple, pedalling between Poppa's and the farm on the bike Alec had loaned her. The entire district had no doubt this was personal sabotage on Alec's part. Bicycles were comic, and to see someone like Joe taking them seriously was naturally offensive.

Then he wouldn't take his jersey off. He'd overheated. There'd been that stupid incident with the boys in the fossil pit—Denise told it to Sheila without sparing Alec one bit. This was the new style between them, a completely frank dissection of the man they loved or had loved. They might have been sisters discussing their brother. The cave was the final straw. 'He doesn't even particularly like the shower box,' said Denise.

'Always had baths,' said Sheila. 'He went into the attic once, had to crawl across the rafters to pull through a light cord which was hanging too low. I remember we had to yank him out by the legs, he was panicking. Pip had one leg and I had the other.'

The humour was partly possible because a heart attack had been ruled out, as had all the other sinister stuff. Georgia's kick had resulted in a syndrome in which some of the symptoms of a heart attack were mimicked. Alec's collapse in the cave had most likely been the result of dehydration and stress associated with claustrophobia. He'd swallowed his tongue. Luke had saved his life.

They'd been at the hospital four hours. When the doctor said Alec could go home, Luke realised he didn't know where home was for Alec any more. He asked Denise. Alec was living in her Christchurch townhouse, using a room off her garage as a makeshift office. He was travelling overseas at least once a month. His suitcase was never packed away. 'He complains,' she said, 'but in a sense, it suits him. It means he's never quite moved in. My place is perfect for me, which is why I bought it. I didn't think I had a person like Alec in my future. You never know, do you?'

They all shared a taxi into town, dropping Denise and Alec, who was tired and still off-colour, at their hotel. He'd hardly spoken. He was sheepish about the fuss he'd caused. He was also shaken. Luke stepped out of the taxi to open the door, help him out. 'I owe you a lot,' Alec said quietly. 'My tongue has always got me into trouble.' They shook hands. From the taxi they could see him pause at the revolving doors of the hotel, unwilling to step into their slow turn. Denise held his elbow. Still he wouldn't, or couldn't, make the decisive step. As the taxi pulled away, they were walking slowly towards a side door.

They began driving towards the hostel, which was near the Botanical Gardens. As they passed the main gates to the Gardens, Sheila suddenly asked the driver to stop. She'd walk from there. Luke got out too. He could walk to work, up through the rose garden, then back down to town. Already he'd missed many opportunities to be dropped closer to Lambton Quay, and he sensed Sheila knew this. He took her offer to walk as an invitation of sorts, made under difficult circumstances. Joe was somewhere, perhaps back at their hotel.

The sun had come out and the wind had dropped. They began walking up the sloping drive to the rose garden. Nothing had been said about whether this was the right direction for Sheila to be heading in—it wasn't.

'People get married up here. I went to a reception in the Begonia House.' He pointed to the buildings across the flower beds. They walked to the pond set in paving in the centre of the garden. 'David Tanner was a rose man.'

'They shifted,' said Sheila. 'I told you that, didn't I?'

'Do you still see them?'

'That awful Eileen person. How are you feeling anyway? You saved a life, an amazing thing, Luke. How are you feeling?'

'Actually elated,' said Luke.

'Yes!' She gripped his arm. 'Of course Alec hardly let on, but he knows what you did.'

'He shook my hand. I wasn't expecting much more.'

Sheila laughed and headed off quickly towards the Begonia House. He caught up with her inside, where she was helping a small girl open the door to the warmer Tropical Water Lily House. The girl ran to her mother who'd been sitting by herself on a seat beside the lily pool, her head tilted back, her eyes closed. She'd been napping. She came alive with a jolt as the girl rushed up and threw herself at her. 'How did you get in?' the mother said sharply. 'How?' The girl pointed at Sheila and Luke.

Sheila came forward and apologised.

The mother was younger than she'd seemed from a distance. She was in her early twenties, scarcely older than Sheila's own daughter. She was also embarrassed to have been caught like this—not napping but speaking harshly to her girl. 'That's all right,' she said. 'She's supposed to be with her dad. I said they could give me ten minutes.'

Propped up beside the woman on the seat was a backpack. Inside was a baby.

'You have two!' said Sheila, smiling and bending down to see the baby.

'Three,' said the woman. 'Her brother's still out there. My guess is their dad's asleep, lying on the grass, and the boy is anywhere.'

'I have three too,' said Sheila.

The woman looked inquiringly—he could not say doubtfully—at Luke when this was said. 'I have none,' he said. 'But I love kids.'

'Liar,' said Sheila. The two mothers began to talk in hushed voices about babies.

The girl, over by the far side, was dipping her finger in the pool, pressing lightly down on the half-submerged leaves. There was a notice asking visitors not to do this. Luke leaned over the pond. The water was greenish, filled with swarms of tiny black fish sweeping up and away from the surface. There were other larger, unhealthy-looking fish of various colours. The warmth made him drowsy. He hadn't eaten properly. Elation was unsustainable, though a few other pleasurable feelings were taking its place: pride and also wonder; the wonder of his own success, certainly, but also the wonder that the viability of this complex, wonderful thing—a human being—depended on the position of a single muscle, the tongue. After a few minutes the girl was called by her mother; they were leaving.

Sheila spoke to him from the other side. 'What can you see?'

'No shopping trolleys.'

'That's an improvement.'

He heard the mother moving through the door, the disappearing voice of the girl. They were alone in the room. It wasn't silent. There was the constant hum of the heating as well as the sound of water being sprayed and striking the rubbery surface of some plant. In the ceiling two fans circled. From the pond came swishes and plops as fish moved and breathed, breaking the surface, then dropping sluggishly again. He remembered the frogs from his sister's farm. The pads too were in a sort of gentle, stultified motion. A few of the lilies had grown up from the pond's surface. These swayed and dipped on narrow stalks. The clammy air pressed against his neck. A shadowy, speckled, gelatinous shape cruised near the bottom of the pond, rolled, and was gone. It was like a log made of flesh. 'There are a couple of monsters down there,' he said, pointing into the water.

She walked around to stand next to him, reading aloud the identifying labels on the plants as she moved. They both looked into the pond.

'Whenever we meet,' she said, 'it's always exciting. First, there was Hamish, remember?'

'I do. I remember it all.'

'Seems like another time.'

'Does it?'

'Of course.'

'Why didn't you come?' he said. 'The night I was waiting for you on the farm.'

She didn't face him. She had put a finger to the surface of a broad leaf; her fingernail was submerged. 'Aren't you pleased, the way it worked out?'

'I don't know.'

'How could it have worked, if I'd come?'

'I have no idea. But I was waiting there anyway.'

'I had the children.'

'They were the obstacle then?'

'The obstacle? You make it sound like something that's fallen in your way and you can move it. Stuff you just shift.'

'You gave me some hope, I remember.'

'I'm sorry.'

'Can I ask whether you meant to come?'

'That's too hard, isn't it. I can't remember really.'

'Can't remember your feelings? I find that difficult to believe.'

'Oh, it's easily done. With Alec, for instance, I can't remember now what it was like, what I was like, to be with him.'

'You went in the ambulance today. You jumped in.'

'Yes. But there was hardly a stampede in that direction. I must ring Phil. He took it hard, I think.' She flattened her palm against the leaf. 'You got in the ambulance too.'

'It seemed too much like a tribute to him that he should have both Denise and you in there. I came to confuse the issue.'

She appeared to find the explanation helpful. 'Seems your forte.' She turned to face him at last. 'And what about now? Are you confusing the issue now?'

'Probably. I'm not sure.'

'You see? Neither of us knows.'

'I know I was there, waiting that night on the farm.'

'I know that too,' she said.

'Because you knew I'd be the foolish one, foolish enough to stand in the cold, hoping.'

'No.' She spoke calmly, drawing poise from his agitation. 'Because I came. That's how I know you were there. That night, I came.'

'What do you mean?'

'I walked as far as the house.'

'Catherine and Phil's?'

'I was early. I waited a while near the house.'

'You didn't. What are you trying to do, make me feel better?'

'Finally I saw you leave by the front door.'

'Which way did I go?'

'You went the long way. I guess to avoid the dogs.'

'What was I wearing?'

'Listen, Luke.' She took his arm. 'I was there. I came.'

Through in the gardens there was a burst of laughter. 'Okay,' he said.

She released his arm. 'You walked by the water tank. You were following the fence. You stumbled. You looked back at the house.'

He listened to her description in a sort of trance, following his own movements from that time as if watching an animation slowed down to the speed of its own composition. Each tiny motion had its own page, its own careful image, subtly different from its predecessor. 'You followed me.'

'I followed you. You didn't have a torch.'

'Forgotten it. I'd thought the moon would be enough.'

'I was well behind. It was quite dark. One time you turned back, I was sure you'd heard me.'

'Why didn't you call out?'

'I was going to.'

'I can't believe it.'

'I was going to.'

He took her lead and kept his voice low, with even a touch of amusement in it. 'Why didn't you?'

She shook her head, indicating that he shouldn't ask her again. After a moment she continued, having lost some but not all of her evenness. 'When you reached the shed, you disappeared.'

'I was sitting down.'

'It was then I realised I couldn't go through with it. To walk up and find you there, no. The shed brought to mind everything.'

'What?'

'Phil and Catherine, the night you'd arrived, Alec, the poor boy and the tractor, the children, everything. I couldn't.'

She was silent. Beneath the control and civility they were both, he thought, shattered. Through the vegetation and the murky window at the far end of the room, he saw the outlines of figures moving about the roses. The glass walls were whitewashed and peeling. Someone would enter soon. 'So you went back,' he said.

She dropped her head. 'How long did you wait for me?'

'Hours.'

'I'm sorry, Luke.'

'I thought I heard you coming a few times.'

'Sorry.'

The events of the day after—when he'd walked inside their empty house, looked into things, seen the presents under the tree, opened the freezer—these flashed briefly before him. Did she also know about that? Had she observed him from some hidden spot? No. She was up to her wrist now in the water, still pushing down on the lily pad. 'You know,' he said, 'they don't actually like you doing that.'

'Oh?'

'There's a sign, look. Everyone does it though.'

She lifted her hand out of the water, confused—not by the signs but by his sudden harshness. He took her wet hand and pulled her close against him. He began to kiss her. She returned it at once, twisting her mouth against his as if trying to find the best angle of attack, gripping his shoulders powerfully. He felt the hardness of her hip in his stomach; she was slightly off-balance. They performed a little stagger and he knocked the top of his thigh against the stone lip of the lily pond. It was painful and of course comic—the bungling gave a nice tone to what was happening, which was otherwise in deadly earnest. They remained locked together, though the kiss also contained their grinning. The tip of her nose pressed coolly into his cheek. With Baden, his own smaller frame provided the central focus; Baden, taller, heavier, had to make his own arrangements around Luke. Sheila had pushed herself easily up on her toes, so they were level. Evenly matched, he thought. She broke from him, placed her hands on his chest, tilted her head back—it was the quickest reverie or hesitation or moment of doubt—then she was kissing him as eagerly as before. 'Darling,' she murmured, 'I wanted to. I wanted to.'

'I know,' he said. 'I know, darling.' Once the amazing word had been said it took on ancient meaning, as if this was their word; they had invented it. The word contained their weird history.

She was apologising and kissing him at the same time, helping him swallow her words by smothering his mouth with hers as she spoke. She held his face in both hands—the most astonishing position, he'd always felt, to be held in, to submit to. Here is this face that means so much to me I must display it between my palms, present it to myself as a gift. He felt so vulnerable and trusting—moved to tears. She smiled, still holding him, and rubbed with her thumbs at the tears he was shedding helplessly, happily.

Perhaps they'd heard the door opening and decided not to care, or perhaps this figure had arrived through another door, one not used by the public: whatever the case, neither of them was surprised—and nor was the figure himself, who appeared to be involved in his work as normal—to discover they now shared the humidity-controlled room. Luke and Sheila disengaged. The gardener, his hair tied back in a ponytail, dressed almost military style with brown shirt and boots, was re-positioning a length of hose nearby, smoothing and shaping it with care. He was kneeling up among the plants. His absorption in his task gave them an odd sort of delight. They were watching, Luke thought, someone totally committed to his own life.

Hand in hand, they moved around the pond. The gardener nodded at them, without much interest, as they went. Then Sheila did an odd thing. Letting go of Luke's hand, she went over to the gardener and began asking him about the plants and the watering system. The gardener at first answered while still working at the hose. When it was clear Sheila had more questions, he stepped down onto the paved floor.

'Can these plants survive without this sort of attention? In Wellington, I mean.'

'In Wellington? No. A few might last a while but generally not a hope.'

The gardener was in his early fifties perhaps; the hair in his ponytail was greying. His knees were large and stained. Luke still hung back from the conversation.

'What sort of qualifications do you have to have, do you mind me asking?'

'To work here? I've got horticulture, a Masters.'

Sheila expressed her admiration for this. The gardener explained that some of the workers didn't have much in terms of official qualifications.

'But they're keen,' said Sheila.

'Sure. Some are.'

Luke stepped forward. 'Some are also fond of the weed.' There'd been a news item the previous year about dope in the gardens.

The gardener laughed. 'Bit of that.'

Sheila hadn't enjoyed this contribution. She started telling the gardener about her daughter, who lived in Kelburn, and who used the Gardens whenever she could. She mentioned Georgia was a chef. 'She comes and walks around and feels peaceful. After the stresses of the kitchen, it's a haven.'

The gardener addressed Luke. 'A while back we had a real problem with needles everywhere.'

'Needles?' said Sheila.

'The junkies had a few favourite spots.'

At this, Sheila turned away and moved smartly towards the door. It was left to Luke to thank the gardener and say goodbye.

They stood outside on the grass, unsure of what had to happen next. 'I'm starving,' said Luke.

'You missed lunch.' She spoke coldly.

'We could get something here.'

'I can't.' She was looking off in the direction of the path they'd taken to reach the rose garden. A tour bus was attempting a difficult manoeuvre among parked cars. Behind the little pinned-back curtains, faces were watching from the bus windows. They were too far off to see anything; nevertheless, their presence was inhibiting. He wanted to reach out to her again, take her in his arms. The bus wasn't the crucial factor of course. Something had shifted between them. She was trembling.

'Are you cold?' he said.

'What are you?' she said. Her voice was swift, pressured.

'What do you mean? I'm your . . . friend.'

'Friend? I don't think that covers it. Do we stay in touch? Do we have the same interests?'

'I'm someone who cares for you.'

'I have someone for that already. You have too.'

'What can I say? It's how I feel.'

She gave him a fierce look, then turned away again. Finally she seemed to relent. 'Yes,' she said, more tenderly this time. 'Yes, I believe that.' Her shoulders slumped in exhaustion.

'I'm someone who feels for you,' he said.

The voice was barely audible. However, it was not the crumpled sound of the person he'd met on the farm: 'But then what am I?' There was dejection but also a speculative quality, as if she might at some stage answer her own question.

He touched her lightly on the shoulder, inviting her to face him, which she did not. 'You're lovely.'

'Lovely?' She gave a short dispirited laugh.

The bus had finally made its turn. There was a hiss as its hydraulics were disengaged. It sat quietly.

'You're the one I want,' he said.

'But that's you again. That's what you are. You're the one who wants. Who am I?'

Again she'd made this sound somehow disconnected from him. He felt the need to re-admit himself into her thoughts. 'What do you want?' he said quietly. In his work it was a rule never to ask a question to which one didn't already know the answer. He feared the next sentence from her.

'At one point, when we found him in the cave, lying on the ground, I thought he might have died already. One part of me was hoping for that.'

The bus door opened. A woman wearing a visor and holding a clip-board stepped out.

'Here they come,' said Sheila. There was no comedy in the statement, rather a deep note of dread.

'Let's walk,' said Luke.

She looked at her watch. 'I must go. I've got to get back.' The first few steps she took away from him were skips, as if she needed to make good ground, to break completely. Once she was sure of her position, she settled into a brisk walk. The people from the bus were filing out onto the central path which led to the fountain. With her head down, she appeared to be on a collision course with them. At the last moment, she looked up and veered off across the grass, threading her way between the flower beds and disappearing down the hill.

Dead duck

He was late to the O'Keefe briefing, which failed to resemble the one he'd imagined in several respects. First, the Secretary, trapped somewhere due to travel problems, wasn't there, though the Deputy was. Second, Roger Angland was present.

'Hello,' said Roger. 'How's your brother doing?'

The question was baffling. At first he thought something

might have happened to Andy. He realised quickly they meant Alec. On arrival, Luke had spent a few minutes in the office toilets, trying to compose himself. The Deputy, sensing Luke's confusion and taking it for family grief, chimed in with noises of concern about this brother before Luke put them right. The message had become scrambled but he thought he should upgrade the relationship to account for his state: Alec became an old family friend.

'How old?' said Roger. 'Not in terms of friendship, I mean, but age.'

'Early sixties?' said Luke.

'Ah,' said Roger, nodding sagely.

One of the others—it was Charles Fuge, in his fifties now—patted Roger on the shoulder. 'Don't worry, Rog, we'll give you a great send-off when it's your turn.'

Fuge's job was to stick close to the Deputy Secretary—'minder' didn't quite cover it, since Fuge's ultimate loyalty seemed always moot. Strange to think of that concept now—it had been their topic years before, when Luke was a fresh recruit and Fuge had put him in his place. Since their time together at The Hague, Luke hadn't crossed swords with him, though he'd succeeded him in Moscow, where Fuge, as First Secretary, had certainly left an impression. He'd taken on the unofficial project of researching the art nouveau building in which the Embassy had been housed for over thirty years, Mindovsky's Mansion. Apparently this became Fuge's main job—a source of tension between him and his overworked colleagues. For some reason the research was never completed. He wanted the restoration budget to be massively increased—such work was ongoing, but since the plumbing and wiring overhaul in the seventies nothing major had been done. Fuge's particular interest was in the stained glass. The grand reception room was his focus. He was certain an image of Pan was buried there. (Several years later, when work was carried out and a book published on the Mansion, this proved correct. A reproduction showed an elegant figure, with a finely etched bare abdomen and shapely calves, wearing a purple cloak.) Before leaving, Fuge was said to have taken all his papers out to the stable and burned them. On the relief above the stable doors—a horse's head—scorch marks could still be seen.

Unprompted, certain other pieces of the Fuge story had come Luke's way. He'd been to school with the Minister. In his twenties, he'd taken to wearing a cape around town. After Moscow, Fuge had gone to Seoul, which had finally killed off the desire for postings. 'It must be acknowledged once and for all,' he'd said on his return, 'that the purpose of diplomacy is to prolong a crisis. I find myself more and more interested in solving the damn things.' He was no longer impressively gaunt, had put on a lot of weight, wore colourful ties and had tried to abandon all aspects of that earlier persona. Self-styled as 'Chas' now, which naturally his opponents refused to use, his beak still protruded, albeit from a fleshier face, and he was still periodically quite vicious. His punishing fondness for quotations also remained.

Roger smiled. 'Actually, Charles, the killer years are between forty-eight and fifty-eight. The nastier cancers and so on. Until I hit seventy-five, touch wood, I'm in for a pretty good run.'

Under the guise of providing proof of Roger's chances, but transparently an attempt to settle a long-running office dispute, Fuge asked how old his mother was. 'An amazing survivor.'

Roger accepted the verdict with a gracious nod but said nothing.

At this juncture the Deputy returned the meeting to its business. He spoke to Luke: 'Asked Mr Angland here to come in because we remembered he'd shared a spot with the Ambassador.' This had the ring of untruth. Though the Ministry was like a very old extended family, with a long and peculiar memory, there was generally a poor grasp of such basics as who had been where with whom and when. All of that tended to mix in the mind. The only person who would remember such details about a career was the owner of that career, and even then Luke had, among his seniors, come across strange blanks. Occasionally whole continents had drifted off. Roger himself would have done the reminding in this case. 'The opinion seems to be that O'Keefe's been shoulder-tapped.'

'Kneecapped,' murmured Fuge.

There was one other at the meeting. Sitting beside Fuge, though leaning as far away from him as possible without leaving her chair, was a woman in her late twenties, whom Luke might have met before, from the Prime Minister's Office. Fuge might have been trying to read her notes. She'd greeted Luke with a friendly smile, perhaps suggesting their connection was greater than he could recall, but they'd had no opportunity to speak. He didn't even know her name, because there seemed to be a policy in the room of ignoring her—an extraordinary act, since she was strikingly attractive. She kept pinning her red, wavy hair behind one ear, from where it would slip again.

'The beloved Opposition party has made him an offer he can't refuse.' The Deputy gestured towards the whiteboard where a number of circles within circles had been drawn, names filling them. The Deputy loved the whiteboard. 'Basically it's time for the sheriff to turn in his badge.'

'Though he can keep his spurs,' said Roger.

'Does he have spurs?' said Fuge.

'He loves his paraphernalia.'

The Deputy spoke over the laughter. 'The recall has been rescinded.'

'He won't come back?'

'The reprimand stays. The recall is a dead duck. We're advising that the Ambassador stew a little. He'll come clean soon. He must. That won't be easy for him or for his new party The PM is quite keen on the idea.'

'What idea?' said the woman from the PM's Office.

'The idea of the stewing of the dead duck,' said Fuge.

She showed signs of not enjoying all this but was distracted at that moment by some tedious request for information from the Deputy, which forced her to look through her papers. No, she would have to get back to him on that. The Deputy stroked his temples and closed his eyes—usually his signal that it was time for everyone to leave his office. He opened them again, and did, in fact, look a little surprised to find them all there still. The headache may even have been real. He stood and moved to the window. 'You say this friend is all right?'

It took a few moments before Luke realised this was addressed in his direction. 'He is.'

'Good, I'm glad.' The Deputy walked over to the whiteboard, gave it a quick satisfied inspection, then pressed the button to copy it all. He tore the sheet off. 'Good,' he said to no one in particular.

After the briefing, Roger caught up with Luke. 'All right?'

'Yes.'

'Look awful.'

'I always look like this on Sundays.' He studied Roger. 'You came in on a Sunday. Why's that? And please don't tell me they called you.'

'Kerry was a very interesting man. I find myself interested still.'

'What did he do to make himself interesting?'

'I don't know. He seems to be just one of those people. You keep an eye on them, and then it crosses that line and it seems they're following you. Neither of you making a special effort. Anyway, you're linked. Do you know the sort? Perhaps you're too young to have these figures in your life.'

The obvious analogy was too painful to consider. 'The links began with the posting?'

'Oh Christ, before that. He was two years ahead of me at school! Isn't that Charles Fuge a shithead?'

Luke said he agreed.

'He was baiting the girl before you arrived.'

'Who was that girl?'

'She is the beauty, Maude Weenink. You might know her father, the eminent Rick.'

'Justice Weenink.'

'The same. When Miles Pearson was diagnosed, you know

what Fuge said to everyone? The bad news is they discovered prostate cancer. The good news is they found his dick.'

'A cruel streak.' He was still considering the connections. Rick Weenink had been on the team at The Hague, and Maude, just out of school, the girl everyone wanted. Her father had been the one in tears in the side room, who'd spoken of the emotionalism of court work. Fuge had used a quotation about redheads. It had come from Mark Twain—as a number of Fuge's did. (It had been Luke's weakness to always track down the source of a quotation.) Why had Fuge gone on the attack with this girl? 'The purpose of diplomacy is to prolong a crisis,' said Luke. 'Who said that?'

'I've heard it before,' said Roger.

'Yes, but can you remember who said it?'

'No. Not one of Fuge's, is it?'

'He used it when he came back from Seoul.'

'Something he lacks, isn't it? A soul.'

'So you and O'Keefe have kept in touch?'

'Not really. From time to time. When he was back, you know. He was okay to you, wasn't he, at the Mission? A dullard but an interesting one, I think. At least for me, maybe because he was my year, I find him worth following.' They'd begun to walk towards the lifts. 'Bugger about your friend.'

Should he tell Roger the true story of Alec? It would take too long. 'Yes, but he's going to be okay.' The lift arrived. Luke had left some things at his desk which he needed to collect. He held the doors for Roger, who got in.

Roger was one of the few people he'd told about his first time in New York, the murder. It had never been a secret and if anyone asked there was a version available that provided basic facts. After a year or so, no one asked anyway. The story took its obscure place somewhere in the Ministry's erratic collective memory. But four or five years ago, Luke had told Roger Angland, one of the stalled figures whose working life was fixed in parallel connection to the 'glamorous' part of the job, who watched the progression of bright and not-so-bright people come and go—and come and go. At some point he might have thought Roger lived off such crumbs, but this wasn't why he'd relived his own crisis for him. He'd tried to be as full as possible in the telling. It had come about when Roger had mentioned Kerry O'Keefe, who. Their assessments showed a good deal of fellow feeling. Neither could quite credit the O'Keefe career. On its reach, Roger was naturally more knowledgeable than Luke. Of course it was no more necessary to show initiative or even efficiency to advance oneself in Foreign Affairs than in any other line of work. The choosing of the best and brightest at age twenty-two failed to guarantee long-term excellence. Casualties abounded. By thirty-two many recruits had matured sufficiently to question their own life choices. People got out. Ran screaming from, as Roger said. Often leaving others less able to man the pumps. They'd talked about Kerry's interest in military matters—the classic sign, Roger offered, of an arrested development. Kerry might have been the glue between them, but Luke had also been drawn to speak because of a closeness he felt to Roger. He liked him, and felt he was liked. Naturally there was always the possibility he was committing an error in being so free. Roger was viewed as unreliable by most. No doubt he'd heard many confessions. But nothing had happened by way of damage or repercussion. The adventure with Sheila was perhaps something Roger would not only enjoy but possibly throw light on. 'He told you, didn't he? O'Keefe rang you.'

Roger was steel. 'I don't know what you're talking about.'

'He was asking your advice, I bet. He wanted guidance. And the reason you came in today was to make sure you got the right result for him, wasn't it? You came to help him.'

Roger stood in the lift; he was pressing the button. Luke had his arm over the door.

'He called his old friend. I wonder what you said?'

'The Nats are not people I'd like to spend time with. But Kerry's lonely now his wife's gone. He gave her half, after just three years of being together. He spoke of it in months, thirty-six months, nothing. Half of everything. That didn't seem fair. He said he'd asked her what she wanted with one testicle.' Roger pressed the button again. 'Can I go now, please? It's fucking Sunday. Poor old Kerry. But you know mostly he was shocked that she didn't want him any more. That's a massive blow. Never underestimate the power of rejection, even if it comes from someone you don't particularly care for.'

Luke released the door on Roger, who waved before he went down.

Someone called for the lift to be held. Luke turned to see Maude Weenink hurrying down the corridor, looking at her mobile phone. 'Sorry,' he said. He introduced himself. They shook hands.

'What do you think is going on with O'Keefe?' she said.

'I don't know.'

For a brief moment she looked close to tears. She pressed the button for the lift. 'I'm sorry about your friend.'

He thanked her, feeling again the falseness of his position. 'How long have you worked in the PM's Office?'

'Two weeks.' She'd spoken challengingly; that now disappeared. 'Does it show?'

'Not at all.'

'I'm not sure why I was even sent in for this. On my way here I thought it was a sort of promotion. A vote of confidence. Gosh, they think I can handle this, and on my own too. You know what I think now? That it's a rather unimportant matter. They rang me just before I went into the meeting to tell me what was happening, O'Keefe's defection and everything. I was literally about to enter the room and I got my briefing. I didn't sleep last night. I'd worked all day on it.'

He was naturally sympathetic to her plight—it had been more or less his own—and touched by her honesty. 'Me too.'

'Really?' The lift had arrived. She hadn't got in it yet.

'I was with your father at The Hague,' he said. This statement hardly registered with her. She nodded absently. As Justice Weenink's daughter she was no doubt insulated from all such claims. There might have even been a kind of deafness around the words 'your father'. She was also still absorbed in O'Keefe. Maude was beautiful, in a vaguely Spanish way, if the hair could be excused, with large, intelligent eyes—the same as her father's—a full mouth. On her neck she carried a scar, which her fingers had gone to at various times in the meeting. 'Years ago, over the French testing.'

'Rick was always getting approaches.'

For a moment he thought she meant the French. Her use of her father's first name caught him by surprise. She was thinking, of course, of the appeal of O'Keefe in the political sphere. 'Do you think your father was tempted?'

'I don't know. Flattered, I'd say. Everyone wanted him. He found that funny, that no one could guess his possible affiliations, right, left, centre. It went on over years.'

'They say O'Keefe is lonely. They got him at the right time.'

'We know his wife, ex-wife, a bit. She worked for Rick. A lovely person but you wouldn't want to be on her wrong side.' She stepped into the lift. 'When were you at The Hague?'

He told her the year, a one-sentence account of the case, and then the doors closed. He had a sudden sharp memory that Maude had done something disappointing to her father back then, or shortly after. He wasn't sure he'd ever known the details. Not a scandal, more like a diversion. Whatever it was, she appeared completely rehabilitated now. Her slight inexperience perhaps suggested a later start to her public service career than might have been the case if she'd gone straight from university. He would have to ask Roger.

A chef's hat

Fog covered the windless city, closing the airport, hiding whole hillsides. On the harbour the fog sank almost to water level, letting the tops of buildings show. Every conversation began with this subject. The fog was an unexpected visitor and got talked about in these terms. When was it leaving? Why had it come? Couldn't it take a hint? Ships on the harbour sounded their horns. When the fog failed to lift by midday, despite the sunshine, there was an exciting sense of existing within a sealed environment, at once familiar and new. Catherine and Phil met Luke for lunch at a place near his work. They'd been walking around the Mt Victoria lookout. 'Heads in the clouds,' said Catherine happily. They were all going to Georgia's graduation ceremony that night. They gave Luke his invitation. He didn't look at it. He had to decline, he said. He was just too busy. They talked for a while about Ambassador O'Keefe and about his son, whom they'd known years back. Luke glanced down at the invitation, a nicely printed card with a chef's hat elegantly embossed in gold at the top. David Lange was set down as the guest speaker. Immediately he regretted giving his answer but felt a switch now on this basis would seem opportunistic. He let the conversation drift off onto other topics. Alec was apparently back to normal.

'Gave us all a scare,' said Phil.

'Lucky you were there,' said Catherine. 'I had no idea our diplomats were so well prepared. How clever of you. Clever, clever, clever!'

'With Alec, there's never a dull moment,' said Luke.

'I'm afraid I wasn't much use,' said Phil.

'Claustrophobia!' said Catherine. 'Very odd. Sheila never said a word.'

Luke repeated the story he'd heard about Alec having to be pulled by his legs from under the roof. Phil grinned but gave the impression of not really believing it.

Catherine too grew pedantic. 'Who was on the other leg? Pip, did you say?'

'Yes.'

There was talk about when this might have taken place and how old Pip would have to have been. It was always good not to admit having heard news of people's friends before they had.

'Pull the other one,' said Phil, without the conviction that he was deploying the phrase correctly. He hadn't fully recovered from the previous day. Obviously he was still in the city too. The prospect of leaving the next morning might have lifted his spirits but the fog worried him. He'd already asked Luke what the pattern was—whether these conditions meant tomorrow would be clear. Luke replied that he didn't know, that this wasn't a pattern as far as he was aware but a fairly unusual event. Phil took this news personally. He sat hunched over his food.

Luke asked about Katie and her hostel—improvements here abounded. She had managed to change rooms, to the quieter side. And in the neighbouring rooms she'd found a couple of girls who seemed likely to become great buddies. There was genuine relief on the part of her parents, while still the outline of former anxieties. Luke spoke enthusiastically of her deeds at the rock-climbing place, both in climbing and in helping Georgia down from the wall. He saw the pleasure they took in hearing all this again.

Towards the end of the lunch Luke tapped the invitation. 'Perhaps I can come,' he said. 'I would like to.'

'Lange will be there,' said Phil.

'Will he? Lange?' he said. He inspected the card.

'He's lost so much weight,' said Catherine.

'He's unwell.'

'Then Georgia's food will help!' said Phil.

'The finger food will all be done by the class,' said Catherine. 'Alec's already said that he's considering it dinner.'

Phil laughed encouragingly, keen to see this Alec reinstated.

'We heard you were at the Gardens yesterday, after the hospital,' said Catherine.

She seemed not to be fishing. However, for a moment he tried to think who might have supplied this information. He thought back to David Tanner in the public library. Had someone from the tour bus identified them? Someone up for the weekend, spying Sheila among the flower beds.

'Sheila said the roses were stunning,' said Catherine.

'They are,' he said.

'We should go there,' Catherine said to Phil.

'Probably running out of time, hon. I'm supposed to be going with Alec to the War Memorial. Maybe we should cancel that. Alec was still dead keen on it this morning when we talked, but maybe it's too soon, after yesterday. I don't think I could persuade him though.' Phil turned to Luke, helpless. 'So much to do. No wonder I start to feel funny. We haven't stopped since we got here. Missing Parliament is a shame. Poorly timed by us.'

'Next time,' said Luke.

'In another fifteen years,' said Catherine. 'Once he's recovered from this trip.'

'With Katie up here there's more sense to a trip,' said Phil.

'Not sure if Katie would be that keen,' said Catherine.

Phil had a worried look on his face. 'I wonder how I'm going to get there.'

'Where?' said Catherine.

'The War Memorial.' He checked his watch. 'Are there buses?'

'I can drive you,' said Luke.

They both protested about this but were happy when Luke overruled them. He had plenty of time owing him at work. The Secretary was still out of town, unable to fly in, and Luke had his car since he was driving to the airport to pick up Baden later on. This of course was also in doubt because of the fog. There was likely to be no substantial wind for another twelve hours at least.

'How can you come to the graduation if Baden's arriving back tonight?' said Catherine.

'He'll be in no condition when he comes in,' said Luke. 'I'll drop him at his place, put him to bed.'

'I don't want to be a killjoy, but I think his chances of getting in are pretty slim.'

Luke felt a pang of guilt upon hearing this and experiencing a sort of relief. Another 'free' day, he thought, would be useful. He'd tried without luck to reach Sheila at their hotel. She and

Joe had apparently gone biking, hiring one bike. They'd taken the ferry across to Eastbourne. That would be an atmospheric ride across the harbour, with Matiu Somes Island a blur, the lights of the city vanishing behind them. He sensed a missed opportunity of vast proportions. He saw Joe coddling the bike, wiping the dew from the seat for Sheila.

Alec had left Denise in Kirkcaldie's, where he said she was living the life. 'Their stamina for shopping is a wondrous thing.' From the back of the car he asked whether anyone had some Panadol. Luke produced some from the glovebox.

Phil took it as bad sign. 'How are you feeling?'

'I'm in no mortal danger, Philip. Yesterday I'd missed breakfast. I didn't make that mistake today.' He swallowed the Panadol. There was no mention of the claustrophobia or the sweating.

Luke offered to stop to buy Alec something to wash down the pills, but Alec said he was fine. They'd stood in the department store for so long and in proximity to some bird cages—though he hadn't seen the birds—and the noise of caged birds had always got to him, he told them. 'The infernal chirping. Is there anything worse? My headache is almost gone anyway. Denise claimed to find the birdsong, which is what it was to her, a very happy sound. I suppose I also had red wine at the lunch yesterday. A mistake.'

'I can't drink much of it myself,' said Phil.

'It was a great lunch though,' said Alec. 'Our two girls in top form in their new lives. Thank you for coming, both of you.'

'Wouldn't have missed it,' said Phil.

'Nor me,' said Luke.

'And as for the chauffeuring, Luke, I must say you've gone over and beyond your duty here in taking us two old codgers to see a war memorial. I was willing to pay for a taxi even if Phil was scared of the expense. It was my treat after yesterday's little escapade.'

'The great thing about hosting visitors to your own place,'

said Phil, 'is that it makes you do the things you never do. Is that right, Luke?'

'That's right,' said Luke.

'The strange thing in this case, I mean of today,' said Alec, 'is that it's hardly the same place. This fog is something. I woke up this morning and wondered where I was.'

'Quite incredible,' said Phil. 'What do you think our chances are of flying out tomorrow?'

'I'm not a local. But it's not flash, is it?'

'I'm supposed to get my rams tomorrow,' said Phil.

The two men talked farming until they pulled into the car park beside what were now university buildings. 'The old museum,' said Luke.

'I remember this,' said Phil. 'We came on a school trip.'

'That would have been a big trip, Philip,' said Alec.

'Overnight ferry.'

'Yes,' said Alec. 'What a trip.'

They stood on the steps, looking up at the inscription in stone above the entrance which included the phrase 'built by the people'. 'I know about progress,' said Alec, 'but this is impressive, isn't it? Still bloody impressive.' Of course he meant Te Papa. Some students walked out from the doors and sat down on the steps, stretching out, their bags around them. They weren't especially objectionable but Alec was clearly put out by these figures. He stared at them, made a disapproving noise. Phil, ever alert to his friend's moods, spoke consolingly: 'At least they didn't tear it all down.' He turned to face the Carillon, the tower which formed part of the War Memorial.

'No,' said Alec, slowly following Phil's lead and abandoning the students, who'd remained unaware that they were part of this grand historical survey.

They walked down the stone steps to the Memorial. Luke had been a few times with foreign dignitaries. He'd been responsible for coordinating several wreaths. No one in his family had been in the services, as far as he knew. 'Did your relatives fight?' he asked Phil.

'An uncle was in Egypt, I think. My father was just too young. Alec's father went, didn't he, Alec?' Alec was a few steps ahead of them, within easy hearing distance. He chose, however, not to respond. Phil continued on his behalf. 'The Solomons mainly, I think.' Another ship's horn sounded, like a cow. He looked out over the city. 'That fog isn't moving, is it.'

By the Tomb of the Unknown Soldier, a middle-aged woman was walking her dog. She had it on a leash and she carried a small plastic bag bearing, it seemed by its shape, evidence of recent activity. The dog, a terrier, was sniffing at the Tomb and manoeuvring itself threateningly, while the woman assumed that pose, often seen in such scenarios, of complete innocence. Alec was taking it all in. It was a moment of pure provocation for him, a stark arrangement of facts, none of which Alec could stand. To Alec's intolerance of domestic dogs could be added his equally dismal view of their owners; that this pair had been brought into contact with such a space seemed almost malicious on the part of the world. He wouldn't have had to be thinking of his father, his war service, for this affront to work on him. That he'd been primed by Phil's casual mention of the Solomons, and also by the hapless appearance of the students on the steps of the old museum, only underlined the woman and dog's predicament. Luke feared for them both. Alec and Phil had stopped. It seemed clearly the moment before hostilities. Maybe even Joe, the vet, was involved.

Alec stepped towards the dog, bending down and holding out his hand. It approached at once. For a moment it seemed possible that Alec would pick up the dog and snap its neck. Instead he allowed the dog to smell his fingers, and then he was rubbing it under the chin. 'Good boy,' he said. He stood up and spoke to the woman. 'Nice day.'

'Foggy,' said the woman. In possession of the bag, she didn't want to chat. She gave a tug on the leash and walked off through the trees.

Phil and Luke came forward. 'Hardly a place for dogs,' said Phil.

'Oh well,' said Alec, 'we're in the city now.'

Luke somehow felt accused. He'd almost been responsible for a dog pissing on the Tomb of the Unknown Soldier. 'I don't think they should let dogs up here,' he said.

Alec was walking around the Tomb, silently reading the text cut into the marble. 'It's a karanga,' said Luke. He thought the word might enrage Alec, but Alec simply nodded and continued to follow it—a phrase in Maori was followed by its English translation. There was something textual that had bothered Luke. At one point the break in the English version seemed sloppy, creating an unwanted ambiguity: the line read 'you were away sorrow', followed by some Maori, then the line was picked up: 'aches into me'. The 'sorrow' should surely have been carried forward. He was about to raise it when Alec took a couple of steps back and exhaled loudly. It had the sound of someone catching his breath. Phil, concerned, shot him a look.

'Certainly a powerful statement,' said Alec. He was visibly affected.

The bronze was a dull, lead-grey colour, beaten or burnished in places to a dark rust. It evoked the metal of warfare: shell-casings but also belts and buttons, pressed flat into this final heavy lid.

'It's a beauty, isn't it,' said Phil. He wandered over to a plaque and read aloud the statistic. Nine thousand lost, without their identities determined or bodies recovered. 'Out of thirty thousand who died, across all the wars of the last century. Nine thousand is a lot. I had no idea it was that high.'

Alec was silent, looking at the Tomb. Perhaps his scare yesterday in the cave was part of this moment.

Luke went inside the Memorial. 'Let all know this is holy ground' began the inscription at the entrance. It was cool and chapel-like, with a high ceiling and a series of small alcoves dedicated to each of the services. Each alcove had a brass plaque, lit by two deco-style brass lamps, and above it the flag or ensign of the service. The focus of the space was a kind of altar on which stood a large bronze statue of a woman with two children.

Alec was at Luke's side. He pointed to the first alcove, the Royal New Zealand Air Force. 'There,' he said. 'No. 4 Servicing Unit, RNZAF.' They approached the plaque together.

'Your father?' said Luke.

'Equipment officer, worked with No. 15 Squadron.' He pointed to where the name of the squadron appeared on the plaque. 'Island called Ondonga, New Georgia. When the Japs flew over from Bougainville the first time to say hello, they hadn't finished the foxholes. That was a wee bit uncomfortable.'

Phil was standing with them now. 'He talked about this did he, your dad?'

'You piece it together,' said Alec. 'I tell you one thing, he hated if you complained about the rain. On the island it rained every day. It was a quagmire apparently, mud everywhere. Boy, he got wild if you said a word about it being wet.'

'Is that right?' Phil laughed, rather more from the excitement, Luke thought, at hearing Alec talk of his father than from the actual material.

'Plus he could never face another pear, tinned or real.'

'Ah, that was their diet, I suppose.'

Alec put his finger to the paper poppy someone had stuck into the small crown at the top of the plaque. He seemed unhappy with it and quickly checked along the wall to see whether the next plaque was decorated in this way: it wasn't. He plucked the poppy out and shoved it in his pocket. 'Bit scruffy,' he mumbled.

They walked slowly along the wall, pausing to read each plaque. Phil tried to remember which part of the armed forces his uncle had been in but couldn't decide between Infantry and Navy. He recalled there'd been a good deal about boats in the stories that had come his way but these might only have been connected with transportation. 'Bit useless not to remember properly,' he said. Alec stepped up onto the raised platform where the statue stood, seemingly having missed it or perhaps ignoring it. He was studying the Roll of Honour book, a leather-bound volume behind glass, opened to a page of names. He stayed there for some time while Luke and Phil looked at the sculpture of the woman and her two children. Carved into stone above the sculpture was a verse which Phil began to read aloud: 'If I climb up into heaven thou art there—If I make my bed in hell behold thou art there also. Gosh, don't quite follow that.'

'Yes, I'm not sure where that's from,' said Luke.

'If I make my bed in hell. That's pretty full-on.' Phil nodded towards the bronze trio. 'Where do you think they made their bed?'

At first glance the sculpture was heroic. The shape of the female head, turned to one side in sadness but also forbearance; the short hair, the strong brow and the wide-apart stance—all this suggested the fortitude and sacrifice which were part of the text at the entrance mentioning the holy ground. Up closer, other things came into view. Notably the children: the girl's straining calves as she reached up to her mother, wanting perhaps to be carried; the stoicism of the girl's older brother who looked off into the distance but whose hand had caught his mother's hand at his shoulder, so that he was under her protection, under her wing. He was in fact in a better position than the girl whose needs had not been met and whose pose, in effect, stood in for the unexpressed drama, or trauma, of the mother. The mother could not be carried by anyone, could not be consoled by anyone. Her averted gaze—she couldn't look at either of her children—was suddenly less heroic and more human, or humanly heroic perhaps. Naturally, the absent figure should have dominated the composition. The soldier, the father, the husband, was the only person who, by his return, could lift things. For Luke, however, this imagined act of completion was not uppermost. The three figures present were the ones who mattered. Their lives were fully in front of the viewer. Despite the plaques naming the squadrons and units, despite even perhaps the Honour book naming the men, it was this group—bodied and touchable—who gave the room its great pathos. He'd always thought it a courageous act, to place them at the centre of the Memorial. Had 1964, when the Memorial was opened, been an enlightened time?

Alec joined them in front of the sculpture. 'Who have we got here?'

'The mother and her little ones,' said Phil.

Alec was making a show of looking for the identifying label; there was none. 'Yeah, but who?'

'They represent all the mothers and their children,' said Phil.

'Oh. A representative woman.' Alec peered. He was intent on the satire. He might just as well have been back at Te Papa, trying to rile the host. 'She's a tall old thing, isn't she.'

'I like the little girl,' said Luke. He began to say something about the statue.

Alec turned away. 'You should look at the Roll of Honour up there. That's men who died. You could be a general or a private, made no difference.'

'Except if you were a general you probably would have had a better chance of making it,' said Phil.

It was insubordination. Alec bristled. 'We don't know that. Step up and have a look at the page, Phil. Starts with a general and ends with a private. Those are men who gave their all.'

Phil, for once, stood his ground. 'Yes, Alec, and these are the women and the children who also gave their all.'

Alec saw his new approach. He smirked. 'Ah, well, yes, some of them carried on.'

'What?'

'Not all of them. Some of them of course had a fine old time, didn't they?' He gestured towards the statue. 'Who's to know if she wasn't carrying on?'

Phil shook his head, disbelieving, and walked up to the Roll of Honour display. Luke took the excuse of looking for a toilet to get away from Alec.

Phil was still not fully recovered when they walked back to the car. He gave Alec a few monosyllabic replies—hardly more than grunts—when asked in a transparently peacemaking way by Alec about Catherine's plans. Alec, unbroken, had looked across the road where it was possible to see into some newish apartments. He'd then launched into a tiresome and largely one-sided conversation about inner-city living. 'Better than television,' he said. 'Look, all the channels!' A couple was reading the paper in their lounge. Through another glass wall they saw a towel rack where three bras were hanging. In yet another window a man was brushing his teeth. Phil remained silent. 'If I climb up into heaven thou art there,' said Alec, laughing and sweeping his arm in the direction of the apartments. 'If I make my bed in hell, behold thou art there also.'

Phil tramped on, head down. The fog over the southern hills seemed lighter. The shapes of roofs could be discerned. Luke made a call on his mobile to the airline but couldn't get through. Baden was only two hours away. Maybe he would be able to land after all.

In the car, aware now that he might have gone too far with Phil, Alec assumed again some seriousness. He talked about Georgia's graduation, and he thanked Phil for Katie's actions at the rock-climbing.

'Nothing to do with me,' said Phil. 'Don't know why you're thanking me.'

'She's your daughter and a great credit to all involved,' said Alec.

'Katie's her own person. I didn't ask her to do what she did.'

'Didn't have to,' said Alec. 'That's my point.'

'Probably the person to thank anyway is Luke here, and not just for driving us up here either. He saved your bacon yesterday and I wouldn't have been any use whatsoever.'

'Of course, yes.'

'There was no one else with the knowledge and the presence of mind to act like Luke did, unless maybe Joe.'

'He saved me from Joe, the vet,' said Alec.

'He saved you,' said Phil.

'Of course he did, I won't forget it.'

'Phil,' said Luke, 'Alec has already thanked me.'

'Not sufficiently,' said Alec. 'Always in your debt.'

'Anybody could have done it,' said Luke.

'No, no,' said Alec. 'Phil is right. Absolutely. Bloody stupid of me too, of course. Really clever.'

They were silent for a time, then Phil—deciding it was time, or simply unable to sustain such a rare mood for him—re-emerged from his fully justified sulk. He suggested that the three of them should find a nice pub, have a drink. Alec said it was a wonderful idea. Luke also accepted. There wasn't much point in going back to work again. He took them to Courtenay Place where Alec and Phil chose a place—Luke himself never went there; at night it was all vomiting secretaries and bank tellers wearing their ties on their heads. Or was that out of date? Whatever the population, the vomit was a constant.

They were upstairs in a corner booth, overlooking the street. Luke and Phil faced Alec, who'd bought the first round.

'We should call the girls, call Catherine and Denise. Get them along,' said Phil.

'Of course. Great idea,' said Alec. He began to search for his phone, patting his pockets. 'I was surprised to see that dog up there today.'

Phil put down his pint and spoke to Luke. 'You didn't think they should be allowed up there. You said that. I agree.'

'I thought you showed great restraint, Alec,' said Luke.

'If it had lifted its leg, I was ready to swing the mutt far out into the trees.' The three men laughed and drank. 'You heard the story of course of Denise's pets, didn't you.'

'No,' said Phil.

'You didn't? Oh, it's not worth telling really then, not with Luke. What's happening with that poor bloke of yours, O'Keefe?'

'I'd rather hear about Denise's pets,' said Luke.

'The knives are out, aren't they, and for what? The trouble is we don't want to hear the truth.'

'What rubbish, Alec,' said Phil, grinning. 'Did you see the things O'Keefe said? He's an embarrassment to the country.'

'To the country? There's no such thing. No one believes in the idea any more, Phil.'

'For a minute there I thought I was back at work. Can we please hear your story?' said Luke.

'Our apologies,' said Alec. 'It's just we get carried away when we come to the big city. Right, Phil?'

'Right. We sniff the air here and we change.'

Alec grinned. 'Taking my cue from your sniffing, then, this all happened a few months back, with Denise, who had a cat and a dog.'

'Luke has a cat,' said Phil.

'As did Denise. And a dog. You remember it, Phil? The time you visited. The little thing that ran round her place. Oh, Christ.'

'What happened?' said Phil.

'We were both going to be gone. Me on my trip—to America, I think. Denise was off to Australia to see her mother. So, you know, I had the little beggar in its . . . box.'

'Cat box,' said Luke.

'Cat box. You've dealt with this too.' Alec raised his pint. 'Okay. I got the little beggar in the box. Took a piece out of me too.' He inspected his hand. 'I thought I'd do the double act, didn't I? Be clever. Didn't tell Denise. Take the dog too, see.'

'The dog and the cat,' said Phil.

'They were both out the same way. The cattery, the dogger . . . the pound. Dog pound, is that where they go? So in with the cat, in the box, in the back. You know in Denise's little car, it's a hatch, there's a cover. Good as tits on a bull, but the cat is under the cover. I had my truck in the garage.'

'Where's the dog?' said Luke.

Alec drank some beer. 'See, this is the fellow with a cat.'

'In with you, is it?' said Phil. 'In the car.'

'In with me. You remember, it was a little bloody dish-rag of a thing.'

'It was a small dog, Alec, a pedigree, as I remember. Denise talked about it to us.'

'Oh, that dog probably cost more than the car.'

'Off you go in the car then.'

'Off we go. Off to the cattery.' Alec drank again. It wasn't the beer he was relishing. 'You wouldn't believe it. The bloody cat.'

'Trying to get out?' said Phil.

'I turn around, the bloody cat sticks its head out the box. Sticks its head out the box, up goes the cover.'

'What about the dog?' said Luke.

Alec smiled at Luke. 'You're ahead of me again. The bloody dog. One look at this bloody cat, they hate each other. One look. Out jumps the cat.'

'Out of the box!' said Phil.

'Trying to make a run for it.'

'You're still driving, Alec, at this stage?' said Phil.

'I'm driving. Oh, I'm going a hundred, way out past Darfield. I'm overtaking a truck. With two animals. The bloody dog thinks it's Christmas. With two animals. Going mad.'

'What'd you do?' said Phil.

'Wait on.' Alec looked out the window, not, it seemed, for dramatic effect this time. He was puzzled by something. 'What was it I had to do just before? I'd lost something.'

'You were going to phone Denise and Catherine,' said Luke.

'Is it too late? I suppose we could have another round.'

Alec's confusion contained an echo of what had struck the previous day. For Phil it was a question of keeping him on track with a command. 'Finish the story first,' he said. 'What did you do?'

'Finally, I get over into the far lane, where I can slow down. Did I say the cat tried to take cover down beside my seat? With the dog going crazy. Me, the great cat protector. I turned off a side road and stopped. I opened my door. The cat takes one look at freedom and bolts. Absolutely bolted. Well. The dog. He thinks that's a good game, doesn't he. Chase the Cat. I swear, I have never seen that dog move so fast. It's legs are—they're not proper legs as such, are they? I have never seen an animal so low to the ground make such good time. Like a rabbit or something. The pair were dust, they were gone.'

'You lost them. Did you call?'

'Did I call? I did everything I could.'

'Did you run after them?'

'I ran and ran and ran.'

'You lost them.'

'I lost the cat. No way a bloody cat is going, despite the song, to "come back".'

'What about the dog?' said Luke.

Alec shook his head. 'That was a long drive home, I tell you.'

'What did Denise say when you got home?' said Phil.

'I never told her about the dog. I told her about the cat. She knew I was taking the cat, but she didn't know I was taking them both out that day.'

'Why didn't you tell her? You mean you went home and when she was saying, "Here boy, here boy", you sat there?'

'Of course I went out looking for it then.'

'For the dog?'

'Denise was very upset, Philip. Very upset.'

'You went out looking round the neighbourhood for the dog you'd lost out by Darfield, thirty kilometres away?'

'I put in a good couple of hours.'

'You're amazing. That dog was miles and miles away, wasn't he?'

'The dog was dead, Phil. Back where I'd been trying to chase down the cat, I came round a corner and the dog was lying on the road. Knocked down by a car.'

'Fuck,' said Phil. 'And you left it there.'

'I picked it up. I'm not so heartless, no matter what you believe. I picked it up in my jacket. It would have fitted in a bigger pocket. I wrapped it in my jacket. I brought it home in the box.'

'In the cat box,' said Luke.

'It fitted easily. I walked back to the house after two hours' searching. I went into the garage. I opened the cupboard where I'd put the box. I took it out. I opened the box, picked up the dish-rag, the dog, the precious dog, and I went inside.'

"'I found him,'" said Phil.

"'I found him, dear. Look what's happened, something awful's happened.'"

Phil stood up suddenly. He looked down at the table. The glasses were empty. It wasn't clear whether he was ready to walk out on Alec or get another round. The question as to whether he should find his friend truly appalling or rather wonderful was being played out across his features. His mouth was set tight. He rested on his fists against the table, quivering.

'Denise just cried for a long, long time. I had a few . . . I had some tears myself was the strange thing.' Alec turned abruptly to the wall and looked down. Anyone looking across the bar might have suspected he'd dropped something. It wasn't immediately apparent even from up close what was happening. Alec had moved his forearm across his eyes.

Phil sat down. 'All right now,' he murmured. 'Okay now.'

Alec coughed loudly and shook his head, trying to clear it.

'Tough position to be in,' said Phil.

'My mistake was to take them both,' said Alec. He coughed again to find his voice.

Luke offered to buy another round. When he came back the men were talking about people he didn't know. There was nothing in their manner to indicate what had just happened. Alec seemed completely his old self, as did Phil, cheerier perhaps than he'd yet been on the weekend. The beer had helped.

'Do you know he's a bigger jetsetter than you?' said Phil. 'Off to America again soon, is that right, Alec?'

Luke asked where he was going exactly. Alec said the names of the cities, which took in both coasts. 'I was in New York last time, at a big conference. We went on a tour of the United Nations building.'

'That was his old place,' said Phil, nudging Luke.

'She's a big set-up all right. They weren't in session but it was a good opportunity. Of course I remembered what happened when you were there, Luke. It pays to keep your wits about you.' Alec touched his pint glass but didn't pick it up. Luke wasn't sure whether he was being got at again. 'We went out for a meal, a few of us, one night. Two fellows from Norway, I think, or Finland perhaps, came down from the hotel wearing tennis shoes and nylon jackets, as if they were off for a run or something. They couldn't believe us, thought we were off our rockers. See, the rest of us had gone to a bit of trouble with dress shoes and leather jackets. We were only going to be there that evening. They begged us to go up and change. They were convinced we were going to be mugged because of it.'

There was the sound of a mobile phone ringing. Both Alec and Luke touched their pockets. 'And did anything happen?' said Phil.

'Of course not,' said Alec. 'But maybe we were lucky. Just as Luke here wasn't.'

'Statistically, I read somewhere, the city is safer now,' said Phil.

'Apart from the odd terrorist attack,' said Alec. 'Is that you, Phil?'

Phil looked surprised. 'Me? My God, it could be. I'd forgotten I had ours. Catherine gave it to me this morning.' He pulled the phone out and looked at it. 'Haven't got my glasses.'

Luke took the phone from him, pushed the talk button and passed it back.

'See?' said Alec. 'Even Phil. We're all failing.'

Phil talked to Catherine on the phone before handing it to Luke who turned it off. 'We should get going,' said Phil.

'He's received his orders,' said Alec. 'Company to move at once.'

'It was Denise who wanted us back, apparently,' said Phil.

'Her job is organisation.'

'She was worried about you.'

'What nonsense.'

'Wants you to get some rest before tonight.'

Alec shook his head. 'The thing with the dog, when I lost it, gave me an insight into her character. Poor old Denise. A lot was invested in that direction.'

'People love their dogs,' said Phil.

'Of course they do. No, but I meant I saw it for the first time.'

'What?'

'Her. Denise. It woke me up. I saw she was there.'

'She was there for a while before that, wasn't she?'

Alec appeared to miss this. 'In her own right, she's very . . . impressive.'

They took final sips from their beers, which had hardly been touched, and stood up. 'What will this dog do, Luke?' said Alec.

'What dog?'

'I meant fog, the fog. What's the story?'

'No idea.'

'Phil needs to get back for his rams. I've offered him a lift with us already.'

'You drove up?'

'Flew. There's a little Piper Cherokee belongs to a bloke I know. He loans it out. Four-seater, very tidy. We came into Paraparaumu, then hired a car. It's the way we'll go back. No fog up the coast.'

'Do you think it's still a good idea, following yesterday?' said Luke.

'I've been checked out at the hospital, subjected to every test. There were people obviously hoping for the reverse outcome, but I'm afraid I'll be with you all for a bit longer.'

They walked out of the bar into the daylight. 'I'm not good with small planes, as you know,' said Phil. 'Catherine's not much keener.'

'Suit yourself,' said Alec. He looked up, as if searching for a version of himself already in the air. The two others did the same. The grey sky had closed again.

Not especially human

The rare media appearances of the ex-Prime Minister, who had amyloidosis, an incurable and, as often repeated, 'potentially terminal' blood disease, never failed to shake the viewer. Lange was a different colour, almost bronzed, with a leathery sheen. As Roger Angland had said, he had something of the look of a Bog Person; and that Person's sense of injustice also at being put on view once more. Luke thought too of the propositioning History professor, the runner, whose bald skull—presumably from years of jogging in the elements—was similarly glazed. An unhealthy polish topped this, perhaps the fittest fifty-five-year-old on campus. Lange's eyes bulged and his mouth sucked between words, indicating a terrifying dryness. There was nothing sly in this illness. It stamped itself with almost tropical exuberance across his features. Tiredness hung from him. He waited for the questions with gloomy good grace, the sense always prominent that he hoped this one would be the last. The characteristic move of his—seen in the Oxford Union Debate—to push his glasses back against the bridge of his nose, which in earlier days announced an advance, the prospect of a parry if not a *bon mot*, had grown agonisingly slow. The wandering finger seemed to take an age to find the glasses, and once it had pressed there it remained, like a man pinpointing a headache. His answers, deemed rightly not to have quite the old élan, were often assisted by the interviewer in a way that was thoroughly depressing. His deeds were recited, his fights re-enacted in front of his eyes. The interviewer knew his—Lange's—moves and his lines, and gave them back, urging the man himself to mouth them. Occasionally Lange rose to it, even once or twice adding a new witticism, a fresh turn. The overall impression was of an exhibit, however, an example of something startling which had passed into history. In asking the question, one was doing little more than pushing a button, as at Te Papa, to hear words already well known. He was hardly a contemporary any more. Roger Angland again had commented that it might have been

Norman Kirk, dead in 1975, who'd been hauled out in front of the cameras, or even Micky Savage, exhumed and made up and asked what he felt of the current Labour.

The present world still had private connections of course to this declining figure. While his adult children were never brought into the conversation, Lange's young daughter was almost always the interview's final shot. How, in her father's view, was she coping, since that must be hard? Behind the large glasses, the eyes, moist from the outset, had thankfully a kind of refuge. Having witnessed it once, Luke didn't care to listen or to watch again this particular manipulation.

In driving to the polytech for the ceremony, he wondered if his hero was indeed improved. Lange was undoubtedly reduced and ravaged, and yet Luke had an image of the tanned, sick man speaking with surprising force from his seat in much the manner of some Roman emperor whose time was slipping away, offering a few final and devastating observations on the foolishness of the world while those around, many of whom had plotted against him, adjusted the glowing adjectives of his obituary. If this was farewell, Lange was not being quite valedictory enough, it seemed. The goodbye had also been a long one. Since diagnosis a few years before, he'd had lows, crises, but had proved prone to rallying. To give an address to the polytech's graduating cookery class was surely another example of his refusal to accept he'd stopped. It also made Luke think of a colleague's story from the late eighties, when she'd been at a formal function with the then Prime Minister. She was directly opposite Lange at the dinner table. When desserts were delivered, he noticed she wasn't eating hers. He asked if she had a problem with it, perhaps to do with rhubarb. She told him she liked rhubarb but that she was full. He finished eating his dessert, then leaned over and said, 'Would you mind if I had yours?' She did not deny her Prime Minister. Hard to think now of such an appetite.

The hall was full. He spied Catherine waving to him from near the front. They were all in the same row: Joe and Sheila, Catherine and Katie and Phil, Denise and Alec. The men were in suits and ties. Alec stood and leaned across the group to shake Luke's hand. Georgia was backstage somewhere. The first two rows were empty, reserved for the graduates. As well as cooking, other classes—food technology, hotel management, tourism—were also graduating. Luke sat down between Sheila and Catherine. Joe was on the end of the row, hovering with his camera. Catherine asked about Baden, whose flight had been diverted to Christchurch. He was being put up in a hotel for the night. Not a bad move, since post-flight he was feeling, as he said on the phone, not especially human.

The lights dimmed. Members of the academic staff filed on stage. Luke discovered he was nervous. The first sight of Lange would, he felt, come as a shock, no matter how thoroughly his condition had been canvassed by TV cameras in the past year. Luke wondered whether he was prepared for it. And there was Sheila, who sat beside him. He could feel her shoulder against his—a pressure accounted for by the general squeeze in the row. She'd thanked him for coming, then turned to answer some question from Joe. A woman entered from the side of the stage and went to the podium. She introduced herself as the Chief Executive, gave an overview of the evening's events, and asked the audience to welcome students from the performing arts programme. First, however, one change had been forced on them: unfortunately, David Lange had been unable to make it down from Auckland due to the fog. He sent his apologies, and just a couple of hours ago an email had come in. The Chief Executive held up a piece of paper.

'I would like to read Mr Lange's words to you all. He was happy for this to take place. I'm afraid I won't be able to deliver the message with anything like the author's wonderful style, but I hope you'll get some idea of what he meant. "The current weather in Wellington is rather appropriate since I find myself more and more in a fog these days. What encourages me and gives me hope is to be in the company of young people who have achieved something and who dream of doing great things. A great thing, I should say, might be to form a successful catering company and increase our nation's GDP; or it might be to make a fine meal for a small group of friends. It might be to run a large and shiny hotel with little soaps in every corner and an accounting system which allows guests with that weakness to abscond occasionally with the bathrobes; or it might be simply to welcome a visitor with warmth into one's own home. What clears the fog in my head these days is to think of your young minds let loose on the world, allowed to create, improvise, and imagine new ways of being great. I congratulate you all on what you have done and I'm filled with excitement at what you can still do. Kind regards, David. PS: Most annoyed to miss the event as I understand the catering will make Bellamy's look like McDonald's.'"

The words had scarcely ended when a piercingly high female voice came from backstage. Several of the staff jumped in their chairs. Luke felt Sheila move suddenly. The students, dressed in traditional Maori costume, came forward. The instant calculation was already done in Luke's head; there were three, perhaps four identifiably Maori students in the group of twenty. Some lovely bodies though. Joe was taking photos. Alec stared, unreadable but apparently gripped, as was Denise. The group began a song. The female students, at the front, were swaying their hips. Catherine and Sheila were grinning. Phil nodded his head in time to the stamp of the male students' feet. Only Katie, for whom this might have been less novel than it was for her elders, remained impassive. She caught Luke looking at her and raised her eyebrows, perhaps as if to say, 'We've been through all this a million times,' or, 'When will this end?' The Maori song had segued cannily into 'Blue Moon', with the boys falling to their knees and the girls, acting haughtily, shimmying away from these beseeching figures, averting their faces. This had the audience laughing and applauding. Luke glanced up at Joe and realised he was having his own picture taken. Joe gave him the thumbs-up and re-trained his camera on the stage, where the students were ending their set with a haka. Phil's leg was pumping up and down.

The awarding of diplomas and degrees was accomplished with impressive speed, the students almost jogging across the stage. Joe, under pressure from a battery change, wasn't sure whether he'd even got Georgia's moment. He swore and let the camera dangle from his wrist, then he swore again. Someone behind told him to sit down. He slumped into the seat, inspecting the camera. Luke thought back to the bike incident on the waterfront. Joe appeared to be the sort, otherwise well balanced, who in connection with inanimate objects revealed something of his seething nature. Sheila was not consoling. Indeed, she asked again whether he'd got the photo. He shrugged, defeated. Catherine leaned across. 'Someone will have it,' she said. 'Didn't she look wonderful! What a great gal you've got.'

'Happened so fast,' said Joe.

'Did you check the batteries before?' said Sheila.

'I'd charged them up.'

'How can that be right?'

Joe stared ahead. The staff were filing off the stage, having heard a final speech from the Chief Executive encouraging everyone to stay on for refreshments. Alec stood up, the first to do so. He was looking to the back of the hall as though he needed to be fed at once. Denise motioned that he should sit back down, but he pretended not to notice. Now everyone around was beginning to move. Alec had not heard any of the camera conversation. 'We'd like a copy of course,' he said, gesturing towards Joe. 'Wouldn't we, dear?' Denise nodded, smiling.

'Weren't the performers something?' said Phil.

'Loved "Blue Moon",' said Catherine.

'A break with tradition, wasn't it?' said Alec.

'Very clever,' said Denise.

'Some would have disapproved,' said Alec. 'The people who can't take a joke.'

'What joke?' said Sheila.

'The people who police these things. They don't like you to muck around with what's theirs.' Alec was addressing these comments to Luke, while also casting looks in the direction of the food, which they could now smell. 'I'm starving.' He moved off. Sheila seemed on the point of calling out after him. She raised her arm.

Catherine might have spoken to intercept her. 'No Lange,' she said. 'Luke only came because of Lange.'

'Such a shame,' said Phil.

Luke had started to explain himself when Georgia ran up. She hugged Sheila, then Joe, because he was closest to her. She ended up hugging everyone. 'Where's Dad?'

'Feeding,' said Katie.

They all turned towards the back of the hall, where a crowd was pressing together to get at the tables. Luke wondered whether something like the same image was in everyone's head. This was confirmed, partly at least, when Sheila spoke. 'They may as well have tossed it all from the back of a tractor.' Joe was showing Georgia the camera and talking about the batteries. She was laughing, telling him it didn't matter. 'Did you see them do "Blue Moon"?' she said. 'What a crack-up! And did you see Harry? He had to keep pulling up his pants.' Talk followed about which one was Harry and how he was known to Georgia. Luke drifted off in the direction of the food and found a way through to a table. Phil appeared at his elbow, with two cans of beer. He gave one to Luke.

'They're on the point of killing each other, don't you reckon?'

'Alec and Sheila?'

Phil drank from his can. 'He's offered them a lift home tomorrow, can you believe it. Since we said no thanks, he's offered the seats to Sheila and Joe!'

'What did they say?'

'They're considering it. With the fog, they're waiting to see what happens in the morning. Joe has to get back for work. The four of them in a small plane, my God.'

'It is extraordinary, given the situation.'

'I'd be afraid.'

'Of what Alec might do? He'll have Denise there beside him.'

'I don't even think he should be flying, not after what happened at the museum. Denise should persuade him it's all a bad idea.'

'Is she capable of that, persuading him?'

Phil opened his beer. 'She hasn't known Alec as long as we have.'

'Meaning she trusts him? And you don't?'

His brother-in-law looked unhappy at this conclusion. 'You've seen how he is this weekend.'

'Volatile.'

'Poor Alec.'

They were being bumped away again from the food table, where Luke had managed to grab a couple of small things which turned out to be prunes, cleverly augmented. Luke spotted Alec across the room, eating from a plate and talking with a middle-aged woman who looked familiar. Alec was offering the woman food, which she accepted. They both looked as though they were enjoying the moment. Luke pointed it out to Phil, who was also sure he'd seen the woman before. Then it came to Luke. 'It's the CE,' he said. 'The person who spoke, who read Lange's email.'

'What could he be saying to her?'

From a distance it was clear Alec was being utterly charming. Again, the likelihood that this same man was anyone's opponent, anyone's enemy, the object of anyone's fear and concern, seemed preposterous. 'Whatever it is,' said Luke, 'he's got her quite literally eating out of his hand.'

Phil examined unhappily his crostini, which balanced a sun-dried tomato on brie. 'Do you remember Margaret Leeds? I don't think you met her.'

The name echoed somewhere but Luke couldn't place it. Phil explained this was Alec's lawyer who'd taken his case against the cheese factory. He looked around, as if for a place to stow the crostini. 'After Sheila left, it was Margaret who helped out.'

'Helped out how?'

'Cooked, cleaned, you know. Helped. Catherine was sure it went further. Alec himself never said a word, of course.' Phil looked over in that direction again, where the CE was laughing and touching Alec's arm. 'This was a very smart career woman, a pocket rocket she was called, and someone who'd never take a backward step.'

Luke asked what had happened finally with the cheese factory. Phil said the factory had previously stated that, following another inconclusive round of negotiations during which it was understood a substantial sum had been offered, one far above what anyone else had been given, they would never again deal with Alec. He'd been labelled a menace and unreasonable beyond sense. By this stage he was no longer on the farm at all, having let it out. He was living mostly in Christchurch—with Denise as it emerged later, Alec again failing to allow the story of his life to be told in anything like its full detail.

'The pocket rocket didn't last?' said Luke.

'Margaret was gone as quick as she came. The house was, at the end, like some haunted house, some horror house. We went there. You could hardly see the house. Covered in branches and vines. We peered through the windows. There was stuff everywhere, leaves, rubbish. A couple of windows had been broken by a falling branch. Possums must have got in, rodents. He still had the furniture in there, the sofa was torn up. Puddles of water all over. Newspaper blown about. Terrible. Catherine was quite upset by it. We could see into the kitchen. One of the cupboards was open. Food, packets of things all over the bench and the floor, spilled, pulled apart. There was a smell. We wondered whether the fridge had been emptied properly, and there was the freezer too.'

Mention of this gave Luke a momentary fright. He'd lost his appetite. 'How did he finally sell then?'

'We don't know everything, but it was done. Maybe he did it on a whim. He took very little for it, I know that.'

'The big offer was not seen again?'

'The story is he went to them and basically handed it over—the house, the land, the plant, everything. There's the idea he sold for a song because of Sheila, to stop her getting much.'

At that moment they saw a worried-looking Joe hurrying from the hall. Luke tried to find Sheila in the crowd. Phil said he was off to get another beer. The first one had been consumed in perhaps three gulps. Luke had the impulse to leave also. The evening belonged, as Lange had said, to these young people. The chances weren't great of his own fog clearing. Still, the message from the ex-Prime Minister had brought him to the brink of some awkward emotion. It had only been the eruption of the students' performance that had saved him. He began to move towards the exit.

'They cooked all the food themselves.' Sheila was in front of him, bearing a plate. 'Have something. Were you leaving?'

'Just for some fresh air. I saw Joe leave.'

'Popped out to get some batteries. I must find Georgia.' She held up a pastry. 'At first I was disappointed she was only going to learn to cook. Big arguments over that. I thought she could have been an architect or a designer. She was always good at maths, which a lot of arty people aren't.'

They talked for a while about Georgia's plans. Sheila gave no sign of wishing to return to the moment in the Begonia House. She spoke while looking around the room. She'd leave him soon.

'On the subject of cooking,' he said, 'when you went off to university, you had to do a lot of preparing meals ahead for the family, didn't you?'

She waited before answering. The impression was she didn't particularly appreciate the topic. Perhaps she suspected him of some ulterior motive in bringing it up. Though Sheila was altogether more confident in her speech and manner, there was still that suspiciousness. Of course she was right, he thought, to hold on to that, especially now with him. 'I did. Of course they had to fend for themselves too. I'd like to say Georgia picked up a bit of her current skill in that time, but she was too young. It was Pip who did the most.'

'I remember you had meals ready in the freezer. You even had the days of the week on the lid.'

'Alec was hopeless of course.' She gave a laugh, though she didn't seem too light-hearted. 'To live with a man who can actually prepare a meal without assistance. It's a true wonder.'

He had it in his mind to tell her exactly what he'd found in the freezer, in the container marked for her ex-husband. It would be a sort of revenge for the night he'd spent waiting for her. His final faint too. The rodent on the table and he sprawled on the floor. He'd returned the package to the freezer afterwards. He could tell her of his care in sealing the container, untangling the tape and fixing it in place again. Yet the image of the house decaying, filled with rot, open more or less to the elements and animals, made him pause again. It was the place they'd first sat together and she'd mentioned she was leaving. Suddenly his discovery that day he'd gone to find her all those years ago seemed, if not insignificant, then superfluous. It belonged to an unhappy time. What was the point in returning there? Clearly she wasn't there any longer. Nor was he. Perhaps she'd cured him. Was he no longer a syncopist, no longer a fainter? He'd wondered for years whether his condition was similar to the alcoholic's—permanent and requiring eternal vigilance. A year went by and you didn't allow yourself to think, That's it, it's over, you made it through. Instead you thought, Well, that didn't happen then, but don't get so cocky, just wait. So you waited, half-expecting at any moment to feel it. Except he didn't feel it now—and moreover didn't feel the half-expecting-it feeling either. There was nothing about him that was faint.

'Oh look!' said Sheila. 'Here's good old Joe.'

There was something in the expression—slightly ironic in its fondness but also completely committed, unshakeable even—that settled things even more completely for Luke. Sheila seemed visibly to relax. Joe was waving, making his way towards them, brandishing the camera above his head victoriously.

'Please don't fly with Alec,' he said to her quickly. 'Tomorrow if the airport's closed, wait another day. Don't go up with him.'

She turned back to him, smiling. 'But what do you think could happen?'

'Don't do it.' The aim was not to unsettle her again. He believed in what he was saying.

She leaned close and kissed him on the cheek. 'He's agreed.'

'Who has?'

'Alec has agreed to give me half. We won't be going to court. It's over. You're the first to know, actually. He just told me. He came up and said it. It's finally over.'

'Congratulations.'

'I can't believe it.' She seemed immensely tired at that moment.

'He meant it then?'

'Yes, he won't go back on that.'

'What a relief.' He thought of the affidavit, which he'd done nothing about. Now she'd have no notion of the level of his commitment, none of them would. They'd triumphed without him, which in fact seemed right.

'I don't care about the money, you know,' she said, revived once again and patently happy. 'What this means is we all move on.'

At a certain time in his life—well, always—he might have flinched at this, and pitied the speaker. Who ever moved on? But at this moment it seemed somehow possible, or if not that, then hopeful, certainly desirable, and admirable. Had his feelings really arrived here: in admiration? 'So that's it then.'

'Oh, there was one condition. He wants a photo. I need to ask Joe to take a photo of us. Alec, me and Georgia. That was his condition. We can suffer that.'

Joe arrived, brandishing his camera. 'We're all set,' he said. 'What shall we start with? I'd like to get one of Georgie on stage. Would she go back up, do you think? Probably her mother could ask her nicely. Or not.'

Luke said he would leave them to decide on things. He shook hands with Joe and exchanged kisses with Sheila.

'Good luck with that problem,' said Joe. The reference was cloudy for a moment, though Luke was nodding his thanks. He must have shown enough confusion, since Sheila helped out. She explained that Joe meant the disgraced ambassador. 'Will he survive?' she said. He was already moving away. He repeated his ignorance of the outcome for O'Keefe. She took this with raised eyebrows, waiting for an elaboration.

'There's a game being played,' said Luke.

'Always is,' said Joe.

'Joe's baying for his blood,' said Sheila. 'But he seems like a nice enough man to me.'

Support from this quarter was a surprise. It aligned her with Alec, of course, though there wasn't a question of anything tactical, Luke thought. Joe shook his fists in the air in mock frustration. He looked for a moment as though he wanted to pound on her head. Yet Sheila's judgement, in the climate of the room, which was naturally positive, celebratory, had a definite force to it. At the UN, O'Keefe had been as understanding and supportive, to use the jargon, as any employee might hope for from management. He was hardly a force of darkness, though the argument could certainly be made that he was one of stupidity. What Sheila was settling by her pronouncement seemed to be O'Keefe's irrelevance in the room. It was an affectionate dismissal. She was waving to her daughter, and moving towards her.

A serious contender

The airport was still marginal the following morning. Baden was on the redeye, which was cancelled. However, a few planes had got in after that, the weather lifting and closing in again. Luke decided to drive out anyway. He couldn't work, had phoned in to say he was delayed at the airport. The sense of things hanging over him was strong. The fact of Baden coming in from the air was a literal part of this. He'd had a dream that night in which he was belaying someone who refused to come down and indeed refused to be identified. The figure clung determinedly to the wall, unmoving.

The monitor showed the flight was delayed. He looked at magazines in the crowded bookshop for a while, then queued for coffee. Low-grade hostility, familiar to him from any number of airports, was one strain; another was a sort of politeness, kindness even, as those who'd waited and suffered longest grew wonderfully accommodating. Someone ahead in the line offered to mind the luggage of a woman who, struggling with an infant, had knocked fruit drink all over herself. With terrific luck, a table at the wall-length window came free as he was passing. He'd made eye contact with its departing owner, a woman in a business suit, who acknowledged the claim with a nod. At the same time, another man was approaching from the other side of the table, unseen by the woman and closer to the prize than Luke. Unable to move very fast with his tray, Luke felt sure it was a lost cause. However, the table was his—the claim held, and the woman stayed beside it until Luke was there. The other claimant gave up.

'Very kind of you,' said Luke. It was only then that he recognised who'd done this. 'Hello, Maude.'

'Hello, Luke.' They shook hands. 'Stranded?'

'Waiting for someone.'

'Me too.'

There was a folded newspaper on the table. He glanced at it almost from reflex. Roger Angland had pointed out this feature of their work, the quick recce when almost any bit of paper came within view. The finest practitioners of this surreptitious art were able to extract print while conversing face to face with the target almost as if the person was transparent. Roger himself was one of the best. Luke had a long way to go.

'There's a tiny thing inside,' said Maude. 'If you're looking for O'Keefe.'

'I was. Sorry to be so rude. I was actually with him for a short time at the UN.'

'You were at the Mission?'

'Briefly.'

'One of my dreams.' She looked out the window and gestured

towards the planes stranded on the tarmac. 'I was going to give up on my one, but now apparently they're trying for it. They're in the air. It's the third time though, so what hope?'

He put his tray on the table. 'Have you got time? We could sit together.'

'Been here an hour, I was looking for a change of scenery. If I come back in five, will you be here?'

When Maude returned, he'd taken in the O'Keefe article. He'd also made a quick dash to check on Arrivals, leaving his briefcase to guard the table. Baden's flight was finally on its way, due in thirty minutes. Through the window, activity had begun. Service vehicles were gathering around a couple of the planes. The sky hadn't noticeably brightened. Maude looked striking, revived. She'd re-applied her lipstick, brushed her hair. The scar on her neck made her beauty even more complete somehow. He asked her whether the plane she was waiting on was coming from Auckland, since a flight was now listed. She hurried off to check and when she came back she squeezed his arm. 'You're my lucky charm,' she said. 'Due in twenty minutes. What did you make of the O'Keefe?'

The hundred-word article in the newspaper quoted the PM saying that all future inquiries regarding the Ambassador should be directed to the majority Opposition party in the House. The journalists would by now have the story. Luke said to Maude that he'd always considered the PM a supreme tactician.

'That sounds bad when you say it like that,' said Maude. 'I'm in awe of her. By the way, I just saw Charles Fuge sitting by himself, reading some papers. I don't think he saw me. Is he a friend of yours?'

'Not at all.'

'He might have wanted to come over and join us. If you thought that was helpful, I wouldn't mind. I need to walk to the gate anyway.'

Luke shook his head. 'Fuge can be alone with his papers. Gosh, we're all here, aren't we?' He thought of his sister and Phil, who'd booked for later in the morning, and the others, perhaps now making their way up the coast to fly out of Paraparaumu—unless Joe and Sheila had changed their minds.

'I don't think Rick will appreciate an audience. He knows him a bit.'

'You're waiting for your father?'

'An inglorious and premature return, I'm afraid. Skiing in Aspen. He's done his Achilles.'

'Painful.'

'The second great blow he's received. After the Supreme Court snub.'

Luke dimly recalled Weenink's name being bandied about during the selection process. He'd been an outsider—which is what he asked Maude about now, whether her father had considered himself a serious contender.

Maude laughed. 'I thought you'd worked with Rick. He always considers himself a serious contender. At everything he does. Even skiing. He has problems with anyone who doesn't take themselves as seriously as he takes himself. Me, for instance.' People had begun to move in the direction of the gates. Maude checked her watch.

'PM's Office looks pretty serious to me,' said Luke.

They were both standing now, gathering their things. Already a group had spied their table and was closing in.

'He hopes I've come right,' said Maude, smiling. They took a few steps, then she stopped. 'Actually, Luke, do you mind if I duck around the other way?'

'Our friend Fuge?'

'Chas and I have a history. Am I telling you something you already know?'

'No.'

'Childish way to behave, I know. But I can't bear to run into him. That meeting yesterday was a nightmare.'

'I didn't notice anything.'

'Precisely. It would have been preferable for us both if he'd stabbed me through the heart with his pen.' She pressed his arm warmly in goodbye and was about to skip away behind the food counter.

'Do you know the saying, the purpose of diplomacy is to prolong a crisis?'

She stopped and considered him. 'One of Charles's.'

'Yes.'

'I used to tell him to stop with those quotes. It's like telling jokes. Unbearable.'

'He had some early success.' He recalled the Montesquieu and the Cicero from The Hague. 'Where's it from, do you know?'

'Oh, it's Mr Spock.'

'Mr Spock?'

'From *Star Trek*. It's Spock. Charles was a great fan. He used to read the novels as well.'

'I'm very pleased to know that.'

'"Sometimes you just have to bow to the absurd." That was a particularly annoying favourite. He applied for a place at Rick's firm and was knocked back. He's convinced I was behind it. I only knew about it afterwards. After the rejection, he wrote Rick a letter saying it was the first time ever in his life he'd been turned down for something. At the point in the letter you might have expected him to say this has been a learning experience, a character-building experience, Charles wrote, "I wonder whether a mistake has somehow been made." Priceless! He believed that it had been an administrative error. Perhaps that is the definition of bulletproof. Actually, I'm sure he was only ever interested in me because of Rick.'

'Of course it might have been the other way around.'

'That's the charitable view, I suppose. Charitable towards me, I mean. In my defence, I was really young and Charles was . . .'

'Not.'

'I was going to say he was a force. No one sees that now.'

'I wouldn't be too sure.'

'Well, goodbye again, Luke. No doubt we'll meet again.'

The image he had now of creepy old *Star Trek*-loving Chas Fuge, with cape, sweeping up Maude Weenink, the beauty, was startling. He was certain that Roger Angland, who knew everything, knew nothing of this, which would have been remarkable but for that capacity of intelligent, watchful, gossipy people, in their pursuit of the finer points, to miss obvious things. Recently he'd been reading about the lives of Aldrich Ames at the CIA and Robert Hanssen at the FBI, the two most notorious double agents for the Russians, whose spying had gone undetected for years. There was nothing of national interest in what he'd learned, though he still felt in possession of a small and fascinating file.

Baden came down the concourse with a sort of hop to his step. It took Luke a few moments to realise he was trying to see past his fellow passengers, to see Luke. He appeared fantastically eager. It gave Luke a shock. Baden was often lugubrious in his movements—this was the sort of curiosity in a physio that was noteworthy, deeply attractive: something about playing against type, but doing so unselfconsciously. It was endearing to register the bad posture, the slight goofiness. Now, however, he was almost airborne, colliding with Luke, knocking him back. They kissed quickly and hugged. Neither was in a hurry to break off this contact, despite the onlookers. Both were laughing, with joyful glistening eyes.

'Where's your Chinese reserve gone?' said Luke.

'Felt like I was never going to get home,' said Baden. 'Is this really Wellington?'

He was carrying plastic duty-free bags full of bottles. Luke took these. 'Do you want to get me drunk or something?'

'Not immediately,' said Baden.

From his shoulder bag, the head of a stuffed animal appeared, as if called.

'Who's your friend?' said Luke.

'Just someone.' He tried to push the head back down inside the bag.

'Persistent thing, isn't he?'

'For Zoe.'

Zoe was Baden's niece, a girl who'd sometimes stayed a weekend at his place and been the unwitting source of a couple of memorable arguments between them. Her presence had prompted Baden to have thoughts about what they were missing out on. For Luke the issue of children was simply a non-starter, though it had proved impossible to convince Baden of his sincerity. Here was a subject about which one would always be accused of repression: the more equanimity one maintained in the face of questioning, the greater the repressive mechanism believed to be operating. 'Bit young for Zoe, surely? She's almost a teenager, isn't she?'

'Teenage girls live with bears. They tell their secrets to them.'

He tried to think whether anything along these lines had emerged from his own niece's suitcase when they'd taken her to the hostel. He hadn't seen it, though he'd left before everything was in place.

They began to walk in the direction of the baggage-claim area. 'There's a whole pile of boxes to collect with my suitcase. Samples and rubbish.'

'So it was a hit? You made deals or whatever you were making? You sold them on it?'

'Luke, they loved the product.'

'They loved you, I'm sure. Nice Asian boy.'

'Me? Oh, they thought I was very nice. But seriously, the product is about to take off.'

'How could they refuse you?'

'Did I tell you about our night on the town?'

'You did. With the cripples.'

'My God.'

'Sounded dangerous.'

'Actually, you're around that environment for a few days, you start to see things a bit differently.'

'Nightclubs?'

'I mean the disability scene. You begin to see the world in a completely different light. I'm used to injury, of course—rehab, whatever. But being at the expo, there are minds being applied to problem-solving where you didn't even know there was a problem. I was talking to this one guy who was in a wheelchair. I said to him, "My God you have all these things coming in, new laws, things getting better for you guys, all these inventions," and he said to me, "Hey, listen, we're the future!" Am I talking too much, too fast?'

'A little,' said Luke. 'It's good to have you back, you know.' There was no strain in the statement that couldn't be accounted for by sheer exhaustion. Baden was studying him and suggested that he looked tired. 'I am. Family, you know.'

Baden squeezed his shoulder. 'Poor thing.' It was what Roger Angland had said too.

Suddenly it felt extraordinarily good to have someone like this.

'I never thought I'd make it. But basically the world needs re-designing. See that guy over there? Look at him. What the heck is this slope on the floor for? Feel we're on a slope? We're walking uphill now.'

Baden was right. People all around leaned slightly forward. Through a window, Luke saw holes of blue sky and a New Zealand flag on top of a distant airport building folding up on itself, then unfolding in the wind before collapsing again.

Baden was continuing excitedly. It struck Luke that his mood was not a result of coming home to him but of being away from him. This garrulous, invigorated person was what Baden became once he left Luke's influence. He'd seen hints of it before, when they were in larger groups. Perhaps this wasn't so unusual; even the brightest couples, believing themselves unobserved, could descend into bleak silence, reviving immediately upon contact with others. Still, he knew Baden could blossom, and he was not required for this to occur; his absence may even be one condition. It had been a dispiriting discovery at first, then one which lodged as fact. Now it might even make things easier.

'At least there are no stairs, but that guy is hauling himself up an incline, why? Because the person who designed this walkway, or didn't design it, was like you and me: able-bodied, walking. This morning I took some cold medicine because I caught something on the plane or somewhere and it's sped me up. I'm zingy. But anyway, in the future, in the very near future, that man won't have to kill himself trying to catch a plane. His world will be incorporated into ours, or ours into his. How are you anyway? How are you? Are you working today? I didn't know if you'd come or not.'

'Of course I'd come.'

'Do you have to go in? You look unwell to me. I think you should call in sick.'

'I think so too.' Luke looked over to where Baden had indicated this emblematic figure. He was ten metres or so in front of them. His head was bobbing up and down with the effort of turning the wheels on his chair. A man in his fifties perhaps or a little older; the hair was silver, distinguished but youthfully so, and swept back in waves. His vigour was propelling him at a fast clip. He was overtaking some of the crowd. A few had to move aside to let him through. It was an impressive performance, gutsy and inspiring, with just a suggestion of something amiss. The figure in the wheelchair had great dignity, perhaps, and also a certain recklessness, a will towards harm even. Beside him, Maude Weenink was trying to keep up. Of course Justice Rick 'Marbles' Weenink was going to be a serious contender even in this, his new role of Man with Disability. He looked perfectly capable of, if not intent on, running someone over.

Luke glanced up at the point Charles Fuge's face appeared, moving the wrong way down the concourse against the strong tide of disembarking travellers. Several flights had come in at the same time. For some reason, rather than wait a few minutes for its dispersal, Fuge had chosen to walk through this surge. He was doing so with obvious difficulty—bustled and jostled, unhappy, but unwilling to concede right of way. It was perfectly in keeping with that personality, and there was something in it that Luke found admirable. The obstinacy was horribly self-centred, of course. Fuge was a pig. Against the swell of people, he moved from near-miss to near-miss. In his thoughtlessness, he was the cause of much inconvenience. People looked at him with justified hostility. He was breaking the social contract. He was being a pain. He was an idiot. The walk was the same as it had been at The Hague years before, when Fuge had turned away from the woman painter in the forest, having offered what he took to be a perfectly good suggestion about how to fix her work. The common perception of diplomacy, with its shadings of smoothness, slipperiness perhaps, evasion but also assistance, care, consensus, was not to be dismissed. What Charles Fuge carried, however, was a different strand, one equally as valid and prevalent in the service, though not as widely appreciated: brute force. Maude was right. As he made his way, barging through the throng, he appeared almost blind, or rather as if his eye was on some other thing. Whether it was on Maude herself or her father, Luke didn't know.

Luke saw him again briefly, at the moment Fuge seemed to have seen the Weeninks, at which Fuge's face appeared to suffer a setback. His mouth hung open for a second. He looked desperate, haunted, like a man chasing a phantom and finally catching up with it. What now? Without knowing any of the particulars, Luke believed he could guess at once the kind of compulsion that tied these three figures together. Then Fuge was lost in the crowd, as was Weenink's bobbing head. There was a glimpse of Maude's hair before she was also gone.

He was aware he'd picked up pace to keep the Weeninks in view. Baden was a few metres behind. He slowed. There was a look on Baden's face which brought him to a stop. It wasn't a look of abandonment exactly. Puzzlement maybe. Certainly irritation. He'd seen the look frequently over the past few months. It had taken only a few minutes for this kind of tension between them to reappear. Usually he was averse to scenes—they both were—and one wouldn't take place now, not in the airport. Yet he was also glad to receive the message so quickly. He didn't need to receive it again—this was what he decided. He would put no more effort into prolonging the crisis.

Baden too seemed to have understood what had happened. He slouched under the weight of his luggage. Suddenly there was nothing for either of them to enjoy in this moment. They were leaving each other. The bags—here they were—the bags were packed. It was a defeat. Though they'd almost certainly be friends, it was the end of them. Both saw the necessity of it—and the misery.

When Baden came alongside, Luke reached out and took the heaviest bag from him, more or less snatched it from him to prevent any objections. Baden was taken aback at first. He wore an expression of shock, as if someone—a stranger—had grabbed the bag from him. He made a move to retrieve it. But Luke had it firmly in his grip. He swung it out in front of him. Baden was watching him, still clearly unconvinced. They walked a few more metres, approaching the escalator which would take them down.

Finally Baden nodded in the direction of the bag. 'Weighs a ton,' he said.

Yes, Luke thought happily, it did.

Several minutes before, not long after Maude had made her escape, Charles Fuge had spotted Luke and come over.

'Who have you got?' said Fuge. 'Not the Tongans too?'

'Picking up a friend,' said Luke.

'Lucky you. I had a call before to say one of them was on a respirator onboard. We've got an ambulance standing by. It's never straightforward with them. Health issues always.'

'Any move on O'Keefe?'

'You saw the PM's bit today? Not much more for us to do, I'd say.' People had started emerging from the gate area—mainly businessmen jogging for the taxis. 'My lot won't be running. The last time I had them over, we had a diabetic coma in the back of the car. Fortunately, I knew what to do. I knew all too well, unfortunately.'

Luke couldn't remember Fuge being diabetic when he'd first met him. Perhaps the diagnosis was fairly recent and the invitation was there to ask more. The subject didn't appeal. He needed to move to the gate where Baden's flight was about to come in. Fuge, too, was showing signs of wanting to leave, though he also seemed reluctant finally to break, as if he had something to say but couldn't quite bring himself to it. 'Well, goodbye, Charles.'

'Got the call on your flight, have you? Are you sure? I've had a couple of false alarms already, although I rather like the fog.'

'My one's come in.'

'Excellent. You know I had lunch last year with Kerry O'Keefe when I was over there.'

Here, it seemed, was the business he'd come across for. Luke said something about not having seen Kerry for ages but that he had a strange, sneaking sympathy for the man in his present position.

Fuge took a moment to consider this. 'At lunch, for some reason your name came up. Kerry had a lot of time for you, said you gave him a book. Napoleon, I think. I thought you were having a go at him perhaps.'

'He was interested in Napoleon.'

'Yes. Poor old Kerry. He gave me the run-down on things, the murder. Awful stuff for you get tied up with on your first go.'

There seemed no reason to keep the truth from Fuge. Mendacious people often had that effect. 'For a while I thought about it a lot. Now hardly ever.'

'It would set you back, though. You've recovered well, haven't you, Luke? I mean, from a rocky start. You've done okay in your postings and so on. I remember when we were at The Hague.'

'Funny, I was thinking about that too, with Maude Weenink at the meeting yesterday.'

The name had an impact. At the moment he heard it, Fuge was looking off through the crowd. His flow was arrested. He spoke distractedly. 'Rick was there, of course. Marvellous man.'

'I remembered the quote you used about Maude. "When

red-headed people are above a certain social grade, their hair is auburn."'

'Is it Twain?'

'It is, and you quoted it to me at The Hague.'

'Did I? How extraordinary for you to remember it.' He didn't look pleased.

Luke hadn't really expected an explanation. He remained convinced that for some reason Fuge had wanted to get at her, put her in her place. This made a sort of sense if Fuge had already been smitten, all those years ago, and perhaps been rejected at first by the nineteen-year-old Maude. To have joined that line was, by all accounts, nothing to be ashamed of, except if you were near forty and Charles Fuge. Of course he'd also been rejected by the father.

'Do you still faint?' said Fuge. 'Is that all settled now?' Here was the fight-back.

'It is.'

'Excellent. Can't have been much fun.'

'It was okay with a soft landing.'

Fuge smiled weakly, which was all this deserved. 'Funny thing, I was involved with a fainting once. Years ago. It was at the Trooping of the Colour. A very hot day, one of those London scorchers. We were all waiting for the Queen, you know. Quite like the Queen actually, a good egg, except in the business of her sister and the divorce. Anyway, the man was standing just in front of me. I remember he half turned towards me, as if he wanted to get past. We looked at each other, and I was about to let him through when his eyes rolled back in his head. Never seen it before but they do literally roll back. He fell right into my arms. Amazing. I caught him. People around didn't quite know what to make of it. Looked a bit like one of those games, I suppose. You know, where the person must trust the other person completely and just let oneself fall back. If you flinch, you've cheated, you lack faith. Might have seemed like that. Then they cottoned on. "He's fainted! Someone's fainted here! Step back, step back! Give the man some air!" Quite a lot of friendly shouting. Everyone was quite wonderful really. Very kind, with water bottles and so on. We laid him down carefully on the ground. Ended up holding his head actually. Head on my knee. I was made chief carer. Perhaps they thought I knew him. Everything came through me.' Fuge smiled at this memory of himself in command. 'A special shock to see someone faint like that. As if the person has vanished, gone!'

'Was he all right?'

'Oh, he came to very quickly. Bit confused at first. "You fainted, mate." "You fainted, dear." He got the picture. Stood up smartly. Very apologetic for the fuss he'd caused. Then people started shaking his hand. A lot of people wanted to shake his hand. Quite strange.'

'Quite nice.'

'Yes, and odd too. Hard to be bothered by the Trooping of the Colour after that. I was more or less obliged to shake his hand as well. Poor bloke probably wanted to get out of there. When you fall like that, when there's all that uncontrolled weight, the body is terrifically heavy. He wasn't a big chap, but when he lost it he almost knocked me down. But I managed to hold on. I caught him.'

'Safe pair of hands.' The phrase belonged to Justice Carling, whom they'd both been with at The Hague. Carling had been killed a few years later in a car accident.

Fuge got it at once. 'Yes! Good old SPH. Dead now, of course. Actually been trying to remember the name of a painter, Dutch.'

'Paulus Potter.'

'Who? That was the one. Odd name as well.'

'Seventeenth century.'

'Oh, don't know a thing about it. Paulus Potter: his name came up again somewhere.' Here was almost certainly a reference to the Weeninks. 'All those functions and openings, ghastly really. You followed me to The Hague and you followed me to Moscow. Like a shadow, aren't you?'

Though he'd spoken with a smile, there was, as with most

of what came from his mouth, an unspecified accusation here. Luke resisted it. Yet he wanted at least to provoke something in Fuge. What was his plan for the Mindovsky Mansion if not an artistic one? 'They found Pan, you know, at the Embassy.'

'I know. Of course I knew he was there all along. I'd done the research.'

'Will you go over and take a look?'

'No. What's the point? They found him.'

'It's a beautiful image.' This statement was nothing like an enticement; Fuge showed little sign of taking it in. Luke recalled Maude's use of the term bulletproof.

As if this thought had been communicated, Fuge returned to her also. 'Maude is certainly the most interesting thing in the PM's Office right now, don't you think? Magnetic.'

The last word was uttered with a different tone, the usual deadness replaced by something strangely tremulous. Luke couldn't help feeling that his own use of the phrase 'beautiful image' was in part responsible for setting this off. Charles Fuge now looked capable of anything, even confession. Luke thought of Alec Moore. The two men, Alec and Fuge, occupied different worlds, mutually hostile ones probably, but shared something stylistic perhaps: a vast and impenetrable egotism, and, given the right trigger, a readiness to crack open completely. Maybe, however, this apparent vulnerability was still part of the egotism: an ability to perform one's pain—and then of course quickly to recover from it. No tears were in the offing.

'Is it true you lit a fire in the stables?'

Here Fuge looked at Luke with surprise—surprise at the challenge, perhaps, but also surprise that was shading almost visibly into pleasure. He was displaying the thoroughly acceptable habit of enjoying hearing about a time when one behaved badly. 'No,' he said. 'It was in the courtyard, just outside the stables.' Behind the flatness of the response, Fuge seemed content. This, Luke believed, was also the satisfaction in having it confirmed that one was talked about, that actions taken years before were still being felt, even unpleasantly, as reverberations. 'I do have a fondness for the Russians, though. The clicks on the phone-line. They cared at least.'

There had been no further opportunity for clarification of the life Fuge had led, or for Luke to gauge how negligible or far-reaching its effects had been. Travellers, some relieved to have arrived, others anxious to get away, were flooding the area, getting between them, making it hard to continue the conversation. Perhaps this was for the best. They were separated by a family group with a large amount of luggage. A moment later they found themselves reunited one last time, swept together briefly by the press of people.

'Ideal conditions,' said Fuge.

'For what?' said Luke.

'How are you feeling? All right?' The inquiry carried no more than a routine touch of malice. It had to go unanswered. Their final separation had occurred. Fuge was beginning to use his elbows to get where he was going.

Acknowledgements

I would like to thank Creative New Zealand for the award of a Scholarship in Letters. This provided momentum and breathing space. I also gratefully acknowledge the generosity of friends and family who loaned me parts of their lives. The way fiction returns such gifts is hardly straightforward. And there is a certain kind of novelist who thinks wishfully that everything has been loaned to him. A whole lot, of course, is just stolen. Still, I hope my gratitude doesn't appear too faint. Thanks to BC especially.

DW